PRAISE FOR *The Last Green Valley*

"Mark Sullivan has done it again! *The Last Green Valley* is a compelling and inspiring story of heroism and courage in the dark days at the end of World War II. Fans of *Beneath a Scarlet Sky* will savor this novel based on an extraordinary and little-known tale of the war and its aftermath."

—Kristin Hannah, #1 *New York Times* bestselling author of *The Nightingale* and *The Great Alone*

"Mark Sullivan weaves together history and memory in an epic journey of love and resilience. One of the most riveting, page-turning books I've read in a long time."

—Heather Morris, author of the #1 international and *New York Times* bestseller *The Tattooist of Auschwitz*

"Sullivan again demonstrates his gift for finding little-known embers of history and breathing life into them until they glow and shine in ways that are both moving and memorable."

—Pam Jenoff, *New York Times* bestselling author of *The Lost Girls of Paris*

THE LAST
GREEN
VALLEY

THE LAST GREEN VALLEY

A NOVEL

MARK SULLIVAN

LAKE UNION
PUBLISHING

Text copyright © 2021 by Suspense Inc
All rights reserved.

Published by Lake Union Publishing, Seattle

www.apub.com

Amazon, the Amazon logo, and Lake Union Publishing are trademarks of Amazon.com, Inc., or its affiliates.

ISBN-13: 9781503958760 (hardcover)
ISBN-10: 1503958760 (hardcover)

ISBN-13: 9781503958746 (paperback)
ISBN-10: 1503958744 (paperback)

Cover design by Shasti O'Leary Soudant

Interior images courtesy of the Martel family.

Printed in the United States of America

First edition

For all the grateful refugees who renew this nation every day.

With love in our hearts, there is nothing
we cannot overcome.

—*Chen Yeng*

PREFACE

People told me I would never find another untold World War II story like that of Pino Lella, the hero and basis of my historical novel *Beneath a Scarlet Sky*. I honestly believed I would, however, and paid close attention to the dozens of letters and pitches I received from people telling me other stories from that time period.

They were all wonderfully interesting in their way. But none of them matched my criteria, which were that the underlying tale had to be inherently moving, inspiring, and potentially transformative to me and so to readers.

Then, in November 2017, I was asked to speak about Pino to the noontime Rotary Club in my hometown of Bozeman, Montana. A retired dentist came up to me afterward to outline a story a local man had told him. It caught my attention immediately.

Two days later, I put the man's address in my GPS and saw it was less than two miles from my own. The closer I got, I felt odd, and I had no idea why. It wasn't until I pulled into his driveway and got out of my car that I realized I was no more than two hundred yards away from the home where I'd first heard Pino Lella's story nearly eleven years before. That story changed my life.

I went to the door, knocked, and my life changed again.

Within fifteen minutes of listening to the particulars of the story of the Martel family, I was more than interested. By the end of two hours, I believed I had a tale to tell that would be a worthy successor to the tale that inspired *Beneath*. And I'd heard it in the same little neighborhood where I'd first heard Pino's story. What were the odds of that?

For the next fifteen months after that first meeting, I interviewed survivors and researched and traveled to critical locations in the story, including the ruins of an abandoned farmhouse in deeply rural, far-western Ukraine. From there, I retraced the dangerous and remarkable journey of a young family of refugees on the run westward in a wagon with two horses, often caught between the retreating German armies and the advancing Soviets in the final chaotic year of World War II.

I trailed the Martels' route through present-day Moldova, Romania, Hungary, the Czech Republic, and Poland, where the way split: one continuing west and another doubling back east more than eleven hundred miles to the former site of a deadly Soviet POW camp set in the bleak postwar rubble near the Ukrainian border with Belarus.

Along the way, I interviewed participants and eyewitnesses to the "Long Trek," as well as Holocaust, military, and refugee historians, who helped me to understand the context in which the Martels' story unfolded and why. I also listened to the recordings of people, long dead, describing the ordeal and felt in awe of the grit, humanity, and spirit they showed in the face of seemingly insurmountable challenges and odds.

Even though I had all that information and understanding when I sat down to write this book, there were holes in the tale not completely explained by the limited material I had to rely on.

To bridge those gaps, I have been forced to draw on my own suspicions and imagination to bring the story more fully to life. What you are about to read, then, is not narrative nonfiction, but historical fiction based on an extraordinary tale of World War II and its aftermath.

As I am finishing this novel, the world is engulfed in the crisis of a century, and the way forward seems as dangerous and unclear as it must have been for the Martels when they set out on their journey. It is my dream that their story will give comfort and courage to the afflicted and a better understanding of what ordinary people can endure and achieve even when all seems lost.

PART ONE: THE LONG TREK

Chapter One

Late March 1944
Romanian Governorate of Transnistria

A cold wind blew in the dawn light. Bombs echoed from the north and east. The rumble of war was getting closer by the minute.

Twenty-eight-year-old Adeline Martel struggled out the back door of her kitchen in heavy winter clothes, carrying a crate full of cooking utensils toward a covered wagon harnessed to two dray horses in front of her modest home in the remote, tiny farming village of Friedenstal.

A damaged German Panzer tank clanked and rattled past her in the early-morning light, upsetting the horses. Trucks filled with wounded German soldiers streamed after the tank. Adeline could hear their cries and tortured sufferings long after they'd passed, and she could see more trucks and more horse- and mule-drawn wagons like hers coming from the east, silhouetted with the rising sun at their backs.

"Mama!" cried her younger son, Wilhelm, who'd run out the back door behind her.

"Not now, Will," Adeline said, puffing as she reached the back of the large V-shaped wooden wagon with oiled canvases stretched over a wooden frame to form a bonnet for shelter.

"But I need to know if I can bring this," said the four-and-a-half-year-old, holding up a rock, one of his latest prized possessions.

"Bring your wool hat instead," she said as she found room for the crate along with a second one that held dishes, cups, and baking tins beside a third that contained crocks of flour, yeast, salt, pepper, lard, and other essentials for their survival.

Emil hustled around the other side of the house, toting a keg-shaped barrel with a lid.

"How much?" she asked.

"Eight kilos dried pork. Ten kilos dried beef."

"I left space for it back here."

Another tank clanked by as her thirty-two-year-old husband grunted, hoisted the small barrel into the back, and began lashing it to the wall of the wagon.

"I'll get all the onions and potatoes from the cellar," she said. "Bedding's packed."

"I'll get the big water sack filled," he said before another bomb hit to the northeast.

Their older son, six-and-a-half-year-old Waldemar, came out from behind the house, pulling a small replica of the larger wagon about a meter long with the same high sides and back and the same wooden axles and wheels with tin nailed around the rims.

"Good boy, Walt," Adeline said, pointing at the wagon. "I need that." She took the handle from him and turned the little wagon around. "Follow me. Fast now. I need your help."

The boys followed her to the root cellar and helped her frantically dig up their stock of potatoes, onions, and beets. Then they moved them to the little wagon and hurried back to the larger one. There were more German trucks and crippled armored vehicles on the road now and dozens of covered wagons and horses, all heading west, all trying to outrun Joseph Stalin's armies, which were on the attack again.

The air stank of horse dung, engine exhaust, spilled petrol, and toiling humans. The din, the cold wind that spoke of a coming storm, the sickening mélange of smells, and the nervousness of the horses all conspired to put Adeline further on edge as they loaded the contents of the root cellar into burlap bags while Emil lashed a large rubber bladder of water to the side of the wagon along with the bucket from the well.

Overhead and to the south several kilometers, a German fighter plane roared past them, belching smoke from its engines.

"Mama," Walt said, "I don't like all the loud noises."

"That's why we're leaving," Emil said as he loaded the burlap bags into the big wagon, then looked at Adeline in irritation. "We should have been up and gone with my parents."

"We weren't ready to go with your parents at four a.m., and as usual, they weren't waiting for us," Adeline replied sharply. "And . . ."

"And what?"

She watched another tank go by, took a step closer to him, and said quietly, "You're sure, Emil? Running with the Nazis like this?"

Emil responded in a whisper. "We can stay and wait for the bear that we know will kill us, or rape you and kill me and the boys, or imprison us all in Siberia. Or we can run with the wolves that will protect us until we can make our escape west. Escape the war. Escape everything."

Three days before, a German SS officer had knocked on their door and offered them protection if they would gather their belongings and move west. After the visit, they had argued for several hours. Now, Adeline gazed at him, still in turmoil over the decision, but feeling what she always did about Emil: his moodiness and quietness aside, he was not only a good man, he was a tested man, a fighter, and a survivor.

"Okay," she said. "We run with the wolves."

"What about our little wagon?" Walt demanded.

"We'll find room for it," Emil told him.

The raw wind gusted. A curled brown leaf from the previous autumn lifted from the dead grass to Adeline's left, spun, looped, and danced across the stubble and around her and the boys in a curious, stuttering pattern before the gust sighed and the leaf tumbled softly to earth. It reminded her of a night long before when she'd seen money appear on the wind, a single crumpled bill that had danced before her in the same curious manner as this leaf, as if in response to some desperate and primal prayer.

Adeline went back to the kitchen one last time, finding the leaf and that memory all oddly upsetting, as bittersweet as it was mysterious, as awe-inspiring as it was frightful.

Like every big change in my life, blown by the wind.

Around the house, Emil finished tying the little wagon to the rear of the big one.

"No one steps on it, right?" he said to his young sons. "You want to come out the back, you wait until I've taken it down."

Walt nodded. Will said, "When are we leaving, Papa?"

"As soon as Mama returns," he said, "and your grandmother and aunt get here. Go use the outhouse if you need to."

Both boys ran out behind the house while the two geldings, Oden and Thor, danced in place, again spooked at tanks passing so close. Emil had to soothe and coax them until they finally calmed. The horses were fit and well cared for. They were used to pulling plows and weight. If he slowed them down to handle the heavier loads on the steeper hills, and barring lameness or, worse, a wreck, Emil believed the pair would take his family a long way.

He paused to study the house he'd built single-handedly, fighting all thoughts of pity or remorse. A house was a house. There would be others. Emil had learned the hard way to detach from the idea of possessing anything for long in his life. But he stared at the roof for a moment, seeing himself two and a half years before, loading tin roofing sheets and trusses into his wagon in a town called Dubossary, some thirty kilometers to the west.

He shook off the memory and turned away from the house and that roof.

"If God giveth, Stalin taketh away," Emil mumbled, and refused to give the home he'd built any more attention. In his mind and in his heart, the house had already crumbled to dust or been burned to ash.

Whoomph, whoomph. Artillery fire began to the north. *Whoomph, whoomph.* The explosions were not close enough yet to make the ground shake, but he soon saw plumes of dark smoke in the northeastern skies, no more than nine or ten kilometers away. For the first time, the true stakes of the journey that lay before him and his family became clear, sending him staggering, dizzied, against the side of the wagon. He was thrown back to a day in mid-September 1941, when he'd gripped the side of this same wagon, feeling relentless nausea and the noon heat and hearing the grasshoppers whirring as he gagged out the poison that had welled in his gut. He'd glared up in rage and shook his fist at the sky with such bitterness, he'd gotten ill all over again.

Remembering that day and still clinging to the side of the wagon, Emil gasped at the way his heart ached. *I remember this. How it felt to have my soul torn from my chest.*

———

Adeline ran from the house with a few more things. The boys were exiting the outhouse.

"Are we leaving now?" Will asked.

"Yes," she said. She rounded the house and saw Emil hunched over, holding on to the wagon with one hand, gasping, his eyes closed, his features twisted with pain as his free hand clawed at his chest.

"Emil!" she yelled, and rushed toward him. "What's wrong?"

Her husband startled and stared at Adeline as if she were part of a nightmare and then a desperately welcome dream. "Nothing."

"You looked like something was wrong with your heart."

"It hurt for a second there," he said, standing up and wiping the sweat gushing from his forehead. "But I'm all right."

"You're not all right," she said. "You're as white as snow, Emil."

"It's passing. I'm fine, Adella."

"Mama, here come Oma and Malia!" Will cried.

Adeline's concern left her husband and lifted when she spotted her mother at the reins of two old ponies pulling her wagon at a steady clip through the loose and shifting caravan of refugees and defeated soldiers all heading west.

Lydia Losing's face was harder and more pinched than usual, but the fifty-four-year-old was still dressed as she'd been dressed for the last fifteen years—in dark grays and widow black. As she was wont to do, Lydia was jawing at Adeline's sister, who was thirty-five and leaning slightly away from their mother, nodding and smiling without comment, a common-enough posture between the two of them. Malia had been kicked by a mule as a fifteen-year-old, which had left her childlike in some ways and wiser than most in others. She looked at Adeline and winked.

Another cannon barrage began, this one close enough to shake the ground beneath their feet. Four German fighters ripped across the sky, followed by six Soviet planes on their tails. Machine guns opened fire above them.

"Whoa!" Will said, thrilled.

"Mama!" Walt said, and grabbed Adeline around the waist.

———

"Everyone in!" Emil shouted, and ran to untie his horses from the tree.

When he was up on the bench with the reins in his hands and had checked to see that Adeline was beside him and the boys under the bonnet behind him, he yelled to his mother-in-law, "Let's get as far away from the battles as we can today!"

"As fast as my ponies will take us!" Lydia called back.

Emil released the wagon's simple lever brake and clucked up the horses, which leaned hard into the load, the wagon rolling slowly at first, and then gathering enough speed to slip into a gap between other wagons and groups of refugees on foot who stood to the side, all their belongings in burlap sacks, staring in envy as the Martels passed.

At the west end of the village, they passed Emil's parents' home, his childhood home. The front door to the old place was open. There was nothing worth saving in the yard.

Emil refused to let a single memory of his childhood or their more recent life in Friedenstal come up. That was over. The person it had happened to no longer existed. As far as he was concerned, that fractured life was now rubble.

———

Next to him, Adeline gazed into passing yards, seeing the ghosts of relationships past, of children playing, and parents singing at harvest, their entire way of life tied to and celebrating the seasons.

She remembered a happier time: 1922, being seven, and bouncing in a wagon like this. Adeline had sat in the back by baskets of food her mother had prepared as they rode out to the fields where the men were cutting wheat. It was almost October, but the air was still warm and smelled of everything lovely in her life. She took the basket to her father, the chief of harvest, as he worked on a mechanical threshing machine.

Karl Losing had a soft spot for his younger daughter and grinned when she brought him lunch. They'd sat side by side in the shade of the thresher, looking out over the golden hills of grain, and ate fresh bread with dried sausage and drank cold tea.

She remembered feeling completely safe and totally in love with her surroundings.

The Last Green Valley

"Will we always live here, Papa?" young Adeline had asked.

"Forever and a day, child," he said. "Unless, of course, the stinking Bolsheviks have their way, and we're thrown to the wind and the wolves."

In their wagon, rolling toward the far end of Friedenstal some twenty-two years later, Adeline recalled vividly being upset when her father had said that. For a time, she had walked around looking over both shoulders for fear wolves would burst from the forest and hunt her.

She felt the same way when they left the village, heading west with the rising sun and cannon fire still rumbling behind them, past fields waiting for plowing, and trees budding, and birds whirling and whistling above the bluffs, and dreams destroyed, buried by the realities of famine and war.

More German fighter planes raced across the sky, heading toward the battle lines.

"Where are we going, Papa?" Walt asked, sounding worried.

"West," Emil said. "As far west as we can go. Across the ocean, maybe; I don't know."

"Across the ocean?" Adeline said, surprised and a little frightened by that idea.

"Why not?" her husband said, glancing at her.

She said the first thing that came to mind. "We can't swim."

"We'll learn."

Will said, "But *why* are we going west?"

"Because life will be better there," Emil said.

A horse whinnied and then screamed in the shifting chaos of carts and wagons and tanks and trucks behind them. People began to yell and to shout. Walt scrambled to look back.

"Someone's wagon got hit by a Wehrmacht truck, a few behind Oma's wagon," he said. "A horse, too. It all tipped over, and the horse broke its leg and can't get up."

Emil clucked to Oden and Thor, and they hurried to close the gap with the wagon ahead.

Will still seemed upset. He climbed into his mother's lap, snuggled against her chest, and said, "Tell me what it will look like, Mama."

"What?" Adeline said, hugging and rocking him.

"West. What will it look like?"

Stroking her son's face, Adeline gazed into Will's eyes, smiled, and said, "We're going to a beautiful green valley surrounded by mountains and forests. And snow up high on the peaks. And below, there will be a winding river and fields of grain for bread, and gardens with vegetables to feed us, and Papa will build us a house where we'll all live together forever and ever, and we'll never be apart."

That seemed to soothe Will. The little boy relaxed.

"I think there will be other boys to play with," he said.

Adeline smiled at his expression, so innocent and hopeful, it made her heart swell. She tickled him, said, "I imagine there will be many boys to play with, and lots of work to be done, too. But we'll be happy, and you and your brother will grow up to follow your hearts' desires."

"What does that mean?"

Emil said, "That you'll be who you want to be, not who you're told to be."

"I'm going to be just like you, Papa," Will said as his eyes drifted shut.

Adeline glanced at her husband, who smiled, and then over her shoulder at Walt, who had lain down and was dozing.

She looked back at Emil, whose smile had fallen into something more pained.

"Are you sure you're okay?"

He belched. "There, that should do it. Probably what I was feeling back there."

After a few moments, she said quietly, "We'll find it, won't we, Emil? A valley like that we can call home? A place we'll never leave?"

Emil's face tightened further. He wouldn't look at her when he shrugged and said, "Someone once told me that if you keep praying for something, you can't help but get it someday."

"I told you that," Adeline said, smiling. "And Mrs. Kantor told me."

"I know."

"It's grace, Emil. God's answers to our prayers. You still believe in grace, don't you?"

"Adeline, with what you and I have seen with our own eyes, there are days I don't know if God hears us, much less answers. But I'll tell you something I do believe in."

"What's that?"

"Wherever we end up, it's going to be better than the hell we've already lived through."

The caravan crested a rise onto a plateau and turned north, giving Adeline one last long look back at their abandoned life. The cold wind had turned blustery. She heard cannons again and saw smoke rising from the ridges beyond the village.

"You're right," she said. "Anywhere will be better than that."

Chapter Two

November 1929
Schoenfeld, Ukraine

The light bulb flickered and died. But fourteen-year-old Adeline Losing had anticipated the cut in electricity at the small school she attended. She had already lit the kerosene lantern above the sink in the school kitchen where she worked after classes were over.

Scrubbing the last big pot of the day, Adeline felt hungry, a common-enough state in her recent life. She glanced at a bag filled with fresh potato-skin shavings on the counter, wondered how her mother might cook them, felt even hungrier, and then dried the pot and put it back on the shelf.

Two hours, Adeline thought, drying her hands. *Two hours of my life for a few rubles and a kilo of peelings. Is it worth it?*

She'd no sooner asked the question than she told herself to stop that line of thinking. Questioning your work and what you got in return for it could get you in trouble if you said it aloud under the rule of Joseph Stalin. Even thinking about it too much might let the words slip out by accident. And then where would she be?

Thrown to the wind and the wolves, as her father liked to say. That was where she'd be. Thrown to the wind and wolves in some far and frozen place.

Adeline put on her heavy wool coat, a gift from a dead aunt, telling herself, *Not me. I am going someplace better in my life.*

She got emotional at the thought of a better place. Somewhere she and her family could lead a better life than the unfair and cruel one they'd been given.

She didn't know much about this future life, but the simple idea of "better" made her smile and feel not as tired as she might have been.

Adeline wrapped her head in a wool scarf, picked up the lantern and her bags, and went to the kitchen door. She opened it and stepped out into a cold, dark night. Shivering, she locked the door, and then held up the lantern and set off west for the other side of town and home.

Hurry to it, she thought, and quickened her stride. *That's what Papa always says. If you want things, hurry to it. If you want things done, hurry to it.*

She'd never known anyone who hurried to it more than her father. He was up before everyone and last to bed, and in constant motion every minute in between.

Adeline kept up a steady, hard pace through the deserted streets of a farming colony that dated back four and five generations to when Catherine the Great reigned. Even in the late 1700s, the farmlands of Ukraine were among the most bounteous on earth, with rich, black soil that could yield bumper crops if properly sown and tended.

The peasants living there at the time, however, were poor agriculturists, and so the empress began approving the immigration of thousands of German families. These ethnic Germans, or *Volksdeutsche*, were given land and made exempt from taxes for decades in return for their agricultural skills and yield. They came in waves, farmed and prospered in self-imposed exile across Ukraine, providing wheat for Mother Russia for more than a century.

The *Volksdeutsche*, especially the so-called "Black Sea Germans" who lived between Odessa and Kiev, never fully assimilated into the Russian culture. They built their homes and laid out towns and villages like Schoenfeld as replicas of the ones they'd left behind in Germany, erecting churches to perpetuate their Lutheran faith and schools to educate their children and keep their native tongue alive.

But multiple generations removed, the Black Sea Germans had become isolated from Germany and its culture, almost completely disconnected from their roots. All in all, however, life was very good for the Black Sea Germans and for the roughly one million other *Volksdeutsche* living across Ukraine until 1917. Before the Bolshevik Revolution, Schoenfeld had been a thriving colony of ethnic Black Sea Germans who regularly produced high-yield crops that helped feed themselves and Russia.

But no longer.

By that evening, as young Adeline hurried through town, most of the other old families had been banished from the colony, thrown out of their houses and off their lands, replaced by people from the city who did not know how to farm at all. That was the main reason the Soviets decided to allow Adeline's family to remain in their ancestral home: her father was the only one left locally who understood how to bring in a big grain harvest. Without him, the idiots from the city would be doomed to one crop failure after another, and everyone around would starve.

But we're safe, Adeline told herself halfway through town. *Mama said so. They need Papa, so we're safe for now. And we should have enough food for the winter.*

Adeline stopped, lifting the lantern higher and peering at the form ahead of her, dark and lying still in the high dead grass. She took a cautious step, and then another. Reaching out with the lantern, she took a third step, and then froze.

The dog, a big mongrel, had been killed, its throat cut, and left to die in a halo of its own blood. The blood was wet, not yet frozen. It shimmered there in the lantern light, and that scared her even more. Someone had only just killed the animal.

Adeline raised the lantern and peered all around, seeing nothing but the pale skirt of light about her and shadows and darkness beyond. No movement. No sound but the beating of her heart in her ears and her own voice in her head.

Tell Papa!

She took off at a run, the lantern held out and to the side as she passed a horse barn that used to belong to her father's friend on the long lane before the final turn and home.

She spotted the second dead dog moments later, a small terrier, throat slashed and cast in the ditch. Adeline knew the dog, a friendly yapper, and wanted to cry. She'd seen him only just that morning on her way to school.

They killed two!

Terrified now, she ran even faster and fought dark imaginations, all of them feeding into another until her mind was flooded and swirling with the murder of the two dogs. She finally made the gate to her home, a beautiful wooden house her great-grandfather had built almost a century before in a modest Bavarian style, with a sweeping shake-shingle roof, two gables, and red trim along the soffits. Kneeing open the door bar, she pushed inside and used her heel to shut the door behind her.

"Put that lantern out," her father called from the table where he was repairing a leather harness for his plow horses with two glowing lanterns hanging from the rafters above him and a blazing fire at his back.

"Papa, I—"

"Put your lantern out, girl," Karl Losing said. "Fuel's rare these days."

"Listen to your father," her mother, Lydia, called from the kitchen beyond him. "And where are those peelings? I expected you long before this."

Adeline swallowed her frustration and blew out the lantern as her eleven-year-old brother, Wilhelm, came in from the back with wood for the fire. She hung the lantern on a hook by the front door and put away her coat and scarf before hurrying with the potato peels past her father and brother into the kitchen where Lydia had a loaf of bread coming hot from the wood oven.

"Peelings," Adeline said, putting the bag down. "A whole kilo. I measured."

"You done with the onions to go with them, Malia?" her mother said, setting the bread tin on the stove to cool.

"If I was, you would be the first to know, Mother," Adeline's older sister, Amalia, said in her odd cadence. She had her back to them and was chopping onions slowly but steadily.

"Set the table, Adella," her mother said. "And fill the pitcher from the well."

"I have to tell Papa something, Mama."

"You'll do as you're told."

Adeline knew it was impossible to reason with her mother once an order had been given, so she grabbed the pitcher and went outside to the pump in the backyard. The temperature was dropping, and her hands were stinging when she returned and put the water on the table. She set spoons for five around the table and around her father, who kept at his harness, engrossed in his work. Once there were cups and bowls laid out as well, Adeline stood squarely in front of him.

"Papa," she said.

"Can it wait for dinner, child?" he said, never looking up at her.

"Can't you see your father's busy?" her mother called.

Adeline felt unseen, unheard, and something in her broke. She burst into tears. "Papa, please! You need to listen to me!"

At last, her father took his attention off his leatherwork, looking puzzled by the outburst. "What is this? Why the tears? What have you got to be sad about today?"

"On the way home from school," she blubbered, "I saw two dead dogs. Their throats had been cut. The blood was fresh."

Her father's face fell. He set the harness on the table and said softly, "Calm down, Adella, and tell me where you saw them."

Her crying slowed. She wiped at her tears with the frayed sleeve of her sweater.

"How far from here?" he said.

"The second one three hundred meters?" she said. "Maybe less."

Her father studied his leathery hands. Adeline had always thought him larger than life and full of fire, but now he seemed suddenly smaller, less sure of himself.

He glanced at his wife, who stood in the kitchen doorway, worrying her apron.

"It's someone else, Karl," she said. "One of the new fools flapping his jaws."

He swallowed hard and nodded. "Let's pray so."

Adeline could not help herself. She went around the table and threw her arms around her father. He said nothing, just rubbed her arm for several moments before saying, "I have to finish my work before supper, girl. Go help your mother."

She kissed his cheek and drew back. He smiled softly and touched her face before returning to the harness with the awl, the big-eyed needle, and the leather cord.

Adeline went back to the kitchen where her mother was stirring onions and potato peels in a cast-iron skillet.

"Mama," she said.

"It's for one of the fools," her mother declared.

"What is?" Malia asked.

Adeline started to reply, but her mother looked over her shoulder sharply at Adeline and shook her head.

"Nothing, sweetie," Adeline said.

Malia said, "I'm not going to break, you know."

"I know."

"I'm better than ever."

"You are," their mother said. "Better than we could have hoped."

"Thank you, Mama," Malia said, and seemed to lose her train of thought. "What am I doing next?"

"Sitting down, dear," Adeline said. "We're going to eat."

"Oh," her sister said, brightening. "I like that."

Aside from Malia and Wilhelm, the mood at the table that evening was somber. Adeline and her parents feared what the dead dogs meant.

There was no insane man on the loose with canine bloodlust in Schoenfeld. The OGPU, Stalin's secret police, was well known to arrange to have dogs murdered so their barking would not give the police away when they came in search of political prisoners during the night.

At one point during the meal, Adeline was stunned to see her father's spoon shake and his food fall back into his bowl.

Her mother put her hand on his elbow. "You brought in the best harvest they've had in six years, Karl. There are grain shortages everywhere else. They cannot do without you."

He did not look convinced. "They don't want you to do well, haven't you heard?"

He stared at the table a moment, and then smashed it with his fist. "First the Communists killed all the smart people who made things work in the cities. And now they want to make doing good at anything at all a punishable crime! What has happened to the world? How did we end up in an asylum?"

He looked at his stunned wife, daughters, and son, who were all slightly cowering from him. Ordinarily, Karl Losing was a quiet, well-tempered, even affable man. But now his shoulders were slumped, and there was anger and then despair in his voice when he said, "You don't grow grain, people starve. You grow too much and feed too many, and you become an enemy of the people. How is this right?"

"It's not right," Adeline said.

"Not a bit," Malia said, surprising everyone. "If you work hard, Papa, if you hurry to it, you are doing the right thing because God rewards your hard labor."

Their father's eyes misted as he gazed helplessly at his brain-injured older daughter.

"Yes, sweetheart, but that was when life made sense. Now there's nothing but madness."

———

They came at three o'clock the following morning with heavy fists and batons pounding on the front door, waking the entire family up. Lydia began to cry almost immediately, and so did her older daughter.

"What's happening?" Adeline's little brother said sleepily from the trundle bed below her.

"Shhhh," she said. "I'll go see."

Adeline climbed down from the bed in the dark.

"Papa?" Adeline said when she'd reached the short upper hall and saw the silhouette of her father starting down the steep stairs with a lantern.

"Stay there, child," he said softly, gazing back at her. "It's okay."

But she could not help herself and followed him, creeping two stairs to look down and to her right where her father stood before the door, trembling.

"Open up!" a voice called in Russian.

He bowed his head, set the lantern on the ledge, and drew back the bar. A baton came out of the night, striking her father low in the gut. He buckled, staggered backward, and fell.

Adeline screamed, "Papa!"

He doubled up, rolled over in agony. Two big men in dark long coats came in.

"I am Commissar Karpo of the OGPU," said the third man behind them, smaller, older. "Comrade Losing, you are hereby charged with being a kulak."

"You mean someone who knows what they're doing?" he gasped.

One of the bigger men kicked him.

"No, comrade," the commissar said. "I mean someone who steals from the people and from the state."

"I've stolen nothing," Adeline's father said. "I gave you a good harvest."

Commissar Karpo looked at his men. "Search it. Out back, too."

"What are you looking for?"

"We'll know when we find it."

Lydia, Malia, and Wilhelm gathered behind Adeline on the staircase, terrified as they watched the secret policemen handcuff Karl and leave him sprawled on his side as two of the goons tore the lower house apart. Ten minutes into the search, one of them came back with a big sack of grain.

"Found it in a bin in the shed," he said.

The commissar smiled. "And you say you steal nothing, Comrade Losing?"

"A man has a right to provide a little extra for his family in return for all his hard work."

"Wherever did you get that idea?"

Lydia pushed by her children and went weeping down the stairs. "Please don't kill him."

"Kill him?" the commissar said, amused. "No, your husband will go to work now where he will learn to think better of his fellow man. In Siberia."

They gave her father an hour to gather his warmest clothes. He was permitted to hug his wife and each of his children before they led him toward the door.

Lydia wept. "How long will he be gone?"

"That is not my decision," Commissar Karpo said.

"What is to become of us?"

"What becomes of all kulaks," he said, and turned away.

"I will come back!" Adeline's father shouted as he was dragged off into the night. "I promise you all I will come back!"

Chapter Three

Late March 1944
Twenty-five kilometers east of the Transnistria-Moldova border

In the Martels' wagon, trailing another wagon, and hundreds more ahead of them all mixed into the semicontrolled chaos of the retreating German armies, Adeline could remember her father disappearing into the darkness of that terrible night as if it happened yesterday.

I promise you all I will come back!

Nearly fifteen years of waiting had passed since that night. Adeline could still recall the raw loss on her mother's face in the days and weeks after her husband vanished, a wound that had grown deeper with each passing year of not knowing, of trying to keep hope alive.

Adeline glanced over her shoulder, saw her boys dozing with blankets around their shoulders and across their laps. Despite the quickening wind, she got up to stand on the wagon bench beside Emil as the horses took them clip-clopping down the road. Looking back over the top of the canvas bonnet, she saw her older sister sitting next to her mother in their wagon, head up, swiveling, taking it all in, seeming fascinated by the newness of the landscape and the ever-changing convoy.

But not Adeline's mother. Lydia was slumped behind the reins as if her shoulders bore a lead weight, staring at her ponies, lost in years of unanswered prayers. Lydia had never stopped believing Karl would return. When they were finally thrown out of their ancestral home in 1930, she had insisted on writing a letter to her husband, telling him where they had gone and why. She left it behind a loose stone in the foundation where he always used to secret his valuable things.

Recalling the years of hardship, toil, and loneliness her mother had endured after their father was taken and after they'd been turned into the streets, Adeline felt her heart ache with pity. And what about Wilhelm, her younger brother? She had no idea what had become of him after the Germans drafted him to fight three years ago. It was the same story with Emil's older brother, Reinhold. Drafted into the Wehrmacht, taken from his family, Reinhold had been sent west to defend Paris and had not been heard from since.

Adeline looked past her mother's wagon and saw six or seven others behind her, all driven by women, all with those same hunched-over shoulders and gritted expressions, all widows of Stalin. Her mother was not the only one leaving loved ones behind that day. Yes, this trek west under Nazi protection was a new beginning for Lydia and for all the other single women in the caravan. But it had to be the end of their hopes as well, an end to their dreams of ever seeing their husbands come home.

How do you live with that? Adeline wondered sadly. *How do you survive?*

"Adeline," Emil said, tapping her leg, "get the boys ready. There's a storm coming. We're going to get hit hard."

Adeline looked north and saw the bruised clouds coming fast. She woke the boys and helped them into their patched woolen overalls, jackets, and hats, before pulling wool leggings up under her smock and dress and putting on a heavy wool sweater under her coat. She took the reins from Emil to let him change. He'd donned the last of his woolens when Adeline felt the first snowflake hit her cheek.

He retook the reins as the snow flurries became big flakes that began to stick and plaster the horses' flanks and withers. He told Adeline to get under the bonnet and the tarp with the boys.

A kilometer farther on, the snow became driving sheets of white spiraling out of the northwest and hitting them sideways. The horses turned their heads away from the wind, which made reining them and keeping the wagon on the road difficult in the increasingly treacherous conditions. The snow came slanting in even harder, stinging Emil's eyes and cheeks. With every gust, the wagon creaked and groaned, and the bonnet stretched and squealed across the bowed wood frame.

Emil looked back at his family. "I want all of you on the right side against the wind, so we won't tip over. And check the knots holding the cover to the frame, Adella."

While Adeline got the boys shifted over to the right side and checked the knots, Emil wrapped his scarf around his neck, mouth, and nose and pulled his cap down low over his eyes. But the snow now rode on a shuddering gale. It pounded him, found the collar of his coat, and crawled down his back. It stung his knuckles through his mittens and gnawed at the exposed right side of his face until his skin was raw and then numb.

The horses plodded on with their heads held left and low, leaving their right shoulders and flanks exposed to the wind that grew more frigid and gustier by the moment. Realizing his horses were at risk, he pulled off to the side of the track and gestured to his mother-in-law to do the same. Other wagons ground past him.

Adeline and the boys were huddled on the wagon's right side beneath the blankets. She had her back to the side of the wagon, which was now shaking violently. She looked at him in alarm. "Will it hold, Emil?"

"I don't know," he admitted, rummaging in a box before coming up with leather blinders for both horses.

He threw his forearm across his eyes, then fought his way back to Oden and Thor. He buckled the blinders to their hackamores, shielding their eyes from some of the brutal sidewinds. Then he went back to Lydia's wagon, got her ponies' blinders, and put them on. Looking back along the track, he saw a gap in the line of the convoy.

Emil jumped back aboard his wagon, grabbed the reins, and snapped them across the horses' rumps. The wagon slid sideways for a few meters in the snow, then straightened and began to roll forward. The blinders seemed to be helping. Both horses had their heads more upright and their ears forward and alert. Emil saw their earlier cue, and ducked his own head low and left, absorbing the brunt of the weather across his right shoulder and side.

He kept sneaking quick looks toward the snowed-in track, catching glimpses of the wagon in front of him a good thirty meters, and little else beyond or to the sides. Everything had gone white and billowing. Emil sensed they were moving across wide-open farm country with little to block or slow the winds. In the woods or where the land was broken, he was sure they would have stopped the trek, told everyone to take cover in a creek bottom or a ravine.

A huge gust howled toward them, smashed the Martels' wagon broadside. They went up on two wheels and slammed back down. The boys and Adeline screamed.

Thor and Oden felt the jolt, heard the screams, and dug in with their hooves, taking short, choppy strides fast enough that the wagon's rear end swung in the snow, almost throwing Emil off and causing him to drop the reins. Thor and Oden ducked their heads away from the oncoming gale and snow, and before Emil could stop them, they had gone right, off the track, and were gaining speed across bouncy terrain.

The snow and wind were blinding as Emil reached forward again and once more tried to grab the reins lying over Oden's rump. But they'd iced up and slipped through his mitts. He thought about the brake on the left front wheel but feared flipping or breaking an axle in this uneven ground. His horses were spooked, disoriented, and at a canter now, quartering to the storm as they went, throwing wet snow and mud behind them. The wagon pitched, bucked, and slid as the blizzard pounded them.

"Stop them!" Adeline shouted. "We'll crash!"

Emil took off his left mitt and leaned and reached as far as he could, snagging the reins with two fingers. He soon had them wrapped three times around his right wrist before grabbing forward on the reins with his bare left hand, bracing his feet, and driving himself backward against the weight of his runaway horses.

He yanked at the bits in their mouths, forcing their heads lower and lower, until they finally slowed and stopped. Their sides heaved and quivered with exertion and fear. They blew hard through their noses and coughed, stamped their feet, and again turned their heads from the storm.

"I want to go home!" Walt said.

Emil ignored him, tied off the reins, turned his back on the weather, and climbed up on the bench to look behind him. All he could see was white and swirling. No trees. No hedgerows. No other wagons. No track. Nothing but the storm.

"Emil!" Adeline shouted. "Which way do we go?"

He thought about all the bucking and sliding they'd done, the mud and snow clods the horses had kicked up, and said, "We'll follow our tracks back."

It worked for the first few minutes. He was able to see where they'd come from but understood how fast the snow was falling and how quickly the wind was covering their tracks. He wanted to urge his horses to go faster, but he was having trouble seeing.

And then he couldn't make out their wheel tracks at all. Everything was snowed over. The snow was up to the axles of the wagon. *If I keep it up . . .*

Emil did not like thinking about ifs. He decided instead to zigzag forward from the last trace by dead reckoning, hoping to come upon tracks the storm had not yet erased. But with the wind churning the heavy snowfall, there was nothing. He finally turned the wagon broadside to the wind, stopped, and set the brake.

"What are we doing?" Adeline asked.

"Waiting out the storm," he said. "We can't be more than five hundred meters from that road, but I have no idea where exactly. When we can see, we'll find it. We'll catch up to the trek."

He climbed down and unharnessed the horses. He brought them around on the leeward side of the wagon, tied them to it, and then climbed into the back of the wagon.

"You look like a snowman, Papa!" Will said from under the blankets.

Emil looked down and saw he was coated head to toe in snow.

Walt started to laugh. So did Adeline, who said, "Take it off or brush it off. You'll get us all wet if you get under the blankets with us."

Emil struggled to get his coat off, then shook it out the back and laid it to the side.

He did the same with his boots and pants, and then slid under the blankets next to Walt. It was warm, and even though the wagon was getting buffeted, the bonnet and his frame seemed to be holding. They were safe for now.

The wind ebbed a little and then a lot. For a good fifteen seconds, the bonnet above them luffed. Then a gust hit before another lull and then another howl. Emil gazed across the heads of his boys at his wife, frightened and transfixed by the weather.

"We'll be okay," he said.

———

Adeline roused slowly from her nap, at first not understanding where she was, only that her body was warm, and she was breathing in bitterly cold air. The horses shifted against their leads and the wagon, bringing her fully awake. She opened her eyes, saw it was still day but no longer snowing. Emil was already up and gone.

Will stirred, said, "Are we there yet?"

Walt said, "Does anything look green out there to you?"

Adeline tickled Will, and then got out from under the blankets and onto the bench. Her breath threw clouds. The sky was clearing. The sun said it was midafternoon. Everything as far as she could see, and she could see quite far, was sparkling and brilliant white, so dazzling, it hurt her eyes to look for long.

Emil came around the side of the wagon, leading Oden and Thor. "Can you fetch some grain?"

"Yes. Where are we? Where's the road?"

"I think it's near that thin tree line way over there," he said, gesturing with his free hand. "But we'll go up that little hill to get a better look."

"I don't see any wagons or vehicles."

"We will from up there," he said, harnessing Oden. "I promise you we'll be on that road before dark and caught up to the trek before you know it."

When Adeline jumped down, the snow was up to her knees in places, but she could see where it had drifted deeper. After she'd gotten the horses a full can from their single sack of oats, and Emil had harnessed Thor, they set out for that hill ahead of them.

"You think we'll make it to the top?" she asked. "We don't want to get stuck."

"We'll get as close as we can, and I'll climb from there."

In the wake of the storm, the air had turned so bitter, the blowing snow writhed like smoke around the horses' legs and the wagon wheels. Emil stopped them well short of the base of the hill, which was drifted over.

"I'll be right back," he said, and handed her the reins.

Adeline watched her husband march into the drift, only to go as far as midthigh, which delighted both boys, who laughed.

"Papa got stuck," Will said.

"Not for long," Adeline said as Emil fought and kicked his way up to shallower snow and then went steadily up the hill.

He was about three-quarters of the way up when, over the boys' talking and the horses' jingling their harnesses, Adeline heard a low rumble to the south, back toward the tree line. She got up on the wagon bench, shielded her eyes, and saw six German Panzer tanks about a kilometer away, grinding through the snow in their direction.

"Thank God," she said to the boys. "Once they drive through, they'll pound down all the snow, and it will be easy for us to get from here to the road."

The sound of the tanks seemed suddenly to get louder and closer, so close she barely caught the sound of a voice yelling. Then she realized the sound was not coming from the south, but from the north.

She whipped her head around, seeing Emil leaping down the hill toward them like some spooked goat, his knees pumping and his lower legs snapping forward, getting buried in the snow, and then vaulting up and out again. Even with seventy meters separating them, she could see the terror on his face.

"Adeline!" he screamed.

"Mama! Look on top!" Walt yelled.

Up the hill and behind Emil a good two hundred meters, the barrel of the cannon of a Soviet tank appeared, followed by its huge turret and armored hull, treads chewing up the snow and the semifrozen earth below.

"Run!" Will screamed. "Run, Papa!"

Emil glanced over his shoulder, hit the deep snow at the bottom of the hill, staggered, and sprawled forward on his face. The tank stopped, pivoted, roared down the hill toward them.

Emil was already back up on his feet, swimming and throwing himself forward again and again, not seeing the tank stop on a terrace on the hillside a quarter of the way down. Another Soviet tank appeared, and a third. They clanked down to the first tank and stopped.

Emil, meanwhile, had flailed free of the deep snow and charged the wagon like some crazed snow creature. He scrambled up onto the bench, grabbed the reins, and yelled, "Hold on!"

Grabbing a buggy whip, something he almost never used, Emil lashed at the rumps of his horses while pulling the reins hard left. Oden and Thor coiled and drove forward, sending the wagon sideways before heading due south.

"There are Panzers in front of us," Adeline said, holding the side rail for dear life.

"What?"

"From the tree line, coming our way. They're in a low spot now. Six of—"

A punching roar cut her off, followed by two more in tight succession as the Soviet tanks opened fire. The horses screamed and bolted from the noise, galloping south even as the first Soviet rounds hit down range near that low spot, blast after blast after blast throwing ice and snow and fire that spiraled into the bitter air.

"Turn back!" Adeline shouted. "We'll be safer behind the Soviets."

"We'll be dead behind the Soviets," he shouted back, and whipped his horses again.

The Panzer tanks ahead of them returned fire, three guns simultaneously followed by two and then one, all of them brilliant enough flashes at the muzzle that the horses began to slow, not knowing what to fear, until Emil lashed at them again.

German shells erupted on the hillside behind them. Oden took charge then, broke back into a gallop, bringing the wagon sliding behind him until Thor found his stride and cadence. The wagon gathered speed. The wheels sliced and plowed through the snow.

Another Red Army tank had reached the crown of the hill behind them and fired its cannon before the other three tanks followed suit. The Soviet rounds again hit shy of that low spot where the Panzers lay, spewing flame and rock, but causing no damage. Emil could see the Panzers moving now, churning up out of the low spot and through the smoke and the snow blackened from the blasts, turrets pivoting for drift, cannon barrels rising for windage.

The German tanks began to fire on their own now, moving independently and evasively north across the snowy flat before pausing to send a round at the hillside, which was getting farther and farther behind the Martels. The Soviets opened fire again.

Four hundred meters separated the young family from the closest two of the six Panzers, which had slowed to a stop as their cannon barrels adjusted.

Emil never stopped whipping his horses toward the oncoming German tanks, even when the Russian rounds hit and exploded between them, hurling pillars of flame and charred debris and snow into the sky.

Adeline and the boys were screaming behind him, but he couldn't stop. The two closest Panzers were prowling again, coming toward them. The ground between Emil and the tanks narrowed. He reined his horses farther right, trying to get out of their way, and then lashed Oden and Thor as he never had, cruelly and with purpose, again and again, with every inch of his being.

A Panzer to their right fired its cannon, causing the horses to veer left. Emil pulled them back right, only to have the nearest German tank fire over their heads from less than one hundred meters away. The roar was deafening. The energy of the muzzle blast battered horse and man alike. The horses lurched. Emil felt it like a heavy vibrating punch that had him loopy as he tried to keep whipping the horses.

They shot through the gap between the two Panzers.

They were well beyond them when the Soviets opened fire again. The German tank that had been closest to them was hit and blew up, throwing fire and black smoke above the stark white fields.

A German army truck was suddenly right there four hundred meters in front of them, crossing left to right, heading to the southwest. The track. The road.

Emil finally stopped whipping his horses. His ears were still ringing, and he felt dizzy when he turned his heaving, coughing horses into the ruts created by the passing truck. Only then did he glance over his shoulder at his wife and children lying amid the jumble of their once carefully packed wagon. They were all gaping at him, in shock at having just survived a battlefield, still cowering at every blast in the fight raging behind them. He smiled and nodded, then looked back to his horses, saw their rumps were bleeding from open lash wounds, and felt so bad, he choked back sobs.

Chapter Four

Every muscle in Adeline's body trembled. Her ribs hurt. Her throat was sore from screaming. Her ears buzzed, and everything sounded hollow and far away.

She could tell Will and Walt were just as stunned and overwhelmed by what they had endured, and her first instinct was to comfort them. But then she realized Emil was hunched over, shoulders shaking, and crying. She shook free of the daze, got up on all fours, crawled to him, and hugged him fiercely.

"You saved us," she said, barely able to hear her own words. "You saved us all."

Emil wiped at his eyes with his forearm, and then gestured at the blood trickling from their horses' wounds before gazing at her in deep sorrow and regret.

"I know how you love them," Adeline shouted. "But they will heal, and we are alive because of what you and they had to do."

She did not know if he could hear what she was saying, but he seemed to feel it. Some of the tension drained out of him. Then he kissed her, got down, and gathered snow that he spread over the lash wounds. Each horse quivered violently at the sensation, blew repeatedly at the pain, and then gradually settled the more snow he caked on.

Adeline's hearing was starting to return when he climbed back onto the wagon. He lifted the reins gently and barely touched their tails to get them moving again. The cannon fire had stopped. It appeared that the Panzers had driven the Soviets back after leaving two of the four Red tanks burning hulks on the far hillside.

She felt a tug on her sleeve. Will was up on his knees behind her.

"Can you hear?" he asked.

"Getting better."

"I hear," Will said, smiled, shook his head like crazy, and waved his hands around his ears in a way that made her laugh.

His smile in reaction to her laugh lit her up even more, made her grateful for every breath. They'd been through a blizzard. They'd been through the middle of a tank battle. And they'd survived! All four of them. Banged, bruised, but nothing major broken.

Adeline wanted to laugh and sing and cry all at once. She didn't know if she'd ever felt so . . . so alive! Walt got up beside his brother, looking confused as he pointed to his ears.

"Make it stop, Mama," he said, wringing his mittens together and barely holding back tears. "Will that happen every day, Mama?"

She realized how upset her older boy was and shook her head while throwing open her arms to him. Walt hesitated and then went to her, and she held him tight. He'd seen so much in just the six hours since they'd left their home. It was a lot for a six-and-a-half-year-old boy, she thought, and held him closer. Then she felt Will hug her from behind, laying his cheek against the nape of her neck, and nothing else mattered.

Adeline beamed through tears that she blinked back to see Emil gazing over at them all, as happy as she'd ever seen him. *Is that what it takes to feel like this? To come so close to death, you want to burst for joy because you feel so glad to be alive?*

That joy did not leave her. Every single tree or abandoned shack or rock wall or windmill that they encountered sticking up out of the vast snow-coated landscape she admired in true wonder; they were all gifts that she would take with her and never forget.

———

To Emil's surprise, they caught up to the back of the trek within an hour. The SS had called a halt during the worst of the storm, and the caravan was now rolling along in fits and starts, with fewer starts than fits. Adding to the mess were German reinforcements and supply trucks traveling the same routes, but moving against the westward-bound trek, headed east toward the ever-shifting battlefront right behind them.

"How far are we going today, Papa?" Walt asked.

"We don't get to say."

"Who does get to say?"

"Our . . . escorts," Emil said, unable to hide his distaste. "The Nazis. The SS. For some reason, they were assigned to protect us on the way west. They will tell us when to move and when to stay."

"Why can't we move when we want?" Will asked.

"Because we are refugees of war now, people who left their lands behind. We have nothing, so we get to say nothing."

Emil felt a helplessness he hadn't felt in a long time. He had liked being fully in charge of his life in Friedenstal. He did not like being told what to do and never had, though he was not stupid or vocal about it in response.

He knew he was at the mercy of the Nazi escorts, with zero say in the direction of his near future. But it was best for his family. Of that he had no doubt. If they'd stayed behind, waited for the Russians, his family would have been torn apart. He would have been sent east to the camps and Adeline with him, leaving the boys orphans of the state.

Emil knew he had made the right move for their survival. But he still chafed at being at other men's whims, especially when they were men he despised.

For the next five kilometers, they lost altitude, and the snow dwindled. With darkness approaching and the temperature turning bitter, they caught up to and passed Lydia's wagon, with the boys yelling about their adventure in the storm and outrunning the tank battle, which frightened their grandmother and astonished their aunt Malia.

The trek slowed yet again. Word came from the SS that the Wehrmacht had halted all westward travel for the night so troop transports and lorries heading east could pass, bringing reinforcements and supplies to the front. Wagons began to pull off to camp.

Emil saw a wagon with a distinctive bonnet ahead, by a line of trees off to the side of the route. "Look who's camped ahead. We'll sleep there."

He pulled their wagon in near a wagon with a cover cleverly woven of dried reeds.

A stooped, shuffling man who looked years past his age appeared, bearing a hatchet and a bundle of firewood, oblivious that they were near him. He dropped the wood near a smoldering fire in a ring of rocks by his wagon and seemed lost. As Emil often did upon seeing his father, he felt a certain sadness; Johann Martel had suffered mightily under Stalin.

"Opa!" the boys cried. "Grandfather!"

Will and Walt clambered out of the wagon and ran over by Emil's father and the fire to get warm and tell him about the tank battle and how the horses had saved them.

Johann smiled at the boys, and with his thick hands patted their shoulders uncomfortably. Emil climbed down and started to see to his horses.

"You and your mother will cook supper?" he said to Adeline.

"And Malia," Adeline said. "Should we build our own fire? Or ask to share?"

"I'll ask."

Emil tied Oden and Thor to a tree, then unbuckled them from their harnesses, gave them more oats, rubbed salve into their wounds, and apologized again for whipping them so. When he was done, he went toward the fire. Before he could get there, his mother, a hard, flinty woman in her sixties, appeared around the back of her wagon, as if she'd been hiding there, waiting for him.

Karoline Martel gestured at her grandsons squatting over by the fire.

"I expect you'll be feeding them from your own stores, Emil."

"We will," Emil said. "Though it hardly makes sense to start two fires."

His mother scowled slightly. "It can't all be on your father."

"Agreed," he said, then called to Walt and Will. "Boys! Go find all the dead branches you can before it gets too dark and drag them up here. I see some down there by the stream. Nothing wet, now."

His sons looked ruefully at the roaring fire but then got up, and, as boys are wont to do, made it a game. Even at four and a half, Will was the more competitive of the two.

"I'll find more than you, Walt!" he cried, and took off.

"Who cares about finding more?" Walt called as he ran after his little brother. "You have to bring back the biggest one."

"And before dark," their father yelled.

They went off toward the stream, laughing and shrieking, the terror of the tank battle forgotten for the moment. Emil ignored his mother's disapproval and watched them go, his heart warmed that his sons could find a way to play and laugh while trying to outrun a war.

Johann coughed, then coughed deeper, rattling from his chest. He paused, but then was racked by a longer coughing fit that finally brought up mucus that he spat out on the ground. He took a step with a bewildered expression on his face.

"You should sit now, Johann," Karoline called over, looking concerned and then glaring at her son. "You see, getting the wood has already weakened him."

"It's just a little cough, Karoline," Johann said, but sat on a stump, his back to one wheel of his wagon. "I've been through worse."

"It's a little cough that almost killed you in the mines," his wife shot back.

"A little cough set me free, didn't it?"

"And look at you," she said, still bitter that he'd been taken from her by Stalinists in the middle of the night and sent to Siberia, just like Adeline's father.

Johann, a farmer, had been a man used to living outside, but they put him to work below ground. He spent nearly seven years in the mines, digging coal, before his cough began, and then spread to other prisoners. By his own account, Johann almost died twice while more men came down with the mysterious ailment. The Soviets in charge of the mine feared they'd lose their entire work base and decided that instead of treating or killing the sick men, they'd set them free, kick them out of the camps, tell them to go home.

Sick, feverish, Emil's father had boarded a freight train in the middle of summer and rode west for weeks in blistering heat before finding his way back to southern Russia. He was emaciated, racked by coughing, and filthy with grime when he knocked at Karoline's door. She had not recognized her own husband.

Neither had his son, who thought his father had aged forty years in the seven he'd been gone. And it wasn't just the mysterious lung sickness. The years in the mines of Siberia had done something to Johann, broken him somehow, robbed him of his inner fire. In the years after his return, he'd often be found staring off into the middle distance, transported to some dark past he rarely spoke of. Emil's mother said he would often awake screaming at night, feverish and drenched in sweat.

"Where is Rese?" Emil said.

"Your sister's sleeping," she said. "All the jolting in the wagon that last bit made her sick to her stomach."

"Emil?" Adeline called before Emil could reply. "Are we good for the fire?"

Emil turned to see Adeline, Lydia, and Malia bringing pots and cooking supplies.

"We're good," he called. "And the boys are bringing more wood."

———

Adeline nodded, but as she came closer, her attention left her husband and darted to her mother-in-law, focusing then on Karoline gazing at the fire. Try as she might, Adeline could not help thinking of a small bottle of cream and feeling a familiar bitterness spoil her stomach. She mentally put her armor on, went to the fire, crouched, and with a stick began drawing glowing coals off to the side.

From childhood, Adeline had been by nature a warm, giving person, with hardly ever a cross word to say about anyone. But her mother-in-law was not anyone. Karoline was a cold, heartless being. Adeline could not stand being around her and avoided the woman as often as possible.

"No hellos?" Karoline said out of the corner of her mouth.

Adeline looked up, forced a smile. "Oh, hello, Karoline. I'm sorry. Mind's on supper. Thank you for letting us use your fire. It's very nice of you."

Karoline studied her a moment, and then moved her focus to Adeline's mother. Lydia greeted Emil's mother, and thanked her for the fire as well, knowing that acting subordinate tended to make Karoline less testy. Adeline put the pot on the coals and heated a stew they'd made from potatoes, onions, and salt pork.

"Put these in, too!" Malia cried, rushing over with a bunch of baby wild asparagus. "I found them near our wagon! Like someone planted them just for us!"

Adeline's older sister seemed so delighted, not even Karoline's presence could stop Adeline from smiling and taking the asparagus from her. It had been twenty years since Malia had gone to feed the family mules and been kicked, two decades since she'd lain in a coma when no one thought she had a chance of living. But Malia had spirit and woke up, certainly changed in many ways, but also the same as she'd ever been: sincere, kind, loving, and oddly funny. Adeline had adored her as a child and adored her still.

The boys returned, pushing their little wagon, now filled with two big broken branches, up the hill from the creek bottom.

Emil walked over, and in the glow of the fire, walked around the two branches, studying them. "Well," he said at last, "I think Walt's branch is bigger."

"What?" Will said.

"I told you!" Walt crowed.

"But," their father said, "given the fact, Walt, that you have two years on Will, and eight kilos, I declare it a tie."

"What?" Walt said.

"A tie!" Will said, dancing around.

Walt looked dejected until Emil reminded him that firewood would be needed every night until their journey was over, and Adeline went over to give him and his brother a hug.

"Why'd you hug us, Mama?" Will asked.

"For getting the firewood."

"Should we hug you for making dinner?"

"Yes, please," she said, teasing him. "And for everything else I do for you."

A girl's voice grumbled loudly behind them. "Stop with all the hugging. It's giving me a headache on top of my stomachache."

Adeline looked across the fire, past her mother-in-law, and saw Emil's sister, twenty-one-year-old Theresa, who was climbing down from their wagon. Known as "Rese," she was dressed as Adeline and the other women were, in heavy, dark wool jackets and long smock skirts, but unlike the other women, Rese wore her golden hair down rather than wrapped in a kerchief or wool scarf.

"How do you feel?" her mother asked.

Rese had her hands jammed in the pockets of her jacket. "Like I'm freezing and there's a nail in my head and I want to puke."

The boys started laughing. Adeline smiled. She liked Rese. As with her own sister, you never knew what she was going to say.

Sure enough, Malia tapped her head and chimed in, "Could be worse. You could have a mule kick your skull."

Rese stopped, tapped her lower lip. "I will not argue with you, Malia. A mule kick to the skull would be worse than wanting to puke when you've got a nail in your head."

Will and Walt laughed at her again. Even Emil chuckled until Karoline said, "That's enough, all of you. Don't encourage her. Rese, do you ever think before you speak?"

Emil's sister walked past her mother, dismissively. "What fun would that be?"

"My God, what have I created?" Karoline said.

Adeline caught a flicker of pain crossing Rese's face before she smiled and said, "You didn't create me alone, Mother."

Her mother gasped at her impudence. Johann smiled.

Rese held her cold hands out to the fire. "And think: if God had a hand in it, too, if being born is a miracle like you once told me, Mother, then I am a miracle, and I am everything I am supposed to be right now. Right?"

Karoline was staring at her like she was speaking another language. Malia broke into a huge grin.

"Johann," Karoline complained, "where does she think these things?"

He shrugged, still smiling.

"In her brain," Walt said.

Rese laughed, pointed at Walt. "I like how my little nephew thinks."

Karoline threw up her hands, looked to the first stars in the night sky, and said, "I give up. She's beyond me."

Rese came around the fire and talked to the boys while Adeline stirred the stew. When she was done, Rese came over and whispered, "Ever notice how it's always about Mother? What did 'I' create? What did 'I' give up?"

"Now that you mention it."

"Deep down, I think she doesn't like other people because she doesn't like herself."

"I gave up trying to understand your mother a long time ago," Adeline said, and retrieved the pot from the coals.

Lydia brought bowls that Adeline filled with piping hot stew.

"That smells great," Rese said. "Can I have some?"

Her mother heard that. "You have your supper here. Biscuits and dried meat."

"Biscuits and dried meat?" Rese complained. "It's cold out, Mother. I'd rather eat what they're eating."

"I'm sure you would," her mother said. "But if we all eat like that now, we'll all be starving before this journey's over."

There was a long, uncomfortable silence that was finally broken by Malia, who looked up from her stew bowl, smiled at Karoline, and said, "Thank you, Mrs. Sunshine."

Adeline turned and walked away to not be seen smiling, but Rese howled with laughter. Emil was trying not to, but soon had his head thrown back, chuckling. His father had his head down, snickering, before Lydia and the boys joined in. Everyone around that campfire was laughing, then, feeding on each other, their worries and pains forgotten. Everybody, that is, except Adeline's mother-in-law.

When Adeline looked back at Karoline, she had stood up. Her lower lip was twisted with scorn as she spat venomous words at Malia.

"You've forgotten the Horror?" Karoline said in a harsh whisper. "You've forgotten what it's like to starve, haven't you? Of course you have. You'd *have* to have only half a brain to forget what it feels like to have an empty belly for weeks on end. The things you'll do to keep living."

The laughter died. Lydia said, "That's not right, Karoline."

"Your daughter's not right in the head," Emil's mother said.

"You spiteful woman. You—"

Malia put her hand on her mother's shoulder, then looked at Karoline without a trace of self-pity or anger. "No, I am not right, Mrs. Martel. Not as right as you. But I have more than half my brain left, so I remember the Holodomor. I remember being so hungry, we ate field grass. Mama and Adeline and our brother, Wilhelm, were right beside me, on our hands and knees and crying because Papa was taken east two years before, and we had nothing, and we were all choking at the way the grass cut at our throats and swelled in our bellies. I remember that plain as day."

Adeline's right hand had gone to her throat, for she could suddenly taste the gritty chaff from the grass stalks coating her tongue and felt a pang of the abdominal pain that built in her gut after days on a grass-and-weed diet.

Karoline appeared shocked to be talked to this way by a younger woman, even more so as Malia went on. "But we kept eating the grass and anything we could find because we wanted to live. I ate worms and bugs and a dead bird because I wanted to live. Even with my head kicked in, I wanted to live so someday I could eat a bowl of good stew like tonight. What did you eat to survive the Holodomor, Mrs. Martel? What did you do to live through it?"

Emil's mother stood there, staring at the ground for a few moments before glaring at Malia. "You have no idea," she said, and walked off behind their wagon.

———

The rest of them ate in uncomfortable silence. When the dishes were done, Will came over and hugged his mother's skirt. "I'm tired, Mama."

"Bedtime," Adeline said. "Bedtime, Walt."

Their older son was dozing by the fire. Emil went to him, meaning to wake him, but then squatted and scooped him up and carried him to the wagon. The boy never stirred.

Adeline had already laid out the blankets inside beneath the bonnet. Emil handed Walt to her. She laid him on one blanket before covering him with another. Adeline helped Will in beside his sleeping brother and promised him a second blanket when she returned.

The fire was dying. Only Johann was still up, sitting on his stump and staring into the fading embers of his life. Beyond Emil's father, other campfires had already gone to coals, and voices in the surrounding darkness dwindled with each passing minute.

Emil looked above the trees to the clear night sky, seeing the tapestry of stars and feeling suddenly small, insignificant, as if his life meant little. A truck passed. A German soldier yelled that the bridges ahead would open before dawn and the convoy would begin moving soon after. That worsened Emil's mood, made him feel like a pawn, made him want to retreat and fight at the same time.

"Emil?"

He startled. Adeline had crept up on him.

"What are you looking at?"

The trance was broken. "The moon and the stars."

"What about them?"

"When I was a boy, I'd go outside almost every night to look at them, and now I rarely think about them at all."

Adeline stepped into Emil's arms, rested her cheek on his chest, and held him.

"Give thanks. We made it through the first day," she said.

"Somehow," he said, seeing himself whipping the horses over and over.

"Because of you and because of God."

He pressed his face to her hair. "We'll get farther away from the tanks tomorrow."

Adeline kissed him, said, "Stay strong, Emil."

"Always."

"And pray for us. God helps those who ask."

Emil offered only a noncommittal grunt. "I'll check the horses."

He did not wait for a reply but went to Oden and Thor, feeling irritated, and thinking, *Pray? A waste of time. You do what you want, Adella, but I'll figure my own way, thank you. No reason to get God involved if he does not exist.*

Emil had been raised Lutheran just like his wife. Miraculously, she had retained her faith through thick and thin, but Emil's had been taken from him piece by piece over the past fifteen years of calamity, persecution, and situations no man should ever have to face, making decisions no man should ever have to make.

He tried not to but had another memory of himself the day he lost his faith completely, saw himself shaking his fist at the sky, lonelier than he'd ever been. Emil shivered as he tried to block out that hated time and saw to his horses, checking their lead ropes and halters. They fluttered their noses and puttered their lips as he put more salve on their wounds.

When Emil returned to the wagon, Adeline had already retrieved the rest of the blankets and spread another across Will. She was lying down beside their younger son. He blew out the lantern and climbed in beside Walt before reaching across both boys to squeeze Adeline's arm good night.

The night fell cold and silent for a moment before Will whispered, "Tell me again, Mama, about where we're going."

"It's a beautiful place," Adeline whispered sleepily. "It's surrounded by mountains and forests. And snow up high. And below there will be a winding river and green fields. We will live in a warm home, and every morning I will bake bread for you, and there will be a big garden in the back, and we'll have so much food, we won't know what to do with it all."

Emil had closed his eyes and was trying to listen to his wife, trying to see such a magical place in his mind. But despite his every effort, images from the day cycled and wormed through him, made him deaf to Adeline's description of paradise. He relived the tank battle before drifting toward sleep and hearing the echoes of Malia's voice from the campfire. *What did you eat to survive the Holodomor, Mrs. Martel? What did you do to live through it?*

Chapter Five

In his fitful dreams that night, Emil was twenty-one again and wandering through the misty streets of a small city northwest of Friedenstal. He weighed less than fifty-five kilos by then, not an ounce of fat left on his frame. Though the sensation of hunger came and went, he ached constantly and everywhere, joints, muscles, and bones. Deprived of fat reserves, his body was beginning to eat him from the inside out.

Apathy had begun to set in as well. A fog seemed to shroud Emil's mind as he roamed far and wide in yet another desperate hunt for food. His most recent meal had been three days before when he'd gone out beyond the city limits and into the farm fields where he'd found a shriveled, soil-caked pumpkin that had survived the winter and other scavengers. After washing it in a stream, Emil had eaten pumpkin until he was beyond full, sat in the sunshine feeling fat and happy, and then promptly slept right there on the bank. When he awoke, he ate the rest of the pumpkin and smiled at how his belly had distended again.

But that was days ago, Emil thought as he searched the streets for something new to eat. *How much longer can this go on? How much longer can I survive?*

Emil had been fending for himself since his family was thrown off its land in Friedenstal, more than three years earlier.

His father, mother, and his sister, eight-year-old Rese, had gone to live in Pervomaisk, a city to the east on the Bug River. At first, Emil had been lucky.

He had farming skills and had little problem finding work on a collective farm as a field laborer.

He was quiet by nature, but he did not miss much. As a boy, he'd learned that the key to survival under Communism was to be silent, do your job, and not aspire to leadership of any kind. Within three months of his parents' leaving him to his own wits, he had learned that people who spoke up, people who tried to do things better or tried to teach others a better way, tended to vanish or to die young.

Emil slept where he could that first year on his own, and he made enough to keep food in his belly. The second year, 1931, was even better when he was given a tractor to drive.

But in the fall of the following year, Joseph Stalin decided to quash all opposition to Soviet rule in Ukraine. He withheld almost all food to the region. His goal was to starve its entire population.

———

As Emil trudged through Birsula six months into the Holodomor, he had the wind in his face, and he was lost in a series of dull, repetitive thoughts of fear and want. He didn't realize that he'd wandered to a road that ran along the rear of the rail yard and the train station.

Emil had not wanted to come to this place ever again, but there he was, and he looked all around now, seeing newly starved corpses and the near dead sprawled against the fence that surrounded the rail yard. Scattered among them and still standing, the merely starving and desperate clung to the chain-link fence, looking at a small mountain of wheat not eighty meters away.

Four armed soldiers stood around the huge wheat pile while others worked at it with shovels, turning the grain over, exposing the kernels to the mist so when the sun returned and beat down on enough food to feed the city for weeks, it all would simply rot. Emil did not want to look at the wheat, but he could not help himself. He went around a weeping woman holding her dying child and to the fence where he gazed at the grain as if it were a mirage or dream.

He fantasized what he might do with his pockets and hands full of that wheat. He could almost smell the bread in the oven.

One of the soldiers laughed. Emil heard him, shook off the fantasy, and then saw him. *Cigarette in his mouth. Hacking laugh. He's not starving, is he?*

The more Emil thought about the well-fed Russian soldiers deliberately destroying food in front of starving people, the more a primal anger flared in him. What had he ever done to Joseph Stalin? What had any of his family done to Joseph Stalin? Why would you kick good farmers off their land and then deny food to innocent people?

Why would a just, kind, and benevolent God let this happen?

Since the Horror began, Emil had been to the rail station twice before, and each time he'd left feeling helpless and doubting the existence of a power beyond himself. Before he could sink into those dark feelings this time, he remembered his father telling him that God helps those who help themselves.

But then a weaselly voice inside him said, *Trust in no power but your own, Emil. If you want to be saved, save yourself.*

At once unnerved and emboldened by that voice, Emil decided he would have to venture outside the city again. He would walk and search until he found food or dropped dead in his tracks. He pondered which direction to go in. To the east, he might find an unharvested beet or turnip patch. But he decided instead to head west toward farmland that had creek bottoms running through it.

From his days on the farm, Emil knew that by early March, creek bottoms that had not flooded were often green and lush with edibles if you knew what you were looking for. He might find the baby ferns his mother used to pick and cook or pickle in brine. Or baby asparagus shoots. Or mushrooms. Or freshly laid duck eggs. Or the carcass of a winter-kill rabbit, still frozen in the last of the snow.

Or he might walk until his legs would not work anymore.

Emil had seen the way starving people went from walking and talking to suddenly tipping over on legs that would no longer support them. Then they just lay there, some of them mewing like newborn kittens, begging their mothers for milk.

Go west, he thought, and tore himself away from the fence around the rail yard. *Those creek bottoms.*

But within blocks, Emil knew he would not make it to the first of the creeks nearly five kilometers away. Or if he did make it, unless he was lucky and found food immediately, he'd probably die there. He was simply too weak to walk all that way and then forage.

All he really needed was just a little food. A little food and he could make the walk with enough energy left to find his next meal and the one after that.

It began to snow. Emil sat down by the side of the road to conserve his energy and to decide whether to seek shelter or food. Across the street, in a little park, he noticed a starving woman, who stumbled, sprawled, and did not move. He felt sorry for her, and if he could have helped her, he would have. If he'd had food, Emil would have given her some. But he was beyond being shocked at people suddenly collapsing. He saw it happen nearly every day now.

The image and voice of the cackling, well-fed soldier from behind the train station filled Emil's mind, made him angry all over again. That Russian soldier would smoke cigarettes today. That Russian soldier would destroy food and eat well today while he, Emil, had nothing.

Nothing.

He fumed on that, understanding that other people in the world were not starving and that even some local people in Birsula were getting more than enough food on a regular basis, local people allied with the party, with Joseph Stalin.

Oddly, Emil did not feel more resentment, more helplessness. Instead, that weaselly voice deep inside him said, *Go, steal from them, Emil. The party men. Steal from them and save yourself.*

The thought at once terrified and thrilled him. Emil knew if he were caught, he'd be sent to a work camp. Or shot. But he didn't dwell long on those options or the fear of them, because he knew he would soon die if he did nothing, and he rather liked the idea of stealing from the bastards watching him starve to death.

———

There was an inch of wet snow on the ground by the time Emil had walked through the city and found a large dacha behind a high wall. He used to see the man who lived in the house often out on the collective farm. One day the prior December, he'd seen the same man enter through the gates of this dacha.

Emil knew the man was a high-ranking party member overseeing grain production in the region. Everyone in agriculture within fifty kilometers of Birsula worked for him. Emil didn't know the party leader's name and didn't want to. He was the cold bastard who'd driven them mercilessly to bring in a big harvest the year before. He was the same cold bastard who'd given it all to Stalin. And Emil was betting that he was the kind of cold bastard who could feast while his neighbors were starving to death.

For a fleeting moment, he remembered the commandment "Thou shall not steal," then dismissed it. This was different. He was doing it to survive. And he knew for a fact that others had done much worse to survive the Horror. He'd heard of children disappearing all over Ukraine. He'd heard of people eating their young.

All Emil was doing was stealing from someone who had too much.

He went to the alley that ran behind the man's house and others on that side of the street, meaning to look at the back of the home, close to the kitchen. If there was a kitchen, there would be a pantry or a larder. There would be food there he could steal.

Emil entered the alley at dusk, no longer thinking about how hungry he was or how tired he was. His heart raced as he anticipated figuring out how best to break into the kitchen after the man and his family and servants had gone to sleep. When would that be? Four, five hours?

He'd be smart, though. He'd wait five hours and then check the doors and the windows. Surely one of them would be left unlocked in the spring after a long, cold winter. If he had to, he'd break a pane on a basement window. He'd get inside and—

Ahead of Emil, well down the alley in back of the party leader's house, the gate opened. A woman wearing an apron brought out a garbage can, set it by the gate with others, and then returned inside.

At once all thoughts of burglary left him. The scraps of a man who ate well could not compare to the contents of the man's pantry, but at twenty-one, Emil had already been so badly beaten down by history and circumstance that he was past begging for better fortune.

After waiting a few anxious moments for the cook to return inside and giving in to fantasies of pork gristle or an old ham rind or a soup bone he could gnaw and crack for marrow, Emil stole toward the garbage can, so focused on the object of his desire that he did not see the other man emerge from the alley's deeper shadows, moving fast toward that same desire.

———

Finally, they saw each other and stopped ten feet apart, the garbage can midway between them and to their left. It was getting dark now, but Emil knew he faced a much taller and bigger man. The height was undeniable, but the illusion of bulk could have been the long coat the shadow wore and his wild hair and unkempt beard.

His whisper came raspy, menacing in Russian. "That's my can, friend. My alley, too. Take another step, and I will kill you."

Emil stood his ground, studied the man's silhouette closely, and said, "If I don't take a step, I'll die."

In his years fending for himself and especially since Stalin had ordered the Holodomor, Emil had witnessed many bare-knuckle fights and even crowd brawls over food. And he'd had to defend and fight for himself more times than he could count. From every fight he'd been in or watched, he had learned lessons and had come to recognize that where you hit a man was far more important than how hard you hit him. The ones who survived and thrived in food brawls knew where to strike a man to break him down, not to merely hurt him, but to injure him badly enough and painfully enough that he was out of the fight, at least for that day.

No matter their size or shape, Emil had noticed that the toughest men completely lost their humanity once they decided to fight, completely lost their basic compassion for fellow human beings. They seemed to turn calm, cold, animal, able to shut out everything except thoughts of crashing into one of those critical targets on the human body that will take a man to his knees or leave him sprawled and unconscious; with a weapon, preferably, but if not, then with the heels of the hands, or the outer forearm, or the shins leading, because these bones were unlikely to break easily. Emil had also noticed that once these fighters had decided on their weapon and target, they rushed to get close to their opponent, attacked immediately, trying to smash into the one and only spot as they threw their entire weight through the other man.

It's how a David can beat a Goliath. Emil stopped thinking of the man opposite him as a human. He became a shadow, the shadow man. Raising his body erect, Emil lifted his arms and rushed the shadow man, trying to make it appear as if he were going high and for the head.

Emil caught the shadow rising and, with his left forearm locked before him, went low at the last second, exploding forward off the balls of his feet, feeling his elbow and forearm smash into the bigger man's torso near the bottom left of his rib cage. He swore he heard ribs break along with the grunt the man made as the air was blown from his lungs. Emil felt his own shoulder wrenched as he crashed through the shadow man and sprawled facedown on the snowy ground beyond him.

Hearing moans and gasps of pain, Emil got to his feet, the calm gone, the adrenaline pumping now, allowing him to ignore the fire in his now-useless left shoulder, and to see the shadow man on the ground in the snow near the garbage can, arched to his left side and writhing, unable to think about anything but pain because his lower ribs were broken and his liver had been bruised.

Emil had seen another man deliver a similar blow in a food riot in November and had never forgotten it. And the shadow man had said he'd kill Emil if he went for the garbage can.

Stepping by the writhing form, Emil used his good right arm to pick up the can by its handle, and then walked away before his humanity and concern could return. He felt he owed the man nothing.

———

Several blocks later, in another alley, behind another house, the snow began to taper off. Emil took shelter in an empty woodshed that caught a slat of light from a window. He pried off the lid from the can and meant to set it down quietly. But the stench of rancid animal fat hit him, and he dropped it with a clang, fighting not to gag as he stayed frozen for a full minute before forcing himself to tilt the can into that slat of light and look inside. Whatever pork gristle, ham rind, or soup bone there might have been was now coated in rancid grease.

In another time, in another place, Emil might have thought about returning to the alley where he'd left the shadow man and going through with his burglary plan. But that weaselly voice inside his head stopped him, asked, *How badly do you want to survive?*

It took only a moment for Emil to shift his entire perspective in life, to harden top to bottom before he made this silent reply: *I will do anything to survive.*

He steeled himself, then began plucking items from the can and licking the rancid grease off them. He would be nauseated and sick soon, but he did not care. If he could keep enough of the fat down, he'd have enough strength to go to the creek bottoms in the morning.

Chapter Six

Adeline awoke in the dark to the sound of cannon fire. Not far. Eight, maybe ten kilometers to the northeast, close enough to throw orange flashes in the lower sky. Horses began to whinny and to nicker as shouts went up in the darkness. A vehicle approached. A voice came, amplified and crackling.

"*Raus!* Everyone up! The bridges at Dubossary are clear of eastward traffic! The trek leaves within the hour!"

Adeline scrambled to get her sleepy boys ready and fed and their bedding stowed. More cannons fired. She felt sick to her stomach. They had to move, but they couldn't go anywhere until Emil had the horses in their traces.

As she set out cold bread and water for the boys' breakfast, she looked over at her husband and saw him moving in the lantern light, head and shoulders slumped as they'd been too often lately. After yesterday, after leading them to safety, he should have been walking around with his shoulders back and his chin up. She longed to see Emil like that, bright-eyed and ready for anything, the way he'd been when she first met him in 1934.

Life had been hard for him in the decade since, for the both of them. But when had he begun to change? When had he started doubting everything?

Adeline's memory flickered to a February night in 1935 when money had floated out of the darkness to her. She had been outside their apartment building in the bitter cold, racked with pain, and empty of tears. Through an open window above and behind her, and for the first time since she'd known him, she had heard Emil choking and sobbing in despair.

We both doubted God that night. How could we not have?

But, Adeline decided, that night wasn't when he changed into the man working with his head down among the horses. That night wasn't when her husband had seemed to lose faith in anything but himself and his own back-breaking will to work.

Adeline thought about it some more. And then she suspected she knew, seeing herself light a lantern not long after their return to Friedenstal, in September 1941. They were living in Karoline and Johann's house while Emil built their home at the other end of town. Walt was almost four, Will almost two. Emil had gone with the wagon and horses to get supplies for the roof and windows in Dubossary, the town that now lay ahead of them. Emil had planned to be gone a day and a half, two at most, but he'd been absent more than three, only to return to their bed before dawn on the fourth morning.

Adeline remembered her husband's face in the lantern light. At first, he had appeared tired, and then aged, and then lost as he climbed into bed.

"Where have you been?" she'd asked. "I was worried sick."

"I was held by the Germans for a day and a half."

"What? Why?"

"I don't know. I don't know why anyone does anything anymore."

Adeline had wanted to question him further, but he'd gazed at her with bloodshot eyes and said, "I don't want to talk about it. Ever. I want to sleep. I need to sleep if I'm to get the roof on before the snow flies."

Emil had rolled over then. She'd stared at his back a long time before blowing out the lantern. In the dim light, she recalled someone saying that the eyes are the windows to the soul and thought of her husband's a few moments before.

Wounded, she'd thought. *Scarred.*

Then she'd heard him crying for the second time in their marriage.

———

Fifty feet from his wife and sons, Emil moved in a dark trance as he harnessed the horses for their second day on the road.

Dubossary? I haven't been there since . . . How is it possible they're taking us this way instead of more to the south?

And yet here he was, before he left Ukraine forever, preparing to face a town he wished he'd never seen. At some level, however, it felt just, deserved. That thought and tortured others spun relentlessly in his head as he finished with the horses.

Wagons in the caravan were already moving out. Dawn was upon them.

"What's bothering you?" Adeline asked as she finished loading the back of the wagon.

"What?"

"You're walking around like the weight of the world is on your shoulders."

Emil adored his wife, but her comment angered him. He felt it flare inside. Before he could let it out, though, he caught himself and gestured at the horses' flanks.

"I'm just worrying about them. I don't want an infection. Without them, we're in trouble."

She studied him a moment before nodding. "We'll watch them closely."

A few minutes later, with Adeline beside him and the boys sitting on the folded oilskin tarp behind the bench, Emil held the reins and gently clucked up Thor and Oden. The wagon began to roll and bump again.

———

Adeline stood up on the bench and looked over the bonnet, watching Emil's parents' wagon roll in behind them, and her mother's wagon after. Johann had the reins with Karoline beside him looking like she was preparing for another storm. Behind her, Rese lay on her back beneath blankets.

Lydia had finally relented and let Malia have the reins of their wagon. Her older sister was sitting with her back ramrod straight and her head swiveling, a massive grin on her face. Adeline broke into a smile. Malia, as far as she was concerned, was one of the best parts of her life. Red Army cannons may have been firing to the north, but she was getting such a warm, good feeling from watching her sister drive that she did not care.

Can happiness be that easy? Finding little joys in the worst moments? Isn't that what Mrs. Kantor used to say?

Before Adeline met Emil, she had worked as a cook and maid for an older widow named Yudit Kantor, who'd been kind to her and taught her a lot about life. Thinking of Mrs. Kantor, Adeline decided that, for today, happiness was that easy, and she took a mental picture of Malia in all her glory that she prayed she would remember forever.

Later that morning, progress snarled due to more wagons and more retreating ethnic *Volksdeutsche* joining the trek from the north. The Martels inched down a slick, snow-and-mud-covered, winding dirt road that descended to an intersection where a German officer stood on the hood of a truck, directing traffic.

The closer they got, the more details of the man Emil could make out: stocky and bull-necked with a close-cropped head beneath a distinctive black cap and a long dark-gray coat that flapped open to the wind. Emil wanted to deny the sudden unease that swept through him, wanted to deny that the officer was who he appeared to be. But the way he stood, the way he moved.

It can't be, Emil thought, tasting acid at the back of his throat.

A solid hundred meters before his wagon came under the German officer's direct attention, the man's mannerisms and voice conspired to convince Emil otherwise.

It's him, SS Hauptsturmführer Haussmann.

Fear burned in his gut before exploding into terror. *It's him! Haussmann. How is this possible?*

For a moment, Emil felt paralyzed. Then he wanted to turn his horses and wagon around and flee the Soviets via another route under the protection of different Nazis. He'd heard of people going northwest toward Poland. But there were too many carts and vehicles around him to try to leave.

"What's wrong, Emil?" Adeline asked.

He didn't hear her at first, then looked at her. "What?"

"It's cold, and you're sweating like you were out plowing. The sweat's freezing in your beard."

"I don't know," he said, feeling more panicked.

Then he thought, *My beard! My winter hair!*

The last time he'd been face-to-face with the Nazi SS captain standing on the hood of the truck ahead of him was two and a half years before, near the end of summer 1941 in the town of Dubossary, less than ten kilometers from this very spot. That first time, Emil had been working day and night to erect the walls of their new home. He had cut his hair and beard completely off to deal with the toil and heat.

Haussmann won't know me. I'm a different man now.

"Emil," Adeline said again.

"I don't know why I'm sweating, dear," he said, trying to smile as he wiped the sweat from his face and adjusted his wool cap low enough to put his eyes in shadow and yet high enough not to provoke the SS officer's ruthless attention.

When it came time, Emil turned his face slightly toward Captain Haussmann, his eyes darting from the man's too-familiar face to the death-head emblem on his cap and the collar badge that indicated he'd been promoted to *Sturmbannführer*, a major now.

Sturmbannführer Haussmann snapped his arm to his right. Despite his self-assurances, Emil's heart was slamming in his chest as he waved once, and then guided his horses past the bumper of the SS major's truck.

Only when he was sure they were out of Haussmann's sight did Emil allow himself to breathe deeply and to admit he felt weak and dizzy.

"Take the reins," he choked.

Adeline grabbed them. "What's the matter?"

"Gonna be sick," he croaked, and vomited over the side.

"Awww," Will said behind him as he retched.

"I hate that," Walt said.

When he was done, Emil had Adeline keep the reins and sat in misery beside her. The closer they got to Dubossary, the more he kept telling himself he could get past the ravine, through the town, into Moldova, and westward without thinking about what had happened to him there. But that was Haussmann back there. There was no doubting it. He would remember that man's face forever. In his mind, he heard people crying and saw Haussmann, enraged, shouting in his face.

What are the chances of Haussmann being here? Why am I being tortured like this?

It had been two and a half years since the trauma of that night in mid-September 1941. But Emil felt the impact as if it were yesterday, the hollow aloneness he'd suffered after witnessing what one man could do to another, and seeing his own weaknesses revealed as starkly as they could be, in the form of a fist shaking at the sky.

In the last few kilometers before they reached the town, Emil refused to look north toward the ravine. He kept his head focused on the wagon in front of him. But some of his inner turmoil must have been showing, because Adeline rubbed his back and said, "How are you feeling?"

He glanced at her, praying she wasn't seeing the tears he felt about to well.

"Better," he said hoarsely, and looked away. "Just thinking."

"About what?"

Emil hesitated, swallowed, forced a smile. "That valley of yours."

———

Adeline had hoped he'd open up about Dubossary, but she smiled at his answer.

"It's your valley, too."

"And mine," Walt said from behind them.

"I'm going, too," Will said.

"We all are going," Adeline said.

"I think there will be lots of fish in the river," Will said.

"Lots of them," she said. "Everywhere you look, fish to catch and eat. Right, Papa? Hasn't that always been your dream? To sit by a river and catch fat fish to fry?"

Despite believing that would never happen, Emil managed to laugh. "Just me and a fishing pole, sitting on the riverbank. Not a chore to do. Now that would be something!"

"What about you, Mama?" Walt asked. "What do you dream of having there?"

She thought about that. "A vegetable garden. A flower garden. A root cellar. And chickens for fresh eggs. And . . . well, no. You can't ask for everything in life."

"What?" Emil said.

"It's silly."

"Tell us," Will said.

Adeline didn't want to but finally replied, "I want a doll with a pretty dress."

"A doll?" Emil said, surprised.

"I never had one growing up," she said, raising her chin. "Is that too much to ask for?"

"No, Adella," he said, and patted her thigh. "It's not too much to ask for a doll."

That made her happy, and she grinned for a moment before gesturing ahead and saying, "They're splitting the trek ahead again."

Emil looked up the road a hundred meters and saw another German officer on the hood of a truck, directing traffic. To his relief, it was not Haussmann but a captain he'd never seen before who waved them toward the center of Dubossary and the north bridge over the Dniester River.

The caravan slowed to fits and starts as they inched toward the crowded town center. When they got there, Emil could see the remainders of a high barbed-wire fence and empty buildings beyond.

Hearing the crying in his mind again, he kept his eyes on the livid scars on his horses' haunches, wondering if his memories of this cursed town would ever leave him, if he'd ever be free of that night when—

He heard a whistling sound that grew louder before the town was rocked by a massive explosion just to the north, and then another.

"Emil!" Adeline shouted.

"They're shelling the town!" he said, fighting to keep his horses under control.

Ahead of them in line, horses began to buck and rear up at the blasts. Others must have stampeded out of town and toward the bridge, because the trek moved much quicker.

Three more artillery rounds hit behind them as the Martels came free of the town proper, Emil urging his horses on at a trot and then a canter. Ahead, two other covered wagons had gone off the road and flipped. Four more were lurching away over the rough terrain, their horses spooked and galloping from the roar of the artillery.

"Papa!" Walt cried. "We're going too fast!"

59

Emil was already pulling hard on the reins. Thor and Oden slowed and settled to puffing and snorting as they passed an SS soldier waving them toward the chaos at the mouth of the bridge. Wagons and German army vehicles already crowded the span over the river, all heading west. A long line of those who'd already crossed the Dniester snaked toward the southwestern horizon. Emil berated himself for not waking earlier, for not being on the bridge at dawn.

"There's smoke and fire back there!" Walt said. "They hit something big, Papa!"

"Mama!" Will said in a whiny voice.

"Not now, Will," Adeline said, climbing up on the bench to look behind them.

Emil was not interested in what was happening back there. His entire focus was on that bridge and getting as far west of the river as fast as possible. But there were too many vehicles, horses, wagons, and refugees on foot at the east entrance to the span. The caravan laced, tied up, and then unknotted with maddening slowness. People were screaming at one another. Two old men in adjacent wagons lashed at each other with buggy whips. The air stank of sweated horses and frightened humans.

"I can't see my mother or Malia!" Adeline said.

"I can't help them," Emil said, gritting his teeth.

"Malia was driving!"

"I can't help her, either. Where are my parents?"

"To our left four wagons and one behind. Rese's between your mother and father. She looks as scared as I've ever seen her."

"Do you blame her?" Emil said, seeing an opening and urging his horses through it and onto the ramp that climbed to the bridge.

———

As they reached the high spot on the span, Adeline peered back toward Dubossary again, seeing flashes and more blasts and plumes of smoke rising before German artillery finally responded with cannon and mortar. Bombs erupted to the north where Stalin's Second Ukrainian Front of the Red Army was preparing to storm the town.

"Mama, I have to go pee," Will said.

Before she could reply, she saw her mother, eight wagons behind them, sitting stone-still beside her older sister. "There they are!" Adeline cried. "Malia's still got the reins!"

Walt shouted, "Mama! Papa! Planes!"

Adeline's attention jerked upriver, seeing Soviet fighters flying low over the Dniester in waves. The first four broke toward Dubossary, and their machine guns opened fire, strafing the Wehrmacht positions. The second wave did the same. But the third flight of four came at them.

"Get down!" Emil shouted, let go the reins, grabbed Adeline by the shoulders, and half dove into the wagon beside the boys.

The four planes did not open fire on the wagons on the bridge; instead, they buzzed them and followed the retreating trek west, tracking the convoy before disappearing. The fifth wave of Soviet fighters did the same, and as the Martels finally rode off the bridge into the country of Moldova, they heard the rattle of machine guns far, far ahead of them and out of sight.

"I thought that was it," Adeline gasped, sitting up beside Emil who'd already grabbed the reins and was urging Oden and Thor back into line. "I thought we were done."

———

Emil had thought much the same as he clucked up his horses into a trot to keep pace with the wagon ahead. Even with the bombs still exploding behind them, now that he was beyond Dubossary and getting farther from it, a place never to be seen again, he felt somewhat emboldened by their escape.

"We are not close to being done," he said, and pulled Adeline tight beside him. "You hear? The Martels are not close to being done."

Adeline grinned and kissed him. He looked like the old Emil! He sounded like the old Emil! She loved him when he was like this, refusing to give up in his own quiet, stubborn way.

Will said, "I have to pee."

Walt's voice was shaking. "Did they almost shoot us, Mama?"

"No," she said, spinning around and seeing her older son trembling and his hands clenched in fists. "They didn't shoot at us. They shot at the town and somewhere up ahead."

"Are they coming back? Are the tanks?"

"I don't know."

There was a long silence before Walt said, "I want to go home."

"We have no home now," Emil said.

"Yes, we do," Adeline said firmly. "Our family is home. Wherever we're together is home. This is home. It doesn't matter if we're on the farm or in the beautiful green valley as long as we're together."

"Can I go pee in the green valley?" Will asked.

Adeline frowned, took one look at her younger child—up on his knees, fidgeting while his swollen cheeks turned red with strain—and burst out laughing. "You poor thing."

"It's not funny!" Will said. "I'm going to pee my pants!"

"Ahh, don't do that!" Walt said, and started to laugh along with his mother.

"Then stop the wagon," Will said.

"I can't," Emil said. "The pace is too fast, and I don't want to be left behind. You'll just have to hold it another half hour at least."

"I can't, Papa! I'm pinching it with my fingers right now!"

"Pee out the back of the wagon, then," Adeline said, trying to stop laughing.

Will gave her a sour look before grinning at the idea. "Okay!"

As he crawled toward the rear of the wagon, Walt said, "That family behind us is going to see you pee out the back, Will. You'll probably hit their horses in the face."

Will paused, craned his head up, and saw an older woman at the reins of the wagon behind them. There was a teenage girl beside her and three more kids beneath the bonnet. And their horses were less than a meter away at times.

"I can't, Mama," he said.

"You'll never see them again," Emil said, chuckling now.

"I still can't," Will said. "Forget it. I'm just going to wet my pants."

"Don't you dare," Adeline said, biting her lip to keep from laughing again. "You'll sit in your stew for hours, and then you'll break out in a rash. Crawl back by the little wagon, the kitchen box in the corner. There's an empty glass jar in there. You'll pee in that."

Will loved that idea and went scrambling back to the corner.

Emil glanced at her.

"I'll clean it," she said. "Unless you have a better idea?"

Emil smiled and shook his head.

Will found the jar, turned his back on the trailing wagon, and fumbled at the buttons to his wool pants. He got them undone and was reaching inside when he realized Adeline and Walt were watching him.

"Turn around," he said, frowning.

"As you wish," Adeline said, turning to look ahead. They were out on a floodplain that was just greening. There was a lull in the battle behind them.

"What do I do when I'm done?"

"Hand it to me, and I'll dump it over the side."

The trek was still moving at a steady clip and was nearing the far side of the floodplain where the road climbed a bluff. After a minute, Adeline said, "Are you done back there?"

"No."

"No?" she said, twisting around to see him with his pants fully unbuttoned and pulled down to his thighs.

Will was still frowning. "It doesn't want to come out, Mama. It's like it's scared!"

Adeline burst out laughing again. Walt looked, made a disgusted face, and clamped his hand across his mouth to hide his amusement. Emil glanced over his shoulder, and he started laughing, too. It was contagious. There was no stopping it.

Even Will started laughing so hard, tears streamed down his face and he was having trouble holding the jar in front of him. Then a short shot of pee squirted from him and hit the oilskin tarp beside Walt.

Adeline shrieked with laughter. Walt screamed as he rolled away, "Piss in the jar, idiot!"

"You pee any more on that tarp and you'll clean it, Will," Emil said.

Will clamped the jar over his groin. "I couldn't help it," he chortled.

Adeline turned around again. She had forgotten how good it felt to laugh like this, the tank battles and the bombardments forgotten for the moment. Laughter was like a hot shower for the soul after a long, cold day.

"Ahhhh," Will said.

"He's peeing!"

"Thank you, Walt," Emil said. "Congratulations, Will."

Adeline started laughing all over again. A half minute went by.

"He's peeing a long time," Walt said.

"Enough," Emil said.

A few moments later, Will cried, "I'm empty, and the wagon behind us is back there pretty far, Mama. I'll pour it out. You don't have to do it."

"Thank you, Will," she said. "And find a place for the jar that's not in the kitchen box."

"Okay," he said. "And I'll find a rag to clean up the pee on the tarp."

She looked at Emil and winked at him.

A few minutes later, Will crawled into her lap, snuggled into her, and said, "When are we gonna get there?"

Adeline kissed the top of his head and smiled. "In God's time."

"That's long," Will said.

"Sometimes. And sometimes God works in the blink of an eye."

"And most times he doesn't work at all," Emil said. "Sometimes God is so deaf, you'd know he wasn't—"

Adeline shot him a sharp look and said, "That's enough."

"What? They might as well learn the truth young, Adella."

"And what truth is that?" she said in a tone that warned him he was on thin ice.

Emil hesitated, said, "God is not going to be there for them at every turn."

"Of course he is. If they ask him."

"I'm just saying a man has got to look out for himself and what's his, Adeline. If some invisible God has a hand, I'm all for it. But I've learned from experience not to expect it, and neither should you, and neither should the boys. And I don't want to talk about this anymore."

The wind shifted now and blew a little harder, forced her to rewrap her scarf as she watched Emil at the reins. *Is he still scarred by Dubossary?*

Every time she'd brought the subject up after that morning he'd come home back in September 1941, he'd gotten angry and walked away, just like his mother had the night before.

He said he was held by the Nazis. What happened? Is there a part of him I don't know? And never will?

Chapter Seven

Those questions did not leave Adeline's mind until she forced herself to remember the laughter they'd just shared and their survival of both a tank battle and a bombardment. She was feeling grateful as they got farther from the border and the sun arced toward the western horizon. Every single tree or abandoned shack or rock wall or windmill that they encountered seemed to shine and catch her attention.

"What's that, Mama?" Will asked, pointing straight ahead and down the road.

Adeline stood, shielded her eyes from the low-angled sun. Large, twisted, hulking things stuck up out of the ground in and to either side of the road. She could see men and animals moving about among them.

Closer, they became lorries and other vehicles, bent, torn, riddled with machine gun rounds. German soldiers whipped mules to drag debris off the road. They rode through the destruction caused by the Soviet fighter planes earlier in the day. Adeline was shocked, seeing maimed corpses frozen in the grotesque positions in which they had died. They'd gone by the third dead soldier before she realized her sons were seeing it. She looked back. Will and Walt were staring at the scene, wide-eyed and horrified.

"Sit back now and don't look," she said. "You don't have to be seeing this at your age."

"Leave them be, Adeline," Emil said. "I want them to see this, understand what one man will do to another."

"Why?" she demanded.

"So people getting killed in war is real to them. Not something you see from far away. It should be something burned in their minds young."

Adeline stared at him, feeling irrationally angry. "I want to protect them from that, Emil."

"You can't."

She shook her head. "Sometimes I love you more than anything on earth. And sometimes I don't understand the half of you, Emil Martel."

He nodded. "That sounds about right."

Before darkness fell, they stopped and pitched camp near the road. Emil's parents and sister rolled in beside them shortly afterward, followed by Lydia and Malia. They did not bother with a fire that second night. They ate dried meat and water and the last of the bread Malia had baked the night before they left on their journey.

Emil again worked salve into his horses' wounds by lantern light, brushed them, and told them how much he appreciated their hard work.

As Adeline got her sons back under the blankets inside the wagon, she could hear him talking to the horses. "I'm sorry, boys, but it was life or death. Our lives and yours."

She took off her boots and stockings and put them at her feet before sliding in beside Walt, who'd been very quiet much of the rest of the day.

Emil climbed in with the lantern.

"Mama, I wish God's 'soon' was tomorrow," Walt said.

Adeline hugged him tight, said, "I do, too."

Emil blew out the lantern as the wind shifted southwest. Temperatures began to rise.

"Day two," he said. "We made it."

"Together," Adeline said, and smiled sleepily in the dark.

They had made it, just as they had time and again throughout their marriage, and just as she had before she met Emil. Emotionally and physically drained by the past thirty-six hours, Adeline nevertheless prayed and gave thanks for her family's miraculous journey so far before plunging into deep dark sleep. When she finally dreamed, it was as if time had been hit by one of the tank rounds and more than a decade had vanished altogether.

―――

October 1933
Birsula, Ukraine

Eighteen-year-old Adeline stood on her tiptoes in a kosher butcher shop in the little town, watching in wonder as the butcher wrapped a whole fresh chicken in paper. Fresh chicken. When was the last time she'd seen or even allowed herself the thought of something like that?

And she was sure she was going to taste it. Well, of course. She was going to cook it, wasn't she?

Adeline could not have wiped the grin off her face if she'd tried. Roasting a fresh chicken. Eating a fresh chicken when only months before . . . And now, here she was, living the high life!

The butcher put the package on the counter. "Tell Mrs. Kantor she is a blessed woman. The first chicken I've been able to offer in months. A miracle you walked in when you did."

"Thank you, Mr. Berman," Adeline said, smiling and putting the chicken into a sack slung over her shoulder.

She hurried outside, excited. A chill breeze hit her in the face, reminded her that winter was not far off, though the thought did not concern her as much as it might have a year ago, or the year before that.

After Adeline and her mother and sister were thrown off the family farm, she was sent to work on a collective farm in the rolling hills outside Birsula, a small town roughly two hundred kilometers north of Odessa. For months, in stifling heat and biting cold, she'd gone shoeless into vats of mud and straw, mixing them for bricks with her bare feet. There were times she thought her legs were going to snap off like icicles beneath a winter eave, and other times when she'd grown so despondent, she'd wondered if she'd ever have even a glimpse of a better lot in life. Then to add to her misery, Stalin had cut off the food in the fall of 1932.

As Adeline left the butcher shop with the chicken, she could remember being so hungry during the Holodomor, she'd hallucinated chicken, swore she saw steaming plates of her mother's egg noodles and carved roast fowl appear in the air right before her eyes. Later, she'd been so weak, she collapsed in the mud vats on a frigid day, contracted pneumonia, and barely survived.

As bad as the months of starvation had been to her, and as sure as she'd been that no better life would ever find her way again, late in her recovery from pneumonia, Malia heard about a job in town, a job indoors. Adeline got the job, and in what felt like a snap of the fingers, her circumstances had changed for the better.

Almost six months now, she thought, carrying the chicken as she ducked into a wide alleyway, passed the rear entrance to a bakery already closed for the day, and walked along the back fences of a row of large homes. She went through the gate of the third one and up the steps to a back door.

Inside, she kicked off her boots, put on the slippers she was supposed to wear indoors, and brought the grocery sack into the kitchen. She'd no sooner set the sack down than a woman's cheerful voice called out in Russian from another room, "Adelka, is that you back so soon?"

"Yes, Mrs. Kantor," Adeline said, pulling on her apron and going into the front room where an old woman sat by the window with a blanket across her lap and a black sweater about her shoulders.

A teapot and simple service were on the table in front of Mrs. Kantor. A woman in her late twenties was sitting opposite Adeline's employer. She wore a plain brown dress, shawl, and scarf. A large book lay on the floor beside her.

"Esther, this is my secret treasure," Mrs. Kantor said. "Her name is Adeline. I call her Adelka. The things she does in the kitchen are wizardry!"

Esther laughed. "You mean witchery?" When Adeline frowned at that, Esther waved her hands. "No, no. I'm not suggesting . . . Oh, never mind. What are you cooking today, Adeline?"

"Whatever she found out on her daily tramp," Mrs. Kantor said before Adeline could answer. "She finds what's available, and then I don't know what she does back there in the kitchen, but it's magic."

Adeline bowed her head, smiling. "Thank you, ma'am. I love cooking."

"It shows."

"So?" Esther said. "What did you find today?"

Adeline picked her head up, looked from Esther to Mrs. Kantor, and swelled with excitement. "A whole fresh chicken!"

Esther gasped. Mrs. Kantor clapped her hands against her thighs. "No! Where?"

"Mr. Berman's shop. I happened to walk in just after the chicken was killed!"

"Kosher?" Esther said.

"Yes, ma'am. I mean, I guess so. From Mr. Berman?"

Mrs. Kantor made a whooping noise and shook her bony fists overhead. "I am going to invite my son and his family! This is a cause for celebration!"

To Adeline's surprise, Esther did not share her employer's enthusiasm. "Are you sure, Mrs. Kantor? When so many are still going hungry?"

The old woman sobered, but then nodded. "I know people are still hungry, dear, but I am also sure that if Moses himself had happened upon a chicken while he was wandering in the desert, he would have hidden it from all the tribes of Israel and eaten it with his family."

Esther snorted even as her hand flew to her mouth, saying, "Mrs. Kantor!"

"What?"

"You're lucky the rabbi isn't here to hear that."

Mrs. Kantor threw back her head, cackled. "Well, there are some things rabbis shouldn't hear about, but as far as real chicken soup, I think he'd back me."

"If you ladle out a bowl for him!" Esther said.

"That's right!" the old woman brayed, and looked to Adeline. "How big is our chicken, dear?"

"A good size, ma'am."

"Enough for my son, his wife, and daughter? And my friend Esther?"

"Oh, Mrs. Kantor, I couldn't," Esther said. "I just dropped by to say hello."

Mrs. Kantor shot her a look. "You dropped by when a chicken appeared in the middle of the desert, so to speak."

Esther laughed. "Well, it would be . . . so nice to just have a taste."

"You'll have more than that," Mrs. Kantor said. "I have the appetite of a mouse. How long should it take, Adelka?"

Adeline thought it through, said, "By sundown? Maybe a bit after?"

"Plan on a bit after," the old woman said to both Adeline and Esther.

Esther grinned and got up. "I have some chores to finish, but I will come back."

When Esther had gone, Mrs. Kantor cocked her head at Adeline, said, "Well?"

She startled, having been so caught up in the two women's banter that she flushed, bowed quickly, and said, "Sorry, Mrs. Kantor. Is there anything you need before I start?"

The old woman's face softened. "I need a nap, dear. Please, put that book on the shelf in the kitchen. And before you boil the bird, would you run to my son's house to tell his wife the news?"

"Yes, ma'am," Adeline said, picking up the book.

"You know where they live?"

"I do."

"Clever child," she said, rearranging the blanket in her lap. "Go on, then. Do you have enough wood for the oven?"

"I think so," she said, and ran back to the kitchen.

She put the book on the shelf before lifting the lid on the box where the wood was kept and saw it was lower than she'd remembered from that morning's fire.

"I'll need to get more wood while I'm out, ma'am," she called, dropping the heavy lid.

The vibration caused the book she'd brought into the kitchen to slide off the shelf and fall to the floor behind her.

Mrs. Kantor called, "Be quick about it!"

"Yes, ma'am!" she called back as she stooped to pick up the book, seeing it was a bound collection of illustrations and paintings, and open to one that depicted a beautiful green valley surrounded by snow-peaked mountains with a river winding through it. Growing up in flat Ukraine, Adeline had never seen such a setting and found it so enchanting, she gazed at it for a long moment.

"Are you going, girl?" Mrs. Kantor cried.

"Right now!" she yelled, slamming the book shut and putting it back on the shelf with a different, heavier book on top of it.

———

She got her coat and boots back on, the image of the painting still lingering as she ran through the streets to Mrs. Kantor's son's house and went to the back door. She found the cook, informed her she had the afternoon and evening off, and then asked her to tell the doctor's wife that they were all invited to eat with Mrs. Kantor after sundown.

Next, she went to a market area to buy eggs for the noodles, then crossed to where men sold firewood, but they had already left for the day. Adeline went to another spot where she could ordinarily find wood, but there was none to be had.

Glancing at the sun angled toward the western horizon, Adeline was suddenly and desperately aware of time slipping away. Five people coming to dinner at sundown and not enough wood to boil the chicken and simmer the soup.

Adeline imagined Mrs. Kantor getting upset and firing her as she hurried back to the house, feeling frightened, feeling like life was about to slap her down again, steal away something she'd fought so long and hard to have. As she entered the kitchen, that fear was all around her. After years of starvation and hardship, she couldn't find enough wood to make chicken soup, and now she would be let go.

"Adeline!" Mrs. Kantor called.

"Yes, ma'am," she said, hearing the quiver in her throat.

"Is my son coming?"

"I believe so," she said. "I told the cook."

"All of them?"

"Yes."

"What about the firewood?"

Adeline felt the fear spiral and ignite again. As it burned stronger, she felt weaker.

"Please," she whispered, shutting her eyes. "Help me."

"Adeline?"

She opened her eyes, meaning to tell the old woman the truth and ask for her forgiveness and advice, when she happened to glance at motion in the alley outside the kitchen window. She blinked and then smiled. "I'm getting it just now, ma'am!"

Adeline ran outside and after a young, broad-shouldered man bent over as he walked, an impossible load of firewood on his back.

"Excuse me!" she cried. "Can I buy some of your firewood?"

He did not slow. "No."

"Oh, please, I have money."

"It's already paid for," he said, walking on. "The baker owns it."

A wave of dread swept over Adeline, and she cried, "Please, sir, can't you sell me just a few pieces? I'm going to lose my job if I don't get some wood for our oven. Please?"

For one horrible moment, she thought he'd keep going, but then he stopped and turned to peer back at her. "Lose your job?"

"I need to boil a chicken," she said, struggling to regain control of herself.

"You have a chicken?"

"The woman I work for does."

"She must be quite a woman."

"Her dead husband was a doctor, and her son is a doctor."

He thought about that. "Okay."

"Okay?"

He nodded, lowered the bundle off his back. "The baker won't know how much I cut."

Adeline clapped with delight. "Oh, thank you! Thank you!"

The young man stood there a moment, watching her. Ever so slowly his weary expression broke, and a smile overtook his face. "How much do you want?"

"Four big pieces, please. Oh, you're so kind."

He untied his bundle, got four stout pieces for her.

"You've rescued me," she said, handing him the money. "Thank you forever!"

He took it and said, "If I knew firewood would make a beautiful young lady like you this happy, I would have bought an ax a long time ago."

He was grimy from work and stank of it, too, but she liked the way he smiled and the way he looked at her, as if he really saw her. She realized she liked his smile and eyes so much, it embarrassed her, made her blush, and she looked down.

"I'm sorry," he said. "I shouldn't have said that."

"No," she said, still looking down, but smiling. "It was nice and funny. Thank you, but I have to boil the chicken and start the egg noodles."

"What's your name?"

She hesitated. "Adeline. Adeline Losing."

He smiled again. "That's a pretty name. I'm Emil Martel."

PART TWO:
THE PURE BLOODS

Chapter Eight

When Emil awoke in the dark on the third full day of their exodus, a thick warm fog had rolled in, blanketing the land. He fed and cared for his horses by lantern light, rubbing more salve into their lash wounds. Though he could not see thirty meters in any direction or hear anything like a big engine, he felt anxious, like tanks or planes with machine guns could burst out of the fog at any moment.

His instincts proved correct. He'd no sooner gotten Oden and Thor back in their traces than whistles began to blow in the fog. That German voice came over a bullhorn, warning that Soviet forces were close and moving their way. The caravan would roll in fifteen minutes.

"The boys haven't eaten," Adeline called from beneath the bonnet.

"They'll eat as we ride. We all will."

She nodded. "I'll get everything tied down except for dry food and water."

As Adeline turned away, Emil smiled at her the way he'd smiled the first time he met her, out in the alley behind Mrs. Kantor's house, desperate for firewood for her chicken soup. From the very beginning, she'd made him feel needed in almost every way.

Maybe that's all I really need in life, he thought. *Adeline's love. My boys' love.*

When the wagons began to move in the warm fog, there was the predictable chaos made worse by the mud that soon caked the horses' underbellies and flanks and spotted the lash wounds on their haunches. It coated the spokes, wheel rims, and axles as well.

For the next few hours, it seemed as if the trek were a ghostly, segmented, snakelike creature, appearing and disappearing in the fog, sliding and twisting in the muck. In the slick, near-blind conditions, wagons began to drift, crash, and overturn. It took all of Emil's skills to keep their wagon and horses moving forward.

Twice that morning they encountered wagons buried up to their axles in the mud.

One of them was Emil's parents' wagon, so he'd pulled over and helped get them unstuck and rolling again. His mother, Karoline, was more civil than usual. His father, Johann, seemed unbothered by the foul conditions. Rese had been unable to leave her bed since Dubossary.

"She sleeps and can't keep anything down for long," Karoline said.

"I'll make something for her stomach when we stop tonight," Adeline said. Emil's mother wouldn't look at her but nodded.

They rode hard and long that day, through the city of Chisinau, Moldova—where slave laborers, men taken by Hitler from every country he conquered, were building fortifications for the Wehrmacht—and out the other side, hearing stories of other battles brewing to the southeast. The fog burned off before noon, revealing land that had been occupied, conquered, and reconquered over the past few decades. Romania held dubious title to the land at the moment, a payment Hitler made to the Romanian dictator Ion Antonescu for allowing German troops to travel east to conquer Stalin in the summer of 1941.

Emil did not care about politics or who controlled the land he and his family crossed that day. All he wanted was to be so far west, he'd never meet another Communist as long as he lived. He could tolerate traveling under Nazi protection for the time being, but when he saw a chance to get west of the murdering, inhuman bastards, he planned on doing just that. In the meantime, he kept a constant eye out for Major Haussmann.

Was it Haussmann back there? Was I imagining him? No. It was him. But why would he have been outside Dubossary? Of all the SS men in Ukraine, why was he the one directing traffic there? Why was he the one to point us into the town?

Those questions threatened Emil's sanity at some level, so he flung them aside unanswered, told himself it was just one of those cruel coincidences in a lifetime. After Haussmann had done his dirty work in the early days of the German occupation, he'd been assigned in some capacity to protect the ethnic Germans fleeing west. End of story. Emil might never see the man again, and if he did, he'd make sure he, Adeline, and the boys were heading in the opposite direction.

That third evening of their journey, the caravan finally ground to a halt and camped in the countryside twelve kilometers southwest of Chisinau. Cannon fire rumbled throughout the night, close enough to wake Emil and Adeline again and again.

The fourth day of the trek, it rained early, which churned up more mud. They barely made fifteen kilometers' progress. The fifth night, bombs fell so close, the Martel clan abandoned its wagons and took refuge in a large road culvert.

The culvert trembled with each explosion. They could hear the shrieking of horses and the cries of those without shelter. But they remained safe. From that point forward, Emil looked for a culvert or some reinforced concrete work like a bridge abutment to camp near or under.

———

A week into the ordeal, the trek was maintaining a ten-to-fifteen-kilometer gap between them and the Wehrmacht rear guard trying to hold back the forces of the Soviet First and Second Ukrainian Fronts. But the fear of being overtaken was constant. The Soviet tanks could come from another direction. Or the Red fighter planes might return.

"We're trapped between two armies," Emil said to Adeline late the seventh night.

They were camped by a bridge abutment west of the Moldovan town of Hincesti. The boys were already asleep, and Emil's stomach was the fullest it had been since they'd fled. He'd dug a horizontal hole in the dirt bank a good meter from the base of the concrete abutment. The boys had gathered wood, and he built a fire before feeding the glowing coals into the makeshift oven. From their precious stock of flour and yeast, Adeline and her mother made dough, which they put in pans and slid on top of the coals.

The freshly baked bread, even with the burned crust, had tasted so wonderful, Emil had been content for a good twenty minutes. But then his fear of the tanks and the planes returned.

"Didn't you hear me?" he whispered louder to Adeline, who was about to get under the blankets by the still-warm oven. "We're trapped between two armies. Hitler's crippled men in front of us with a few able men behind us trying to stop all of Stalin's soldiers."

He felt breathless. "When I really think about where we are and what we're doing and what could happen to us in the days ahead, it's like my thoughts speed up, Adeline. They run and repeat in circles, like a storm in my head."

Adeline came over and hugged him. "Everyone feels like that now and then. I remind myself what Mrs. Kantor told me once: 'There is a safe place in the eye of every storm.'"

"I've rarely found it," Emil said.

"You did when those tanks started shooting last week. You've gotten us all this far safely, haven't you?"

For some reason, Emil could not embrace that the way Adeline did. "We've got a long way to go before I'll feel like I've got you all safe."

"Then come get some sleep. Dawn will be here soon enough."

Emil wanted to climb under the blankets, close his eyes, and take a rest from all of it. But then he heard voices, men's voices singing and laughing up the bank not far off from his horses and wagon. He felt drawn to them.

"Emil?" Adeline called softly.

"I want to check the horses," he said, and with his lantern climbed up the bank to the road and the bridge.

Thor and Oden were tied and hobbled where he'd left them. The wagon appeared untouched. But the singing and the laughing had only gotten louder and more raucous. They were singing an old German drinking song. He had not heard the song in years but recognized it from his days working in a brewery in Pervomaisk, the town where the boys were born.

Emil began to walk toward the singing. He didn't know why. Maybe it was just to be near and hear other men trying to survive the same predicament. His father aside, he often felt like the only people he had to talk to were women. The closer he got, the more he heard alcohol in their song. Emil was not a big drinker, but he always enjoyed making wine and beer. And, on occasion, he enjoyed the easiness brought on by a glass or two or three.

The singing died off into rough laughter about the time he stepped into a clearing on the other side of the road. A fire burned before a half circle of wagons like his own. Four men he did not recognize were drinking from tin mugs. The biggest of them, a tall, rangy fellow in his early forties, saw Emil approaching and stopped talking. Then they all did.

Emil held up his hands. "I didn't mean to interrupt you," he said in German. "I heard the singing. I guess it's been a while since I've heard men singing over drink."

The rangy one said, "Sounds like your wife's got control of your drink."

The other men laughed, and so did Emil, who said, "It came down to a small cask of homemade wine going with us or a small wagon I made for my sons last Christmas. The wagon won on a three-to-one vote."

The rangy one smiled and beckoned Emil closer. "Come, have a drink. I am Nikolas. What is your name, friend? Where are you from? And how old are your sons?"

———

Emil told them. Nikolas introduced the other men in rapid fashion, so he caught few of their names. But up close, in the firelight, he noticed the quality of their clothes. They were all wearing newer wool coats, pants, and hats. A mug of red wine was handed to him. He drank from it and felt like he'd been given a short reprieve from the fear of the Soviets.

He learned that Nikolas and his friends were all refugees as well, running from Stalin under the protection of the SS. They were from the town of Rastadt, west of the Bug River. Emil told them he had lived in Pervomaisk, north of Rastadt, for several years before returning to the family farm in Friedenstal.

"Ever been to Bogdanovka?" Nikolas asked. "It's not far south of Pervomaisk."

"I remember a collective farm from that area," Emil said. "We bought barley from them when I worked at the brewery in Pervomaisk."

"What did you do there?"

"Most of the physical work. Hauling grain. Pouring grain. Mixing."

"How did you get on the trek?" Nikolas asked.

Emil looked at him, puzzled. "Uh, German officers came to our village and told us the Soviets were coming and if we did not wish to die, we had two days to pack."

"No, I mean, what qualified you? Were you *Selbstschutz*?"

Emil knew what he meant, and it made him uneasy. Nikolas was asking him if he'd been a member of the *Selbstschutz*, a militia group the Nazis formed after the German invasion in 1941. Recruits to the *Selbstschutz* had all come from the ethnic-German population in the region.

In the Romanian-controlled Governorate of Transnistria, one of the *Selbstschutz* missions was to protect the *Volksdeutsche* communities and colonies from marauding Romanian troops. But Emil also knew there was more to tell about those militias and the things they had done. Much more.

A good part of him wanted to leave right then, but instead, he said, "There was no call for *Selbstschutz* or that sort of thing in Friedenstal. It is a tiny place in a sea of grain fields. The Romanians never bothered us."

Nikolas nodded but kept watching Emil, who felt the need to fill the silence.

"Were you *Selbstschutz* in Rastadt?" he asked.

"All of us," Nikolas said, and raised his mug to the other men. "It's how we showed we were good Germans worthy of being brought home to the Fatherland. With the documents to prove it. You have them, yes? These documents, Emil?"

Emil nodded. "Since the first days of the invasion. Proving it was not difficult. My mother had our family Bible going back generations all the way to Germany and all of our birth records from the church."

"They didn't draft you into the Wehrmacht?"

"They wanted to at first, but I told them that I was the last useful man left in my family, and I would be a better farmer to the Germans than a soldier. They told me to go back to our farm, start growing, and we did."

"How lucky for you," Nikolas said, but he didn't sound satisfied.

Emil drank more of his wine and was offered a second cup and a third while the militiamen sang, got maudlin over the lives they were leaving behind, and anxious about a future away from the Soviets. Near the bottom of Emil's third mug, one of the men called it a night.

Emil knew he should be getting back to his family. But then Nikolas poured him a little more. Last one, he promised himself as the other two men waved off Nikolas's offer and announced that they, too, were going to sleep.

"We never know where life will take us," Nikolas said when they were gone.

"I am trying to live life," Emil said. "Not life living me. Not anymore."

"You are drunk, my friend."

"A little," Emil said, raising his mug. "Thanks to you."

Nikolas clinked his mug, and they drank and then lapsed into silence the way men are wont to do. Emil was pleasantly studying the glowing coals of the dying fire and thinking he really should go back or he was going to have a headache come morning, when Nikolas spoke.

"How many?"

Emil looked over to see the man staring at him. "How many what?"

Nikolas curled his hand into a gun shape, closed his left eye. "How many Jews did you have to shoot to get your land back and be on this trek?"

Emil felt as if he'd been punched and must have looked it.

Nikolas smiled and nodded. "Uh-huh. I thought so. You had to do something for them, the Germans. Everyone did. Otherwise they wouldn't be taking you with them, protecting you and your wife and your sons. You were a shooter just like me, weren't you, Emil?"

Emil had a vivid memory of himself staring at a Luger in his hand. His head swirled, and his stomach boiled. He'd had far too much wine.

"I knew it," Nikolas said smugly. "I see it in your face, Emil. How many?"

Emil shook his head, but Nikolas was having none of it. He came closer, loomed over Emil. "How many stinking Bolshevik Jews did you have to shoot to get a spot on this trek?"

"None!"

Nikolas sneered at him. "Bullshit. Hell, I got no problem saying it, and neither should you. We did a good thing, a noble thing, wiping the earth free of those lice-ridden kikes. That's how it started for us. The Romanians sent all their Jews to that farm at Bogdanovka, and the Yids started to die of typhus because of the lice crawling on them. Could have become an epidemic. Could have killed everyone for hundreds of kilometers—German, Russian, Ukrainian, everyone—if they didn't keep it contained. The Nazis knew they had no choice, so we, the Rastadt *Selbstschutz*, had no choice. Took us eighteen days to shoot them all and twenty days more to boil or burn their clothes."

Eighteen days shooting? Emil thought in horror, staring at the man's newer clothes before he staggered a few feet to his right and vomited up Adeline's bread and four mugs of wine.

"There you go," Nikolas said. "We've all felt that way, one time or another, because of what we did. Get it out; you'll feel better. And the way I see it, we had no choice, right?"

Emil turned, glared at him, acid burning the back of his throat as he said, "You had a choice. And I've never shot or killed anyone in my life. We're on this trek because of an old Bible and because I'm a good farmer and smart with my hands. Thanks for the wine."

He picked up his lantern and headed by dead reckoning back into the darkness with Nikolas yelling drunkenly after him, "Bullshit! I saw it in your face. It takes a man like me to know a man like you, Emil. You see them when you're sleeping, don't you? Hear them, too. All the lice-ridden rats you put down!"

———

At that, Emil began to run blindly, trying to put space between himself and Nikolas, and terrified that Adeline might somehow be hearing the ravings of a drunken killer. He tripped and almost went down but caught his balance and slowed. The shouting had stopped.

"I never . . . ," Emil muttered shakily after he'd lit the lantern and found the road to the bridge. "Never."

He passed his horses and scrambled down the embankment. Then he extinguished the light and crept toward the sleeping forms of his wife and children. None of them stirred when Emil slid under the blankets behind Walt.

He lay awake on his back with Nikolas's cruel voice echoing in his head: *I saw it in your face.* In his mind, Emil heard people crying, then the flat cracks of guns, saw their flashes in the darkness beyond Captain Haussmann, who stood there, thrusting a loaded Luger at him.

That memory was seared so deeply in Emil, it took his breath away. He felt hollow and alone, a sense magnified when he thought of Nikolas shooting Jews for eighteen days.

He's a threat to me. I don't know why yet, but he's a threat. I can feel it in my bones.

Emil closed his eyes, understanding that he needed to stay far away from Nikolas and he needed to rely on himself to do it, certainly not on a God who'd create a man who could shoot innocent people for eighteen days on end.

And then he was fearfully wondering if meeting Nikolas and seeing Haussmann were part of some bitter punishment for that night outside Dubossary. He drifted toward sleep, thinking, *Once you decided, Emil, you were as guilty as Nikolas.*

Chapter Nine

Four more days and five nights passed, and the Martels were seeing as many retreating Romanians as Germans. Whenever they passed a group of marching Wehrmacht soldiers, Adeline found herself searching their faces, hoping against hope to see her younger brother, Wilhelm, Will's namesake, among them. Or Emil's older brother, Reinhold. But she never did.

Emil had turned quiet and brooding since they'd camped below that bridge west of Hincesti. Adeline had learned to give her husband distance when he was like this and focused her attention on supporting him and the boys as they passed through muddy low country laced with creek bottoms, and then climbed forested ridges made treacherous by lingering ice and snow.

Parts and pieces of the broken German war machine had been discarded on both sides of the route. They saw unburied frozen soldiers being pecked by crows. And charred abandoned tanks. And transport trucks buried up to their axles in muck. And the blasted black barrels of artillery cannons that the Wehrmacht had decided to blow up rather than leave for Stalin's forces to use against them.

Now some twelve days into their ordeal, members of the trek had begun to die from exposure, weakness, and disease. Not an hour passed when they weren't rolling by a wagon pulled off to the side of the route so survivors could bury their dead.

"When I was getting water this morning, a woman told me they think it's typhus," Adeline said when they were about to turn northwest toward the Romanian border town of Iasi.

"Lice," Emil said, thinking of Nikolas. "The lice carry it."

"I checked both boys last night."

"We'll check everyone every night until this is over."

The caravan halted. Word soon came back that tanks and forces with the Soviet Second Ukrainian Front were now moving to the west-northwest, trying to split German Army Group South into two pieces. The SS men protecting the trek kept them stalled for two hours before directing the caravan south, away from Iasi.

The sun came out an hour after they changed routes, which Adeline took as a good sign. The temperature warmed the farther south they rolled. As the hours passed, the boys dozed under the bonnet. Emil was at the reins, looking all around and taking in their surroundings.

"What are you looking for?" she asked.

His brows knitted. "I don't know that I'm looking for anything. I'm just looking around because I never intend on coming back this way ever again."

"Does that make you happy or sad?"

"That I'm never coming back here? Happy."

"Good. I thought you'd forgotten how to be happy."

He looked at her, his mouth slightly agape. "I'm sorry, Adella. I just get caught up in my worries about you and the boys and whether we should have come with the Germans or, I don't know, gone our own way to freedom."

"Do you know the way to freedom?"

"I figure I'll know it when I see it," he said, and smiled.

He glanced over at her. She smiled at him. "Remember Mrs. Kantor?"

"Wasn't for her, I wouldn't be in love with you."

"Awww," she said, forgetting what she wanted to tell Emil and scooting over to give him a kiss on the cheek.

He put his arm around her, and she snuggled against his chest as the sun rose high overhead and the air turned even warmer. Despite his dark moods, Adeline felt so safe in Emil's arms, and the wagon and horses were moving so smoothly in rhythm that her eyelids got heavy, and soon she was dozing, too.

———

October 1933
Birsula, Ukraine

In Adeline's dreams, Mrs. Kantor and her guests had all raved over the chicken and egg-noodle soup. Esther called it "a triumph," which made Adeline blush because she thought so, too. She had taken half a bowl for herself and could not remember the last time anything had tasted so good. And there was that handsome, funny young man who'd sold her the firewood.

Emil. He made her smile. Maybe her life was changing for the better again.

She saw Emil pass by on his way to the bakery the evening after the chicken feast and the evening after that. She got irritated that he had not once looked toward the house where he knew she worked. On the third evening, he did the same thing, and she felt hurt in a way that surprised her because, really, she'd only spoken to him for a few minutes. What had she expected, anyway?

Adeline was at the sink, furiously scrubbing pots ten minutes after he'd gone past her for the third evening in a row, when she happened to look up through the kitchen window and saw Emil standing at the rear gate, looking awkward. He waved.

Adeline waved back, dried her hands, checked her hair in the mirror, and went out. "More wood to sell?" she asked.

"Uh, no. Uh, you need some? I can make sure you've got enough."

Adeline smiled. "You can drop by a little every day if you like."

Emil blushed, smiled, and then nodded. "I can do that. I . . . I'd like that."

Their conversation never ended from that day forward. Granted, it stopped during the day when they were apart and working, but together they picked back up right where they'd left off, both of them mooning over each other like fools. At times, Adeline felt like they could complete each other's sentences, and her heart physically ached whenever they parted.

But when Emil asked her to marry him on the first anniversary of their meeting, Adeline was conflicted and asked him for time to think about it. She loved cooking and taking care of Mrs. Kantor. And she had a steady paycheck for the first time in her life and made more money than Emil did gathering firewood. On the other hand, she adored Emil. He was funny, hardworking, and even though he had not stayed in school as long as she had, he was smart, street-smart, the kind of man who would survive. But would he grow and thrive? Would she have a better life with him than a life alone?

The next morning, Mrs. Kantor noticed her fretting, and Adeline explained her predicament, finishing, "I have it so good here. You are kind to me. We have enough to eat, and you've given me a warm place to sleep. What should I do? He collects firewood for a living."

Mrs. Kantor gazed at her for several moments before replying. "I shall be heartbroken if you leave, Adelka, but it is better to be a poor wife than a rich maid. You have said Emil is a good man, which means you will know love if you leave me. You will have children if you leave me. You will have a family. And what a family it will be!"

Her employer had said this last statement with such enthusiasm that she almost knocked over her water glass. This caused Adeline to burst out laughing, which very much pleased Mrs. Kantor.

"Keep laughing," she said, wagging a finger at her. "Laughter keeps you young at heart. Laugh at least once a day. Twice is better."

"That's easy," Adeline said.

"Not always. Can I give you some other advice that has helped me in life?"

"Please," she said.

Mrs. Kantor waved her to the chair across from her where her friend Esther had sat. Adeline took the chair tentatively, but then smiled at the older woman.

"My dear," Mrs. Kantor said, "I have come to believe after eighty-one years on this earth that our job in life is to endure, to be kind, and to constantly put the past behind us and not dwell too much on the future. If you must look back, try to find the beauty and the benefit in every cruelty done to you. If you must think about the future, try to have no expectations about it. Trust in God to guide you through. You understand?"

Adeline did not understand everything the older woman was saying, but she nodded.

"Good," Mrs. Kantor said. "Because when you do that, my dear, you will know God's blessing and deserve every happiness and abundance this life has to offer as long as you give part of your abundance to others less fortunate. Do you understand?"

Adeline was still not fully grasping what Mrs. Kantor was telling her, but she nodded again. Her uncertainty must have shown in her face because her employer sighed.

"I'm trying to give you the keys to a long and happy life, Adeline," Mrs. Kantor said. "Listen again. Our job in life is to endure, to be kind, and to constantly put the past behind us and not dwell too much on the future. If you must look back . . ."

The old woman's voice blurred and faded, replaced in Adeline's dream by another memory, a later memory, one far more bitter and scarring.

January 13, 1936
Pervomaisk, Ukraine

Feeling weaker and more helpless than at any other time in her life, twenty-year-old Adeline gazed down at her baby boy, dear sweet Waldemar, fussing in her arms, still trying to nurse at her painful, dry nipples, his own arms so tiny, and his skin so thin and close to the bone, she wanted to break down sobbing and did.

Emil put his arms around her shoulders. "My friends are trying to find cream for him. We will find some; I'm sure of it."

"We'll both go ask strangers," she said, panicked. "Anyone and everyone. Find your mother first. Get her to come take care of her grandson while you and I try to keep him alive."

The couple had relocated to Pervomaisk shortly after their marriage because Emil's mother had moved there and said there was work in the small city four hours east of Birsula. Emil got a job first as a field hand and then in the brewery. Life as newlyweds suited them despite their humble living arrangements, and soon Adeline became pregnant.

Back in August 1935, more than six months into her term, Adeline was still working in the fields. The month had started out wet, and then turned hot. The mosquitos along the aptly named Bug River were thick as she worked, so she never knew which bite passed the disease. But by the first of September, as she entered her seventh month, Adeline was suffering the debilitating symptoms of malaria. The first attack began with a pleasant, heavy feeling at the base of her neck that led to drowsiness and then to a delicious sleep in a darkness so complete and comforting, only painful joint ache and a soaring fever could wake her.

Day after day, Adeline burned up, hallucinating her father's long-awaited return as new fevers spiked and then broke, drenching her in sweat. Within minutes, she'd be chilled to the bone and shivering so violently, blankets could not warm her.

She'd fall asleep finally, only to have the same pleasant, heavy feeling at the back of her neck again as the malaria cycle started over. With each new attack coming six to eight hours apart, Adeline became weaker, unable to keep food down. She lost weight. She feared for the baby growing inside her but could do nothing until Emil found a doctor who gave her quinine.

Improving steadily by the end of September and through October, Adeline had not had a malaria attack in nearly twenty days when November took the calendar and the birth of her first child loomed. On the twelfth of that month, she was sewing a blanket for the cradle Emil had built. The baby was active, kicking all the time, something she adored.

It was early afternoon, but she was very tired and set her handiwork down and closed her eyes, almost immediately feeling the familiar, hated, lovely pressure at the base of her skull. She slept the dreamless sleep and awoke to malarial fevers different from the previous bouts, higher temperatures and headaches so bad, she thought the pain would break her eardrums.

Emil would later tell her that he had to soak her in wet sheets while she spoke gibberish to people he could not see. She took more quinine, but it did not knock the disease back as quickly as it had before. On the fifth day, while in fever and suffering through a long, hard delivery, she gave birth to a son they named Waldemar.

He was small at birth, under two kilos, but even as sick as she was, she'd experienced the most intense joy of her life seeing her firstborn child, holding him to her breast and seeing him feed on her milk. He was everything she'd ever wanted or hoped for. When Emil had thrown his arms around the both of them, she'd felt more complete, and happier than she'd ever been.

But the malaria would not let her go. Adeline was symptom-free one day and feverish the next. As it does, malaria chipped away at her, wore her down.

During another attack between Christmas and New Year's, she became distrustful of ever feeling good again. Then her breast milk trickled to an intermittent seep.

Waldemar was struggling, barely getting enough to survive by the start of the second week of January 1936. Adeline's fevers had stopped finally. She was eating and beginning to get her strength back. But she was barely able to give her baby a single feeding a day let alone the seven or eight he needed to thrive.

They'd taken the baby to the same doctor who'd given Adeline quinine, and he'd told them the baby needed milky fats immediately. He recommended they either find a wet nurse or get fresh cream from a dairy to feed to him until her strength and milk returned. But they could not find a wet nurse, and cream had so far been impossible to come by in Pervomaisk in the dead of winter.

"I'll go out again," Emil said.

"I'm going with you," Adeline insisted.

Emil went to fetch his mother. Karoline had fallen on her hip before Christmas and was walking with a cane.

"He's very weak," Adeline told her.

"I can see that," her mother-in-law said.

Adeline started to give Karoline instructions, but the older woman held up her hands. "I've raised a few of these myself already."

Adeline and Emil went out into the streets and walked for hours that day, asking anyone and everyone how they might find cream for their sick child. Though there was a black market on such things, after nearly nineteen years under Communist rule, no one was able or felt confident enough to tell them.

Emil had to work that evening. Adeline walked with him to the brewery. Outside, she started to cry. "I can't give him milk. That's why he's dying. This is because of me."

Emil grabbed her, held her tight. "We'll find out a way to—"

"Emil?" a man said.

They looked up to see a fellow worker of Emil's from the brewery.

"I found your son some cream," he said. "I left it with your mother at your apartment."

Adeline's spirits soared. She kissed Emil on the cheek and ran home while he went to work. She reached the modest apartment building where they lived, climbed to the third floor, and went into their flat.

"Where is it?" she said before shutting the door.

Her mother-in-law said, "Where's what?"

"The bottle of cream," Adeline said.

"Oh, what does that doctor know?" Karoline said. "I tried to give the baby a spoonful, and he spat it up as soon as it went down. Same thing the second and the third time. So I drank it."

Adeline stared at her mother-in-law incredulously. "You drank it?"

"Not all of it," Karoline sniffed, a little indignant. "And like I said, it wasn't doing him a lick of good. And besides, I haven't had real cream in five years, maybe more."

Adeline shrieked. "You . . . you hateful witch, get out of my house! You just killed your own grandson!"

"I did nothing of the sort," Karoline shouted. "Anyone with two eyes can see he's so far gone because you can't give him *your* milk! My sipping some cream has nothing to do with it!"

She slammed the door behind her.

In the end, eight-week-old Waldemar was too far gone. When Adeline gave him some of the remaining fresh cream, he did indeed throw it up and every spoonful after. Then he developed a cough that further weakened him. Two evenings later, Emil came home to find Adeline cradling the baby in her arms. He was swaddled and laboring for breath.

"He's dying now," she said. "He won't open his eyes anymore."

"No," Emil rasped. "He's not dying."

"He is," she said. "I can feel it. Can we hold him together?"

Sadness swallowed her husband whole before he came over beside her and they held their infant son between them, grieving for hours before he took his final breath and let it go in a slim, devastating wheeze that tore through the last bit of strength holding Adeline together. She began to choke, sob, to moan with a pain she'd never known, worse than giving birth to him, more primal, the agony of her heart cracking.

Emil stayed strong for her, held her through the worst of it. He sat by her for more than an hour, and never broke, never even uttered a word until she said, "We have to bury him. We need a little coffin."

He hesitated, and then said, "I haven't been paid yet this month. We don't have the money to buy the lumber."

Adeline gazed dully at him. "What?"

"We don't."

"Then?"

"I don't know," he said in total defeat. "I don't."

"We can't just bury our baby in the dirt!"

"I know, but I—"

Adeline pushed her swaddled dead child into her husband's arms. "Hold him. I . . . I can't be in here right now. I just can't."

She got up on wobbly legs, took her coat and hat, and went out into the predawn. It was mid-January in north-central Ukraine. It should have been bitter and snow-clad. But the cold and the storms had not yet come. Everything around her was bleak and shadowed in brown and gray as she sat on the front steps of the building, looking southeast, trying to spot the first hint of light on the horizon.

But Adeline saw only darkness there, and her grief fought against her numbness.

She bowed her head and prayed.

"You must have taken him from me for a reason," she said, trying not to blubber, but not succeeding. "I don't know why . . . I don't know why you let me get sick, why he had to die. But please don't make me put my baby in the cold dirt like something you throw away. Please don't make me do that to my blessed little boy."

Unable to go on, Adeline sat there in the dark, tears streaming down her face, arms wrapped around her knees until she saw a rose-hued glow appear low in the sky to the east. Then she heard through an open window above her the tortured sound of her proud, stoic husband crying for the first time in their marriage.

That cored her out, put her in an otherworldly daze in which she faced the sky where fingers of that glowing rose color were growing, extending. Adeline was so battered by that point, she barely noticed the coming dawn as she questioned how much pain a woman could go through before her mind broke as badly as her heart.

From above her, she heard Emil hit something in their apartment and then curse God. Adeline put her face in her hands. She had heard what happens to couples when a child dies like this. She wondered if her marriage was over and felt worse than abandoned. She felt tossed aside, trash, nothing in the eyes of heaven.

A breeze began to blow. Chilled, Adeline lifted her head, wanting to pull her coat collar tighter around her neck. Though she remained in dark shadow, the rose fingers of dawn had become long and beautiful now, the tips almost over her head as the sun finally began to rise, throwing a weak crown of golden rays on the horizon.

She watched it grow stronger, thinking, *How can something as beautiful as this happen on a morning as vicious as this?*

The breeze gusted. Out of the corner of her eye, she caught something move on the stiffened wind, tumbling, twirling, and dancing in an odd stutter. It fluttered and lifted and then fell as the gust sighed, spiraling to a stop about a meter in front of her.

Adeline gaped in disbelief at the yellow-and-white twenty-ruble note, more than enough money for Emil to build Waldemar a coffin.

She started to sob all over again.

———

"Adella," Emil said, shaking her shoulder softly. "Easy now."

Adeline startled awake, looked around for a moment in total confusion before settling on Oden and Thor pulling the wagon and then back to Emil. "I was having a bad dream."

"A nightmare," he said. "You were all shook up."

"You slept longer than I did, Mama," Will said behind her.

"And me," said the second Waldemar, born in October 1937, twenty-one months after the first child died.

She twisted around on the bench and found her boys lying on the folded blankets, elbows up, chins in their palms. She smiled, leaned over, and kissed them both on the foreheads.

"Why did you do that?" Walt asked.

"Because you and your brother are the miracles your father and I and God made," she said. "And because I la-la-la love you."

Will laughed, and so did Walt before he looked past her, and his face fell. "There are six tanks up on that hill in front of us, Mama," he said.

Adeline turned, put her hand to her brow, and made out the German Panzers sitting atop the rise, three on each side of the convoy. Their cannon barrels were all pointed up at an angle and aimed out over the caravan.

Will said, "I'm keeping my fingers in my ears until we get past them."

Walt frowned and then put his fingers in his ears, too.

Adeline said, "Putting our fingers in our ears is probably not a bad idea."

Her husband did not reply. Emil was now fixed on something closer than the tanks, ahead and to the right of the convoy. She could see a wagon pulled over off the track and a Wehrmacht vehicle parked beside it. Several men milled about outside.

She glanced at Emil, who'd turned his attention to the other side of the route. But when they got closer, he was watching them again, intently now.

Up the slope, the Panzers' engines roared. The tanks began to roll, spread out in two rows, their tracks digging up mud and hurling it into the air behind them. Adeline stuck her fingers in her ears, her attention on the Panzers, which picked up speed, coming toward them.

Oden and Thor began to shiver, tremble, and snort. They remembered.

"You're okay, boys," Emil called in a soothing tone. "They're just bigger horses."

Adeline had forgotten the wagon and the Wehrmacht vehicle until they were almost to them. She glanced at Emil who was staring intently at two of the men by the vehicle.

One was a tall, lanky man in heavy wool civilian clothing; the other an SS officer. They stood in semiprofile, watching the oncoming tanks.

Chapter Ten

Nikolas and Sturmbannführer Haussmann turned their backs to the tanks coming to their right and the mud being thrown into the air behind them. Emil wanted to give Adeline the reins and climb into the back with his sons.

But his wagon was fewer than twenty meters from the two men. There wasn't even enough time for Emil to lower his head and look away, hoping they did not recognize him.

The tanks veered off. Major Haussmann studied the wagon in front of the Martels and then Emil a moment before shifting his gaze to Adeline where it lingered before looking to the next wagon in the line. Nikolas barely scanned Adeline and the boys behind her before fixing on Emil and giving him a knowing smile and nod as they passed. The gesture felt oily, like honor among thieves, and turned Emil's stomach.

"Who was that man?" Adeline asked. "Why did he smile at you like that?"

"I have no idea," Emil said, wanting to look back.

"He nodded to you."

"Did he? I thought he smiled. Probably just being friendly."

He glanced over at his wife, who was skeptical. "It didn't feel friendly."

Walt and Will started moving behind Emil, which gave him the excuse to look over his shoulder and through the bonnet to the route unfolding behind them. Nikolas and Haussmann were staring after him.

"They're watching us," said Adeline, who was also twisted around. "Who are they?"

Emil glanced at his wife, shook his head. "I don't know."

"The SS officer looked like the same one directing the caravan the second morning."

"Did he?"

"Emil, you remember faces. You always do."

"I must not have given him much attention, Adella," he said, looking back again. "Anyway, they're out of sight now."

But neither Nikolas nor Haussmann were long out of Emil's thoughts the rest of that day's ride. They passed more Panzer tanks and crews to either side of the route and more soldiers digging in along the hillsides, and even more Romanian soldiers setting camps.

The Martel clan stopped for the night near a creek running with cold, clear water. Along the banks, the boys easily found wood for a fire that their grandfather soon set ablaze. Emil dug another oven for Adeline in the creek bank. She made bread while her mother and sister brewed a soup of onions, potatoes, turnips, and strips of dried pork. Walt found another handful of wild-asparagus stalks that they also put into the pot.

As the sun set, it threw fingers of dramatic reds and purples overhead.

"That's pretty," Emil said. "The sky."

Adeline looked up from her cutting board and started to smile before cocking her head, puzzled, and then saddened.

"What's the matter?" he asked.

"I don't know. I have seen beautiful fingers like that only one other time that I can remember," she said, and hesitated, her eyes welling with tears.

"One sunset looks like another to me," said Rese. "When can we eat?"

"You're up?" Emil said.

"I feel like I've slept for a week," Rese said, and yawned.

"You have slept for a week," Adeline said, pushing her grief aside.

"Which is why I'm hungry."

"I'll get her a bowl," said Karoline, who had marched over.

"I'm fine, Mama," Rese said. "I am more than able to carry a soup bowl."

"Here," Malia said, handing Rese a steaming bowl. "The potatoes might still be a bit crunchy, but that should fill you up."

Adeline handed her a piece of bread. Rese smiled and thanked her. The boys were next, then the women, oldest to youngest, followed by the men. Emil waited until the very last to eat, but there was more than enough left to fill his belly that evening.

As they ate, the sky faded into night. They fed the fire and turned up the lantern. The wind picked up, whistling through the tree branches and causing the fire to roar, crack, and spark so violently, a small volcano of glowing embers burst forth and floated high into the sky.

———

On the other side of the blaze, in the shadows thrown by the wind-bellowed flames, Emil caught movement down in the creek bed. A man soon appeared, coming up the bank, carrying a rifle on his shoulder and a bottle in his hand. He walked toward the fire, revealing the olive-brown winter uniform of a Romanian army soldier. He was short, about five foot six, and in his midtwenties.

"Good evening," he said in German, smiling and looking at them all in this strange, lit-up way while raising the bottle. "I am Corporal Gheorghe of the Third Romanian Army. The moon and stars have brought me to you with honey wine. I was crossing the creek, feeling cold, and saw your fire. Can we trade? Wine for warmth?"

Emil sensed immediately that there was something not quite right about the man. Why had he been in the creek bed? Where did the wine come from? When he glanced at Walt and Will sitting by their mother, both boys were frowning, distrustful. But not Adeline. She seemed amused by their visitor.

"I'll take some honey wine, Corporal Gheorghe, please," Rese said.

"You will not," her mother said.

"I will," Emil's father said.

"I will, too," Adeline said. "Where did you get honey wine? And how does a Romanian corporal know how to speak German?"

He walked up by the fire, smiling at them all as he twisted the cork from the bottle. "I stole the honey wine from an SS officers' camp just up the road." He went to Johann and poured some in his cup, saying, "Do you know what the stars and the moon and the Almighty One say I am going to do when the war is over and I get to go home?"

Emil wanted to tell him that he didn't care what he was going to do after the war was over and that stealing alcohol from SS officers was one of the dumbest moves he'd ever heard of.

But Adeline's older sister, Malia, said, "What will you do?"

"I will be a beekeeper," the corporal said. "Make honey. Sell honey. I love honey."

He moved with the wine to Karoline, who shook her head and gestured to her daughter. "None for Rese, either."

"I'm twenty-one, Mama," Rese protested.

Karoline glared at her, said, "This is not about age, Rese, and you know it."

Rese went into a huff, crossed her arms, shut her eyes, and said nothing.

"Why a beekeeper?" Malia asked as he poured Adeline and Lydia some wine.

The Romanian raised his eyebrows at Emil, who shook his head. The corporal made a sad face with a pouty lower lip before walking over to Malia, saying, "Bees and honey are good for men and women and little boys. If you eat honey, you're strong, never get sick. If you get stung, it makes you even stronger. And you eat the royal jelly? You live and live and live. And a beekeeper, he does not have to work so hard all year. It's a good dream. Every night, I dream the war is over. Crazy Stalin, loony Hitler, all gone, dead, to hell. In my dream, I throw my gun away, go home, raise bees, make honey, and find a good woman to make happy."

He smiled at Malia. "My wife and I will live long. No war. Just love everyone. Make sweet honey together, right?"

She blushed, dropped her chin, said, "That does sound like a dream, Corporal."

"Dreams come true," he said, grinning. "You know this, yes?"

She looked up in confusion and then glanced at her mother. Lydia shook her head and said, "Dreams are nonsense, Corporal Gheorghe. They don't come true."

"No, no, dreams come true," he said, taking off his helmet and gesturing to a still-livid scar above a slight crescent-shaped depression in his skull above his right ear. "The old Corporal Gheorghe? Before the mortar hit? He hated life. He suffered every day, dark and angry, and listened to scared voices in his head. *Why me? Why not me? Who will shoot me?* The old Corporal Gheorghe did not believe in God. He did not believe that dreams come true."

The Romanian soldier put his hand over his heart, and his eyes widened. "But then the mortar bomb hit, knocked me cold. I woke up and everything was different. I was part of everything and everyone. I saw it. I felt it. I understood! Private Kumar was right! Dreams come true if you hold them in your heart and act from your heart. Every night, right here in my chest, I know I was born to make honey, find a beautiful woman, and make more honey."

He laughed, touched the scar with his right hand again, and closed his eyes, his face as blissful as a man's face could be. "I can wait. I have patience and peace and am not afraid. I know in my heart I am already a beekeeper. No matter what, I am a beekeeper."

Emil had concluded by then that the Romanian was a raving lunatic or a drunk or both. He felt a little hostile as he said, "You did not tell us where you learned to speak German."

"Oh, my grandmother was Austrian," he said, opening his eyes. "I went to live with her for several years after my mother died."

Malia said, "And where were you when the mortar hit?"

The rapture drained out of the corporal's face. His face clouded. His hand dropped from his heart and grabbed the bottle of honey wine. After pouring a generous slug into his mouth, he swallowed it, shivered, and stared at them all with a haunted expression.

"Stalingrad," he said. "The Elbow of the Don."

Over the course of the next hour, while the fire burned down to embers and they consumed the rest of the honey wine, the beekeeper told his story of the longest and bloodiest battle ever fought on earth. Despite not trusting the man, Emil could not help listening closely as Corporal Gheorghe described leaving his hometown of Barlad in eastern Romania and being ordered onto a troop train in his summer uniform in July 1942. The beekeeper left the train two days later and then marched for nine days to a position near the town of Serafimovich more than one hundred kilometers northwest of Stalingrad.

"It was steppe country south of Cotul Donului, the Elbow of the Don River," he said. "Open. Few trees. Lots of wind. Hot then, too. Private Kumar, that crazy little Indian, he thought the wind and the sun were just fine. I hated it."

A soldier in the Romanian's platoon, Private Kumar worked hard digging trenches, foxholes, and pads for machine gun nests and cannons. As they dug into their position on a ridge about two kilometers from the elbow of the river, Corporal Gheorghe learned that Private Kumar's father was an expatriate from India who owned a textile company, had lived in Bucharest for thirty years, and early on married Kumar's mother, a beautiful Romanian woman. They had three children. Kumar was the oldest.

The Romanian drank again from the honey wine, said, "Private Kumar was even shorter than me but he was twice as strong. And later, when it got colder than cold? He would not shake. He'd just sit down, shut his eyes, make this little smile, breathe deep and slow for ten minutes. And then he'd be fine and go back to work. Finally, I asked Kumar if he was praying. He said, no, he was meditating. I told him I had no idea what he was talking about. He said praying was where you talk to God. And meditation was where you listen."

He paused, smiled. "At the time, I thought Private Kumar was kind of nuts and—"

"I thought you were going to tell us about the battle." Lost in all this rambling talk, Emil had gotten to his feet, intending to care for his horses.

"And how I got hit in the head, yes," the corporal said. "It's coming."

Though the Soviet air force bombed Corporal Gheorghe's position several times in the ensuing months, the beekeeper, Private Kumar, and the rest of the Third Romanian Army were largely untested well into the autumn of 1942, which was unseasonably mild and spawned windstorms and tornadoes across southern Russia.

Gheorghe said, "In November, the Red Army came to the heights on the other side of the Don River. Tanks. Cannons. Many divisions."

The beekeeper's face had gone hard with the memory. He said Private Kumar had a vision while he was meditating. In his vision, the Soviets attacked at night, and he was killed.

"I told him not to think that way, that he had to be ready to fight, and Kumar would just smile at me. I went to sleep and had this dream that I lived through the battle, walked right through it, became a beekeeper, and lived a long, happy life."

In the early hours before dawn on November 23, 1942, three Soviet armies attacked the Romanians, who were stretched thin along a hundred-kilometer front from Corporal Gheorghe's position on the Elbow of the Don, east toward Stalingrad.

"The snow and wind had come in, first big storm of winter," the beekeeper said, looking up at the night sky. "I could not hear the tanks, but Private Kumar said he could hear them idling. Then cannons and mortars started thumping and hitting all over our ridge. Private Kumar was over at the other end of the same dogleg trench, not far, maybe forty meters away. I tell you, when the bombs started falling, he just put his gun down and sat there, eyes closed, with that silly little smile on his face."

The Romanian stopped his tale to offer them the last of the honey wine, but they all shook him off. Malia asked, "What happened?"

He gazed sadly into the fire. "At first light, a mortar shell hit Private Kumar, and he was gone, like red snow blowing away on the wind."

"What?" Rese said, recoiling. "Really?"

"Sad but true. And then in the snowstorm, there were big flashes like lightning. And *boom!* I got hit, too, and everything went dark."

The Romanian's gloved fingers went to the scar and the depression on the side of his head before he took his attention off the night sky and stared wide-eyed at them all.

"I woke up, facedown in the snow. It was daylight. My ears rang and buzzed. My head felt broken. I was caked with snow, and I could feel I was injured here in my head and bleeding out my nose and ears. More bombs fell. More cannons fired. Tanks were coming. And riflemen. And machine gunners. But I was dizzy, and time seemed slow until I saw thousands of Soviets in white clothes crossing the river and climbing the hill in the storm. I saw them shoot six men below me and heard them say, 'Take no prisoners.'"

The corporal paused, transfixed and horrified, remembering the moment of his approaching doom. His body trembled, then, not in fear, Emil noticed, but with a strange joy that suddenly seemed to burst from his chest and radiate from his face. He gazed around at them all, grinning like a madman.

"The Russian soldiers, they ran right past me, like I was invisible!" he said. "Then more came, and it was the same. And right then, I knew I was different after the mortar bomb, like something got knocked into place in my head. I was very calm, at peace, and as I surveyed the battle that raged around me, I knew in my heart that Private Kumar was correct. You, me, the fire, the universe, everything is the Almighty One. And when you know that, when you embrace that, dreams come true because you are in the Almighty and the Almighty is in you."

Emil wanted to stop him right there because it all sounded totally insane, but then he noticed how Malia and Adeline and Rese seemed almost entranced by the Romanian.

"What did you do?" Malia asked.

Corporal Gheorghe smiled at her. "I took my rifle, got up out of the trench, and walked through the blizzard, straight through combat."

He claimed he saw dead Soviet soldiers in white coveralls and took a set off one of the corpses. He said Russian and Romanian machine gunners shot past him. Bombs fell. Cannons roared. Tanks clanked by him at less than one and a half meters while he buried too many of his comrades.

Corporal Gheorghe said he walked through battles and the aftermath for days, seeing the brutality, the carnage, and far too many dead—Germans, Soviets, and Romanians, civilians and military personnel alike. He rummaged in the packs of dead Romanian soldiers. If he found food or something useful, he buried those soldiers. To avoid lying in the snow, he slept where the bombs had hit most recently.

"The ground was black, warm, and smelled like oil smoke," he said. "The third or fourth morning, a fog came, and I walked into it. When I came out of that fog, the battle of Cotul Donului was over, and I was very much alive."

He shifted his attention to Malia, widened his smile, and said, "This is why I know I will be a beekeeper and find a good woman and live a honey life."

Adeline's older sister blushed again and giggled. "A honey life."

"Well," Lydia, her mother, said, getting to her feet, irritated. "I've had enough, and so have you, Malia. We must go in the morning to find our own honey life."

The Romanian seemed to find that funny and laughed and bowed. Lydia and a reluctant Malia left the dying fire along with Adeline, who carried Will while Walt trudged sleepily beside her toward the wagon and bed.

Karoline urged Rese and Johann off with her as well. And then there were just Emil and the Romanian soldier in the fire's last glowing light.

"You understand, Martel?" Corporal Gheorghe said. "The Almighty One, God, the Divine, the Universal Intelligence, whatever you call it, is all the same thing. The One hears us and helps us, moves the moon and stars for us if we ask in the right way. And dreams come true."

Emil felt leaden inside as he shook his head and snapped, "There is no God, no Almighty One, no Divine, no Universal Intelligence, no moon and stars moving because of dreams. Just your own hard work and what you build for yourself and what you can hide from. That's it!"

The Romanian touched his head scar. "I walked through war at its worst and wasn't touched after the mortar bomb. I saw thousands die, Martel. But not me. I am here, by your fire."

"If what you said is true, you are a lucky man," Emil said. "I'll give you that. Good night, Corporal Gheorghe. Have a good life."

Gheorghe put his hand over his heart and then rocked back his head for a moment, eyes closed, before opening them and staring at Emil with his hand extended. "I have the feeling I will see you again, Martel. In fact, I am sure of it. It will happen when the moon and stars move."

Emil reluctantly shook the madman's hand. "Sure, okay, and good luck with the honey."

"Not luck," he said as he picked up his rifle and empty bottle. "In my heart, I am already a beekeeper."

He chuckled and walked away, down into the dark creek bottom. As Emil went to check on the horses, he could hear the Romanian corporal talking to no one and crashing through the brush. The night had fallen silent when he crawled beneath the blankets under the wagon.

"Was he crazy, Emil?" Adeline whispered.

"Hit in the head and completely cracked," he whispered back. "Worse than Malia."

He thought she might be angry at that, but instead, Adeline said, "I didn't understand half of what that man said, but my sister seemed to understand all of it. They do see the world differently, don't they?"

"Like I said, hit in the head. Now, go to sleep."

Chapter Eleven

In the chill deep darkness of night, Adeline awoke to a shrill whistle followed by an explosion, fifteen hundred meters away, no more. It tremored the ground beneath them. There was another whistle and another, more violent explosion even closer.

The Soviet Fourth Ukrainian Front was attacking from the east.

"The culvert!" Emil shouted. "Get Will! I'll bring Walt!"

Adeline grabbed her shoes, pulled them on, grabbed Will, and together they scrambled from beneath the wagon, hearing her mother and sister screaming for her.

"Which way?" Malia cried as another artillery round hit.

"Toward me!" Adeline screamed back. "Toward me!"

"Keep yelling!"

There was a tremendous flash as a bomb hit the Wehrmacht encampment close to them. The blast threw Adeline off balance, and she stumbled even as she saw Emil and Walt in front of her and Will, going for the creek and the culvert.

She felt blinded when the blasts stopped but kept going in the direction she'd last seen Emil. Then another bomb went off, and he was right there, holding out his powerful arms to grab Will and then her, and guide them into the cold water and where to duck into the culvert.

Adeline's shoes and feet were soaked and cold in two steps. But when the next bomb went off, she didn't care. The explosion sounded muffled, almost distant.

"I can't see, Mama," Walt said, deeper into the culvert.

"I'm cold," Will said. "Where do I stop?"

"Get to Walt," Adeline said. "And we're all cold, but we're safe for now."

When Will reached Walt, Adeline got beside him and told her sons to turn their backs to the culvert wall and to get their feet up out of the water and braced against the opposite wall. There was a splash.

"Mama!" Will cried. "I fell in!"

"Get up," Emil yelled from close to the entrance to the culvert.

"Yes, get up," she said, her stomach knotting because she knew he was in trouble now, cold and wet. "Come to me."

Adeline felt Will's frigid little hands against her thighs, reached out in the darkness and lifted him up onto her. Her legs and back strained against the pressure, but she hugged her already-shivering son to her chest.

"It's okay," she murmured in his ear. "Mama's got you."

"I'm so cold."

"It's just until Papa says it's okay to go out."

Ice-cold and wet, his fingers sought her cheeks in the darkness. She kissed them, grabbed them in her own dry hand.

"Why do we have to do this?" Walt asked in the darkness. "I don't like being in here."

"Sometimes you have to do things that you don't want to in order to stay alive," Emil said. "As bad as it is, it's better than being with the wagon."

"What if the wagon is gone?" Walt asked. "What if Thor and Oden are dead?"

"I'm cold, Mama," Will said, squirming in her arms.

"Think of somewhere you were very hot," she said. "The hottest place you've ever been. So hot you just want to get into the shade and sweat."

Then they all fell quiet, each of them finding a hot day in their minds. For reasons she did not quite understand, Adeline's thoughts went to August 9, 1941, in the city of Pervomaisk during a heat wave.

———

It was sweltering hot. Adeline carried Will, almost two, in her arms, with almost-four-year-old Walt beside her. She was returning to their apartment from a shopping foray with little to show for the effort. As she walked, her attention roamed everywhere, still trying to learn the world order anew. A week before, the Germans had invaded and now occupied the city, and she'd only just learned that her younger brother, Wilhelm, had been conscripted by the Wehrmacht to fight the retreating Red Army. He was already gone.

There were rumors of other bad changes coming. Every night, out their open windows, they had heard shooting inside the city. But Emil said that life could be better for them under the Germans than it had been under the Russians. Was that true? She was ethnic German and spoke both Russian and German, but felt no ties to either country, and certainly not to Stalin or to Hitler.

"Mama?" Walt said. "It's too hot. I'm thirsty."

"We're almost home. We'll get water there."

"Can you carry me?"

"What will I do with Will?"

"Oh," he said, looking downcast.

"Adeline? Is that you?" said a woman in a tremulous voice behind them.

Adeline, not recognizing the voice, looked over her shoulder and saw a desperate, frightened woman in her late thirties wearing a scarf over her head and peasant clothes. At first, she didn't recognize her. But then the woman shifted her head a bit, and Adeline did know her.

"Mrs. Kantor's friend," Adeline said, smiling. "Esther." It had been nearly eight years.

"Shhhh, I go by Ilse now," Esther said, glanced around and then smiled at Walt and the baby. "Both your boys?"

Adeline thought it odd she'd changed her name but grinned. "Yes."

"A blessing for you. Mrs. Kantor told me about your first child. I'm so sorry."

Adeline felt a pang of sorrow. Five years now and she had come to believe the pain of losing Waldemar would be something she'd carry always. She hugged Walt to her side. "These are my precious gifts instead. How are you?"

Esther leaned forward, put her trembling fingers on the back of Adeline's hand, and in a whisper on the verge of weeping, said, "The Nazis are shooting Jews in Bogopol, just across the river, and I . . . I need your help. Oh God, please, I have no one else to turn to."

———

In the pitch dark of the culvert almost three years later, with the bombs falling less frequently now, Will shivered in her arms and tore her from her memory. "I'm so cold, Mama."

Adeline called, "Emil?"

He called back, "The bombing is still going on, but it seems aimed somewhere else. I think we can get out. Lydia? Malia? Follow me."

"Thank God," Lydia said. "I hate being in these things."

Adeline heard them start down the culvert. "Will, get off me and walk toward Oma."

"In the water?" he said, his teeth chattering.

"Yes. Now."

Will climbed off her. She twisted around on one knee and then stood up into a crouch, the back of her head against the roof of the culvert.

"We're out," her sister called.

"Go on, Will," Adeline said. "Mama's right behind you. Walt, follow me."

A few moments later, they emerged from the culvert. They'd been inside thirty minutes. A new dawn was coming.

As Emil had sensed, the bombardment had not stopped but moved to the east toward the hillsides where the German troops were encamped, far enough away that her family seemed safe for the moment. Adeline grabbed up Will, who was shivering violently.

"Straight to the wagon," she said, and with Walt started up the bank.

They'd no sooner gotten to the top and taken a few steps toward the wagon than she heard the whistles and *whoomphs* of artillery again, as if the Soviets were sending explosives in sweeps along the German front, with different ranges east and west. Another round could be coming their way any moment.

Adeline broke into a sprint to the wagon.

"Climb in!" she said to Will, lifting him. "Get in the back. Take off all your clothes."

"No, Mama," he said. "I'm cold."

"Get in and take your clothes off!" she shouted. "I'm getting blankets!"

Adeline dropped to her knees. She heard planes now followed by more whistles and more blasts closer still to the south. The ground moved.

Walt screamed, "Mama!"

She grabbed the bedding, dragged it out, saw her older son pointing to the east where a wall of fire raged.

"I see it," she said, trying not to panic. "Get in."

Walt clambered up onto the bench and took the bedding from her and threw it in under the bonnet. She got up beside him, only to feel the wagon lurch again.

Up until then, she had not seen Emil working the horses into their harnesses. She helped Will and Walt strip off the rest of their wet clothes and wrapped both boys in the blankets.

Will was bluish and still shivering. Another artillery round exploded closer than before.

"We have to go!" Adeline screamed at Emil. "They're shelling south to north. They're coming at us!"

Emil jumped up on the bench and grabbed the reins.

"Hold on!" he shouted, and then slapped the flanks of Thor and Oden. The big horses coiled and drove forward, hurling Adeline off balance. She fell to her side on pots and pans that bruised her ribs.

She groaned, looked up and out the back of the wagon, seeing Emil's father lashing at his horses with Karoline and Rese behind him under the bonnet, on their knees, holding on to the bench and terrified. Behind them, Malia was driving their mother's wagon, screaming at the top of her lungs and whipping the reins on her ponies' flanks.

Mud flew. They skidded as the wheels floated in the grease. The wagon whipped violently one way and then another. Adeline was sure they were going to jackknife off the route. But Emil and their trusted horses countered the motion and fought through the wet ground on the far side of the creek bed before climbing onto more-stable ground. Artillery shells began to strike back where they'd been encamped, throwing shattered red and orange flames through the dawn.

Thor and Oden picked up their pace. They put distance between themselves and the barrage, five hundred meters and then a thousand. But other refugees in other wagons were on the move as well, streaming out of the woods to either side of the road ahead, and their speed slowed.

Will and Walt pulled the blankets over their heads and fell asleep. Adeline climbed onto the bench beside Emil. They glanced at each other and smiled. She reached out her hand. He took it and squeezed it.

"I'm glad you're so good with bombs falling around you," he said.

She broke into a grin. "You're not bad yourself."

An hour later, they crossed a rise that gave them a view ahead where even more wagons were strung out along a fairly wide road that traversed a steep hillside. Some of the wagons farther to the west had veered off into the left lane. To their right and down the steep bank, there was yet another wreckage. Two wagons had become entangled, and they and their horses and humans had gone over, flipping off sideways and tumbling down the bank.

Men and women were running across the route and down the bank toward the wreckage. By the time the Martels closed on the scene, German soldiers had appeared and were keeping the wagons still on the route moving forward. As they got close, Adeline saw that amid the wagon debris there were crippled horses, dead bodies, and many others hurt and wounded.

She closed her eyes, tried to go far away to that mythical green valley in her mind, tried to see it with rainbows in a clearing sky after a summer rain. But a woman's agony intruded.

"Help me, please," she called. "Please. Dear God, someone help me!"

She heard another woman saying, "We're here. We're helping as best we can."

Adeline opened her eyes and saw two women only a few meters ahead and to her right, on their knees on the road, and working on a woman who'd been brought up the bank. Her face was battered, filthy, and bloody. Both her legs were clearly broken. A bone stuck out of one shin.

"Oh God," the woman groaned. "Help me, please! I have no one else!"

Adeline stared after the woman as they passed, hearing another voice utter similar words in her mind.

———

August 9, 1941
Pervomaisk, Ukraine

That hot day, Esther put her trembling fingers on the back of Adeline's hand as she held Will. "I need your help. Oh God, please, I have no one else to turn to."

"They're shooting Jews?" Adeline said as Will squirmed in her arms.

The fear had Esther frantic as she said, "I have seen it with my own eyes. Old women in wheelchairs shot. Men kicked, beaten. Can we go somewhere safe? Can I tell you what I need?"

"Yes, but we don't have . . ."

"Money? I don't need money. I have money, my dear. Can we please go somewhere that's not on the street? Where I could be stopped?"

Will squawked in her arms. He was clearly hungry. Walt said, "I'm thirsty, Mama."

Esther's desperateness triggered memories of the woman being at Mrs. Kantor's house several times and how kind she'd always been.

"Yes, of course," Adeline said, smiling at the poor distraught woman. "We'll do anything we can to help you, won't we, Walt?"

"I'm thirsty, Mama."

"Well, hold Aunt Est—hold Aunt Ilse's hand. We'll go straight home."

Fifteen minutes later, Walt was gulping water, and Adeline was feeding Will in the kitchen of their tiny, bleak flat. Esther sat in a chair opposite her.

"Thank you, Adeline," she said for the tenth time. "You are a blessing."

"How can I help?"

Esther reached into her purse and came up with a name and an address on a piece of white paper that she pushed across the table.

"This man is a forger," she said. "My cousin in Odessa put me in touch with him. There is a black market now in documents that can erase your past. My mother was Jewish. That could get me shot, Adeline. I paid him half up front to change my papers so my mother was a descendant of German settlers like my father, but the forger lives in Bogopol, and I don't dare go there again."

"You want me to get your papers?" Adeline said, feeling unsure.

"And pay him the rest of the money," Esther said. "I'll pay you, Adeline."

Adeline swallowed hard. If the Nazis were shooting Jews, they'd shoot her for helping one, wouldn't they? But this was Mrs. Kantor's friend. And she'd always been so kind.

"You don't have to do that," Adeline said finally.

"I insist."

"And I still say no," Adeline said, doing her best to smile. "I'm sure you'll pay me back in some other way at some other time."

Esther looked ready to cry. "You'll do it?"

"You're a friend of Mrs. Kantor. It's the least I can do. When do I go?"

"Tomorrow," she said. "He said they'd be done tomorrow."

"Good. Then you'll stay here until I bring them to you."

Esther wept in relief and held Adeline's hand. "You are a good person," she said. "A very good person, Adeline. Mrs. Kantor was right about you."

"How is she?"

"Oh, didn't you know? She passed last year, bless her. I saw her the week before, and when I said I was moving here, she said I should find you. And now I have. And now here you are helping me. It's as if she knew."

Adeline had a great memory of the way Mrs. Kantor used to laugh, and felt deeply sad that her happy soul was gone.

"She taught me a lot," Adeline said. "I loved her."

"And she loved you."

The front door to the apartment opened and shut. Emil, tired and hot from work at the brewery, came and poked his head through the kitchen doorway.

———

Adeline's shoulder shook and shook again. She startled, unsure where or when she was, then saw the refugee wagons strung out ahead of her, and Emil beside her.

"There's another storm coming," he said, gesturing toward the western horizon where dark purple clouds raced toward them.

For almost an hour, the rain came in sheets that forced Emil to drop his head constantly and leave it to the horses to follow the wagons ahead and keep them on the slick route. He huddled into his coat and pulled his hat down over his ears.

"I should take a turn," Adeline said. She was under the bonnet with the boys.

"No use both of us suffering," he said. "Besides, it's lightening up."

It was true. The rain had ebbed from driving to steady to light as the wind picked up out of the south. By the time the trek was halted, they were close to the Romanian border at Barlad.

The lorry with the loudspeaker went around before dark, instructing everyone to prepare their papers, which would be examined before they were given transit documents from the Romanian government. The Martels were exhausted. Right after they'd eaten, they climbed into the back of their wagon and slept.

Chapter Twelve

Emil awoke before dawn to see to the horses. Adeline was up soon after, preparing a breakfast of dried meat, leftover bread, and boiled sliced beets. Not a feast, but far better than grass. More important, their sons had not gone hungry. After their first son's death, she and Emil had both vowed that would never happen.

While Emil ate, Adeline woke the boys, checked them for lice, and got them dressed. They helped her fold and store the bedding before beginning their breakfast by giving thanks.

"We are grateful for this food and our safety, God," she said. "All we ask is for another safe day, maybe a simpler one than yesterday, away from war. Amen."

"Amen," Walt said.

"Amen," Will said.

Emil said nothing. He was looking west up the rutted road to the Romanian border and seeing a Wehrmacht vehicle coming their way. It drove up and parked across from their encampment.

Nikolas climbed out of the front passenger side. SS Sturmbannführer Haussmann, the Nazi of Emil's nightmares, emerged from the rear. Bull-necked, hair close-cropped, he yelled, "I am Major Haussmann, and I have been put in charge of the trek and your safety by the authority of Reichsführer Himmler. I need to see papers for each wagon and each family member. You will show them to me or to Herr Nikolas, who is helping us certify documentation. *Raus!* Or you will not be permitted to cross the border into Romania or to remain under SS protection!"

Fear rooting him in his tracks, Emil found his vision restricted. He saw the SS major and the willing executioner as if down a tunnel. For some reason he heard Adeline in his mind, repeating a phrase her long-gone father had taught her: *Thrown to the wind and the wolves.*

Haussmann and Nikolas crossed the street to inspect the documents of another family camped there. Swallowing hard, moving stiffly, Emil went to the wagon, reached beneath the bench, and found a box nailed to the wagon floor. He opened it, got out an old leather sheaf, and retrieved the documents inside.

When he turned around, Haussmann was in the road, talking to Nikolas. The tall man gestured toward the Martel encampment and followed the major, his eyes meeting Emil's and an oily smile rising on his lips.

The SS major walked up, looked at Emil. "Papers, Herr . . . ?"

"Martel," Emil said, focusing on a point just above and between Haussmann's dark eyes as he handed him the papers. "Emil Martel."

"We share the same given name," Haussmann said. He did not examine the documents, but instead studied Emil, engaged his eyes, saying, "And where did you get these documents, Herr Martel? Who certified you German enough to be protected by the SS of the Reich?"

Emil felt terror looking into Haussmann's eyes, but did not let himself look away when he said, "A German officer where we lived and—"

"What officer?" Haussmann said sharply. "When and where, Herr Martel?"

The change in tone rattled Emil, and he took his eyes off the SS officer's. He heard the tremor in his own voice when he said, "I don't remember his name offhand, Major. He was an officer with VoMi, Sonderkommando R in Pervomaisk where we lived in mid-August 1941. His name is on the papers there somewhere."

"VoMi, Sonderkommando R, hmm," Haussmann said, finally examining the pages in his hands now. "Yes, I see that. On what basis was the certification given?"

"We had our birth certificates and our family Bible. It goes back to when our family came from Germany."

"Hmm," the SS major said, glanced at Nikolas. "I find it hard to believe you have a Bible that survived Stalin's purges. Do you have this Bible with you, Herr Martel?"

He froze a moment. "Me? Uh, no."

"No?" Haussmann said, taking a step closer.

Before Emil could reply, Adeline blurted out, "Karoline does. My mother-in-law."

"She does!" Rese called. "We do!"

"I do!" Karoline said. "It's here!"

Major Haussmann smiled coldly at Adeline, then Emil, before pivoting toward Karoline, who was limping toward him resolutely, leaning on her cane, and carrying an old Bible with Johann shambling behind her.

In a strong voice, she said, "Emil's great-, great-, great-, great-grandfather carried this Bible with him when he left Germany, to answer Catherine the Great's offer of land in Russia. The name of every Martel in our family is in it. That's why we were all certified. And that's why we were given back our land from the Communists. And that's why we're on this trek under your protection, Major."

For the first time in ages, Emil wanted to hug his mother. He glanced at Nikolas, who appeared less smug. And Haussmann had not seemed to recognize him.

Karoline gave her cane to her husband and flipped open the Bible to pages at the back that revealed the entire Martel family lineage scrawled in ink that faded as it went back generation after generation after generation to Germany.

The SS major traced his gloved finger up a page and stopped. "Gustav Martel, born March 4, 1789, in Hanover, Germany. Dies December 12, 1842, in Friedenstal, Russia."

"That's where our land was, going back more than a century," Karoline said. "That's what we've had to leave forever."

If Haussmann felt any pity for her, he did not show it. He closed the Bible, handed it to her, and said, "My apologies, Frau Martel. We will not worry about the authenticity of your papers or blood purity any longer. You are all free to cross the border."

———

When Haussmann turned to hand back the Martels' documents, Emil felt a wave of relief. The SS officer would drive on, never realizing their paths had crossed before. And Nikolas would leave and not give him another thought.

But then the major cocked his head and kept the papers just out of Emil's grasp.

"Do I know you, Herr Martel?" he asked, training his dead eyes on Emil again.

Emil's terror was complete, but he forced himself again to gaze at the man. "No, Major. I do not believe so."

Haussmann stood there, glanced at the papers. "Pervomaisk. No, I was never there. And where is this Friedenstal?"

"Sixty kilometers southeast of Birsula. A small village established from the Glückstal colony."

The major thought about that and then shrugged, shook his head, and said, "I must be mistaken, Herr Martel."

Emil's emotions had swung back the other way so fast after hearing the word "mistaken" that it took a beat for him to realize Haussmann was handing him his papers.

He took them, nodded shallowly, and said, "Thank you, Major."

"You were not taken into the army when we invaded, Herr Martel?" Haussmann said, studying him again.

"My wife's brother was. If I had gone, there would have been no man in our family left to farm our fields. The VoMi decided they'd rather have me produce food than fight."

The SS major considered that a moment, glanced at Nikolas, and then said, "You were not a member of the *Selbstschutz* in your area?"

"We lived in a tiny place in a sea of grain fields," Emil replied. "I know of only one crime there in three years, and that was a Romanian soldier who raped a widow. He was caught."

"Hmm," Haussmann said. "Did you know that all men of ethnic German descent over the age of thirty were supposed to be members of the *Selbstschutz*? And required to take an oath of allegiance?"

"No," Emil said. "I did not know that. As I said, we lived—"

Haussmann barked, "Raise your right hand in a proper salute, Herr Martel, as if you were greeting the führer right here and now!"

Emil felt as if he were being both tested and humiliated in front of his family but threw his arm up and out in the Nazi salute.

"Repeat after me, Herr Martel: 'As a carrier of pure German blood, I swear to Adolf Hitler, the führer of all Germans, to be true unto death, to do my best, and to be absolutely obedient to all of my superiors. Heil Hitler!'"

Swallowing his pride, telling himself to do whatever it took to be rid of this man, Emil recited the oath for the second time in his life and for the second time at Haussmann's command. As he did so, he was seeing the SS major not as he was now but as he'd been nearly three years before, a younger captain shouting at him beside a remote ravine outside Dubossary.

When Emil finished, he stood there with his arm raised, gazing at Haussmann, who finally allowed the wisp of a smile to cross his face.

"You may lower your arm, Herr Martel. Be safe on your journey today."

"Thank you, Cap—Major," he said.

If Haussmann caught him addressing him as Captain, he did not show it. Instead, he nodded to Adeline, and then to Emil's mother before moving toward the vehicle with Nikolas trudging after him. They got in, and as Nikolas drove off, he could hear the two men arguing, though he could not tell about what.

Emil's knees turned to rubber when they were finally out of sight. He walked to a tree and leaned against it, aware that the boys were thirty meters away, Will by the wagon, Walt in it, both somber and watching him closely. He was also as sweaty as if he'd been working hard for hours and as sick in his gut as he'd been the other night talking to Nikolas. *Took us eighteen days to shoot them all.*

Adeline came over, put her arms around him, as the rest of the family joined them.

Emil said, "I didn't want to say that."

"I know."

"I had to. For you and the boys."

"And for you."

"I feel sick."

"Don't," his mother said. "You did what you had to, Emil."

His father nodded sadly, and then said, "We all do what we have to, son."

Emil wanted to argue with his father, tell him that there were lines a man just could not cross, but instead, he said, "Thank you, Papa."

He realized that Rese, Lydia, and Malia were all looking to him for direction. "Let's forget this, please, pack now, and get across the border and away from here as fast as we can."

They listened to him and moved off quickly to pack. Adeline held on to him.

"You're shaking," she said quietly.

"Am I? It doesn't matter. We're okay now."

Adeline pulled back a bit, gazed at him. "Do you know him, Emil? Haussmann?"

He would not meet her gaze.

"Emil?"

"Papa, when are we leaving?" Walt called from the wagon.

"In a few minutes," Emil said, and made it clear he wanted to leave her embrace.

Adeline held on to him, whispered, "I am your wife. Do you keep secrets from me?"

"Of course I keep secrets from you. Some secrets are not to be shared. Some memories are meant to be forgotten. You know that's true."

———

In her heart, Adeline did know that was true. She had seen profound suffering and hardship herself. Though she tried not to, she could summon the brutal emotions at will. Yet many of the cutting details of losing her father, of starvation, and of watching her firstborn die in her arms had gradually disappeared from her daily thoughts, like dead leaves crumbling on the wind.

"I do," she said, softening. "But will you answer just that one question? Do you know him, Emil? Major Haussmann?"

Emil's cheeks sagged before he sighed and said, "Haussmann was one of the captains with the SS group that held me in Dubossary when I went to buy supplies for the roof the September after we returned to Friedenstal."

Adeline remembered Emil coming home that night, how weakened and defeated he'd been. How he'd cried for the second time in their marriage. Her heart broke all over again. "What did Haussmann do to you?"

"You said one question."

Adeline's emotions slashed and sawed until the dominant one took over.

"You don't have to tell me what you went through that night," she said. "Just tell me if Haussmann and that other man are a danger to our boys. To us."

After several moments, Emil said, "They're a danger to everyone on the face of the earth. They kill innocent people and steal good men's souls. And please, Adeline, let's leave it at that. I've been through enough just having to see Haussmann again."

Adeline did not want to leave it at that, but she could see how upset Emil was.

"Okay," she said finally. "And thank you."

"You're welcome," he said, and started toward the horses.

"I love you, Emil Martel," she called after him.

He looked back at her and smiled a little bittersweetly, she thought, before he said, "I love you, too, Adeline Losing."

Artillery roared to the east, closer than before, so close, she heard the hard edges of the blasts, which turned everyone camped around them frantic to leave.

"In you go," she said, scooping up Will and helping him into the rear of the wagon. "Crawl up there with Walt."

She got up on the bench, took the reins, and watched Emil untie the horses from the tree.

"Release the lever," he said.

Adeline eased off the brake, felt the horses and the wagon retreat enough that they could clear the tree. Emil got up beside her, took the reins, and clucked up the horses even as a new salvo of cannon fire sounded to the west.

"They're getting close again," she said as they started to roll.

"I don't care," he said. "Nothing is going to stop us from going west from now on. We'll go day and night if we have to."

———

An hour later, they rolled across the border into Romania on the road to the small city of Barlad. The crossing was heavily fortified and defended by more than two hundred Romanian soldiers, all of them looking anxiously east past the caravan, toward oncoming combat. To get her mind off the morning and the threat of Major Haussmann, Adeline scanned the Romanian soldiers, some of them so very young, but did not recognize any as Corporal Gheorghe from two nights before.

"Didn't Corporal Gheorghe say he was from this town?" she said once they'd passed completely through the checkpoint.

Emil shrugged. "I don't remember."

"He was strange and interesting to listen to, wasn't he?"

Emil's brows knitted. "You haven't given up on him yet? The man's head was hit with a bomb, Adella."

"And Malia was kicked in the head, and even though it's made her special and interesting in her own way, Corporal Gheorghe, well, he was very different. He was . . ."

"What?"

"I don't know the right word. Touched? In a good way?"

"Touched?"

"I said, I didn't know the exact word, but I just can't get his story off my mind, how after the bomb hit his head, he walked for days through the battle unharmed, as if an angel or a spirit were right there with him, clearing the way, protecting him."

"Protecting him so he could become a beekeeper?"

"Maybe. And why not? It's his dream, isn't it?"

Emil's face tightened. "Who knows if any of that's even true? He could have been making it all up. Or because he got hit in the head, that's just the way he thinks. Who knows? He was crazy, and that's it."

Adeline studied her husband without judgment, then looked away from him when the wagon bounced through a rut in the road. She gazed out over the plateau they crossed, seeing Corporal Gheorghe in her mind.

"I think it was true," she said at last. "When he talked about waking up in the ditch, covered in snow, then walking through the bullets, I don't know, didn't he seem to kind of glow, Emil? Didn't he seem happy? Like really happy?"

Emil turned, exasperated, and said, "If I'd had as much honey wine as he did, I'd have been glowing, too. And I don't want to talk about him anymore. Corporal Gheorghe is behind us, Adeline. For good."

She wondered why Emil had reacted so negatively to the beekeeper and his story. But then she set that aside, remembering how the corporal had been flirting with Malia. *He was, wasn't he?*

Adeline had not had the chance to talk to her older sister more about Corporal Gheorghe, what with the disturbing visit from Haussmann, but she smiled when she recalled how Malia herself had glowed in the beekeeper's presence, as if they were connected somehow. Wasn't that interesting? Wasn't that . . . well, miraculous? She decided that if what she'd seen was the spark and first flame of love, then she had indeed seen a small wonder with her own two eyes.

Adeline bowed her head and gave thanks. Although the Lutheran religion and all other religions were banned and the churches shuttered or converted under Stalin, her parents had imbued her at a young age with a strong Christian faith that she'd relied on repeatedly in her life. Her faith had certainly wavered at times but never once left her. She had never stopped believing that God had a greater plan for her and for her family.

She looked over at her husband, rock-steady, strong-as-an-ox Emil, and remembered how he'd trembled in her arms after Haussmann left their campground. She closed her eyes and prayed that her husband still had his faith.

We can't do this alone, she thought. *There's no way to do this without help.*

———

For hours on end, like an inchworm crossing a twig, the caravan stretched out and then squeezed to a stop, stretched, and squeezed through Barlad and into rolling grasslands that reminded Adeline of the country around Friedenstal. Even though there had been no weather to speak of in several days, the creek bottoms remained boggy. Wagons were getting stuck or sliding off the wood planking the SS put down across the worst of the muck.

Whenever the caravan halted, Adeline could still hear the distant rumor of war behind them. And every now and then, German or Soviet fighter planes would cross overhead, reminding her that danger was never far and could be lurking just ahead, around the corner, or over the next rise.

At the same time, she realized that in some ways she was more frightened of what lay ahead of her than of the war catching up to her. Wasn't that strange? She could not figure out why that was true, only that it was.

To get her mind off their uncertain future, Adeline worked with the boys on their alphabets and their math. She made it a game that they enjoyed rather than a chore. She even had Emil laughing at one point, though she could see he remained moody and upset about his encounter with Major Haussmann.

The farther they got from the Romanian-Moldovan border, however, the less Adeline could hear the war. The sky cleared in the early afternoon, and the April sun shone down on them. The boys were napping behind her. Adeline thought about Emil and how upset he'd been earlier. But she also felt proud that he'd swallowed his stubborn pride and repeated that loyalty oath to Haussmann for the sake of her and their sons.

Emil would always protect them. He'd do what he had to do, and so would she, whatever it took to find their green valley and build a new life. Gradually, in the heat, she grew foggy and tired. Her eyes drifted shut, and she tried to remember when she'd been in such a state before, frightened to death by someone like Haussmann and then so relieved, she needed to sleep.

———

August 10, 1941
Pervomaisk, Ukraine

Emil finished buttoning his shirt in their spartan bedroom. In an irritated tone, he said, "I may only have a fifth-grade education, but you should have at least asked me if it was a good idea to help your friend."

"If she's my friend, it's a good idea to help her," Adeline said. "We went through this last night. I am going to get those documents for her."

"What if you're caught?"

"Why would I be? I'll be carrying the baby."

He got angry. "You'll put Will in danger, too? Do you know what these Germans do? My friend at the brewery said he saw a man's head bashed in with a rifle butt for refusing to cooperate with the new regime."

"And Jews like Esther are being killed just because they're Jews. You said the Germans would be good for us. They're no better than Stalin."

"If we get back our land, they are better than Stalin," he snapped as he went to the sink and picked up his razor.

"You just shaved," she said. "What are you doing?"

"Cutting my mustache to look like Hitler's."

"You are not!"

"Watch me," he said. "And then I'm going with my mother and all our family papers and the Bible to ask the Germans for our land back."

A minute later, he turned to look at her with the postage-stamp mustache on his upper lip. He smiled, crossed to her, and tried to kiss her.

"Not with that on your face," she said. "Not even if you get the land back."

Emil gazed at her then, his eyes flickering over the features of her face, while his own showed both tenderness and fear.

"Why are you looking at me like that?" Adeline asked.

"I'm memorizing your face. In case this is the last time I see it."

"Emil!"

"You need to understand the penalty for the game you are playing."

"I'm not playing a game. I'm running an errand for an old friend."

"Good luck with that," he said, left the room, and slammed the door behind him.

She heard muffled voices, Emil's and Esther's, before the apartment door opened and slammed shut. Adeline took a deep breath, believing that she was about to do the right thing helping Esther, and praying that she would be protected while doing it.

After she finished dressing, Adeline went out into the main room, finding it empty except for baby Will sleeping in the cradle Emil built. In the kitchen, Walt was eating breakfast while Esther watched with obvious enjoyment.

"He really eats!" Esther said. "Mrs. Kantor would have loved him."

Adeline smiled as she folded clothes in the main room. "How could she not?"

Esther's face sank toward concern, and she came out to her, saying quietly, "Your husband is not happy, I think, Adeline. And the mustache?"

"He's thinking of what's best for our family and trying to get our farm back."

Her expression sank farther. "I understand."

"But I am doing what's best for you and for me," Adeline said. "I could not live with myself if I did not try to help you."

Esther broke into tears and hugged Adeline. "Bless you."

———

The threat of blistering heat was already in the air when Adeline left the flat shortly after feeding and changing Will. She carried him in a sling she'd tied from two scarves. He rode against her belly and lower ribs and laughed and burped as she started the long walk to Bogopol, east of the Golta district where the Martels lived, and across the Bug River.

At that point, less than eight days after the Nazis took the city of Pervomaisk, negotiations had already taken place between the Germans and the Romanians. The Bug River turned out to be the dividing line. Those in Golta were technically part of the new Protectorate of Transnistria under Romanian control while Bogopol and increasingly the lands to the east lay in German hands. The bridge across the Bug River to Bogopol had already become a major checkpoint when Adeline got in line. She had her papers and Will's papers with her, showed them to a surly Wehrmacht sentry, and spoke to him in German, which improved his mood considerably.

"What is his name?" he asked.

"Wilhelm," she said. "We call him Will."

"I am Willy, too," he said, and waved her through.

As she walked through the central streets, following Esther's directions, Adeline saw buildings being fortified with fences and barbed wire. German soldiers occupied nearly every corner. There were fewer of them the farther she got from the bridge and none on the street of old warehouses where she found the address Esther had given her. She knocked on the door and got no reply. Will began to fuss. She knocked again, louder this time. Still no answer.

"Hello!" she shouted, and pounded on the door. "Is anybody here?"

She heard nothing and didn't know what to do. All she had was the address. Esther didn't even know the forger's name. Will began to squawk and cry.

Adeline admitted defeat and walked away from the warehouse door while teasing the boy's mouth with her knuckle. "Shhhh," she said. "Mama's going to . . ."

She heard a creak behind her. A woman said, "Patience is not one of your virtues, is it?"

Adeline turned around, seeing a much older woman, holding on to her hip as if in pain and peering at her.

"Who are you looking for?" she asked.

As Esther had told her to, Adeline replied, "Ilse Koch."

"Ahh, you're lucky. Ilse Koch only just arrived."

Adeline followed the older woman into a musty, hot, dimly lit building that smelled of grain chaff and up a set of rickety wooden stairs into a loft where an old man wearing a jeweler's loupe was crouched over a drafting table. The woman went to a cabinet and retrieved an envelope that she opened. She looked at the picture and then Adeline.

"That's a problem," she said.

"I'm picking them up for Ilse Koch."

The man lifted his head and loupe. "That cannot happen. She must come herself. We told her that."

"I know but—"

"No buts," he said. "If you are caught with papers that do not belong to you, they will ask questions, and if they ask questions, they could find us."

"They won't find her papers," Adeline said. "I will wait until my baby has pooped, then put the documents under his back and between these two scarfs. If I need to, I'll speak to the sentries in German, get them to talk about their sweethearts back home."

———

And that was exactly what she tried to do. Except going back west across the bridge toward her flat in Golta, she encountered Romanian sentries, who barely spoke Russian and zero German. It was near noon and brutally hot again, but they started to give her a hard time about going back and forth over the bridge in a single day. Then the breeze shifted, and the stench of Will's foul diapers reached their nostrils.

The baby was crying again when she arrived at the apartment door fifteen minutes later. She knocked twice softly. A few moments later, the door opened, and she slipped inside.

Esther closed the door behind her. Walt, who'd been playing on the floor, made a disgusted face. "Will stinks!"

"Thank God he does," Adeline said, reaching into the overlap between the two scarves that held Will, retrieving the forged papers and handing them to Esther.

She held them to her breast and started crying. "Thank you, Adeline. Thank you from the bottom of my heart. You've given me . . . you've given me a future, a life."

"I hate that you even need those papers to have a life," Adeline said. "And I need to clean this little guy right now."

When she was finished and Will was falling asleep in the cradle and Walt was already napping, Esther began gathering her things.

"You don't need to leave just yet," Adeline said.

"It's better that I'm gone before your husband returns."

"Where will you go?"

"To where I have some things stored outside the city. And then I don't know. I'm going to leave that up to a power greater than me to decide. But I've heard about Argentina. Or Palestine. I'd like to end up somewhere like that eventually."

Adeline did not know either of those places but wished Esther good luck and hugged her at the door.

"May God protect you," she said.

"And you," Esther said. "There are no words."

Adeline put her hand over her heart, opened the apartment door, and Ilse Koch was gone from their lives.

———

Mid-April 1944
Central Romania

Near the back of the Long Trek, the Martels rolled slowly westward.

Behind them, the German and Romanian armies were successfully fighting off the Soviets in their initial attempt to invade Romania from the north. Nevertheless, at the town of Onesti, the SS turned the caravan southwest toward Targu Secuiesc.

They had left the rolling grass hills of far-eastern Romania behind them by that point and now climbed into leafless hardwood forests below mountain peaks capped with snow. The weather was wildly unsettled. Rain. Sleet. Hail. Snow. Mud was a constant hazard.

And since there were so few mature men on the trek, Emil felt obliged to stop and help any family of women and small children stuck in the mire or having suffered an accident. If they were in the mud over their axles, he would have them unload their wagon and then unharness Thor and Oden and tie them to the empty wagons' horses to yank them free, all the while supporting the rear end by himself so the wheels and axles would not break under the torque. The sight of people digging graves for the newly dead had become commonplace. Every time Emil saw somebody being buried, he looked away as they passed.

They were negotiating a series of steep switchbacks in the route near the town of Oituz where the mud was thin, more like grease, when they came upon a newly overturned wagon and a weeping woman from Kiev, her three children, and her now-dead father, who'd been thrown in the crash and hit his head on a rock.

"Stop, Emil," Adeline said. "We need to help that poor woman."

He sighed but reined the horses to a halt. He tied Oden and Thor to a tree just starting to throw green buds and detached them from the wagon while Adeline, Walt, and Will went to comfort the woman and her children.

When Emil was done, he started down the hill to detach the woman's horses from the wreck. Before he did, he inspected her wagon and was happy to see that, aside from damage to the wooden siding and material of the bonnet, her transportation was largely sound.

"Emil," Adeline said, coming up behind him, "she wants you to bury her father."

He wanted to close his eyes, wanted to say, *Anything but that.* Instead, Emil remembered that a man can only rely on himself in times of challenge, and he steeled himself.

"Can you get the spade strapped to the side of our wagon for me?" Emil said at last. "I have to tend to her horses first."

By the time he'd unhitched the horses from the overturned wagon, Adeline was back with the shovel. Emil did not look at the dead grandfather as he walked beyond the overturned wagon and the women and children. He selected a suitable spot and started to dig, telling himself, *It's a hole in the ground. That's all it is.*

The soil was looser than he would have thought, but ten shovelfuls deep, he hit roots and rock. It would have taken him a good two hours to dig the hole had not Walt come over, dragging an old, heavy German mattock tool, with a steel pick on one side and a cutting hoe on the other.

"The lady said it was her father's," Walt said.

"That will help," Emil said, and switched to the mattock, picking at the rocks and chopping at the roots.

An hour later, the hole was deep enough to keep the body from being smelled and unearthed by animals. Adeline and the woman wrapped her father in a blanket. Luckily, the man had been old and did not weigh much. Emil was able to hoist him up on his shoulder and bring him to the grave without assistance.

It's just weight up there. Nothing more than a sack of grain.

He got two ropes under the body. Adeline had one end of one rope, and the woman had the other. On the other side of the grave, Emil held the other ends of both ropes. Together, they lowered the body into the hole. When the corpse came to rest, he told Adeline and the woman to let go their ends of the ropes, and he reeled them in.

He felt sick and started back toward his wagon.

"Emil," Adeline said, "we have to say a prayer."

"You go ahead," he said. "It'll be dark soon, and I want to get their wagon up on the road before then. I'll bury him when you're done. My condolences for the loss of your father, ma'am."

He didn't have to look at Adeline to tell she was not happy with him, but he walked off toward their wagon anyway. As he lashed the two ropes to the side of the crashed wagon, he could hear his wife leading the woman and the children in prayer.

"Our Father, who art in heaven, hallowed be thy name," Adeline said, and the rest joined in. "Thy kingdom come, thy will be done on earth as it is in heaven . . ."

Emil forced himself to stop listening at that point and ran the other ends of the ropes up the hill to his horses. Once he'd tied them to their harness, he waited until another wagon passed and then eased the team forward. With creaks and groans, the overturned wagon came upright on the other side of the ditch. Scouting ahead on the route, he found a low spot in the ditch walls that would allow a wagon to cross. He attached the woman's horses to the wagon and then led them up and across the ditch before tying them up on the other side of the road.

He walked back and saw Adeline walking toward him in disapproval. "That was rude and insensitive, walking away like that."

"No, Adeline, it was practical. I dug the hole. I paid my respects. I got her wagon back on the road, and now I'm going to bury her father. By the time I'm done, we will be near sundown and looking for a camping spot. And thank you for helping her."

Adeline swallowed, but then nodded. "I don't give you enough credit, Emil. I'm sorry I said anything."

Chapter Thirteen

Days passed and became weeks that all melted into another and another as the Martel clan continued to slowly tack its way through Romania, southwest to Brasov to skirt more mountainous terrain and then northwest on a steep and winding route toward and through the town of Sighisoara. The ground war had faded behind them for the moment, though Soviet bombers were a frequent threat as they tried to destroy the Romanian bridges and exit routes available to the Germans.

Spring had fought winter and won by the time they reached central Romania. In the valleys, the leaves were out, lime-colored and shimmering on warm breezes. And the snowpack in the Carpathian Mountains to the south was in full retreat. High and low and on both sides of the route, wildflowers bloomed in disarrayed carpets of scarlet, canary, and violet. They filled the air with sweet, intoxicating scents that could trick the mind into believing there was no such thing as war, no such thing as hatred between men or countries or religions.

They came over a rise south of Targu Mures to find a beautiful new vista breaking before them, a verdant dale with gentle, forested slopes and lush meadows of wildflowers and grass.

"Is this the beautiful green valley, Mama?" Will asked.

"Not yet," Adeline said, "but it is beautiful."

"Oh," Will said, sounding discouraged.

Adeline tousled his hair and said, "This is the beautiful green valley where you get to live today, Will. So be happy and thankful for it."

Glancing at his younger son and seeing him break into a grin, Emil smiled and felt good inside for a change. For more than two weeks, he had seen neither

Major Haussmann nor Nikolas. As the roads westward became choked with retreating traffic, the SS had been diverting different parts of the caravan, sending them on multiple routes west. The two men could be gone from his life forever. And good riddance.

After another week of hard travel, they were passing through the city of Cluj-Napoca, and Emil was starting to feel hopeful that at long last their luck had changed for the better. In Cluj, the trek was divided yet again, with some refugees directed north to the train station in the city of Dej and others westward. On a hot afternoon, some six days after that division, the Martels entered Oradea, a city in chaos.

Oradea bordered Hungary. Even though Germany, Hungary, and Romania remained Axis partners in the last days of April 1944, there was intense competition for train and road space. When they arrived, a full Wehrmacht division had just come off the most recent train and was trying to move east. Foot soldiers, lorries, and artillery clogged the medieval streets of the city, which had been heavily bombed recently.

The Martels and the rest of the trek inched forward and through the knots of traffic until, hours later, they reached a small plaza in front of the rail station, which was choked with wagons and horses and many Black Sea Germans who looked distraught. Several of the women were hugging their horses and crying, and Emil could not figure out why. A loudspeaker blared.

Emil recognized the voice and felt sickened. He did not have to see Major Haussmann to know it was him.

"You will proceed by train from here to Budapest, where you will find shelter until your next train north to Silesia," Haussmann said. "Your wagons cannot come on this train. It does not have enough flatbed room. Your horses cannot come, either. The Wehrmacht is taking them as payment for your safety. You will be allowed on the train with what you can pull or push or carry by yourselves and no more. Repeat: whatever you can carry or pull or push by yourselves and no more. You have two hours to gather your necessaries and board the train."

Not hearing Adeline's complaints and worries, Emil stared at his horses, already feeling the loss of their calming, dependable presence. He loved horses, especially that pair; how much heart they had. Images of their efforts rippled through his mind, none stronger than when Thor and Oden had galloped for him through the tank battle that first day of the trek, fearless, courageous, as if they had been veteran warhorses familiar with the roar of cannons and the destruction of explosions.

"Emil!" Adeline said sharply.

He frowned and looked over to see tears dripping down his wife's face.

"What do we bring?" she asked. "How much can we carry? What did we bring all this so far for, anyway?" She flung herself into his arms and sobbed. "They want us down to nothing, Emil, people with no pasts!"

Emil held his wife as she trembled and shook, feeling as helpless as she did.

"No, Mama," Walt said, rubbing her back. "We can take more than we can carry. We can use the little wagon. Remember?"

"It holds a lot," Will said.

Up to that point, Emil had regretted taking the little wagon with them. He'd had to unlash it from the big wagon's back wall every night and then relash it in place every morning before they set off. Now? The toy he'd built for the boys' Christmas present was the most useful thing they had left.

Even so, being Emil, he decided to modify it before they set off. Up front, he left the wooden handle in place but used his saw to cut pieces out of the side of the bigger wagon and removed its corner brackets, which he used to fashion into a push bar at the rear of the little wagon.

He removed the oilskin bonnet from the big wagon and cut a rectangular piece out of it, using the piece to wrap his tools, which went in the forward bottom of the little wagon. Adeline set aside a skillet, a deep pan for boiling water, two bread tins, two large bowls, four small bowls, five spoons, and all six of her kitchen knives.

Emil cut off two more sections of the bonnet and wrapped the cutlery in one and the cooking utensils in the other. Those went on top of the tools. Food and dry goods, along with bedding and the few extra clothes they owned, went on top and forward in the little wagon.

He gave the rear space to Adeline's mother and sister. When they were done putting their things in, he laid several coils of rope on top, and then tied down the rest of the oiled canvas as a cover. On one side, he hung the large water bag they'd been using since Friedenstal. He tied the well pail beside the water bag while Adeline rummaged around in the back of the big wagon, looting as a sailor might a sinking ship. Emil had stopped searching for treasures. He already considered what was left in the bigger wagon cast to the wind, open game for wolves and vultures.

That's how it always was and always will be, he thought a little bitterly. *We come in with nothing, and we go out with nothing.*

Adeline brought out an envelope that held their wedding picture and a few other photos. He smiled when she showed him.

"We were so young," he said.

"Weren't we? And innocent."

"And look at us," Emil said. "Still in love."

Adeline gazed at him with watery eyes and nodded.

German soldiers appeared. One of them started to untie his horses' leads.

"Whoa," Emil said. "Hold on a second."

The soldier glared at him. Emil ignored him, went around to the front of the animals and lowered his head between them, feeling their warm breath on his ears and how good it was to be near them, such magical creatures.

"Thank you, both," he whispered. "You saved us. We will never forget you."

"Raus!" the soldier barked in annoyance. *Hurry up!*

"Okay, okay," Emil said, and stood back.

The soldier took the leads. Emil patted Thor on the shoulder. Walt, Will, and Adeline stroked Oden's flanks as the pair began to walk after the soldier. Too quickly, the horses, the big wagon, and the rest of their belongings were gone.

———

The Martels all stood there in the daze of yet another catastrophic loss.

Emil made peace with it first. "Adeline and Malia are on the push bar. I am pulling the handle. I want Will on the left side of the cart and Walt on the right. Oma Lydia follows. Get in position!"

Emil looked over at his father, who had brought along a small cart that was used in their farmyard. Johann was at the push bar with Karoline and Rese pulling on the handle.

They moved slowly toward the waiting train and the crowd trying to find refuge on it. Others had small carts or wagons like themselves. The less fortunate had crafted packs from their wagon covers and staggered forward under impossibly heavy loads. Too many went to the train with nothing but the ragged clothes on their backs.

Emil led them away from those in the crowd fighting to be in the freight cars closest to the engine. They went instead to the far rear of the train. The last car's doors were slid back, and it was fairly empty yet. They used ropes and brute strength to hoist the loaded carts into the hold, which smelled of straw and unbathed humans. Then they lashed the two carts together and to the wooden wall in the rear corner of the boxcar.

Will and Walt climbed up and sat on the resulting platform like proud princes. Their aunt Rese flopped back across the top of her parents' cart, folding her hands across her stomach, and closing her eyes while more and more refugees began climbing into the boxcar with the last of their belongings.

The space was soon uncomfortably full. The SS left open the sliding doors on both sides of the car and hung lengths of heavy chain across the openings. Adeline understood why. They'd need the air. As people had crammed into the car, the air had gotten thicker with stale human sweat and fear of the unknown. She herself began to feel closed in, cornered, claustrophobic.

"I'm going to try to stand by the door for a minute," she told Emil.

"I'll go with you," Malia said.

"I'll go, too!" Will said.

"You'll stay with Papa," Adeline said firmly, fighting the panic growing in her.

She began to slip and to slide forward through the crowd, excusing herself, but insistently stepping over someone's feet or around their backs and between their belongings. She had to get to fresh air or she'd scream. Finally, she reached the open door and held on to the door frame, gulping the fresh air. Malia did the same beside her.

"I couldn't breathe," Malia said. "I wanted to fight to get out."

"I did, too," Adeline said, and laughed softly, putting her hand to her chest and her still-thumping heart. "I thought—"

The train lurched and almost threw them off their feet. Adeline had to grab her sister to keep her from falling even as everyone in the car shouted in surprise. The train wheels creaked slowly forward over the rails amid nervous laughter, and quickly chatter of what was to come replaced concern over what they'd left behind. Within one hundred and fifty meters after rolling from the rail yard, the train slowed to a stop again.

Both Adeline and Malia gasped at the scene before them. They gazed out across a still and placid backwater of the Crisul Repede River, which perfectly reflected the purple bruised sky, and the roiling thunderclouds and the shafts of golden last light pouring down on the pool beside the gorgeous pale ruins of a large building on the far side.

"It's like a painting," Malia said.

"It is," Adeline said, entranced by the scene. "The roof, the dome is all caved in, and yet it's so . . . beautiful. I wonder what that building was? The way it glows like that."

A woman behind her said, "It was a Jewish synagogue. The Germans blew it up last year."

———

The train started to roll again, picking up momentum, leaving the haunting, beautiful scars of Oradea and Romania behind them. Adeline still did not understand why Hitler hated the Jews as much as he did, no more than she understood why Stalin would starve his own people after killing the ministers and priests and burning down the houses of God.

What possesses men to do such evil? Are they even human? Can't they see that when you kill someone or destroy a holy place, the faith always goes on? Don't they see that in broken hearts and ruins, something always glows?

Feeling the wind building against her face as the train gathered speed, Adeline tried to put all that out of her mind, tried to enjoy the warm wind and the smell of oncoming rain and night. But she thought of Mrs. Kantor's friend, Esther, and wondered where she'd ended up, whether she'd made it to Argentina or Palestine. She could only imagine. Those places sounded so far off, so exciting, so scary, so good, she shivered.

A whole new life somewhere. Free to do whatever we want. In peace.

Try as Adeline might, however, she could not dream up another vision for herself beyond the memory of that painting of that mythical green valley in Mrs. Kantor's book.

"Does it scare you?" Malia asked, breaking her thoughts. "Not knowing?"

They were traveling through farm country in the twilight with lightning and thunder rumbling in the distance. She looked at her older sister. "Not knowing what?"

"Where we'll be when this journey's over."

For a beat, she stared at Malia with great curiosity. It wasn't the first time her sister seemed to know her thoughts or at least mirrored them.

"Not really," Adeline said. "I have faith we will end up where we're supposed to be."

"But where is that?"

"Emil says we'll know freedom when we see it."

"Everything else is just a stop on the way to your green valley?"

"Or a step in that direction. I think that's right."

To Adeline's surprise, her older sister suddenly hugged her tight and said, "Thank you for being here. Helping me. And Mother. I . . . I couldn't bear us all being apart."

Then she burst into tears. "I don't know what I'd do without you, Adeline."

This was the most upset she'd seen Malia in years, and she held tight to her, saying, "You'll never be without me. I'll always be with you. I am your baby sister, aren't I? I need my big sister, don't I?"

Malia relaxed her bear hug and, blinking back tears, gazed at Adeline with an adoring smile. "You do."

———

April 27, 1944
Budapest, Hungary

The train traveled through the night, and in the first light of dawn entered the city. Hungary and Germany had been allies earlier in the war, but in March 1944, Hitler initiated a coup, and his forces now occupied the city. The Martels saw tanks and heavy fortifications ringing the rail yard outside Keleti Station.

Waffen SS soldiers awaited them on the platform. To prevent a stampede, the SS had the train unload boxcar by boxcar, back to front, making the extended Martel clan among the first to debark and push and pull their little wagons down the platform, all the while gaping at the ornate interior of the train station: the carved marble stanchions, the grand domed ceiling, and the spiderweb skeleton of the huge arched window and clock at the far end. Even with all the Nazi flags dangling from the rafters, Adeline thought it was the most breathtaking place she'd ever been.

They moved toward double doors where sentries were checking papers. Will hung onto Adeline's skirt, while Walt marched resolutely beside her. They went through the doors and out onto a plaza where they were hit by a barrage of foreign noises blaring from a bazaar of exotic sights, smells, and languages. Adeline's attention darted everywhere, trying to catch it all, especially the buildings, tall and crafted, intricate and awe-inspiring after their dreary life in rural Ukraine. It was all so fantastic, she thought she might have slipped into a heavenly dream.

Then she saw Emil stiffen, and understood why. Her dreamy state vanished. Ahead of them as they left the plaza, Sturmbannführer Haussmann stood at the top of the stairs that led to a large building with a huge Nazi flag hanging from its upper windows. He was watching his soldiers direct the refugees. As the Martels passed beneath Major Haussmann's glare, Adeline felt the menace of the man even before she dared to glance up to find him gazing down at her family with amusement.

"Send the Martels to the south camp," Haussmann shouted down. "Everyone in that family."

The soldier in front of them stood aside and gestured after several other families already moving south with armed Waffen SS soldiers leading them.

"Why are we going this way?" Adeline said. "The others are going more to the north."

Her husband looked back at her, his face ashen. "I don't know."

They had to walk only several blocks before the soldiers turned left at a wide iron gate in a high stone wall. The families ahead followed, vanishing from Adeline's sight.

"I don't like this, Emil," she said.

"I don't like it, either. But I don't see much choice at this point, do you?"

When they reached the gate, a sentry motioned them through into what Adeline at first took to be a large and beautifully tended garden with dozens of white stones set in patterns before a marble spire at the center of the space. But then she realized with growing unease that the white stones were all monuments. They'd been led into a vast formal cemetery.

Chapter Fourteen

Emil saw the gravestones before Adeline did, flashed on Haussmann that night outside Dubossary, and felt his knees turn to rubber and his gut roil.

"Emil," Adeline called to him.

"I know," he said, not looking back at her, but at the young SS officer turning toward him with a curt nod.

"You may find a spot to camp beyond the state cemetery," he said, gesturing southeast toward a line of trees. "It's a big park, really. With graves. But with the walls and the patrols, this is the safest place for you and your family. In the park to the north, there is no wall, and refugees have been attacked in the night."

Emil took a deep breath. *Maybe Haussmann was just being kind when he sent us here, which means he still has no idea who I am.*

"Thank you," he said, relieved. "How long will we be here?"

The officer looked at his watch, annoyed now. "Until a train frees up to take you north. There will be a truck with fresh water here within the hour, and latrines are being built in the far southwest corner of the park. Use them. We don't want diseases any more than you do."

Emil led them down the lane, past that marble spire, which they all paused to gawk at before heading toward a line of locust trees along a path that curved into a shadowed grove with grassy openings, and in almost every one, a monument or statue in remembrance of some past king or statesman or poet.

There were other families in the first six or seven likely camping spots. They kept pushing and pulling the heavy wagons, but no one complained. Emil glanced back and saw them all transfixed by the place. The trees thinned and the path narrowed as they walked into an open-air mausoleum with grand colonnades of granite and marble flanking the wide path through. On the back walls of the colonnades, there were crypts from one end to the other.

"There," he said, gesturing to two dark, almost charred-looking crypts in the right colonnade. "We can sleep beneath that roof if it rains. And it looks like someone's built a fire there before."

He pulled the little wagon up onto a flat spot there. Adeline looked unhappy and flicked her hand at the scorched bas-relief faces of demons on the crypts.

"I don't like them," she said, looked around, and then pointed down the colonnade toward one with a large angel on it. "I'll feel better there."

"I agree," Malia said.

"Yes," said Karoline.

Emil knew better than to argue with three women and pulled the little wagon over in front of the crypt with the statue of the winged angel. He gave the carving no more than a passing glance before getting back to work.

More families appeared while the Martels unpacked, and they, too, began making camp under the roofs of the colonnades. When their wagon was emptied, Emil left in search of firewood and water, with Walt and Will standing in the wagon as if it were a chariot. Against a steady stream of refugees from the train, he pushed the wagon and his boys back the way they'd come through the park and graveyard.

Near the front gate, the water truck had only just arrived. Emil was feeling happy that he'd get to fill his water bag before the line got too long, when out of the crowd of refugees came Nikolas. He didn't seem to notice Emil at first. But then Nikolas did see them, and he ambled over and used his height to loom over Walt and Will, who eyed him suspiciously.

"Fine young German stock," Nikolas said, and nodded to Emil with that oily smile. "You must be proud of your bloodlines. I know the major was."

Emil hated the man. He knew in his gut that Nikolas was not only a stone-cold killer, he was a persecutor, someone who wallowed like a pig in another man's pain. If Emil allowed it, Nikolas would continue to goad and poke him for weakness, and he would show him none. He knew there were times to fight and smarter times to wait. He said nothing.

Nikolas's smile vanished. He tilted his head slightly and studied Emil.

"There's something about you, Martel. Something that's off."

"Why do you care?"

"Because in the *Selbstschutz*, the militia, it was my job to care, to tell the Nazis the truth behind people who told so many lies. Like you, Martel."

Emil had no idea what power if any Nikolas held over him, but it was better to be safe than sorry. "I'm here for water for my family," Emil said. "Nothing more."

Nikolas looked like he wanted to continue, but Emil pushed by him and got in line. When he looked back, the executioner was gone.

After filling the water bag full, Emil and the boys went looking for enough wood for a cook fire. Deeper into the cemetery, they found branches broken off trees during winter in a thicket near several SS soldiers who were standing around, having a smoke.

Gathering up the broken branches, Emil came near to them and overheard one soldier talking disdainfully. "Why are we guarding these ignorant peasants? These are the future of the Reich? You must be joking."

"According to Reichsführer Himmler, I'm not joking," said another soldier. "Or do you wish to tell the chief of the Gestapo that he is wrong about who is of pure Aryan blood and who is not? Their ancestors left Germany, kept mostly to themselves, and ran big farms and colonies in isolation for more than a century. Who else would have purer Aryan blood?"

Emil took a load of firewood to the wagon, helped the boys with their armfuls, and then returned to gather more.

The loud soldier was still talking. "At least these are almost the last of them. There will be fewer coming now. Good riddance, I say. Get the trains in here."

"No trains to be had for at least a few days," his friend said. "Himmler commandeered them for all the Yids outside Budapest. They're starting at the Kistarcsa transit station. Those are the ones being taken north first."

"Rats," the loud one said, and spat. "Take them all, I say. Be rid of them for good."

"Papa!" Walt called.

Emil picked up one last branch about the thickness of his wrist and walked back to his sons. He didn't understand the exact meaning behind the words "being taken north," but in light of their earlier conversation about the pure bloodlines, Emil got the gist and felt torn apart. The Nazis were still killing Jews, and he and his family were evidently supposed to replace them.

———

Emil and his sons returned to find the long mausoleum almost filled now with families making temporary homes against the crypts and among the statues of long-dead Hungarian royalty.

"I thought we would have the place to ourselves," Emil said, pulling the little wagon and the boys up to their camp.

"We're not so lucky," Adeline said. "Look at the far end, other side."

Emil acted as if he had not heard her as he turned to lift Will and then Walt from the wagon. But as he did, he got two good looks diagonally across the mausoleum courtyard, enough to know that Nikolas was camped there along with two of the men who'd been with him that night around the campfire back in Moldova.

He set Walt down and said, "Stack the wood near Opa. Make it a good stack."

Armed with purpose, Walt reached into the wagon and left with an armful. Will did, too. When Emil looked across the courtyard again, Nikolas was leaning against a carved stone column, smiling over at him, his hand raised in a mocking Heil Hitler salute. Emil did not return the gesture and gave the man no outward reaction before helping Walt and Will with the last load of firewood.

But in his street-smart mind, he had seen that taunting salute as a direct threat to himself and to his family. Whatever the man's relationship to the SS, Emil decided he could not avoid it any longer. It was time to protect his family, and the sooner the better.

He waited until it was almost dark, then excused himself and left their camping area, walked straight past Nikolas and his two friends, slowing to look at them and to spit in their direction. Leaving the courtyard, he trailed a steady flow of other refugees drawn by the distant lights the SS had put up around the camp latrines.

He walked in the darkest shadows, which allowed him to keep peering back toward the colonnades. Not twenty seconds later, he recognized the tall silhouette of Nikolas ambling after him. Emil left the shadows then and let himself be seen the rest of the way to the latrine area, which was crowded. He used that to his advantage, ducking a little to blend in more, and then standing up straight enough to be seen as he pushed toward the long, low latrine tents.

Inside, he did not use the urinals or the toilets. The traffic was meant to be one-way, and Emil walked straight through the tent and out the other side.

He stood at the corner until he saw Nikolas enter the latrine tent at the far end, and then moved fast back in the general direction of the open-air mausoleum, the colonnades, and the encampment, but off the direct route by several degrees. A hundred meters out from the electric lights around the latrine, he stopped, panting in the shadow of a statue and watching the exit from the toilet.

"The only thing a man can rely on is himself," Emil muttered, and felt his resolve harden to a place he'd learned to go during times of extreme starvation and want.

Nikolas appeared in the exit to the latrine, his head swiveling. Emil waited one count, then waved his arm like a windmill as he stepped out in the last good light of the latrine. He paused in profile to the light and then took three long, slow strides into the darkness.

———

Emil took two more steps out of Nikolas's sight before crouching behind a large monument, reaching into his pocket, and pulling out a folding knife he used to slaughter farm animals.

The only thing a man can rely on is himself, he thought again. His heart raced. He breathed deep, trying to calm his nerves as his night vision got better and better.

Gravel scuffed, and pebbles rattled and became slow footfalls coming closer. Emil reset his feet, coiled low, and pressed his left flank into the side of the monument.

Nikolas walked closer, came abreast of the monument, and paused for what felt like an eternity to Emil. Finally, he took a step, and then another, and then he was right there, or at least the tall, dark, sidelong silhouette of Nikolas, towering above and in front of Emil, who exploded from his crouch, driving his legs and propelling his farmer's shoulders and body low and hard against the side of the bigger man's right knee.

There was a crunching noise. Nikolas buckled and fell with a howling grunt of pain. Emil dove on top of him and with his powerful left hand pinned the man's head down, left cheek against the gravel. With his right hand, he held the blade above Nikolas's throat.

"My knee!" Nikolas cried, and squirmed. "Something's broken!"

"I don't care," Emil said, grinding his face into the gravel. "You don't care, either."

"What? I care! My leg's—"

"I have a slaughtering knife in my hand, Nikolas," Emil said, and lowered the keen edge of the blade. "Feel it against your throat?"

The man stopped squirming, the fiery pain in his knee forgotten.

"Don't," he said. "Please. Have mercy."

"I'll give you more than you gave," Emil said. "You have a choice, Nikolas. Stay away, don't even look at me, my wife, and sons, and you live. Or I come back, break every bone in your body, and cut your throat ear to ear like a shoat pig."

———

Not long after, Emil padded into the courtyard of the mausoleum, his heart still pounding wildly as he passed other refugee families sitting by their small fires on his way to his own family's fire, which was already down to coals. Adeline and Malia were cooking over it. The rest of his clan looked on hungrily.

He smiled when he stepped up to the circle, noticing the shadows of the angel statue moving in the fire's glow.

"Where have you been all this time?" Adeline said.

"There was a long line," he said. "Someone said there's diarrhea going around."

Walt thought that was funny. Emil went and sat next to his older son on the marble steps of the colonnade with the statue behind them, put his arm around Walt, and looked at his family, feeling deeply satisfied.

You're all safe, he thought. *You'll never know what I just had to do for you or what I've done for you before. But for now, you're safe.*

———

Adeline helped Rese scrubbing the pots. "You seem better."

"I feel better," Rese said. "Not wanting to throw up. But I have other things to feel bad about. Like Mama says, it's not hard to find something bad in our lives."

"What's bad in yours?"

"Besides Mama?" she said before laughing nervously. "I have no idea if my boyfriend is alive or not."

"A boyfriend?" Adeline said, smiling. "Since when?"

"Since four months ago," Rese said. "When I had to go up to Balta for the week."

Adeline vaguely remembered. "Who is he?"

"A boy from Odessa who got taken off to fight for the Germans," Rese said. "His name is Stephan. He's twenty and the handsomest boy I've ever seen."

Adeline could hear the sadness in her voice. "Does he know where you are? Where you're going?"

Emil's sister shook her head and wiped at tears that flowed down her cheeks. "I wrote to his mother in Odessa, but I never heard back."

"Give it time, Rese," Adeline said. "The war's not over yet."

———

They spent six days camped in the cemetery, and Emil never once saw limping Nikolas look his way. They were nearing the end of their supper on the sixth day when they were notified that a train would take them north to the Warthegau region of Poland, departing Keleti Station at nine thirty the following morning.

Emil did not want to go north to Poland. He wanted to go west, now more than ever. In the short time he'd been in Budapest, he'd talked to enough German soldiers to know that the western Allies were fighting in Sicily and preparing to invade Italy. As far as Emil was concerned, it was only a matter of time before there were other invasions, and soon the western Allies would be sweeping through all of Europe. He wanted to make sure he and his family were in Allied territory when the war ended.

He'd come to realize during the long days in the wagon that much of his life had been subject to a conquering army and a dictator. The Bolsheviks deposed the Czar, and Stalin laid waste to Ukraine. Then Hitler did. And now Stalin had it back. Emil decided he wanted to go where there were no conquering armies, and in his mind that meant west across the ocean, as far from where they started as he could possibly imagine.

"Why are you so cloudy?" Adeline asked as they packed the little wagon.

"I don't want to go to Poland," he said. "I want to go west."

"We'll go west from Poland," she said. "The Germans will give us food and a place to live there. I heard many say that."

"What good are food and a flat if Stalin gets to Poland before the other Allies?"

"I don't know," she said, showing rare irritation. "What is your plan, Emil? Are we going to leave the trek? Go off on our own on foot with no protection?"

He thought about that and frowned. "No, I guess not."

"Then we go north on the train in the morning and go west from the Warthegau as soon as we can."

———

It was unseasonably hot in Budapest that May morning, close to unbearable, especially in the heavy clothes they wore. Adeline put the boys in shorts and stripped them to their undershirts before the Martels pushed and pulled the two small wagons through the cemetery and out onto the main road.

They were not far from the rail station, but there was a slight rise to the street, and the sun was blazing hot. No more than a hundred meters from the station, Rese let go the handle of her parents' cart, put her hand to her forehead, rushed over to one side of the street, and vomited hard and violently enough to take her to her knees. Adeline got to her first.

"I'm all right," Rese gasped. "It's the heat. I just couldn't stop it from coming."

Adeline helped her up. Karoline gave her a rag to wipe her mouth, and Emil gave her water from the bag, which seemed to perk her up before they reached the crowd of refugees trying to get into the station.

"It's an hour and fifteen minutes until we leave, and so many are already here," Karoline said. "Will there be enough room for us all?"

Karoline's fears were well-founded. By the time they got inside and down the platform, many of the boxcars were already packed with people and their belongings.

"This train looks shorter than the one we came in on," said Walt, who was riding on top of the little wagon with Will.

"He's right," Emil said. "Adella, take my place. I'll run forward to guard us a spot."

She came around and took the handle of the wagon while her mother and sister continued to push. Emil disappeared into the crowd and down the platform.

Adeline took glances at the already-full cars as they passed, seeing the faces of people cut loose from everything they'd ever known, some frightened, some resigned, and a few eager with anticipation, which was how she felt. She was wondering what else she might see in the coming days that she'd never seen before, like this train station, the most magnificent building she'd ever been in. She lowered her gaze to see Emil hanging out the side of the boxcar behind the covered coal car and the locomotive.

"I've got space for the wagons, but some of us will have to sit up top," Emil said.

"I'm going up top," Rese said.

"Sick as you are?" her mother said.

"The wind will do me good, Mama, settle my stomach," Rese said. "If I go inside, I know I'll be sick again. Besides, it will be fun to ride on top of a train."

Karoline looked like she wanted to argue, but said, "Suit yourself, then."

With all of them helping, they lifted both wagons into the boxcar and lashed them together and to the wall by the open door. Sweating people were soon jammed behind them, sitting on their own wagons or bags of belongings. Johann, Karoline, and Lydia decided to stay inside with the wagons despite the sweltering heat. After Emil fashioned two ropes with loops that went around the boys' waists to save them from a fall, Adeline let herself be talked into climbing up with them and Malia onto the roof of the boxcar.

A low railing ran around the perimeter of the roof. Rese was already up there, sitting with her thighs wedged under the rail and dangling her bare feet off the side.

"It's not as hot up here," Rese said, excited. "Thank God Mama can't stand heights. This is going to be fun!"

"This is going to be fun," Malia said, sitting beside Rese and sliding her legs under the rail. She kicked her feet a few times in the air with a smile. "And your mother means well."

"Does she?" Rese said. "I get tired of her telling me what to do and how to do it."

"It's just the way she was taught," Adeline said. "You watch, you'll catch yourself doing the same to your daughter someday."

Rese looked a little queasy, rubbed her stomach, and belched softly.

"Oh, I hope not."

The train whistle blew. SS soldiers hurried the last refugees aboard the train. The roofs of their boxcar and the boxcars behind them were now crowded with people trying to get safely seated before the train began to move.

A minute later, it did, belching smoke from its ancient stack, groaning, whining, and then slowly picking up speed. They left the protection of the station's canopy. The sun beat down mercilessly on them as they rolled past German soldiers and artillery pieces chained to flatbed cars in the rail yard.

Leaving the yard, the train looped southwest through the city and then north, roughly paralleling the Danube River while slowly gathering speed. The wind blew the locomotive smoke away from them, allowing Adeline to catch thrilling glimpses of the bridges that spanned the Danube and, high on a hill, the ancient and grand fortress of the Hungarian kings.

Rese began to sing an old drinking song about a soulful wanderer in search of love, and Adeline and Malia and many other people atop the boxcar joined in with her. For a few moments, Adeline felt her spirits lifted, elated almost and yet easy, and she wondered whether this was what freedom felt like.

By the time they'd cleared the Budapest city limits, Adeline had decided that the locomotive was either very old or very damaged, because it tended to belch thick whips of dark smoke and seemed incapable of traveling very fast. But at top speed and as long as you weren't straight downwind of the smokestack, the wind made the powerful sun more than bearable. It was . . . well, nice, pleasant. Almost freedom, she decided.

"I like riding up here, Mama," Will said, grinning.

"I do, too," Adeline said, smiling and pushing her hair out of her eyes.

Walt leaned his chest against the railing to peer forward up the track. "Here comes a tunnel!"

They swung into the darkness, which made the speed seem faster. Will screamed for joy at the top of his lungs, which made them all laugh. In the next tunnel, Rese joined Will, and soon they were all doing it, screaming for joy every time they hurtled from light to darkness to light once more.

At one point, Rese grinned and laughed as she looked over at Adeline and the boys all anticipating the next tunnel. "This is the best I've felt since we left home. I can't remember being this happy ever, Adeline."

"We're on an adventure," Walt said.

"We are, aren't we?" Rese said, looking in love with that idea.

"Yes," Will said, "because you never know how things are going to turn out."

———

Five hours into their journey, nearing the Hungarian town of Tata, the train came to another stop above a grassy opening that sloped down to a small lake that was settled at the other end. One of the engineers came out of the locomotive along with Major Haussmann, who walked past them, shouting that there would be a half-hour delay here while military trains passed ahead. While they were all free to get off to relieve themselves or have a cigarette, Haussmann also told them to stay close to the train.

The sun was intense again now that they were no longer moving.

"Pretty lake," Malia said. "Looks good enough to swim in."

"I'm game," Rese said, grinning and putting on her shoes.

"You're not," Adeline said.

"Watch me," Rese said, standing up.

Malia clapped and laughed. "What if Karoline catches you?"

"Oh, what if she does?" Rese said, winking at the boys as she started to climb down the ladder. "I know how to swim, and she doesn't."

"I want to go in the water, Mama," Will said. "It's hot."

"Me, too, Papa," Walt said to Emil, who had climbed up at the last stop.

"None of us knows how to swim," Emil said. "And I don't want you to drown."

Rese, meanwhile, jumped off the bottom rung of the ladder, and with a wave at them all, she started to trot down through the lush spring grass toward the lake a hundred meters off. Other people were exiting their boxcars, some smoking, some going off to piss. But no one headed toward the water except Rese. She reached shore, turned back toward the train, and waved wildly at them, before pivoting and stepping out into the water. She took another awkward step and a third before losing her balance, crashing forward, and submerging.

Rese did not come up.

And she did not come up.

Adeline felt a ball in her throat start to build before Rese's head suddenly popped out of the lake. She blew out a stream of water, threw back her head, and shrieked with delight before diving under again.

"How did she learn to swim like that?" Malia asked.

"At school in Pervomaisk," Emil said. "When she was a little girl, she took to it like a fish and—"

The train whistle blew. Major Haussmann came hurrying back up the side of the train, shouting, "Back aboard! The track has cleared ahead. Back aboard or you'll be left behind!"

Down in the lake, Rese surfaced again. Emil cupped his mouth with both palms and shouted at her, "We're leaving, Rese!"

She didn't hear him at first. They all started screaming and waving to her. "Come back to the train! We're leaving!"

Adeline could tell Rese didn't believe them at first. They were supposed to be there thirty minutes, after all. But then the train whistle blew a second time and Rese started swimming as fast as she could toward shore. She came up out of the water, held her soaking skirts high, and started running up the hill, following her own path back up through the long grass.

"Come on, Rese!" Malia yelled.

And now they were all hooting at her and calling encouragement. Rese's grin got bigger and bigger the closer she got to them. She was soaking wet, her clothes had grass all over them, and yet it all made Adeline realize that she'd never known someone quite like her sister-in-law. Rese was pretty and smart and very funny. She did not care what other people thought of her when she did crazy things like this. She was . . . well . . . free in a way that Adeline had never known before. Like Emil said, you know freedom when you see it.

Emil's mother's head was sticking out the side of the boxcar, looking at her daughter as Rese reached the bottom of the ladder by the forward left corner of the boxcar.

"What were you thinking?" Karoline yelled at her.

"I wasn't thinking, Mama," Rese said as she grabbed the rails of the ladder and stepped onto the first rung with her right foot. "I was swimming, and it felt great!"

She lifted her left foot to make the second rung when the train suddenly jerked and shuddered and jerked again with enough violence to fling Rese sideways and forward off the ladder in a spiraling fall that caused her to crash face-first in the grass and gravel, her chest and belly below the railroad tie and her shins across the rail. The coupler that held the coal car to their car was right behind and above her.

It all happened so fast, Adeline had barely cried out in response to Rese's fall before the locomotive sighed and the train lurched forward again. The wheels of the boxcar rolled slowly over Rese's legs, severing both of them at midcalf.

Chapter Fifteen

Emil erupted from his position on the roof of the boxcar, bellowing at the engineers in the locomotive to stop the train. Evidently, Major Haussmann, who was riding in the locomotive, saw the accident and shouted the same thing before the brakes hit, sending shrieks from the wheels and rails that were not loud enough to mask the trumpets of horror blaring from the crowded boxcars as Rese convulsed, squirmed, and rolled down the embankment into weeds at the edge of the clearing.

Scrambling to the ladder, Emil could see blood spurt and mist, spurt and mist from the stumps of what had been her legs. *Stop the bleeding,* he chanted to himself as he all but slid down the ladder. *Stop the bleeding or Rese dies.*

He landed hard and spun around to find the SS major almost to his sister. Emil ran to them, stripping his belt as he did.

Haussmann had already removed his own belt and was trying to get into a position to help without being sprayed with blood. Emil did not care; he went straight into the blood and to his knees beside his sister, seeing she was unconscious as he got the belt around her lower left leg, above the stump, and cinched it tight enough to staunch the spurting and the misting. Across from him, the SS major had done the same to her right leg and was now shouting for a medic.

Emil was aware of other people yelling now as he tried to comfort his sister, who was shivering as if it were well below zero while he felt as if he were burning in a hot haze of light.

"Save her!" his mother sobbed. He looked up to see Karoline standing there, her face bleeding from the fall she'd taken from the boxcar after seeing her daughter's legs severed, and his father behind his mother, struggling to keep her on her feet as she keened, one bony hand covering her mouth and the other outstretched in misery.

"Save her," Karoline sobbed again, and then looked up at the blistering sky. "Take me, but save her, God. She's all we have left."

Adeline came down beside Emil. "What can I do?"

"We've stopped the bleeding," Major Haussmann said, putting his bloody fingers on Rese's neck. "But she needs morphine, blood, and a surgeon."

Ernst Decker, a medic and SS sergeant in his late twenties, raced from the rear of the train, carrying a pack while two soldiers followed with a stretcher. Sergeant Decker did not blanch at seeing the state of Rese's legs, but instead calmly asked Emil to move aside, and took her vitals, saying, "How long have the tourniquets been in place?"

"A minute," Haussmann said. "No more."

"I need her in a more stable place," he said. "Not out in the sun like this."

"We'll put more people on top and make room for her in the car," Emil said, and glanced warily at Haussmann who'd gone stony. "I am sorry, Major. She's my sister."

Haussmann seemed to be studying him again. Had he recognized Emil just then? Emil didn't care at that point and returned the stare until the major nodded.

"Do it. Get your sister inside by the door where there is air."

Sergeant Decker got out a glass-and-steel syringe and gave Rese a small shot of morphine, enough to keep her sedated during the transfer. In moments it was done: she was on the stretcher, and hands in the boxcar were lifting her inside and placing her litter across the Martels' wagons where Decker went to work.

Emil was going to climb into the boxcar to help the medic, when he saw Walt standing forward of the coupling and looking down between it and the coal car. He walked to his older son, who peered up at his father in bewilderment.

"They don't look much different except right at the top where the wheels crushed them. Below that, they're the same as they were when Aunt Rese still had them."

Emil looked and saw it was true. The wheels, the weight of the coal, and the rail beneath had all served to cut the legs relatively cleanly.

"What do we do with them, Papa?" Walt said. "Do we just leave them there?"

Emil hated to do it but nodded. "In this heat, they are already gathering disease. They'll be gone in hours once we're gone, probably to buzzards and crows."

He could see his older son was upset by that idea, but Walt finally nodded, walked around Emil, and started up the ladder. Adeline appeared in the open door to the boxcar, saying, "Emil, the medic needs you, and your mother's having a fit."

"Go up on top with Walt," he said as he climbed in. "I'm predicting a meltdown up there pretty soon. He saw Rese's legs."

Adeline closed her eyes and nodded.

Inside the crowded boxcar, the heat was stifling, and his mother was wailing. Emil went to her and told her not to make things worse than they were. "This isn't about you. This is about Rese and keeping her alive."

"I have to do something!" Karoline said. "My God, I can't stand this!"

Emil did not reply for a pause, and then said, "If you still believe in God, Mother, I guess you should pray."

He went to Rese's side, however, confirming his own disbelief in God or in any higher force. No decent spirit would allow such a tragic thing to happen to a wild but innocent creature like his sister. No fair universe would put her on a stretcher near the door of a packed and stifling boxcar in northern Hungary with an SS medic putting an IV line into her arm while her lower legs, feet, and shoes lay below on the tracks.

"Do you know her blood type?" Decker asked.

"Type O negative," Emil said. "I am O negative, too. The Communists tested us all. We were required to know."

"You're a universal donor. I need you to be by her side and slightly higher for the transfusion."

Emil looked past his father and saw several wooden crates stacked there. He went to the owner, a woman with two small children, and asked her if he could use them for his sister. She agreed as long as he would return them so she would not lose her space.

Once Emil had two crates moved and stacked, and he was sitting on them, slightly above his sister, Decker moved quickly, efficiently, like the veteran battlefield medic he was, and soon had blood traveling from Emil's left arm into Rese's right. Haussmann appeared at the door to the boxcar and said, "How long until you have her stabilized?"

"Forty minutes?"

"You have ten," the major snapped. "Be creative."

The sergeant looked ready to argue, but then said, "Very well, Major."

Decker told Emil to stay where he was and that he'd be back in a few moments.

"Don't you have to loosen the tourniquets at some point?" Emil asked.

"If I do this right, we should be able to remove them for good in about ten minutes," he said, and got down from the train. He walked forward and climbed up into the locomotive where Emil could not see him any longer.

Emil looked over at Rese's face, battered, swollen, and filthy from the fall. The siblings were separated by a lifetime; he was more than a decade older, a father to his boys much more than he was a brother to her. It made him feel guilty that he'd often been short with Rese, especially the past few years when her emotions had reeled between hurricane and dust storm, all of it compounded by this trip, her near-constant illness, and now this.

He saw Decker climbing back down the ladder of the engine, wearing one glove that held a smoking tin bucket with a wooden handle that stuck out of it. The medic jogged back, put the smoking bucket on the floor of the boxcar, and climbed in. The smell of the smoke was harsh and acrid. People began to cough and hack. Emil looked into the bucket and saw the iron tip of the poker buried in glowing red, smoking coals from the locomotive's firebox.

"What are you going to do with that thing?" Karoline demanded. "You're not burning her with that thing! She's been through enough—"

Decker turned his back on her, saying, "She's going through a little more to save her life."

He looked at Emil, took Rese's blood pressure. "Better," he said. "Who else in your family is type O negative?"

"I am," said Johann, who'd been largely quiet, watching it all unfold from the sweltering shadows. "Her father."

"You'll be next," he said, and removed the transfusion line from Emil's arm.

When Emil stood, he felt light-headed, but managed to move aside while Decker replaced the needle assembly of the transfusion line and Johann took a seat by his beloved daughter. It was only then, as the medic worked the needle into his arm, that Emil saw Johann shed tears.

Decker saw it, too. "She's going to live because of you and your son, Herr Martel, and because of what I'm about to do. I promise you that."

Johann nodded. "Do it. Some things are worth the pain."

A tired, pretty woman in her late twenties who looked vaguely familiar to Emil appeared at the side door, holding a basket with two infants sleeping in it. She looked in at the makeshift operating table and then up when Adeline called down from the roof, "Marie? Is that you?"

"Adeline?" the woman said, surprised. "I didn't know you were on this train. I came because I heard about the accident and wanted to see if I could help."

"I'll come right down and take the twins," Adeline said.

While Decker cleaned the wounds and prepared them for what was to come, Adeline climbed down. "Emil, you remember my cousin Marie from Birsula? She worked in a hospital there."

"With the surgeons," Marie said.

"Get up here, then," Decker said. "I can use the help." The medic looked over at Emil. "I'll need you to hold her down. I don't have any ether, and even with the additional morphine I'm going to give her, she may buck some."

"You're going to torture her!" Karoline said, and turned away, weeping again.

Marie gazed at the scene. "No time to flap and suture?"

"No."

Outside, Major Haussmann hurried up. "You have four minutes. We are on a schedule from Berlin now. Himmler himself."

The sergeant nodded. Marie gave Rese another injection. Decker put gloves on to pick up the poker from the still-smoking bucket. The tip of it glowed ripe-pumpkin orange.

"Hold her now," the medic commanded.

Emil pinned his sister's right thigh to the blanket below her. Marie took her left. Decker went to the right stump, peered closely at it, and then touched the tip of the red-hot iron to the first of the three severed arteries that had been spurting and misting Rese's blood away. There was a hissing noise and a smell like meat searing before Rese jerked, arched, and screamed from some depth of consciousness not deadened by shock or opiate. She twisted her hips hard and bucked, almost got out from under Emil and Marie's grasp.

"Hold her!" Decker shouted. "Don't let her tear out that transfusion line!"

In a panic, Emil threw his entire weight onto his sister's right pelvis and thigh, and Adeline's cousin did the same. Johann took Rese's arms. Together they pinned her down as Decker went about his brutal business, cauterizing two more major blood vessels in the right leg before turning to the left. By the time he finished, Emil was sickened to tears by Rese's wailing, which by the sixth searing touch of the glowing iron had died to whimpering and delirium.

———

Sergeant Decker handed the fire bucket and the poker down to Major Haussmann, saying, "We'll disinfect and bandage her. The smaller arteries and veins will naturally produce a clot. Barring infection, she'll live for a surgeon in Poland to do a better job."

"Well done, Sergeant," Haussmann said. "Heil Hitler!"

Decker and Marie applied hydrogen peroxide and iodine salve generously over the wounds and especially over the open bone cavities. When they were dry, he released the tourniquets around each leg and watched the wounds. Seeing little seepage, he doused the stumps with sulfa powder, applied layers of pads that he had Marie hold in place, and then wrapped them with roll after roll of tan gauze until they looked like large mittens where her lower legs used to be.

There was a sharp whistle. The train lurched yet again and rolled on.

Marie spun around, went to the open side door, and called up, "Adeline?"

"We've got the twins up here," Adeline called back.

Emil did not have it in himself to think about leaving Rese's legs on the tracks where she'd lost them. As they gathered speed and the lake and the town of Tata were swallowed by spring forests and green meadows, he watched Decker remove the transfusion line from his father, now feeling more anger than pity for Rese's plight.

If she had not gone down to swim. If she had listened for once in her life, she'd . . . she'd be . . . He wanted to say . . . *whole,* but instead thought . . . *not my sister.* Rese had been her own person from her first word as a little girl. Most kids said Mama or Dada. Emil's little sister said, "No." And she'd remained a contrary soul ever since.

A half hour passed and then an hour. The heat and the merciless sun of midafternoon blistered on as they rolled slowly toward Bratislava. Rese's blood pressure stayed steady, and the wounds had been redressed. Clotting had begun.

Emil was feeling sure that the worst of Rese's crisis had passed when Marie said, "I need to feed my boys at the next stop."

"And I have sick men in the rear cars to attend," Sergeant Decker said.

"I'll sit with her," Emil said, right before his sister moaned and arched. A convulsion shuddered through her body, which stiffened and then collapsed.

Decker and Marie rushed to her side.

"What happened?" Karoline asked. "What's happening to her?"

The medic had his stethoscope out, listening to her heart while Adeline's cousin put her hands upon Rese to soothe her.

"Heart rate's up, but it's settling again," Decker said to Emil. "That seizure could have been a lot of things caused by the body's natural way of dealing with shock."

Decker was packing his gear ten minutes later when the train whistle blew and they slowed to a stop for a train to cross ahead of them. Marie had not moved from Rese's side, hands on her thigh and stomach, watching for signs of another convulsion.

It came when the train had come to a full stop, a shorter fit than the first, but no less shuddering. Emil's sister arched and bent with an internal convulsion and then collapsed again.

Rese panted and moaned.

"What's happening to her?" Karoline cried.

"I don't know," Decker said.

"I do," Marie said, reaching up Rese's skirt. "She's in labor."

"Labor?" Emil said. "Rese? No."

"She's broken her water," Marie said, then looked at his mother. "How far along is she, Frau Martel?"

Karoline said nothing for a moment, then looked around, anxious and disgusted that there was no way out of facing reality. "Three, maybe three and a half months," she said, sounding crushed. "She only told me the night before we started out on this insane trek."

"Well, she's losing her baby along with her legs," Marie said, then looked at Emil as Decker climbed down from the boxcar with promises to return. "I'll stay with her. But can you go get Adeline and Malia to come down and help me here? I need to feed and tend to my babies before your poor sister gets any worse."

Emil climbed up on the roof. He helped Adeline and Malia lower the basket holding Marie's twins, then watched until his wife and sister-in-law were safely down the ladder before admitting that he was utterly exhausted, worse than after his longest days in the fields or in the brewery, beyond bone-tired. Having expended every bit of energy and love on his sister, he was drained of everything but the need for sleep.

He sat down between his sons, legs under the rails, feet dangling as Rese's had been only hours before. He hugged Will and Walt, and then, as the train began to roll north again, lay back, put his cap across his face, and fell into a hypnotic, buzzing sleep where he remained aware of certain real noises around him—the talk of his sons, the chop and squeal of the train wheels, and the low thudding chug of the locomotive—even as the awfulness of the accident replayed over and over.

There is no God, his inner voice said. *No force for good would take her legs like that. Our pleas are not heard by some invisible force in the sky. We are alone. We fight for survival every day. We can count on no one but ourselves.*

———

When Emil awoke, they were rolling north of Bratislava, heading toward Trnava. The sun was lower, partially blocked by bands of thunderclouds in the west. They were passing through old vineyards with swollen buds about to flower, and then into lush, rolling green country with small farms in the dells and snowcapped mountains beyond.

He yawned and sat up, seeing hobbled horses grazing in a field and feeling a pang for Oden and Thor. What was their fate? What were they doing for the Nazis?

"This is a nice green valley," Will said, "but it's not ours."

Emil shook off his grogginess and was about to tell his younger son not to believe in such nonsense, that whatever color the land around their new home turned out to be, there was no doubt that it would be harsh and cruel and laced with suffering at some level. He was about to tell Will that these facts were unavoidable in life and that he did not believe there was a place on earth where a true paradise like Adeline's existed.

Instead, Emil said, "No, it isn't. We're going to a place called Lodz, Poland."

"What's it like, Papa?" Will said. "Lodz?"

"I don't know," he said. "We'll all find out together."

They fell into silence, and Emil was hoping the train would stop again so he could go down and check on his sister's condition, when Walt said, "Papa, why did that have to happen to Aunt Rese?"

He sighed and hugged his older son again. "I don't know. Life can be cruel at times."

Walt was quiet for several moments before saying, "At first, I didn't like that we left her legs and feet and her shoes like that."

"I didn't, either," Emil said. "I still don't."

"But then I remembered you said birds would probably find them, and I felt better because her legs would get to fly like a bird."

Emil looked down at Walt, smiling at the way he seemed to see the world, from a slightly off but always interesting angle.

"You want to fly someday?" Emil asked.

Walt grinned. "Maybe. Why not?"

"That's right," Emil said. "Why not?"

"I'm going to build things," Will boasted.

"Like what?" Emil said, interested because he, too, liked to build things.

His younger son pointed at a grand old villa on a hillside. "Like that."

"No, you won't," Walt said. "That's too big."

"It's not too big," Will said. "Right, Papa?"

The villa did look huge, bigger than anything Emil had ever built or been a part of building. Maybe it was seeing Rese's life changed for the worse in a heartbeat; maybe he just wanted to spare his son the despair of never having a dream at all, but something in him told him not to discourage Will's vision of life, whatever it was.

"Why not?" Emil said.

Chapter Sixteen

Rese Martel lost her baby as the sun set over eastern Czechoslovakia that hot day in May 1944. Marie guided and helped Adeline and her sister through the entire ordeal. Karoline refused to participate and sat as quiet as Johann, who stood beside her while their unconscious daughter labored to deliver a stillborn son.

Marie clamped and cut the umbilical cord and handed him to Adeline. Curled fetal, Rese's son, slick with fluid and blood, fit in the palm of her hand. Malia came over, looked at him, and after a moment began to cry.

"The poor thing died sucking his thumb," she said, her hand going to her lips.

Adeline saw it was true and felt her own heart ripped open yet again that day. "A little miracle that never had a chance."

"Miracle," Karoline snorted in disgust behind them. "More like a deadly sin, proof of lust before God and man. Mark my words. The Lord took her legs and that . . . sin in your hands because of her fornication."

Adeline, her sister, and cousin were so stunned by the venom in Rese's mother's voice that they turned to look at her swathed in shadows. So did many other people near her.

Aware of them and not caring, Adeline said, "He's your grandson, Karoline. If you're going to say such things, you should look at him and say it. A quarter of his blood descends from you."

Her mother-in-law leaned forward into a slat of light, revealing one eye and a twitching cheek. "Throw that thing out the train door, or I will."

Looming over her suddenly, Johann stunned the crowded boxcar, roaring, "You'll do no such thing! And I'll hear no more from you, woman! Do you think I survived the mines and the miserable walk home to hear your constant and never-ending shit-stirring? Wanting this. Fearing that. Condemning that. Comparing this. Destroying that. Judging who is good and who is not. All with your acid tongue!"

Karoline had shrunk against the forward wall of the boxcar, her voice meeker when she began. "Johann, I do not—"

"Shut up, you evil, evil bitch!" he bellowed down at his wife. "Shut up, or so help me, God, I'll throw you off this train myself and be rid of you for good!"

There was a long, stunned, uncomfortable silence in which Adeline felt confirmed in every ill emotion she'd ever had toward Emil's mother, but also aware that she should be preparing Rese's son for burial at the next stop.

Karoline said bitterly, "Maybe I'll help you, Johann, do you a favor. Throw myself off this train before Rese wakes up. Be rid of me for good."

"There she goes again," Malia whispered in Adeline's ear. "Turning the tables. Playing the persecuted."

"Do it, then, and be quick about it," Johann replied finally, leaving her side for Rese's.

———

Before full darkness fell over the countryside that blipped slowly past them, Adeline wrapped the baby in gauze Decker had left for them to redress Rese's wounds. Marie's sons, Rutger and Hans, began to stir and squawk in their basket.

Marie asked her and Malia to clean Rese as best they could with the last of the water in a bucket while making sure to keep her bandages dry.

"We don't want gangrene," she said as she sat and lifted the first of her boys to her breast.

Adeline marveled at Marie's stamina. Her cousin was shorter and lighter than Adeline, and yet she seemed so much bigger and certainly strong enough to produce milk for two babies at once.

Malia hung a lit lantern in the doorway of the train, just out of the wind, and began wiping and daubing Rese's lower body with a wet cloth. "Marie, tell us about your husband, the surgeon."

Adeline had corresponded with Marie several times a year, knew parts of the story, and wanted to spare her torment. "Malia, maybe there are better things to talk about," she began.

"It's all right, Adella," Marie said. "The Soviets tried to take Klaus when their army left Ukraine in July 1941, but he managed to hide long enough to be taken instead by the Wehrmacht a year after the Germans invaded."

Marie had been working for Dr. Klaus Werner for nearly two years by then, and he'd taught her enough that she had become useful to him in surgery.

"I was in love with him, but he did not seem to notice," Marie said, taking one boy off her left breast and putting the other baby on the right. "He was twelve years older than me. When the Germans discovered his surgical skills, they drafted him. I wanted to go with him but was told to go help on my family's lands. Klaus said he would write to me and left."

Heartbroken and anxious, Marie waited for months to hear from the surgeon. Then two letters arrived at once in early December, both describing his life at a military hospital south of Stalingrad: the endless casualties, the long, hellish hours trying to save men torn apart by war, and the bleak conditions in which he lived.

"At the end of the second letter, he said he missed me," Marie said, glowing in the lantern light. "He said he missed my smile and the sound of my voice."

"You must have been so happy!" Malia said.

"Joyous," Marie said. "I didn't hear from him again until he knocked at my door on March 24 last year. He'd been given a month's leave from the front and immediately got down on one knee and asked me to marry him."

Malia clapped. "This is so romantic! You said yes!"

"I said yes, and we married the very next day," she said. "I could not have been happier. He had come back the Klaus I knew and loved, more tender than I could have imagined, along with another Klaus I did not recognize: a stranger, haunted by everything he'd survived, a doctor terrified of going back to the war."

She paused, cleared her throat, and went on. "But we experienced true love. That month together I'll cherish forever. We made these beautiful little boys before he left."

The baby pulled off her breast and coughed. Marie lifted him to her shoulder and patted him on the back until he burped. Malia finished cleaning Rese and covered her, felt her brow for fever, while smiling and looking expectantly at Marie to finish the story.

"Does he just love them?" Malia asked.

Marie's face fell. "I've heard from Klaus only once since he went back, last November, before the babies were born, before the Dnieper River fell and we needed to run."

"I'm sure he's just behind us somewhere," Malia said.

Her cousin said nothing for a moment. But then her face rippled with fear and pain as she choked, "That's what I'm afraid of. He's behind me somewhere. Not with me and our sons. Maybe for good."

———

During an hour's scheduled stop near the Czech town of Cervenik, Emil got a shovel from the engineers and, together with Johann and Adeline, went well off the track with a lantern. They dug a hole and placed the dead baby wrapped in gauze inside. They said a prayer and covered him up.

"Thank you," Johann said to Emil. "I am sorry your mother said those things. I'm sorrier I said those things."

"It's okay, Papa," Emil said, and patted him on the back. "It was a horrible day for everyone, even Mother."

His father sighed, nodded, and trudged toward the silhouette of the train.

Adeline fell into Emil's arms.

"I still miss our little one," she said.

"We will always miss him," he said. "He was our firstborn."

As they walked back up the slope toward the waiting train, Adeline recalled what caused Johann to explode in rage. It was literally the first time she'd ever seen Emil's father angry.

"I've seen your mother like that only one other time," she said. "When she drank the cream to cut out my heart before the first Waldemar died. Cold. Heartless. Evil inside, like your father said."

"And she hasn't said a word since he blasted her?"

"Not a peep."

"Well, that has to be a first in her entire life," he said, and laughed, which made Adeline laugh and then hug him.

166

"I love that you can turn my spirits," she said. "You're a good husband, a good father, and a very good man, Emil Martel."

Adeline had hoped her husband would take her words as genuine praise, but Emil's face clouded briefly before he managed to smile at her in the lantern light. "And you are the finest woman I have ever known. I'll sit with Rese first if you want. Let you get some sleep."

Adeline studied him a long moment, thinking again that there were parts of Emil that were still a mystery to her and might always be so. They went up the short slope to the train where they met Sergeant Decker leaving the boxcar after giving Rese a full dose of morphine, enough to hold her through the night.

"When will she wake up?"

"I would think tomorrow," Decker said, and left.

They managed to lift Rese and the stretcher high enough to get their bedding from the wagons below. Emil carried it all to the roof of the boxcar where they found the boys curled up together sleeping, their safety ropes still tied around their waists.

He helped Adeline to get the blankets over and around their sons before doing the same for her. "Don't untie the rope unless the train is stopped," he whispered. "I'll wake you up when it's your time to watch over her."

He moved toward the ladder with the lantern.

"Emil," she whispered sharp enough to turn him. "I love you. And thank you."

Her husband looked at her as if she were speaking another language, but then nodded. "I love you, too. And you are welcome. I guess."

Emil started down the ladder before she could reply. Eyes closed, she lay there, thinking about him before images and sounds of Rese began to appear in her mind: Rese vomiting on the way to the train station; Rese coming up out of the lake water, screaming with delight, so wild and free; Rese falling onto the tracks; Rese screaming when Decker cauterized her stumps.

More and faster images flashed as she fought for sleep: Marie delivering Rese's stillborn son and Adeline holding him, a miracle ended, so tiny and so sad and precious; she wanted to cry at how dizzy and beaten down she felt now atop the train, displaced, a refugee of war with no place to call home other than the one she'd conjured from a painting in a book.

Was it only this morning we left Budapest? Adeline thought as she drifted to sleep. *How can so much hope and tragedy be packed into one day?*

———

Emil woke her in the darkness before dawn as they passed through the Czech town of Puchov. The boys still slept. The train rolled at a walking pace.

"How is she?" Adeline whispered as she got out from under her blankets.

"A few nightmares, but she slept through it," he said.

"Your mother?"

"You mean the Sphinx?"

Even though she'd only just awoken, Adeline couldn't help but laugh again at the idea of Karoline still not talking. She kissed his cheek after he got beneath the blankets and then climbed down the ladder. Johann was waiting to help her over to the open door of the boxcar.

She thanked him and scooted by Marie and her twins sleeping on the floor and went to Rese's side. Putting her hand on her sister-in-law's head, she found it warm but not feverish. She used the lantern to inspect the bandages, which were just soaking through. In the first good light, she'd help her cousin change them.

As Adeline hung the lantern back on its hook, she noticed Rese move, not with a jerk of pain, but a stirring, her shoulders shifting, her jaw going slack and then swallowing before her eyelids fluttered open. Rese's eyes rolled as if she could not focus them. She swallowed, closed her eyes, and then opened them again, wobbling before they settled shakily on Adeline.

"Where am I?" she rasped.

Adeline took her young sister-in-law's hand in her own and murmured, "You're alive, Rese. You had a bad accident, but you're alive."

She grimaced and said, "It hurts. Everywhere."

"Yes, there will be a man here to help with that soon."

Johann came behind Adeline, put his massive hand on his daughter's shoulder with tears in his eyes. "Rese."

"Papa," she said, and smiled as her eyes shut and her head lolled a bit.

Rese took two big deep breaths before she suddenly stiffened and clenched Adeline's hands. Her cheeks drew back, her lips thinned, and her eyes stretched wide.

"I fell," she said.

"Yes," Adeline said.

"I landed by the tracks."

"On the tracks," her father said.

Rese seemed confused before looking toward the ceiling with an expression that fluttered between disbelief and total dread.

"No," she said at last. "Tell me it didn't . . ." Then she smiled crazily at them. "No, I feel . . . feel them! You see?"

With that, Rese struggled upright and looked down her skirt, seeing the bloody, round bandages about the stumps where her feet, ankles, and lower calves used to be. She gaped at them, wrenched her hand from Adeline's, and reached for them.

"They're there! I feel them! They're under the bandages! I feel them!"

Karoline appeared at the foot of the stretcher, facing the doorway, unable to look at her daughter directly.

"Mama?" Rese said. "I feel them."

Adeline feared her mother-in-law was going to launch into her damnation sermon from the night before. But instead, Karoline said coldly, "You're feeling the ghosts of them, Rese," she said. "My mother knew soldiers who lost their legs in the Great War, and they swore they could feel them years later."

Much went out of Rese, then. She blinked at her mother blankly and then at her bandaged stumps. She lifted the left leg, pain rippling through her, and then bent it at the knee. After doing the same with the right, she burst into tears.

"Now Stephan will never come find me to marry me!" she sobbed, and threw herself backward on the stretcher. "Oh God, he'll leave me with the baby! We will be left to beg in the streets of Germany, the freak girl from Russia with no feet and a child!"

Rese went hysterical, inconsolable, tortured and racked with agonies Adeline could not begin to fathom until Marie appeared at her side. The sun had risen. The train was slowing.

Marie took Rese's hand. When Rese tried to pull it back, Marie held her firmly by the wrist and stroked her forearm, saying, "I have delivered many children, Rese, and have two of my own. See them there in the basket?"

Rese's tears slowed, and she opened her eyes to blearily look at the basket Adeline held tilted toward her so she could see the infants in the increasing light.

"My sons are both my greatest blessing and my greatest curse," Marie said. "God gives you children only when he thinks you are ready for the experience of holding your greatest blessing and your greatest curse in your arms at the same time."

Rese winced in pain and reached for her left leg with her left hand.

"My legs hurt like fire. Both of them."

"The medic is coming now," she said. "But do you understand what I'm saying, Rese? God decided that you were not ready to be a mother. I'm sorry."

"What?"

Karoline said, "You lost the baby, Rese."

For a moment, it was as if Rese had not heard her mother and was transfixed on something above Marie. Then the skin on her forehead twitched, her eyes dulled, and she slowly drew her hand from Adeline's cousin's. Wrapping her head in her arms, she turned away and tried to draw up her legs, only to scream and twist in pain.

Sergeant Decker appeared. Karoline said, "Thank God. Put her out of her misery. I don't think I can take any more right now."

The medic nodded, introduced himself to Rese, and asked if he could examine her legs.

"No!" Rese screamed. "No, you can't!"

"I'm going to give you a shot first to help with the pain, okay?"

Rese didn't reply. Decker retrieved his syringe and a vial of morphine and gave her a healthy dose. Within minutes, she'd stopped crying and had rolled over on her back, staring lazily at the ceiling while Decker cut off her bandages and examined the stumps, finding that the smaller arteries and veins had indeed clotted.

"No sign of infection that I can see," the medic said. "You are lucky to be alive, Rese."

She laughed softly. "I admit you got me feeling pretty good right now, but I know when this stuff wears off, I'll rather be dead."

Chapter Seventeen

The train crawled north through hilly and then mountainous terrain in dry, windy heat, past Zilina and Cadca before crossing the border at Bohumin into Poland around noon. Midafternoon, the train stopped in farmland just east of the city of Lodz, which the Germans had renamed "Litzmannstadt."

Emil and Adeline were atop the boxcar with the boys when Major Haussmann exited the locomotive and strode along the train, shouting that everyone was to exit with their belongings. The mob spilled out and away from the train and crossed a county road.

The sun and the wind were near infernal as they brought down Rese on the stretcher and then the Martels' two little wagons and the last of their things. The boys were excited to be off the train after the twenty-seven-hour trip and began a game of tag despite the heat.

Major Haussmann returned, said, "The girl will be taken to the military hospital along with the other wounded soldiers."

"I'll go with her," Karoline said.

"No one goes with her. The rest of you are in quarantine. A fever spread through the train ahead of you, and we can't take the chance of infecting the city."

A young, burly medic named Praeger arrived to help Decker take Rese to an ambulance. She had not spoken in hours, but he managed to get through to her by appealing to her slightly warped sense of humor.

As Decker prepared another injection to carry Rese through the bumpy ride to the military hospital, Praeger squatted by her side and said, "My older sister lost her leg above the knee in a farming accident."

Rese showed no reaction.

"She didn't get over the loss of her leg until she started telling amputee jokes."

Rese scowled in disgust. "There's nothing funny about this."

"No?" Praeger said. "What did the driver say to the one-legged man needing a ride?"

She glared at him. "I have no idea."

"Hop in."

Rese shut her eyes and pursed her lips not to smile.

"What do you call a one-legged woman?"

She opened one eye skeptically. "What?"

"Peg," he said.

Rese scrunched up her lips sourly, said, "What do you call a no-legged woman?"

He smiled at her as Decker thumbed the plunger and said, "Beautiful."

Maybe it was the drugs hitting her or the sentiment, or the soft tone in his voice, or all three, but something in Rese unlocked and softened. She smiled weakly at Praeger before her head lolled, and he and Decker picked up the litter and took her away while Johann called to her with promises that he would come find her once he was allowed.

The Germans took the refugees by boxcar, starting with the one closest to the coal car. The Martels pulled and pushed their wagons behind three soldiers who led them and the other refugees on a dusty, hot road that led out through fields that still lay fallow, awaiting the plow.

Emil was pulling, and Adeline and her mother, Lydia, pushing. Malia had gone to help Karoline and Johann. The boys were trudging along behind. As he was nearest to the three soldiers leading them, Emil could hear most of the discussion they were having.

"Like clockwork," one of them said.

Another said, "More vermin left last night, just in time for this new blood to take their places."

"Clothes and bugs off them first," a third said, sounding disgusted as they crested a rise to see a group of four buildings, two on each side of the road.

A sign said "*Einwandererzentralstelle* (EWZ)."

"Immigration Control Center," Emil said to Adeline.

The soldiers stopped at the center of the four buildings, and Major Haussmann appeared around the front of them.

"Men and women are to be separated here briefly. All boys are to be with their fathers. If they have no fathers and are under the age of four, they will go with their mothers and sisters. Over four years old, they go with the men.

"Keep your papers with you," Haussmann went on. "Your belongings will be tagged and returned to you as soon as it is allowed. *Bitte*, men to my left, women to my right, enter the front doors before you."

———

Emil kissed Adeline, then took the boys by the hands and with his father led the way up to open steel double doors in a brick wall about three meters high with barbed wire strung across the top. On the other side, they entered a courtyard of sorts with soldiers waiting behind long tables and piles of clothes thrown behind them.

"Strip!" a soldier shouted. "Keep your papers and strip. Leave your clothes here, and then give your papers to be protected. Alphabetically. *A* to *M*, left, *N* to *Z*, right!"

Walt stared in fright at Emil. He did not like to be naked, but Emil said, "Do what the officer tells you."

Will stripped off his clothes right away and was dancing about, laughing and ignoring the disapproving looks from the men just coming into the courtyard. Walt finally complied. Holding his hands over his groin, he followed Emil and Will and his grandfather to the officer who was taking their papers.

"Don't worry," the soldier said. "They'll be given back to you on the other side. Through those doors, *bitte*."

Inside, soldiers led them to chairs where their hair was shorn off with clippers. Emil's and Johann's beards—long and bushy from the six-week journey after a long winter—were taken down to stubble, too.

Both boys rubbed their hands across their buzz cuts uncertainly as Emil led them and his father through the third set of doors into a low-ceilinged space with drains set in the concrete floor. More soldiers waved them in, yelling, "When the order is given, you are to close your eyes and cover them with your hands. If you open your eyes, they will be burned by the shower that kills the disease-carrying lice on your bodies. Repeat: do not open your eyes until the second order is given!"

"Did you hear him?" Emil asked both boys who were looking up at pipework and shower nozzles for the first time in their lives. Their home in Friedenstal had had no running water. They were used to drinking and bathing in pail-drawn well water.

"We close our eyes," Walt said finally. "We wait for the order."

More men and boys were crowding into the delousing room behind them. "Will?"

His younger son stood up straight, slammed shut his eyes, and covered them dramatically with his hands.

"Good boy," Emil said.

"Quiet!" a soldier roared. "Listen to the loudspeaker!"

The doors were shut, cutting off all light. The boys clung to Emil until the voice came over a speaker saying, "Cover your eyes with your hands. Tilt your heads down. Close your eyes and wait for the order to open your eyes."

Water mixed with chemicals that smelled like tar rained down on them for several minutes and then stopped. They were ordered to remain with their eyes shut and covered. After what seemed like hours, a second shower began, longer than the first and without the petrol smell.

When the water turned off, doors on the near wall opened. They stepped out into a grassy area in the sun. Eight military lorries were parked four opposite four and fifteen meters apart with their tail ends facing each other. Soldiers were unloading piles of clothes from the trucks.

"Retrieve your documents first," a soldier in uniform yelled. "Then go to the clothes. These have all been boiled clean. There are pants, shirts, coats, and shoes divided into small, medium, and large. Get one or two of everything for now. You will be given more clothes once you have been assigned a place to live."

Emil stood in line only a few minutes before retrieving their documents. It did not take them long to find clothes and shoes that fit them all well enough. Emil was amazed by the feel of the fabric of the pants and shirt he now wore. He'd never worn clothes this fine in his entire life. Except for torn yellow stitches on the left chest, the suit jacket he discovered was almost new.

"I'm hot," Will said.

"Take off your jacket for now."

"I want my shorts."

"We'll find you shorts," Emil said, and was surprised when they did.

With their new clothes on and more in their arms, they were directed to another larger courtyard to wait for their families. Not long after, Malia and both grandmothers came out of the doors on the opposite side of the courtyard, wearing new dresses and shoes, but completely shorn of hair. None of them looked happy about it.

They became unhappier when Will and then Walt started pointing at them and laughing. "I hate lice," Malia said, tying a scarf around her head.

"If we had them, they're gone now," Adeline's mother said.

"Where's Adella?" Emil said.

"Helping Marie find clothes for the babies," Malia said.

———

Karoline put on a scarf as well. She walked to Johann and said, "I don't recognize you without the beard and the wild hair."

"I could say the same," he said.

They fell quiet and stood there awkwardly.

Emil had never truly understood their relationship, tottering between indifference and rancor at times, a marriage that had a gaping wound in it from years spent apart, not knowing whether the other was alive or dead.

Adeline came into the courtyard with one of Marie's sons in her arms and trailed by her cousin and her other boy. She wore a dark-blue skirt now, a gray blouse of fine quality, and a blue-and-red scarf around her head. Even with her hair shorn, Emil thought she looked radiant in the late-day light.

A new life was beginning for them. He could feel it. They'd relied on themselves to get through the abandonment of their lands forever and a long, difficult journey. They had made it to Poland when so many had died along the trek. Rese's accident was a senseless tragedy, but seeing her reaction to Praeger calling her "beautiful" actually gave him hope that his little sister would recover and find a way to a better life.

"Who is that strange-looking man?" Adeline asked, waving one of the baby's hands at Emil as she walked up to him.

"I know who you are," Emil said. "I'd recognize you anywhere, Adeline Martel."

They kissed. He pushed back her scarf to look at her haircut. "It becomes you."

"Don't count on it lasting," she said.

The courtyard filled as more refugees streamed out of the delousing station, wearing their almost-new clothes. SS soldiers appeared and led their group on foot almost three kilometers to a large camp of buildings and tents surrounded by a high wood-and-wire fence.

Inside, they were registered, had their temperatures taken to identify and segregate anyone with a fever, and then were assigned to tents on the far side of a parade ground east of the biggest building in the camp. The extended Martel clan had three tents tall enough for everyone but Johann. Marie and the twins bunked with Malia and Lydia. There were pallets with fresh straw mattresses and blankets, and towels and soap, and a lantern hanging from a pole. After so many weeks outrunning the war, sleeping on the ground beneath the wagon, and huddling in culverts during bombardments, these simple quarters felt almost too good to be true.

And the food! Something savory was cooking, and bread was baking. They'd smelled it all as they'd passed the big building by the parade ground. After arranging their belongings, they were directed back to that building, a sprawling mess hall where they stood in line for egg noodles and pork sausages and onions and applesauce and fresh rolls with butter. The boys were given milk with melted chocolate in it. Emil and Adeline were handed small mugs of hoppy, frothy beer.

"It's a feast!" Adeline said, shaking her head at the plate she carried.

"And all for us?" Malia wondered.

"I never expected this," Emil said as they went to long tables with benches.

Walt dug in the moment he sat down, shoveling in noodles and meat so fast, his mother had to slow him. "But it's so good," he protested, his cheeks full.

"You'll choke to death, and then where would good be?" Malia said.

"Listen to your aunt and slow down," Adeline chided. "Enjoy this gift from heaven."

Wherever it had come from, it felt like a gift to Emil as well. He ate each fork and spoonful of the meal like it was his first. He sipped the beer and smacked his lips. His head swirled a little, and slowly his shoulders dropped.

He looked at Adeline and the boys, and with each sip of the beer—his first taste of alcohol since that night with Nikolas—he felt easier, more relaxed, and more likely to laugh.

When was the last time that had happened? When was the last time he wasn't constantly looking out for his survival? His family's survival? The second day of the trek? When Will had to go pee and he couldn't stop the wagon?

Whenever it was, the weight of being vigilant slipped away with the second beer and allowed Emil to feel good, so good, he grabbed Adeline by the hip, spun her around, and kissed her while the boys and Malia hooted and clapped.

"I love you," he said.

"You're drunk."

"I still love you."

They weren't as far west as Emil could imagine, somewhere across the sea, but the worst seemed over. He felt it in his bones. They'd been through a nightmare but lived through it to enjoy a meal like this with only better days ahead.

After they finished with full and distended bellies, the Martels wandered through the ever-filling refugee camp, finding the latrines and showers and the gates in the fencing that led to the medical clinic and other buildings outside the fence. An hour later, in the gloaming and shadows of late day, floodlights went on, and loudspeakers called them to that parade ground by the mess hall. At one end, there was a low stage of sorts with Nazi flags fluttering to either side of a large radio microphone on a stand.

Major Haussmann came onstage and went to the microphone.

"I trust you enjoyed your meal after your long journey?" he asked.

The crowd roared its approval.

"That was a welcoming gift to you from Reichsführer Heinrich Himmler who himself authorized the treks that rescued you and more than one hundred thousand others. Because you were part of the last trek to arrive, Reichsführer Himmler wanted to be here to greet you personally but was unavoidably detained. The Reichsführer has, however, sent a message that he has asked me to read to you."

The major retrieved a piece of paper from his breast pocket and began to read:

"'I bid welcome to the last of the Black Sea Germans to arrive in the Warthegau. You are very important to the Third Reich and to the führer, good loyal pure German bloodstock returning to the greater Fatherland to strengthen our Aryan roots after a century apart. Know that I consider you a critical part of an expanding German future where Judeo-Stalinism will be completely and permanently destroyed. You are in quarantine now and will be for the next few weeks until the doctors say it is safe for you to join the general population. But you will be given a home soon and a way to be useful to the Reich. I bid you welcome again, and congratulations. Signed, Heinrich Himmler, Reichsführer of the *Schutzstaffel*.'"

Other SS officers began to clap as Major Haussmann lowered the letter and looked expectantly at the refugees, who began to clap as well. Soon all of them were clapping, and some whistled their approval.

Haussmann let the applause build and last a few moments before he held up his hands for quiet. "In a moment, you will get in lines for doctors and nurses to have a quick look at you before we release you to sleep. Tomorrow, you must have your papers with you to prove your German ancestry in order to receive your *Umsiedlerausweis*, or resettlement identity card. Your application must include your *Einbürgerungsantrag*, *Stammblatt*, *Volkstumausweis*, and *Lebenslauf*."

Adeline leaned forward and whispered in Emil's ear. "We have them all?"

He nodded. "Naturalization application, family tree, ethnic identity card, and our life stories."

Haussmann was still talking. "My assignment to protect you is now complete, though I will remain in the area until you are moved to permanent housing. I know it has been a tiring journey, but you are safe now. More important, as Reichsführer Himmler himself just said, your pure Aryan blood is safe now, too."

Music played from the speakers.

Haussmann put himself at attention and shot out his right arm in the Nazi salute.

"Heil Hitler!" he roared. "Welcome to the Third Reich!"

———

Close to the stage, a large group of semidrunken refugees immediately responded with the salute and bellowed "Heil Hitler!" in return. Among the Martels and the other Black Sea Germans, the response was more muted.

Haussmann stood there, looking furious, and bellowed, "Sieg!"

Every soldier in the camp threw his arms out and bellowed, "Heil!"

The major glared at the refugees. "Sieg!"

"Heil!" roared the soldiers and many of the refugees.

"Sieg!"

"Heil!"

By the eighth time, Emil noticed, every refugee, every member of his family, including himself, Adeline, and his two young boys, were calling back to Haussmann and throwing their arms forward and up in unison.

The major stopped, his arm still in the salute, the arms of everyone in the camp still in salute. A record played over a loudspeaker, static and popping that gave way to blaring trumpets and rousing drum tattoos and a chorus of men and women singing "*Horst-Wessell-Lied*," the anthem of the Nazi Party. Every soldier sang along. One by one, every refugee did as well. If they didn't know the words, they acted as if they did while the recording of Adolf Hitler's Brownshirts' street-fighting song played:

> Raise the flag! The ranks tightly closed!
> The SA marches with calm, steady step.
> Comrades shot by the Red Front and reactionaries
> March in spirit within our ranks.

> Clear the streets for the brown battalions,
> Clear the streets for the storm division!
> Millions are looking upon the swastika full of hope,
> The day of freedom and of bread dawns!

> For the last time, the call to arms is sounded!
> For the fight, we all stand prepared!
> Already Hitler's banners fly over all streets.
> The time of bondage will last but a little while now!

> Raise the flag! The ranks tightly closed!
> The SA march with quiet, steady step.
> Comrades shot by the Red Front and reactionaries,
> March in spirit within our ranks.

When the recording ended, Haussmann again strode to the microphone.

"Heil Hitler!" he roared, thrusting his arm out and up.

"Heil Hitler!" the refugees shouted with more enthusiasm.

"Heil Hitler!"

The refugees shouted it back even louder. Emil noticed again that by the eighth time, the entire camp was bellowing "Heil Hitler!" as one monstrous voice.

Haussmann smiled. "Well done. Now, line yourselves up in one of ten rows here for a brief medical examination, and then you may retire."

The Martels got in the shortest line, which led past the stage to a doctor and nurse, wearing surgical masks and inspecting people, one by one.

Emil noticed Nikolas was well ahead of them in the line of ethnic German refugees, almost to the doctor. When Nikolas passed Haussmann, the SS major nodded to him.

"I'm tired, Papa," Will said.

"My stomach hurts," Walt said.

Emil took his attention off Haussmann and Nikolas when Adeline said, "That's what happens when you eat too fast after not eating much for weeks."

The line was moving quicker now. Emil glanced up to see the SS major less than ten meters ahead, still on the stage, as a junior officer came to Haussmann with a piece of paper, which he took and read. As Emil passed him, however, the major picked his head up, made eye contact, and then nodded. Emil nodded back and continued on.

A few moments later, Emil glanced back to the stage and saw Major Haussmann staring after him. Their eyes met. One of the SS officer's brows rose, and a hard smile came to his lips before he nodded and shook a finger at him.

Emil turned, feeling his heart sink into the pit of his stomach. *What did that mean?*

He didn't dare look back, though the question kept spinning fear in his head and gut. It took every bit of will to answer the doctor who examined Emil, Adeline, and the boys after taking their temperatures and asking about fevers or persistent illnesses they may have had in the last three months. Emil told him he hadn't been sick in five years, which was true. And Adeline said Walt had been sick the year before, but Will was in generally good health. The doctor waved them on.

Night had fallen. Will was so tired, Emil put him on his shoulders and carried him back to the tent. As they walked, Walt said, "Mama? Is Heinrich Himmler God?"

"What? No! Whatever are you talking about?"

"You said dinner was a gift from heaven, and the major said it was a gift from Himmler," Walt said. "How does that make sense?"

"It doesn't," she said wearily. "Whoever it came from on earth, it was a gift to us from above. That's what I believe."

For once that seemed to satisfy Walt, and soon Adeline had both boys tucked into bed on their cots in their tent.

"They don't have to go pee?" Emil said.

"They said they were too tired," Adeline said.

"I have to go."

"I do, too," she said.

They left Malia to listen for the boys, took the lantern, and went to the latrine. Emil was done quickly and stood outside waiting for Adeline when Nikolas walked up and stopped a yard away with a knowing smile on his face.

Emil hardened, said, "I guess a busted knee wasn't enough to make you hear."

"I hear just fine," Nikolas said, the smile becoming a gloat. "I heard exactly what Sturmbannführer Haussmann told me a few moments ago. With the hair and the beard gone, he recognized you, Martel. He remembers who you are now."

PART THREE:
THROWN TO THE WIND
AND THE WOLVES

Chapter Eighteen

Adeline exited the latrine and saw a tall man limping away from Emil, who stared after him, appearing deeply shaken in the lantern light.

"What's the matter, Emil?"

"Just tired," he said, though he would not meet her gaze.

"Isn't he the same man who came to our camp on the Romanian border with the major?"

"Was he?" Emil said. "He asked me where the medical clinic was, and I showed him. Are you sure?"

Adeline was almost sure but gave Emil the benefit of the doubt, and they walked back to the tent in silence. He immediately took his coat off and climbed beneath the blanket. She soon put out the lantern and joined him, spooning him from behind.

"They're asleep," she whispered.

"What?"

"You know. If you want?"

There was a long silence. "I'm beyond tired."

Adeline rolled away from him onto her back and closed her eyes. She could feel the tension coming off her husband in waves. When he got like this, she'd learned to give him room. If something was bothering Emil, he'd come to her once he'd figured out a way to solve the problem. It was just the way he was, and she fell asleep telling herself that maybe he was right: some things were not worth knowing.

———

The following day, the Martel family went through five hours of interviews and document inspection. At each of eight stations, they were questioned by as many as six immigration and naturalization officers about everything from their personal history to potential occupations to the value of the lands they left behind. They were also photographed and subjected to full medical examinations that included detailed measurements of their skulls, jaws, and arm and leg bones as part of racial research commissioned by Himmler himself.

At the end of the process, each family was given a framed picture of Adolf Hitler, granted provisional resettlement identity cards, and told they would be moved to more permanent quarters once the quarantine was lifted.

The newest residents of the führer's Greater Germany quickly fell into the military-like rhythm of refugee-camp life. Though the boys had spoken German and some Russian from birth, they were enrolled in a makeshift school within days, learning to spell, read, and write in proper German and to master the basics of mathematics. Except for Karoline and Lydia, the adults were given jobs. Malia and Marie worked in the laundry, while Adeline toiled in the kitchen, which suited her because she adored cooking and learned something new from the cooks there every day. Johann swept the pathways between the first eight rows of tents. Emil was ordered to work emptying the latrines, which he did stoically. As he told himself repeatedly, *My family is safe. The food isn't what it was the first night, but we're being fed and given a place to live. Cleaning the latrines is the least I can do.*

Emil came back to the tent every evening after removing the coverall Haussmann's men gave him and after taking a shower with a strong lye soap that gave him its own peculiar, lingering odor. Day after day turned into the middle of June 1944, and still, Adeline never once heard her husband complain about his shitty lot.

About that time, however, Adeline began to notice the food deliveries coming into the kitchen had dropped in both quality and quantity; and she overheard one of the cooks talking about Rome falling to the Allies and the Wehrmacht in pitched battles against the Allies in France, all of which was drawing manpower and supplies from all regions of the Reich west into France and south into Italy.

When she murmured this all to Emil, he became excited because he said it meant the western Allies had invaded Europe and were coming for Hitler.

"Don't you see?" he whispered. "The Allies? They're our way west, Adella. All we have to do is get to them and surrender."

She looked at him like he'd lost his mind. "You want to walk through Poland and Germany into France, past the Wehrmacht, through the battle, and live long enough to surrender? First of all, you're not a soldier. Neither am I. We can't surrender."

"It doesn't matter. If we can get to the Allies, however we do it, we'd be *their* refugees. We can work for them, Adeline. If I must, I'll clean toilets the rest of my life. Maybe they will send us west across the ocean as thanks for our hard work."

Adeline frowned. "That's a big maybe when I have two young boys, a mother, and a sister to think about, not to mention your parents and my cousin and the twins. And Rese. Do you want your sister to run through bullets and bombs to surrender?"

"No," he said. "We'll carry Rese if we have to. And the bullets will miss us."

"Now you are sounding like Corporal Gheorghe. And you haven't even been hit in the head."

She was trying to be funny, but it got him outright angry. "That's right: I have not been hit in the head. And I am not anything like Corporal damned Gheorghe!"

She held up both hands. "Take time to think it over, Emil. We can't leave the camp's grounds, so we can't go looking for the Allies at the moment anyway."

———

That calmed Emil down for several days until word spread through the camp that the quarantine would soon be lifted and they'd be moving into permanent quarters in the small city of Wielun southwest about twenty-two kilometers. Emil started studying the position of the stars in the northern hemisphere from a book the boys had been given in school.

"You haven't read a book in years," Adeline said. "Why are you interested in that?"

He scowled at her. "I may only have a fifth-grade education, but I can read and write, and I'm not stupid."

She blushed. "I never said you were, Emil. I just wondered."

"If you know the position of the stars, you can find your way at night, Adella, which I think might help us getting to the Allies and becoming *their* refugees."

"Walking at night?"

"Yes. Only at night."

"We'll fall on our faces," she said. "We'll break our noses or our legs."

Emil sighed. "Or we might make our way to freedom."

He tried to spend time every day listening behind the SS officers' latrines for news of the war and trying to figure out how long it might take them to get to the Allied lines. At night, Emil stood outside, studying the North Star in relation to the constellations. But every time he brought up the subject of running west after they were released from the camp, Adeline became more and more upset.

"I won't do it," she said finally.

"You will," Emil replied. "At some point, you'll have to decide where you want to spend your life—in slavery or in freedom—and if you choose freedom, you'll have to run through a no-man's-land with bullets zinging around your head to get there. I don't think there's any way around it. If we want that life, we'll have to risk death for it."

————

They were awoken at dawn on a late-June day, told to gather their things and to report to the parade ground, where Major Haussmann was waiting at the microphone.

"Your quarantine is over," Haussmann said. "The belongings you surrendered at the train station will be returned to you, and you will be given an address, a key, and a map to your home as well as an explanation of the food-rationing system, which is important if you wish to eat. Once in their new homes, adults must report to their EWZ officer to be assigned to jobs according to their skills."

"What about Rese?" Emil's mother fretted.

"I told you, Mama," Emil said. "The doctors said she's recovering and will be brought to us in Wielun as soon as she is able to travel."

They were told to organize themselves by the boxcars they arrived in, with the Martels' boxcar the first to go. Soon they passed through the gates for the first time in five weeks. It was a beautiful, warm summer day. Their little wagon was one of the first to be unloaded from the truck, and everything was as they'd left it, even the dried foodstuffs.

Emil received the key, the map to their quarters in Wielun, and their first ration cards. Emil studied the map, which showed their new homes reachable by one of three routes. He was lost in calculating the distance of each route when he heard Major Haussmann say, "Martel?"

Looking up, Emil saw Major Haussmann standing there, in an at-ease position, gazing directly at him. He felt his gut roil. He'd thought once they were beyond the gate that they were rid of the man forever. But there Haussmann stood.

He lowered the map and said, "Yes, Major?"

"A word before you go, *bitte*," the SS officer said. "In private."

"Of course, Major," Emil said, feeling worse, looking at his wife and kids, wondering if it was for the last time, before following the SS officer down the fence line of the camp, over a roll in the terrain, and down into a deep dip in the field where they could not be seen from the road.

The major pivoted to face him, his Luger drawn, with the same furiously amused expression Emil had seen on Haussmann's face that night in Dubossary long ago. Emil threw up his hands, terrified.

"I knew I'd seen you before, even with all the hair and the beard," Haussmann said. "But with it all gone, I knew it was you, which is strange because I've seen tens of thousands of faces since that night. Yet yours stood out. Why is that, Martel?"

Emil debated whether to remain silent, but then said, "I don't know, Major."

"I do, actually," Haussmann said, laughing acidly. "Your face stood out because it belonged to the first true coward I faced in Ukraine. You remember, don't you, farm boy?"

Emil took a deep breath, said, "Major, that rule was—"

"I don't give a damn about some other coward's rule," he seethed, shaking the gun.

"Himmler's rule," Emil said.

"What does Reichsführer Himmler know, really? Was he in the field with rifles and pistols, solving his Jew problem? No. I was in the field solving his Jew problem. I should have shot you that night, and I didn't. And now, miraculously, I have a chance to fix that."

Haussmann's pistol rose, and Emil, trembling, looked over its barrel at the Nazi. "You're going to just shoot me?"

"I've done it before."

"Wait, please," Emil choked. "I have been a good German since. Please, all I want is a better life for my family. I beg you not to leave my wife a widow and my sons without a father. My wife's father was taken to Siberia and was never heard from again. She couldn't bear being left like that."

Haussmann pulled the trigger.

———

Adeline was still watching the knoll Emil had disappeared over with Major Haussmann when she heard the flat crack of the gunshot and jerked violently. Her hand flew to her mouth, and she staggered left and stabbed out her hand to grab the side of the little wagon.

"No," she gasped weakly.

"Mama?" Walt said, rushing to her. "What just happened?"

Adeline stood there in shock, staring at the knoll and the last spot where she'd seen Emil, silently screaming from the depths of her soul for God to spare and protect him.

Please, God, if there was ever a good man, a good father, and a good husband, it's Emil Martel. In all my years of knowing him, he's never wavered from doing what was right. Not once. He deserves better than this; he deserves—

A second shot shattered the morning.

———

Emil was on his knees, shaking from head to toe, ears ringing, and sure he was about to die because both shots had gone right past his ears and slammed into the embankment behind him. Haussmann wouldn't miss a third time.

He looked up to see the Nazi smiling at him and then lowering the Luger.

"It is enough," Haussmann said. "Seeing you like this, quivering, about to crap your pants. It's enough. I used to have to see them die, watch the blood and the life drain out of them. But about a year ago, I realized I enjoyed the begging and the reaction to the intentional first missed shot more than I did the actual kill. Seeing you destroyed is enough, Martel. Get up. Go back to your family."

Feeling weak as a lamb and distrusting the man, Emil got unsteadily to his feet and looked walleyed at Haussmann. "I can go?"

"Yes, but don't think for a second your punishment is over," the major said. "It will go on well after I am gone. I've made sure of that. And as you and your family suffer in the months ahead, I want you to think about your acts that night in Dubossary. Your cowardice."

He gestured at Emil's jacket. "I want you to think about the clothes you're wearing and the place you're blessed to live in because of people like me. And I want you to decide whether you really do want to be part of the Third Reich, or whether you should go back to living under Stalin and his filthy Yids."

———

Will had begun to cry. "Mama! Where is he?"

Adeline couldn't answer. She was still fixed on that point on the knoll where she'd last seen Emil, still praying to God to deliver him, when she caught movement.

Walt, who'd stood up on the wagon, screamed, "It's him! It's Papa!"

Adeline started running toward Emil as he crested the knoll. Walt and Will did, too. But he held up his hands, shook his head, and ran to them as they slowed.

"What happened?"

"A rat," he said, pale and sweating as if he'd been running for an hour, and gesturing at the wagon. "Let's go. Now!"

She wanted to press him, but she could see he was in no mood to be pressed.

"They said lorries are coming for us soon."

"I don't care."

They assumed their positions fore and aft of the little wagon. Emil began to pull it hard across the open ground. Adeline, Malia, and Lydia puffed to stay with him.

"Slow down, Emil," Adeline gasped. "We can't keep up."

Chapter Nineteen

Trucks rolled by them. One stopped to let them load their wagons. Two hours later, they arrived in Wielun, the very first town Hitler attacked when he invaded Poland in 1939. A sizable portion of the town still lay in ruins from the Wehrmacht and Luftwaffe bombardments. The buildings left standing were either empty or filled with resentful Poles, who glared at the Black Sea Germans as they unloaded their meager belongings and set out to find their new place in the world.

There had been no canvas roof on the rear of the truck, so Adeline had been able to see that the surroundings were largely farmland. Much of it had lain fallow, which surprised her and made her anxious. If crops weren't being raised, how were they to eat? The dry goods they'd brought from the East would last only so long.

She voiced her concerns to Emil as they wandered through the narrow streets and bomb rubble, looking for their new home.

"They said we get ration cards," Emil said. "Besides, I don't want to stay here long. At some point, Adeline, we have to go west."

"At some point. But not now. The boys need a calm life for a bit, and so do I."

They found the address: a gray, dilapidated, three-story, wood-framed building badly in need of repair. The building's front stoop sagged. The door hung crookedly on its hinges and moaned when Emil used the key to open it, revealing a narrow hall and a narrower staircase that ascended into shadow.

There were six apartments inside, two on each floor. The first-floor flats were uninhabitable. Emil's parents and Adeline's cousin Marie and her twins took the second-floor apartments. Emil's family and Adeline's mother and sister would take the third-floor flats.

The air inside was hot and rank with human odor. When they climbed the staircases, the risers made cracking and popping noises as if they'd break away under their feet.

"Is this safe?" Lydia asked, holding the flimsy banister with both hands.

"Let's go up and down one at a time until we're sure," Emil said.

"Do you feel that breeze?" Adeline asked. "It's coming through the wall."

"Beggars can't be choosers," Karoline said as she went into her apartment.

Adeline climbed another flight and opened the door to their flat, revealing a narrow room with three stools, a wooden table, and a kitchen at the far end. The sink was filled with dishes and the floor covered in dead flies and mouse and rat shit. So were the plates of black, unidentifiable food on the table and the globes of the flameless lanterns.

"Looks like they left in a hurry," she said. "Probably during the bombing."

"It stinks in here," Will said.

"It's hot, too," Walt said. "I don't like this place."

"We don't have a choice," Adeline said. "We'll do the best we can with what we've got. But it is hot in here. Go outside, watch our wagon, and stay together."

After the boys left, she and Emil found the source of the stench—two dead rats—in the narrow single bedroom, which boasted a small window, two wooden bunks, and no bedding. The walls were littered with penciled numbers, equations, and geometry proofs she recognized from her school days. A forgotten ragged sweater and a ripped shirt hung from a nail on the back of the door.

"Well," Adeline said, taking in the total bleakness of their new home, "I guess we can only go up from here."

———

Emil tried to smile at her. But he had a growing conviction that this apartment and this building had been chosen for him and for his family by Major Haussmann to make them all suffer for what he'd done to the SS officer back in September 1941. And hadn't he seen Nikolas enter a much nicer building? Of course he had. Nikolas was being rewarded while Emil and his family were being punished.

"No running water," Adeline said when she went to the kitchen area.

"We'll have to find the community well," Emil said. "And latrine."

"This helps," Adeline said, reaching into the corner for a stubbly straw broom and dustpan. "Could you do that? Take the boys to find water? There are two buckets there in the corner. And before you go? Please open all the windows."

She took the scarf off her head and tied it around her nose and mouth. Emil grinned. When his wife got to cleaning, she was a whirlwind. After getting the windows open for her, he took the pails and went downstairs, seeing into Marie's and his parents' apartments, which were also miserable and austere.

Outside, Johann shook his head the moment he saw Emil.

"The windows leak," his father said. "The winter will be cold."

"I'm going to ask for other quarters tomorrow," Emil said.

"We're going to find water," Walt said. "Do you want to come, Opa?"

Johann thought about that. When Karoline started yelling about something inside, he nodded before fetching two tin buckets. In the street, they found a Pole who spoke enough German to direct them to a public well several blocks away.

By the time they'd gone there, waited in line, drawn their water, and returned to the third floor, Adeline had swept up most of the flies and rodent turds and dumped them out the window. She found lye bar soap beneath the stack of plates and pans in the sink. She and Emil used the sweater and torn shirt left behind as mops to scrub the floors and bunks with the soapy water.

Since the boys knew the way to the well, Emil gave them the job of resupplying the water. With the next two bucketsful, they washed the dishes, pots, and pans and then took inventory of the kitchen. Only then did they start to bring up the last of their belongings from the little wagon.

There was no fuel in their stove, but her mother's range produced a flame. That night she baked the last of the Zwieback rolls in her mother's apartment. They also made a soup from the dried foods and two bruised onions Adeline pilfered from the quarantine-camp kitchen before they left that morning.

They waited to eat until after the sun had gone down and with it the summer heat. In the lantern light, Adeline made them all join hands and give thanks to God for their deliverance from the Soviets and for the food and the roof over their heads.

She could tell that Emil didn't share her gratitude. He seemed to be putting on a brave face, but she knew he was brooding about their living conditions.

After the boys had fallen asleep, she said, "This isn't forever, my love."

"I know," he said, "but I didn't expect to leave one bad life for a worse one."

"We'll make a better life for ourselves. You don't expect it to just fall from the sky, do you? A better life?"

"I don't expect anything to fall from the sky. I'm willing to work for it."

"You work harder than anyone I know, Emil."

"Except you," he said, and took her in his arms. "My queen."

Adeline laughed. "A queen with her king and princes in their grand new palace."

"You forgot your green valley."

"Never."

They kissed and held each other for a long time. When they parted to get ready for bed, through the open windows, they saw lightning and heard thunder. They climbed into the lower bunk and held each other as the rain began to drum on the roof. Within minutes, Adeline could hear water dripping and spattering off the floor beside her.

"Nowhere to go but up," Emil said, and held her tighter.

———

The days passed. The boys attended school, made friends, and were soon out in the streets, playing long into the evening. Adeline negotiated the German ration system and managed to put decent meals on the table. When Emil sought out the VoMi officers to ask that they be moved to other quarters, he was denied and told he was being ungrateful for having been saved from the Judeo-Bolsheviks.

Adeline was assigned to work in the town bakery. Emil was put to work in the few fields that had been plowed and planted. He hoed for hours in the heat without complaint, glad for the familiar feel of the farm tool in his hands and the satisfaction he got from a job done right. As a boy, before his family was thrown off its lands and later when the Nazis returned them, he had toiled like this, long and hard, day after day. He liked it. This kind of brute labor suited him. It felt honest.

As he worked his hoe, Emil did his best not to think of Major Haussmann but did not always succeed. He kept flashing back to the fear that had seized him when Haussmann shot the first time, just missing his head. That memory was enough to get his heart tripping in his chest and adrenaline erupting through his veins, clouding his recall of all that had happened, especially after Haussmann's second shot.

What had the major said? Something about the clothes he'd been given and the place they were to live and how he should decide whether he wanted to be part of a Greater Germany. But he could not remember the exact way Haussmann had said it.

Did it matter? With each passing day, he cared less. Haussmann may have put them in a hellhole, but he was gone from their lives. In the meantime, Emil returned to old habits formed back in Ukraine under Stalin. He did everything he could not to attract undue attention. He did his job. He went home. He spent time with his family. He looked at the night sky and dreamed of the West, not as some fictional green paradise in Adeline's imagination, but as a place where he'd be left alone by governments to forge a new life through his own best efforts.

———

As July turned to August and September 1944 approached, however, someone noticed how hard and how diligently Emil was working in the fields. His name was Claude Wahl, a florid-faced Wehrmacht sergeant who'd been wounded near Minsk in July 1941. Soviet bomb shrapnel had broken Wahl's pelvis, giving him an awkward gait and rending him unfit for combat. He had been assigned to VoMi to work with the new ethnic German immigrants and to oversee the farms in the area surrounding the Wielun refugee camp.

Like Emil, Wahl was in his early thirties and had been raised on a farm. He also had a similar work ethic. One day as Emil was leaving the fields, Wahl approached him, talked to him, and then invited him for a beer at his home. Emil felt uncomfortable about the idea and tried to decline, but Wahl insisted.

"Why?" Emil asked.

"Because you are the hardest-working man in my fields, and I want to know how to get other men to work like you do."

Wahl lived on the same street as Nikolas in a nice house with running water and electricity, a far cry from the Martels' living arrangements. The disparity was so pronounced, it turned Emil resentful for his family's lot, and he wanted to leave almost immediately. Wahl would not hear of it, pouring pale beer from a jug into glass mugs.

After his long day in the field, the beer slid clean and cool down Emil's throat, and his opinion of Wahl improved slightly.

"I used to work in a brewery, and this is very good," he said. "Where is it made?"

Wahl beamed. "My father makes beer in the winter on our farm near Stuttgart. This is his hefeweizen beer. Made with wheat just for summer."

"Excellent," Emil said, and when Wahl got out a length of dried sausage and cheese and bread, he found that he liked his boss even more.

"So," Wahl said after Emil had taken slices of each that he washed down with more beer, "what does make a man work as hard as you?"

Emil didn't know how to respond to that. Hard work was all he'd ever known.

"First thing you think of," Wahl said, and grinned. "That's the answer. First thing."

"Starvation," Emil said.

The German's grin faded. "You have been starved?"

Emil nodded. "Twice. By Stalin."

Wahl was pensive for a moment. "And how does starving make you work hard?"

"When you can remember not having eaten in days and having no hope of eating tomorrow . . . when you can remember that feeling, you just work harder to make sure you never feel it again. After a while, it's just what you do."

Wahl thought about that and then smiled. "Well, I don't think I'm going to starve someone to get them to work harder someday down the road."

"Thank you for that," Emil said, and raised the beer toward him.

The German studied him. "Are you just surviving, or do you have a plan in life, Emil?"

"I don't understand."

"A plan. The life you lie awake at night and think about."

"I think about how I can protect my wife and family and what we are going to eat tomorrow and when we will sleep somewhere else."

"That's surviving."

"Then I am surviving, and that is a good thing."

"It is, but let me ask you: What do you think about when you stare at the stars?"

Emil stared at Wahl suspiciously. "How did you know I stare at the stars?"

"Doesn't anyone who has ever lived on a farm?"

Emil hesitated, not knowing how best to respond. But there was something about the man that he already trusted.

He said, "I want to have a time when I am older when I have enough to live without worrying about food or staying warm, and then I want to go fishing. Every day if I want."

"Fishing?" Wahl said, and smiled.

"I used to fish when I was a boy," Emil said. "It was a way to get food when the Communists weren't giving us any. But it was more than that. You never knew when the fish would come. There was . . . I don't know . . . mystery in it."

"I can see that," Wahl said. "But that's when you're an old man. What about now? What's next after you get out of this place?"

"I want to go west," he said, and immediately regretted it.

Wahl cocked his head to one side. "How far west?"

Emil wanted to change the subject but could already tell he'd hooked the German sergeant through the lip, and he wasn't shaking him free.

"As far as I can go," he said finally. "Across the ocean."

"Why? What do you think you'll find there?"

Emil knew his tongue had been loosened by beer and that he was already late for supper and that he'd already spoken too much. But he gazed straight into Wahl's eyes and said, "Freedom. Isn't that all any man wants when it comes right down to it?"

Wahl showed no response at first, his eyes fixed on Emil for several beats before he nodded. "That is correct. And as someone who has taken an interest in you, Herr Martel, I advise you not to repeat that part of your plan to anyone until this war is over."

———

Adeline was furious with Emil when he came home late, smelling of beer, and admitted to her that he'd told Wahl that he, a new immigrant to Hitler's Greater Germany, dreamed of going west, looking for freedom, and a place to fish.

"Are you crazy?" she shouted. "They'll throw us in a prison or worse!"

"We live in a prison," he shouted back. "Look at this place!"

"It's what we have," Adeline said, turning colder. "And if you want better, you should be thinking of keeping us safe, not telling the Germans, 'Thanks for the protection, but we want to go west to the Allies.'"

"I never said that," Emil said. "But you're right. It was foolish. I'll stay clear of Wahl and won't mention it again."

Two afternoons later, however, on August 25, 1944, Emil exited the fields, heading for home, only to find the gimpy sergeant waiting for him again.

"Come have another beer, Martel," Wahl said.

"Thank you, Sergeant, but I must—"

"Come. I have something to show you, something I think you'll find interesting."

Emil sighed and followed Wahl back to his house as the German told him of life on his own family farm and asked questions about Adeline and the boys. Even though Emil was consciously trying to keep his replies curt and vague, the sergeant had a way of making him want to talk openly.

In Wahl's kitchen, the routine was the same as before: beer, sausage, cheese, and bread. But instead of putting the food on a plate on the table, he put it on a cutting board and told Emil to take the beer mugs and to follow him. Emil hesitated, feeling fear. Was this some kind of trap?

Wahl went down a short hallway off the kitchen to a closed door and opened it with a key before turning on a light. He smiled at Emil. "You'll find this interesting."

Emil swallowed and followed Wahl. He entered the room as the sergeant set down the cutting board with the food on top of a metal table. Other than two chairs and a padlocked travel locker, the rest of the room was empty.

Emil thought of stories he'd heard of men back home being lured to their doom by men posing as friends who urged them to speak freely. These same men were tortured before they were sent to Siberia. Were the Nazis the same? Was this what he was facing for talking to Wahl?

"Why are we in here?" Emil asked, hearing the tremor in his voice when Wahl turned his back on him and crouched before the locker.

Wahl worked the lock and did not reply. Emil began to sweat and took a slug of the beer. "Please, Sergeant. What is this about?"

"The way west," the German said, and stood up, holding another box with steel ribbing. He undid the hasp and lifted the lid. "Have you ever listened to a shortwave?"

He removed a radio from the box and set it on the table near the food and beer.

Emil stared. "The SS said they were forbidden here. You won't get shot for having that?"

Wahl laughed. "I would if I had not been a Wehrmacht radioman for many years before the bomb got me. And there are times my superiors here need to contact their superiors in Warsaw or Berlin. But for tonight, no transmission."

Emil frowned. "What's transmission?"

"We can't talk over it," he said, plugging the radio in. "But we can listen."

Emil had never owned a shortwave, which had been forbidden under Stalin as well, so he watched with fascination as Wahl attached the radio to a speaker and then to a line that ran out the window to an antenna mounted on the roof. The sergeant threw a switch, and a red bulb glowed.

"What are we going to listen to?"

"What every man wants," Wahl said.

Chapter Twenty

Woo-wooing noises and harsh static poured from the speaker. The sergeant twisted knobs, and voices soon sounded out of the electric hiss, speaking languages Emil did not understand, a babble that unsettled him, made him aware of how little he knew of the greater world.

After several tries, the sergeant tuned in to a German male voice broadcasting from Berlin that described Nazi victories in France, Belgium, and Hungary where the führer's forces were heroically holding back Stalin's southern armies. Wahl turned the dial on the radio again, stopping at a language Emil did not understand or recognize.

"London," Wahl said, looking over at him. "BBC in English."

The sergeant twisted the dial ever so slightly, saying, "Now BBC German Service. Listen how different the news is from Berlin's version."

The BBC announcer was female, spoke perfect German, and went straight to the point, describing the liberation of Paris and Charles de Gaulle leading troops down the Champs-Élysées, as well as ongoing battles elsewhere in France and Italy, where despite fierce German resistance, the Allies were making significant advances. The broadcaster also talked about Romania's recent surrender to the Soviets and the Red Army's bombardment of Budapest, before shifting to news from the South Pacific.

Emil said, "It sounds like there is war everywhere."

"No, it sounds like Germany is losing," Wahl said, and held up his hands. "See, there, I said it: the Fatherland is losing, and the Allies are winning on almost every front. It's only a matter of time before Hitler gets squeezed between

Eisenhower and Stalin. It's only a matter of time before Berlin falls. And you and I need to be ready for it."

After leaving Wahl's house, Emil had so much to tell Adeline, he wanted to sprint home through the streets. His instinct and experience told him to slow down, to be just some refugee field hand overlooked or dismissed as unimportant by any and all authorities.

When he reached their building, however, Emil leaped up the stairs, pounded past the open doors of his parents' apartment and Marie's, where he could hear the twins crying, and on up the second flight of stairs and into their apartment where Adeline sat by herself at the kitchen table with her head down and her back to the door.

He shut the door behind him. "You won't believe what happened today."

Emil came around the front of her. She didn't look up. He crouched beside her and said, "I heard freedom today, Adella. The voice of it, anyway."

Adeline lifted her head and stared at him with bleary eyes that turned angry. "You've been drinking again. I can smell it."

"One beer," he said. "And you've been . . . crying?"

"Maybe I have. Aren't I allowed?"

He threw his hands up in the air. "Of course, you're allowed, but just listen a second. Where are the boys?"

She looked away, irritated. "Playing. I told them to be here before dark."

"Okay," he said. "We have a friend now. Sergeant Wahl."

Her expression turned incredulous, then hostile. "You don't know that. What if he is more than he seems? What if he is a member of the Gestapo, trying to expose you?"

Adeline was normally such a kind person Emil was taken aback by her tone. "He's not."

"How do you know?"

Emil swore her to tell no one, not her sister, or mother, or cousin, or acquaintance, and then described his second visit with Sergeant Wahl, his shortwave, and the news from the BBC German Service.

"Paris falling means Hitler is losing in the West," Emil said excitedly. "The Soviets have taken Romania, are bombing Budapest, and are nearing Poland. Germany is being squeezed, Adeline. They're losing."

"Why do you believe a radio?" she said dismissively. "I thought we learned to ignore anything said on the radio by a government."

"This was different," he insisted. "This came from the West, from England, where people are free to tell the truth. Wahl says that at some point the Wehrmacht will retreat to Berlin, and when they finally surrender, we want to get to the Americans or the British as fast as possible, or we'll be caught by the Soviets and . . ."

Adeline's anger was gone, but now she seemed preoccupied.

"Don't you see?" Emil said. "Please don't ignore me. Wahl sees it, too."

She pivoted her head to look at him blankly. "Sees what?"

"The West, Adella—freedom, what we want, the Allies—they're coming at us! We need to be ready to go to them, or the Soviets will get us from behind, and we could all be going to Siberia or worse."

Adeline blinked a few times, absorbing what he'd said before her hands fell to the table. "Okay. I surrender. When do we go on this suicide mission?"

"It's not a suicide mission," Emil said, smiling as he sat across from her and held her hands, which were cold despite the late-summer heat. "That is why Sergeant Wahl is so important to us. We will know when the time is exactly right to run, because he can listen to where the Allies are on the BBC German Service every night."

Adeline shook her head as if clearing cobwebs. "Why would he do that?"

"Because he is going west, too," Emil said. "He will help us if he can."

"But why would he do that? Why even talk to you in the first place?"

"He said he just saw me working harder than anyone else and wanted to talk to me about it. There are some good people left in the world, Adeline. Even among the Germans."

"I hope so," she said. "When does your friend think we'll go? Tomorrow? Next week? Before winter?"

"Wahl says the war could be over before Christmas, and we should plan on traveling as soon as the Allies get across the Rhine River, closing on Berlin."

Adeline closed her eyes a moment and then opened them and sighed. "At least, I don't have to think about it anytime soon."

"You do need to think about it. You need to—"

"No, Emil, I don't!" she shouted. "*You* need to think about it! I need to think about other things, thank you very much!"

Emil gaped at her. Adeline rarely raised her voice. His wife could be firm, but she almost never shouted.

"Why are you yelling at me?" he demanded.

Adeline tried to glare at him but looked lost and then burst into tears. "I don't know. I shouldn't . . . but I . . ."

He went over, and she stood up into his arms, sobbing. "I shouldn't care, but I do. I care, Emil. I care. I care. I care."

"What is going on? Care about what? Care about who?"

It took several moments for her to compose herself and step back from him, sniffling.

"I was cleaning this morning. I discovered something."

———

Adeline went to the corner where the broom and dustpan stood. She set them aside before putting the toe of her shoe on the floorboard closest to the rear wall. The floorboard rose enough to allow her to lift it.

Reaching into the space between the floor joists, she came up with a thick, dog-eared book with a cracked and burnished dark leather cover. "It's a Jewish Bible. I think," she said, and then opened the book to show him writing that baffled him.

"What language is this?" he asked.

"Hebrew," she said, tearing up again. "I saw one like this in Mrs. Kantor's house back in Birsula. She called it a *mikra*, I think."

Emil frowned. "But why are you crying?"

She wiped at her tears with the sleeve of her blouse. "I went to the well for water to wash clothes afterward, and I was talking to one of the Polish women who speaks German, and I told her what I'd found under the floorboards and . . ."

Adeline looked lost again. "She asked where we lived. I told her, and she said this whole building used to be Jewish. Then she said that every refugee apartment in Wielun used to belong to Jews. Every single one. And do you know what else she said they owned, the Jews?"

Emil was feeling shaken, though he sensed the answer. "What?"

Adeline lifted the fabric of the sleeve of her blouse as if it were thorny.

"Our clothes," she said, tears streaming down her face. "She said they made all the Jews take off their clothes before they were killed, and we were given their clothes after they were boiled clean. The woman looked like she wanted to spit on me for it and then walked away."

That hit Emil hard, made him recall multiple headlights cutting the twilight.

Adeline said, "Don't you understand, Emil? We're wearing the clothes of good people like Mrs. Kantor and Esther. Maybe the good people who lived right here. People who loved and had children and—"

She choked. "It makes us a part of it, doesn't it? Their hatred? Their murdering? I feel so dirty and ashamed, Emil. I don't know what to do."

At that, Emil had to sit down. His head ached from Sergeant Wahl's beer and now swirled with guilt and regret and hatred. He never asked to wear a dead man's clothes. He never asked that the SS be in Dubossary when he'd had to fetch building supplies. He never asked Haussmann to single him out and . . .

"Emil!" Adeline shouted. "I need you to listen to me!"

"I am listening to you!" he thundered back before lowering his voice. "I hear you, Adeline. You are not part of what they've done. It makes my skin crawl that these are the clothes we've been given. If I could, I'd strip them off and buy others, but I can't and neither can you."

"What do we do? I mean, we're living with ghosts all around us, Emil. We're wearing their clothes and sleeping in their beds. How do we live with that?"

"We won't for long. Until we can buy new clothes, we thank the ghosts for their clothes and their beds, and we go on. If things were reversed, we'd want them to do so. Life goes on, Adeline. They were gone before we got here. It's not like we threw them out ourselves."

They heard the boys laughing and shouting, their feet pounding up the staircase. Emil got a cloth, dipped it in the bucket, and handed it to Adeline. She washed the tears off her face before breaking into a smile and throwing her arms open to Walt and Will who burst into the flat, flushed and sweaty and happy as only young boys can be.

Adeline kept her focus on her family but tried not to ignore whose clothes she wore and whose bunk she lay down on at night. There were times in the weeks and months that followed, however, when she almost forgot, and the clothes seemed hers and not a ghost's, and their apartment belonged more to the living than the dead.

Rese returned to their lives at the end of September. Praeger, the same medic who'd taken her to the hospital, brought her home. Johann was happy, whereas Karoline displayed little emotion when her daughter arrived in a wheelchair, blanket across her lap, glassy-eyed and much older in Adeline's view. Rese seemed more resigned than happy to see her parents and the rest of the family, until the boys came around the corner. Then she got a devilish look on her face.

"Want to see my legs?" she said.

Walt didn't seem to want to, but Will walked right up to Rese and said, "I do."

Rese threw back the blanket to reveal she was wearing artificial legs. "Peggy," she said, pointing to her left leg. "The right's Hopper. They're different lengths, so I need to keep track. Hopper's the longer one."

"Can you walk on Peggy and Hopper?" Walt asked, interested now.

"With crutches," Praeger said. "She can even climb stairs."

"She'll have to," Johann said.

"She's ready," the medic said, and then crouched by Rese's side. "Time for me to go. I am on duty tonight."

"Will you come back?" she asked, acting as if she feared his answer. "It's a long way from Lodz."

"It's not that far, Rese," Praeger said. "Besides, how could I stay away from your beauty and humor?"

Rese blushed before saying, "You'll leave my medicine?"

"Right here," he said, handing her a pouch. "Make it last. And here are your crutches. The wheelchair should go upstairs with her. She needs to be up on the new legs slowly at first, and every day she should practice."

Praeger left then. Rese received a round of applause getting out of the wheelchair and climbing the stairs less with the crutches than the banister. Johann brought the wheelchair up, and she sat in it, sweat gushing off her forehead as she looked around.

"Who'd we piss off to get this place?" Rese asked.

In the month that followed, Adeline tried to visit with her mother and sister and Rese and Marie at least once a day.

Lydia seemed happier now that they were settled into their quarters, as depressing as they were. And Malia always seemed happier, or more amused anyway, when she was living with their mother. After the mule had kicked her, Lydia had held Malia for hours on end, telling her she was going to live and come back to her. Adeline had always understood their bond was special, and accepted it as best a daughter could.

Marie looked exhausted and grateful whenever Adeline knocked on her door and offered to help with the twins, who were nearly six months old now. Her cousin's emotions swung whenever she talked about her missing husband, the surgeon.

"How do I even find him?" Marie fretted and cried one day. "How will he find me?"

Adeline remembered Mrs. Kantor's advice and said, "You have to trust in God that you will be brought back together. Crazier stories have happened, Marie."

"Tell me one."

Adeline told her about Corporal Gheorghe and Stalingrad.

"You believed him?" Marie asked.

"I did. I do."

Adeline never knew what kind of mood she'd face taking Rese for walks, either with her artificial legs and crutches or pushing her sister-in-law in the wheelchair so she could get air. There were days when Rese seemed content, smiling with glassy eyes when Adeline came for her, talking about a future when they were alone. But there were more days when Rese was fully in her misery, berating her mother and father and Emil and God for having saved her.

"I should be dead," she'd say over and over again. "Why live like this? No one will ever want a no-legged woman. I'm useless, Adeline."

"Not to me," Adeline said. "You're brave and alive because you are a fighter by nature like your brother. He gets knocked down by life and gets right back up. You're the same way."

"I'm not, and I hate my life, our life. Have we had one good day in our lives? Any of us?"

"I've had many wonderful days in my life."

"Name one."

"The day Walt was born. The day Will was born. The day I met Emil. The day I found a chicken for Mrs. Kantor. You will have days like these, Rese. I know from experience that the shadows can't last forever. Eventually good fortune will come your way."

———

Adeline tried not to think about Emil's plan to run toward the war when it came close enough and let herself be consumed by her work and her family. But then, out of nowhere, she'd remember the ghosts in her clothes and the apartment, and that would start another cycle of guilt and despair. After a while, these circles of thought seemed to link up and become a figure eight in her mind: guilt of the past arching into anxiety about the future over and over again until she'd think about their food stocks and winter coming, and that would set off another figure eight of starvation memories twisting and spiraling into her singular abject fear of having to go hungry again, to starve again.

Luckily, Emil was able to skim enough fruit, vegetables, and grain from the harvest to supplement their food rations, which were getting smaller each and every week. Emil also went to Wahl's house several times a week to listen to the shortwave and to look at the maps with the sergeant, keeping track of the Allies' positions. They heard about the first V-2 rocket hitting London and the fear that Hitler's superweapon would turn the tide. But then the Allies liberated Luxembourg and launched Operation Market Garden with paratroopers attempting to take the important bridges crossing the Rhine.

Over Wahl's radio, they heard Hitler's call for all men from age sixteen to sixty to join the Home Guard to fight the Allies to the last drop of German blood and about battles all along the "Siegfried Line," the western wall of Nazi fortifications. On October 21, 1944, Emil rushed home to tell Adeline about the taking of Aachen, the first city in the Fatherland to fall.

Emil and Wahl thought for sure they would all be packing and leaving within days. But German resistance proved fierce. More than ten thousand Allied paratroopers died, and another six thousand were captured in Market Garden, and the Rhine did not fall, dashing all hope that the war would be over by Christmas.

During this time, Rese went through a series of wild mood swings where she was her normal caustic self, then sleepy and withdrawn, and then howling with laughter, followed by days where she was deeply bitter, lashing out at whichever closest family member was in range.

"Why did this happen to me?" she asked over and over again.

It wasn't until the end of November, however, that she turned agitated, violent, and then brutally ill. It took Marie and her nursing skills to figure out that Rese, who'd been left to self-administer her medicines, had become addicted to painkillers. Now that her supplies had dwindled, she was going through withdrawal. Marie contacted Praeger, and he sent a new supply of pills to Marie so she could administer them to Rese and begin to wean her off the opiates.

In early December 1944, the north winds blew hard and came laden with snow. The icy gale found every crack and seam in the building, which whistled day and night. They used whatever they could find to stuff and chink the cracks and huddled around their coal stoves for warmth. Emil fell ill with chills, a low-grade fever, and a cough that would not quit. By December 12, he was weak, hacking up mucus, and spiking fevers that had Adeline and the boys frightened because during them he would often scream out at terrors unseen and then cry and moan in inexplicable shame and regret. More than once, Adeline thought she heard Emil say he was doomed and there was nothing he could do about it.

Chapter Twenty-One

In the nightmares and hallucinations provoked by the soaring fevers, Emil traveled back in time and faced torments he had spent years avoiding, denying, and then crated away in the deepest recesses of his mind. But as the refugee lay sweating, twitching, and twisting in his bunk in Wielun, the screws and slats of those crates failed, and the events inside broke free.

———

September 15, 1941
Dubossary, Transnistria

On his way to buy roofing supplies for the house he was building for Adeline and the boys in Friedenstal, Emil had driven his horses into town by a back route, a two-track shortcut that brought him to the south end of Dubossary around three o'clock that afternoon. It began to rain almost as soon as he'd arrived at the lumberyard south of town, and he knew the shortcut would now be too muddy and slick for his horses to navigate while pulling a load in the rain and the dark. Leaving the lumberyard, Emil decided to take the northern route through Dubossary. It was a much longer way back to Friedenstal, but the roads would be better.

He had not been in Dubossary since before his father was taken to Siberia and his family was thrown off its land. As he rode through the town, he was surprised at how much he remembered and how much he did not. Near the town center, Emil saw a high barbed-wire fence he did not recall around several blocks of buildings and two SS sentries guarding a gate in the fence.

Beyond the town limits, all traffic slowed at a German checkpoint. When he reached the front of the line, he showed his papers to an SS soldier, who studied them.

"Are you from Dubossary?"

"Friedenstal," Emil said. "It's about thirty kilometers from here. A farming village."

"Why are you not in the Wehrmacht?"

"I am the only able-bodied man left in my entire family," he said. "The VoMi decided it was better for Germany to have me back on my farm, growing wheat for the Fatherland."

The soldier looked skeptical. "Have you not enrolled in *Selbstschutz*?"

"I don't know what that is."

"A home guard to protect your village against the Romanian swine. And a way to show us that you are a true German and a useful person."

"I'll look into it," Emil said, expecting the sentry to send him along.

Instead, the soldier glared at him. "Bring your horses and wagon over there by those trees. They'll be watched."

"Please, my wife is expecting me. We have two young sons and—"

"This is an order," the sentry barked. "Bring your wagon over there with those others. They will be watched."

"Watched? Why?"

"Because you'll be busy elsewhere," the sentry said coldly. "Proving your worth and allegiance to the Fatherland."

———

Emil did as he was told and led Oden and Thor and the wagon over by two army lorries and several other wagon-and-horse teams tied up at a fence near a two-track path that ran north. The rain had stopped. Clouds broke in the west, revealing a sinking, bloodred sun. The air was cooling, so he put on his jacket and climbed down to hobble the horses. When Emil stood to join several other civilian men there, the stuff of night terrors entered his life for the first time.

He strode up in a dark uniform and said, "I am Hauptsturmführer Haussmann, *Einsatzkommando 12, Einsatzgruppen D*. I understand you wish to demonstrate your loyalty to Germany and to our führer, Adolf Hitler."

Emil wanted to say he did not wish to do anything except go home but nodded along with the other men.

"And I assume none of you has love for the Jew and the Bolshevik?"

The question made Emil uneasy, made him think of Adeline risking her life for that woman, Esther, back in Pervomaisk, and how much his wife had loved her employer in Birsula, Mrs. Kantor. But after the other men shook their heads no, Emil shook his head as well.

Gesturing to the two-track, Haussmann said, "Follow this way north three kilometers. You'll be met by other officers, and I will be following you out there shortly."

"When will we be coming back, Captain?" Emil asked. "I have a wife and sons waiting for me at home."

Haussmann studied him closely for the first time. "I don't give a damn about your wife or your sons. You're in for a busy night, farm boy."

The two-track ran out through fields of ripe wheat awaiting harvest and then climbed into bluff-and-ravine country that in the last red rays of light might have been called beautiful on any other day. The sun set. Twilight was deepening when Emil heard the first shots cracking at a distance, a spurt and then a volley, another spurt and then a second volley. He did not like the sound of the gunfire and wanted to turn back.

He could see several of the other men wished to reverse course as well. But that SS captain said he would be following them out on this same path shortly. Emil supposed he could take off and loop around the path. But would they let him just get his horses and wagon and leave? His gut said no. His gut said they'd probably kill him.

Emil kept walking into the gloaming, smelling the good clean scent of the wind after the rain, and hearing more shots and then shouts and cries that with every step closer became the voices of innocence screaming for mercy.

Emil's feet felt leaden. His breath had turned shallow, and his heart hammered in his chest. *They're shooting Jews and Bolsheviks, aren't they? That's why he asked. Just like Esther said they did in Pervomaisk. Wait, are we next? Are they sending us out here to be shot?*

In the two months the Nazis had occupied Ukraine, Emil had heard of other *Volksdeutsche* being beaten and shot as examples of what happened when locals did not follow their orders. He decided to make a run for it, loop back, and take his chances getting the horses and the wagon. But when he lagged to the rear of the group and started to turn, headlights slashed across him from behind and back toward the fields.

———

Emil felt gut-punched. That had to be Captain Haussmann coming in a vehicle behind them up the two-track. If he tried to run now, he'd be seen. Tasting acid at the back of his throat, he pressed on with the others, up and over a rise where several hundred meters ahead he saw more headlight beams cutting the deepening twilight from left to right. Scrub brush grew on either side of the trail now. A steep hillside rose to his right. The truck headlights appeared to be aimed at something behind it.

As he got closer, Emil saw that the headlights came from six big Wehrmacht trucks parked parallel to each other and thirty meters apart. Beyond the vehicles, in shadows near the far periphery of the headlight glare, there were vague, wavy charcoal forms moving. More guns went off, close enough to make him startle, cringe, and slow his pace when he realized the shooting was all happening on the other side of that hill where all the headlights were pointed.

The vehicle behind them came roaring up. Its headlamps hit Emil from behind and lit up the terrain ahead, revealing SS soldiers milling about the rears of the trucks, and casting aside the shadows beyond them. The wavy charcoal forms had become distinct people now, hunched over, some clothed and others naked, men, women, and children shuffling behind that sidehill toward the darkest edge of night.

"You there, *Volksdeutscher*," Captain Haussmann called. "Climb up in the back. We'll take you the rest of the way."

Emil did not want to get up in the open back of the vehicle. He wanted to get around the truck and flee for his life. But fear of a bullet between the shoulder blades stopped him, goaded him to climb up behind the cab of the smaller lorry with the other men.

The truck went into gear, drove across the last hundred and fifty meters, its headlights cutting deeper into the northern shadows, revealing wave after wave of despondent, weeping people trudging eastward under the watchful eyes of SS soldiers bearing machine guns on the bluff above them.

The truck rounded the hill and pulled over almost immediately into a cut in its north flank, out of the headlight glare. Emil stared in horror over the roof of the cab, seeing husbands holding tight to their wives, mothers leading their terrified children by the hands, and six older men with long white beards waving in the westerly breeze, their backs to the rim of a deep ravine that dropped away into darkness.

Eight SS soldiers were reloading their rifles and pistols about thirty meters from the Jews. There were five of these eight-man units strung out close to the long rim, all of them facing lines of trembling and praying people, some standing to face the guns, some away on their knees, all flanked by the long line waiting to perish.

Please, God, Emil prayed. *Don't let this happen. Don't let them do this.*

A shorter SS officer rushed up the moment Captain Haussmann climbed from the cab. He saluted Haussmann, said, "Heil Hitler." Haussmann returned the salute and said, "How many to report, Captain Drexel?"

"We just began, Captain Haussmann."

"How many so far?"

"One hundred and eighty-seven."

There was an obvious rivalry between the two men, but then the shooting started, and the mothers and their children and the young and the old and the lovers and the loved and the lonely and the lost and the families clinging and the six old men with wispy beards blowing in the westerly breeze all jerked with bullet impacts before crumpling and falling backward into the ravine like so many dolls blown over. Up and down the firing line, from one execution squad to the next, the rain of lead went on until no one at the rim was left standing and Emil could not gape in horror any longer. He rested his forehead on the roof of the cab, every muscle in his body shaking uncontrollably before he felt his insides boil. He lurched and puked over the side of the truck. Several of the other men were vomiting as well.

When the shooting subsided and the crying and wails for mercy began again, Haussmann barked, "All of you: down out of there. You have work to do! *Raus!*"

"I didn't hurl," said a younger guy with an oily beard and a filthy jacket and cap. He smiled, revealing a missing lower tooth. "I want to see more of them Jews die."

"Name?" Captain Drexel purred.

"Helmut."

"Helmut, you're just the sort of eager young man we're looking for in the new Greater Germany," Drexel said. "We will see how you all do tonight. If we are satisfied, we will recommend you to the VoMi for paid assignments in the future."

Helmut grinned at Emil, who could barely climb down and felt imbalanced when he did. The ground seemed to shift under his feet, and everything around him looked distorted.

"Four of you will prove yourselves with Captain Drexel," Haussmann said. "And the other four will come with me."

Helmut immediately went to Haussmann's side as did two others. But four had gone to Drexel, and Emil had no choice but to join Haussmann.

More Jews were being led to the ravine. Children were whimpering. Men and women cried piteously. He could hear them, but he could not look at them.

Please, God, don't make me a part of this, he prayed. *And please don't make me kill anyone. I'm begging you. I am many things, but I am not a murderer.*

"You will each be assigned to a unit," Haussmann said. "You are expected to do whatever is asked of you until we are finished for the night. And then you can go home."

New victims were being led or dragged to the edge of the ravine. Haussmann retrieved a Luger from the truck cab and then walked them to the closest of the shooting units. The eight SS men were grimly loading or cleaning weapons, lit cigarettes dangling from several of their lips. The men smelled unnaturally foul to Emil, as if their hearts and souls had been so corrupted by mass murder that the invisible, evil pus of it was seeping out of their skin and pouring from their lungs. When one of them glanced their way, Emil saw the deadest eyes he'd ever seen in a living man. Then the wind shifted, swung one hundred and eighty degrees, due out of the east, bringing with it the stench of bodies rotting in the ravine.

Emil fought not to gag. *How many are down in there already?*

"Who will prove his loyalty to the führer first?" Haussmann asked, holding up the Luger and waving it.

"I'll go," Helmut said.

Haussmann ignored him, looked at Emil, and held out the pistol by the barrel. "You first, farm boy. Show us you are someone the Reich can count on."

God, please, no. Anything but that.

Emil did not know what to do, or how to reply, so he didn't move. Haussmann's face turned to stone, and he walked over, the butt of the Luger still extended before him, until he was directly in front of Emil.

"I said, take the Luger."

Emil had never held a gun in his life and reached for it awkwardly, gingerly, surprised at the weight of the loaded pistol in his hand when the Nazi let go.

"There," Haussmann said.

The SS captain took a step back and then gestured toward several Jews being led in front of the execution squad, including a young man who knelt by two little girls, who were hugging him and crying. The young man stared defiantly through his tears at the men, preparing for his death.

"Those three Yids," Haussmann said, pointing right at them. "Kill them. Now."

Emil saw the captain as if he were down a long tunnel and heard him speaking a language he did not understand. He looked at the Luger and then up at Haussmann, who said, "Come on, farm boy. Show us what kind of blood runs in you."

Please, God. Don't make me. I . . . These people are good. They're innocent.

"Shoot them!" Haussmann shouted.

Time seemed to slow. As if in a trance, Emil understood they were all watching his every move. He glanced to the young man and the two little girls in his arms.

The young man was staring at Emil now. "Don't do it," he said. "Please, sir, you know this is wrong. You know it is!"

"Kill them!" Haussmann shouted.

Emil looked down at the Luger again . . . and felt hot, salty sweat roll down his forehead and into his eyes, stinging them, blinding him.

He panicked, took a step, and felt himself fall into an unseen hole or shaft of some kind. As he plunged, Emil screamed, "I can't! I can't . . ."

Chapter Twenty-Two

December 23, 1944
Wielun, Poland

Adeline dipped the washcloth in the icy bucket of water as Emil thrashed and sweated after burning up yet again with fever. He moaned, "I can't. I can't . . . see."

"Then open your eyes, Papa," Will said from the doorway as Adeline returned the cold cloth to Emil's fevered brow.

"Shhhh," Adeline said, looking at her younger son sternly. "Your father could—"

"He opened his eyes!" Will yelled, pointing past her. "Look, Mama!"

She did look, and it was true. Emil's eyes were fluttering open, glazed, and trying to focus on her. At last, with a thick tongue, he said, "Sick."

"Yes, dear, you've been very sick for a long time," she soothed. "Eleven days. But here you are. There's no stopping you now, is there?"

He smiled and closed his eyes. "Eleven days?"

"It's Christmas Eve tomorrow, but I feel like I've opened the best present already."

Adeline got him hot tea and some thin soup, not having it in her to tell him that the rations had been cut almost completely the week before. She'd set aside enough flour and sugar to make cookies and a last decent dinner for Christmas, but after that, they had only about a week's worth of provisions left.

The Martels held an impromptu service the next evening with the entire clan crammed into the upper two apartments and the hallway between. Because it was Malia's birthday, they all sang to her before Adeline read the Nativity from the book of Luke in the family Bible and gave thanks that they were all still alive when the war and the trek had taken so many. Emil had listened from his sickbed at first, but then insisted on getting up when Sergeant Wahl came by to give them two large bottles of beer.

Wahl seemed appalled at their living conditions but sat down with them and drank. While Adeline, Malia, and Lydia sang old songs and taught them to the boys, he told Emil about the battle raging in the Ardennes Forest of France where snowstorms had put the Allies on the defensive after eight days of brutal combat. The sergeant also said that he was going to Lodz for two weeks but would be back earlier if he heard the tide of the war had turned toward Nazi collapse.

Later that night, after putting the boys to bed, Adeline wrapped a blanket around Emil and kissed his forehead. "You scared me," she said. "I thought I'd lost you."

"Never," he said, rubbing her arm. "Never ever."

———

With sixty-kilometer-an-hour wind gusts, an arctic blast hit Europe on New Year's Eve. It would be the start of two of the coldest months on record. Temperatures in western Poland dove to thirty-one below zero Celsius. The entire building where the Martels lived shook in the gales. Windchills approached minus forty-five and overwhelmed their individual coal stoves. The four families took to crowding into Adeline and Emil's apartment because it faced south out of the wind. They used their combined coal rations to keep a fire burning hot.

But their food stocks were almost drained, and Adeline was unsure whether new rations were coming anytime soon. On January 2, 1945, Will went down with the fever. The following day, Malia did and then Rese. Emil relapsed on the morning of the fourth.

On the evening of January 6, 1945, Adeline gave the last of the vegetable broth to Emil and Will and the last of the bread to Walt, who had also fallen ill. There was not enough for her to eat. After talking to her mother and her mother-in-law, she went to bed tired, hungry, and determined to go in search of food in the morning.

When she awoke, it was snowing lightly and well below zero. She put on every stitch of clothing she had, took a canvas bag, and went out into the bitter cold. With the hunger building again in her stomach and the memory of real starvation echoing from her past, Adeline went to the edge of town where an SS soldier stopped her and asked her where she was going.

"To Lodz," she said. "To find medicine and food. My sons are sick and starving."

"Where did you get money?" he asked suspiciously.

"I'm going to sell my wedding ring. And my mother's. And my mother-in-law's."

He must have heard the desperate emotion in her voice, because he flagged down the next truck heading north. When she told the driver that her family was sick and starving and she was going to Lodz, he was kind and let her sit up front in the cab.

————

Two hours later, the driver dropped her at the outskirts of Lodz, and she walked into the small city, asking where she might buy food on the black market. She was directed to a shop nearby and went there directly, finding food on the shelves, mostly staples, but more than enough to keep the family all alive.

The shopkeeper, however, refused to take Adeline's wedding ring or Karoline's or Lydia's as payment, deriding them as "worthless."

"Bring me Reichsmarks," he said. "Or better yet, bring me gold."

The next shopkeeper said the same thing and the one after that and the fourth and the fifth. She even went in desperation to the VoMi office, seeking to inquire about rations, only to find it locked and dark.

Walking away, Adeline felt like that fallen leaf that had caught her attention the day the trek began: dried and curled brown, blown by the wind on some strange, haphazard journey that she now saw as futile and meaningless. Her family was destitute. Her husband was sicker than she'd ever seen. And her boys were facing starvation, something she'd vowed would never happen. She felt angry and helpless in one breath and terribly alone in the next. Her throat swelled, and she swallowed at it, determined to forge on without admitting defeat. She knew no one in Lodz except Rese's friend, Praeger, the medic. But how could she find him? She couldn't. It would take too much energy. Adeline knew how hunger worked, the stages of starvation and how they sapped you. Before she lost more energy, she was better off getting a ride back to Wielun to tell everyone that they were going to go without food for a while.

All at once, an overwhelming mix of raw emotions began to well up through Adeline. They made her feel small and discarded by life, displaced, landless, refugeed, and as worthless as the wedding rings she carried. Her heart began to bump and to ache. She got dizzy, and the crown of her head felt hot beneath her scarves, and then she simply couldn't go on. She stopped there in the middle of the street, flurries hitting her face, and gazed up at the leaden sky. She raised her arms and more than prayed. Afire with anguish and desperate love that felt pumped from the very depths of her soul, Adeline beseeched God for aid for her family.

"Please, help me, Lord," she whispered. "I don't know where to go. I don't know what to do. Please, we've come so far. We've been through so much. It cannot have been for nothing. We cannot have been people who were supposed to come this far, only to die. I don't even have grass to give my sons!"

A lorry beeped its horn behind her. She jumped, her heart slamming in her chest, and looked back at the driver who leaned out his window.

"Get the hell out of the road, lady," he shouted. "Do you want to get killed or something?"

Quaking inside, Adeline hurried out of the way, and the truck went past, the driver shaking his head at her stupidity.

———

More lost than she'd ever been and feeling like the weight of the world was now centered between her shoulder blades, Adeline started back through the center of Lodz, past several of the black-market food shops that had turned her down. The snow had stopped falling but still swirled on a stiffening wind. Overhead, the gray clouds were thinning and in places were streaked with pale rose strings that seemed to curve and laze as the late-day sun fought for control of the winter sky.

Adeline ignored the empty pit in her stomach as she neared the far end of the market area, consumed by a whirlwind of questions. *How will I find a ride south with no money before darkness falls? How will I tell Emil and the boys that I have nothing for them? How can I possibly go—?*

A woman with her coat sleeve raised to block the swirling snow hurried out of the first shop Adeline had gone into earlier. She ran right into Adeline and sent them both sprawling in the street.

"I'm so sorry," the woman said in German, scrambling around on her hands and knees to help Adeline up and then to retrieve the bag she'd dropped. "I didn't see you."

"It was my fault," Adeline said. "I wasn't looking where I was going and—"

The woman raised her head to face Adeline. There was instant confusion on both their parts as they struggled to place each other, in the snow, years later, more than twelve hundred kilometers from their last chance meeting. But then they did recognize each other, and they were astonished.

"Adeline?" Esther said. "Is that really you?"

Nodding and bursting into tears, Adeline threw her arms around Mrs. Kantor's friend. "You were sent to me. I had no one else to turn to, and you were sent to me."

———

Twenty minutes later, Adeline was in Esther's large, nicely appointed flat on the fourth floor of a beautiful building, sitting in front of a stove well-hopped with coal and burning fiercely. On their walk and despite her hunger, Adeline had wanted to know how Mrs. Kantor's friend had gotten from Pervomaisk, Ukraine, to Lodz, Poland, but Esther had reminded Adeline in a whisper that her name was Ilse and that she was to stay quiet until they reached her home.

Now, as Esther boiled water for tea and got out fresh bread and two cold cooked sausages, she explained that with the forged identity documents Adeline had helped her secure, Esther received a slot on one of the first protected treks heading west.

"Which is why you have such a nice home?"

"Among other things," Esther said, setting the hot tea before her. "I hate this place, really. In some ways, it's a prison of memories that are not my own."

It was a cryptic thing to say, but Adeline understood. "Other Jews lived here before you."

Esther cocked her head in reappraisal. "Yes. How did you know that?"

"It is the same where we live. I'm wearing their clothes."

"So am I," she replied, and then, as she watched Adeline eat, Esther described coming to Lodz when the ghetto still housed seventy thousand Jews. She would walk by there at times, hear the Jews speaking Yiddish, and want to go to them.

"But I didn't dare," she said, gazing off, haunted more than sad. "Earlier this year, as more refugee treks started to leave the East, the Nazis began to empty the Lodz ghetto. Tens of thousands of them were put on trains in August. They're all gone now."

Tears dripped down her cheeks. "I've lived in their clothes and their homes, torn apart and guilty at first because I knew what became of them, and I kept wondering why I had been saved and not them. But then I saw it differently, defiantly, you know? I had fooled them, the Nazis. I was a Jew; I am a Jew living right beneath their . . ."

She laughed, dropped her head, and shook it.

Tens of thousands? Adeline thought. "You're sure they're all dead?"

"They haven't come back," Esther said. "Do you want more to eat before you go?"

Adeline declined and then got out the wedding rings. "I know they're not much, but could you buy them for Reichsmarks or gold? Then I can bring food back to my family. They're all sick and hungry and . . ."

Esther pushed her hand back, shook her head. "I can't take those, and I won't."

With that, she got up and left the room. Adeline felt horrid; she'd offended or imposed upon the woman somehow.

Esther returned with a wad of Reichsmarks and handed them to Adeline. "This is a debt I'm glad to repay. That should carry you for a while."

Adeline stared at the cash, dumbfounded. She had never held that much money in her life. "I can't take this. It's too much. What will you do?"

"I'm fine," she said. "I have more, and gold, too. I'd spend that money sooner than later if I were you. From what I've heard, the Allies will soon break through the western lines in France. Within weeks, they'll be in Berlin, and Reichsmarks might become useless. You should go now. The black-market stores close at six o'clock, and I have a visitor coming. If you can't find a way south tonight, Adeline, you are more than welcome to return around seven thirty, spend the night with me, and go home in the morning."

"Oh," Adeline said, still feeling weak despite the food and looking regretfully at the fire but getting up. "Thank you. Maybe I will. If that's okay?"

"It's more than okay. Buy your family food, and I'll see you in a couple of hours."

Feeling far better than she had when Esther ran into her, Adeline put her coat back on and her scarf and mittens and left with her empty bag over her shoulder. The flat adjoined an open stairwell. Adeline climbed down the first flight, noticing the echoes her footsteps made, when an older German officer hurried up the stairs and past her. As she descended the second flight of stairs, she heard three sharp raps on a door above her. Adeline paused a moment, heard a door open, and swore she heard him say, *"Guten Abend, Ilse-Schätzchen."*

———

The door shut. Adeline hurried down the last stairs and out into the bitter cold, thinking, *Who am I to judge how Esther manages to survive when she is one of the targets of a war?*

She returned to the first shop of the day and began grabbing bulk items off the shelf and putting them on the counter—flour, sugar, salt, yeast, dried sausage, fresh sausage, dried eggs, dried milk, three bars of chocolate—until the clerk went back and returned with the shopkeeper who'd told her the rings were worthless.

"I hope you have Reichsmarks or gold," he said, eyeing her load. "And a lot."

"Reichsmarks," she said. "And I have a lot."

"Yeah?" the shopkeeper said skeptically. "Where'd you get them?"

"The other side of town," she said, raising her chin. "I found a merchant there who knows the value of fine jewelry. He called our rings 'priceless' and gave me what I asked for them."

With that, she pulled out the wad of bills, paused to let the clerk and shopkeeper gape a little, and then said, "How much for it all?"

———

Feeling more than a little guilty that she was about to enjoy another meal and sleep in a warm, cozy place while her family suffered, Adeline knocked on Esther's door at half past seven.

A few moments later, Esther opened it warily, but then saw Adeline and smiled.

"I'm glad you came back," she said with a slight slur as she opened the door. She was in her robe. "The roads must be horrible and—"

Esther laughed, clapped and pointed at the two bulging bags Adeline carried. "You bought out the store!"

"Thanks to you," Adeline said. "You've saved us."

She went in, set her bags down, and hugged Esther as she was about to light a cigarette.

"Oh dear," she said, hugging Adeline back. "And you saved me, and we all save ourselves every day, somehow. That's why we're survivors, Adeline. That's why we're still here. Now, go over by the fire and get warm again."

Adeline let her go, felt a little awkward, but smiled and went over by the stove.

Esther lit her cigarette, took a drag, and plucked an empty wine bottle off the table before disappearing into the kitchen. She returned a few minutes later with another bottle of wine, cheese, and more bread and dried sausage.

"I'm going to feed you at least twice more before you go," she said. "That way, you'll be strong enough to care for Emil and your precious boys."

After Adeline had eaten her fill and drunk two glasses of wine, she told Esther how Emil wanted them to run for the Allied lines when the time was right.

"I think that time is coming sooner than later," Esther said. "I have it on high authority that the Soviets are forty kilometers from Warsaw right now. I have one bag packed and all my gold sewn into the lining of my coat."

"And that's what you're going to try to do? Get to the Allied side?"

"I've lived under Stalin once," she said. "I won't do it twice."

"Where will you go? Try to go."

"Argentina." Esther laughed. "Don't you like the sound of it? Ar-gen-ti-na? In my dream, I'll meet some handsome Latin man, and we'll be passionately in love and have passionate children. I mean, why not?"

Adeline felt tipsy and said, "Why not?"

"What's the point of living if you don't have a dream like that?"

"I believe that."

"What is your dream? Where will you go?"

Adeline hesitated, but then described the beautiful green valley surrounded by snowcapped mountains in the painting she'd seen in that folio book at Mrs. Kantor's house.

"Sounds like a dream," Esther said. "Where is that valley?"

"I don't know," Adeline said. "Somewhere west, Emil thinks. Maybe across the ocean, in America or Canada."

"Or Ar-gen-ti-na," Esther said, stood up, shook her hips, and drained the rest of the bottle into her glass.

After finishing her wine, Adeline felt more woozy than tipsy, and said, "I think you're one of the bravest, strongest women I've ever known."

"No," Esther said, lighting another cigarette. "I'm not."

"You are. You made it here alone."

"Not alone. Because of the documents you got for me."

"But you used them and got here on your own. And now you'll go to Ar-gen-ti-na the same way. That takes inner courage and strength."

Esther thought, took a drag, then relaxed. "I guess it does. I thank Mrs. Kantor for that."

"I thank her for a lot of things," Adeline said. "I miss her. Still."

"I do, too," Esther said. "Did she ever tell you any of her 'secrets to a happy life'?"

"A few of them."

"I admit I wonder sometimes if all her secrets are real and true."

"Like what?"

Esther shrugged. "She told me once that she believed that life does not happen to you; it happens for you, and that your whole life is a blessed journey of discovery. But you can only see life clearly and relish it when the journey is almost at an end."

"Your life isn't over," Adeline said.

"I know," she said. "But I don't think I'll ever understand why so many people like me were killed or persecuted around me. And I won't ever get why their lives had to end the way they did. Where's the blessed journey of discovery in any of that?"

Chapter Twenty-Three

Early on the morning of January 9, 1945, Emil shivered and coughed in his bed, echoing the rattling and hackings of his sons in the bunk above him. He could see his breath billow and move on the frigid air still finding the cracks in the walls, but he forced himself out from under his blankets and upright.

Chattering, a little dizzy, he made his way to the outer room and then the window to once again look out to see if Adeline was returning. Even as he'd lapsed in and out of fever, he'd known she was gone and that more than a day had passed since she set out for Lodz. But the storm could have slowed her, he told himself as he checked the boys, both asleep, both flushed with fever, though Will's seemed to be lessening.

Will this ever end? Emil crawled back into his own bunk. *I've never been sick like this in my life—more than three weeks now.*

As he pulled his wool hat down and the blankets up around him, the only good he could see of being sick like this was that he and the boys had little appetite, which helped when you had almost no food. Better than being dead, he supposed, but then thought about the clothes he wore and the place he was living and the things he had done to survive the war.

It's like we're being tortured, Emil thought as his fever rose again and his eyelids drifted shut. *Tortured for something I didn't . . .*

———

September 15, 1941
Outside Dubossary, Transnistria

"Shoot them now!" Captain Haussmann shouted.

Emil looked at the young man holding the two crying girls at the edge of the ravine, squinting in the headlights and begging him not to do it.

Emil turned from them, looked at the Nazi, and knew he was about to die.

"I can't," he said, holding the Luger out to Haussmann.

"Can't?" the SS captain said. "Or won't?"

Emil kept his eyes on the SS captain, and said, "Can't and won't."

The Nazi stared at him, then over at the execution squad watching, growing visibly infuriated until he drew his own Luger from his holster, pushed aside the gun Emil had offered him, and pressed the muzzle of his pistol to the bridge of Emil's nose.

"Make your decision, farm boy," the SS captain said. "They die one way or another. Your choice is whether you live or die with them."

An execution squad to the north and behind Emil began firing, further terrifying him until all he could see was the barrel of the Luger and Haussmann's rage before his wife and sons appeared in his mind. His love for them was suddenly overwhelming. Would dying instead of killing these people do Adeline and the boys any good? Adeline would be a widow. Walt and Will would be fatherless. It all hit him with full and violent force, a blow so powerful, it blew away whatever convictions he had always held true, and with them went his belief in a benevolent God. Emil had begged not to be put in this position, and now here he was. There was no God in that, no God at all. There were only Adeline and Walt and Will, and what he would do to survive and protect them.

"Okay," he said coldly to Haussmann. "I'll do it."

The SS captain smiled and lowered his weapon. "A wise choice."

Emil felt outside himself, then, as if his body were a stranger's. He shifted the Luger in his hand and started to turn toward the young man and the little girls.

Someone grabbed his shoulder from behind and shook him. The grip tightened. The hand shook him harder.

———

The nightmare slowly vanished.

Emil roused enough to blearily open his eyes and see Adeline gazing down at him, her hand on his shoulder, a big smile on her lovely face, and her cheeks rosy from the cold.

"I hope you've had a good sleep while I've been gone," she said, stroking his beard tenderly. "I've brought you all something to eat and some coal for the stove. It's already burning. Did you have good dreams of me?"

Emil had a fleeting memory of that moment when he decided to kill the three Jews, that moment when he lost his faith in God, and said, "I'm feeling better just seeing you. I was worried sick when you didn't come home last night."

"I had to wait out the storm and get a ride down this morning after it passed," Adeline said. "Get up, then, and help me cook, or at least keep me company. I have a story to tell you."

He groaned at the idea of getting up into the cold again.

"Up!" she said, smiling at him and tugging at his blankets.

He made it up onto his elbows and winced. "You're a cruel woman, Adella!"

She laughed and tickled him. "Oh yes, I'm putting a gun to your head."

Emil stared at her a moment in disbelief, the memory of that night playing again.

He felt the steel of Haussmann's gun between his eyes again, saw the SS captain's rage, and felt himself go primal, savage, godless, willing to kill two little girls and a young man so he could return to protect his own wife and sons.

Would she ever understand that decision? Emil wondered as he searched Adeline's puzzled face. *How could she? I don't understand that moment myself.*

"Hey," Adeline said in a soothing, concerned tone. "Do you want to just stay there, and I'll bring you some food?"

It was only then that he smelled something savory and almost indescribably delicious in the air. "What's that cooking?"

She smiled and whispered, "Fresh sausage and onions. I want the smell to fill the apartment, seep into the hall, and call everyone to our feast."

"Feast?"

"Feast," she said, smiling and standing. "Now, get up and come out. We'll let the boys sleep as long as they need to."

She left the room. Emil threw back the blankets, sat up, and then stood without feeling dizzy. He walked out into their little living area, surprised at how warm the coal-fired stove had made it and how good the smells were coming from the tiny range where Adeline was turning over sausages and onions. And the table! It was covered with more food and ingredients than he'd seen in years.

"Where did you get all this?" he asked in wonder.

Adeline tapped the edge of the skillet and turned, grinning as she said, "It was a miracle, Emil. You won't believe it."

———

And Adeline was right. At first, Emil did not believe her story of running into Esther after begging God for help and then the woman repaying her with enough money to buy food for a month, maybe longer. As far as he was concerned at that moment, God did not answer prayers like Adeline's because there was no God that he could see or hear or touch. *The only thing we can rely on is ourselves.*

Adeline had relied on herself, and there was a . . . coincidence. That's what it was. Luck strikes everyone eventually. Adeline just got lucky, he decided, and smiled at the smells and the wad of money on the table that Adeline said had been a third again as fat yesterday evening.

"Where did Esther get enough money to give away that much money?" he said.

"I didn't ask, and she didn't say," Adeline replied, going back to the stove even as a knock came on the door and Malia and their cousin Marie poked their heads in.

"What is that smell?" Marie shrieked.

"Heaven," Adeline said. "First course coming up."

———

The Martels told no one else about the food and ate four times a day for the next two weeks while buying double their ration of coal on the black market. Will and Walt both recovered from the fever, and they, too, were gaining weight and growing stronger.

Emil took daily walks in the arctic conditions, going by Sergeant Wahl's cottage and finding it dark every time. He began to worry, because he did not know what was happening in the war, where the Allies were in Germany and the Soviets in Poland.

"I need to hear where they are almost every day, and Sergeant Wahl was supposed to be back a week ago," he fretted to Adeline on January 17.

On his walk late that afternoon, the snow and the winds were building again, and the streets were clearing as people hustled toward shelter. Emil took a chance and slipped through the back gate to Wahl's cottage and tried the kitchen door. Locked.

He didn't want to but packed a big snowball with his bare hands and used it to punch out a pane of glass above the doorknob. Inside, he didn't dare put on a light, but knowing he was in the kitchen allowed him to grope his way to the room where Wahl kept the radio. He turned on the light briefly, saw it wasn't there, and felt his heart sink.

Then he checked Wahl's closet and found it. After watching it done so many times, he had the radio set up quickly. He listened to the BBC German Service and soon learned that the Battle of the Ardennes Forest, or Battle of the Bulge, was over with the Allies victorious. The US First and Third Armies had joined up but were encountering fierce resistance trying to cross the Rhine. And the Soviets had retaken Warsaw.

That last piece of information was all Emil had to hear. The Red Army was less than seventy-five kilometers away. Even in terrible conditions, a tank could cover seventy-five kilometers in a day, maybe less. He considered putting the shortwave in its protective case and walking off with it. The Nazis were losing, but having a radio transmitter was probably still reason enough to be shot if you were caught with it. He reluctantly decided to leave the radio where it was, along with a note to Sergeant Wahl, thanking him for his kindness. Outside, he sneaked around the cottage onto the road that led to his home. A match lit a cigarette on the other side of the road.

Nikolas stepped out and said, "I live up the street, Martel, and I don't think the VoMi would take kindly to a thief breaking into one of their cottages."

"I'm not a thief," Emil said.

"That's what it looks like," Nikolas said. "Hungry people have been wondering where the sudden money and food came from, and I decided to follow you, and now we know."

Emil understood that once again he was in direct conflict with this man. *Is he still in touch with Major Haussmann? Does he have the Nazis' ear here in Wielun? Does it matter with the Germans on the run?*

"You know nothing," Emil said at last, and started walking. "I'm no thief, Nikolas, just checking on my boss's house as he asked me to."

"I doubt that!" Nikolas shouted after him.

"I don't care about your doubt," Emil said, and turned the corner, out of sight.

When he reached home, their apartment was more than warm, and Adeline had fresh bread already out of the oven and was ladling soup into bowls.

Emil shut the door and said, "We have to pack and leave as soon as possible."

She looked up. "I know. They just told us."

"What? Who?"

Adeline set the ladle back in the pot. "SS soldiers. We're being moved closer to Germany the day after tomorrow."

———

German military trucks came to Camp Wielun at dawn on January 19, 1945. As before, they were able to take only what they could load in the little wagons. Luckily, with Marie's wagon and one that had been gifted to them by another refugee family, the greater Martel clan now had four little wagons among them, and they were able to bring along most of the staples Adeline had bought for them in Lodz.

Adeline sat with her cousin Marie and her twin boys on the bumpy ride.

"They're getting nice and chubby," she said, holding Rutger, the bigger twin.

"Thanks to your food and kindness," Marie said, holding smaller Hans. "I think they'll crawl any day now."

"Sometimes that's all we really need to get up and go. Food and kindness."

Driving through Breslau—a vital stop on the road to Germany, and a strategic position with bridges over the Oder River—they saw Wehrmacht troops and the slaves of the Organization Todt, gaunt, weary men dressed in gray with the letter *E* sewn on their left breasts, acting on Hitler's recent order to turn the city into an armed fortress. Two hours later, they rolled into Legnica, a city far more populated and beautiful than Wielun. And yet their quarters were in some ways worse. But they had money, and money always talks. While winter continued to throw ice and snow at them, Emil was able to buy enough black-market coal to keep the entire family warm.

Emil also did everything he could to get news of the Soviets and the western Allies. He struck gold because refugees were often targeted by hustlers and black marketeers. Soon after they arrived in Legnica, while out walking, he met a teenager who offered to sell him contraband cigarettes.

"Captured American," the kid whispered. "Camel. Lucky Strike."

Emil told him he was more interested in a small shortwave receiver.

"Not a transmitter," Emil said. "Nothing illegal. Just a receiver."

"That could still get me shot," the kid said. "It will definitely cost you."

A few days later, he handed Emil a bag in return for half the Reichsmarks the Martels had left. Inside the bag was a beat-up, khaki-green Radione R3 shortwave receiver stolen from a Wehrmacht supply depot.

"Be careful," the kid said. "My friend said there are fuses, but no spare crystals or radio tubes. What you see is what you get."

Emil waited until late that night to turn the radio on and tune it to the BBC German Service. He heard about the latest developments at the Yalta Conference between American president Roosevelt, British prime minister Churchill, and Stalin. He learned that the Soviets had crossed the Oder River to the north and that they were now less than eighty kilometers from Berlin. The Americans and the British were still battling for western Germany and facing stiff resistance. He also heard a word he'd only heard once before, in the cemetery in Budapest: Auschwitz. The announcer described the scene when the Soviets liberated the concentration camp on January 27. Emil closed his eyes, completely overwhelmed at the scope of what the Nazis had done.

He didn't want to, but his thoughts inevitably returned to that night in Dubossary, when Captain Haussmann had put a gun to his head and told him he'd die if he didn't kill the three Jews. He heard himself say, *Okay, I'll do it.* He heard Haussmann reply, *A wise choice.*

Emil fell asleep that night, feeling sick and fearful and wondering if he was doomed to be haunted the rest of his life by that choice.

In the weeks that followed, up late at night, listening to the shortwave, Emil knew when the Soviets took Lodz and when they won Budapest and when the western Allies firebombed Dresden and when the Red Army laid siege to Breslau, only to pause along the western banks of the Oder River, resupplying and preparing to invade eastern Germany. On the night of February 24, he heard about the Allies launching nine thousand bombers over the Fatherland.

Wahl was right, Emil thought, yawning and shutting off the radio. *The Nazis are beaten even if they don't know it.*

He stood and crossed the room, meaning to put the radio in a metal cabinet in the flat, only to trip over a bulge in the flooring. The radio flew from his hands and crashed and clattered across the floor.

"No!" he said, grabbing the radio and trying to turn it on. "No, no, no."

It never ran again.

———

Four days later, on the last day of February, Emil saw Wehrmacht soldiers rushing into lorries and leaving Legnica. He went out walking, saw more jammed trucks departing, and then spotted two Waffen-SS soldiers using razor blades to cut off the small blood-type tattoos they had high under their left arms.

"Those bastards knew they were going to be caught and probably killed for being a member of the SS," he told Adeline when he got back to their flat. "We've got to go in the morning. We've got to get to the Allied lines."

"How?" Adeline demanded. "The Germans have left."

"We'll walk if we have to," he said.

Adeline hesitated only a moment before yet again packing their meager belongings. Her mother and sister did the same. Marie was feeling sick and needed help, but she was not waiting for the Soviets to send her and her sons back to Ukraine, either. When Emil knocked on his parents' door and entered their quarters later that evening, however, he found his mother, father, and sister sitting by the coal stove.

"C'mon, get packed," he said. "We've got to leave early."

Karoline said, "We're not going."

"What? You have to go. You know what they'll do to you when—"

"Do we?" Rese asked. "We'll just speak to them in Russian. They won't know who we are. And besides, I can't walk to Germany, and you can't carry me."

"The wheelchair."

Johann shook his head. "It won't last the trip. This is it, son. We're staying and hoping for the best."

The temperature nose-dived that night. March came in like a lion, with snow that intensified after dawn. While he waited out the storm, Emil kept arguing with his parents and sister, telling them that their best hope was to get to the Allied lines. They wouldn't hear of it. Karoline said she had heard rumors that the Soviets might let them return to their lands.

"Don't believe it," Emil said. "Not a word. They'll say anything. Do anything."

He stood at the window, watching the snowy streets. Every time he saw a convoy of Wehrmacht trucks heading through town, headed toward Germany, he ran down to ask for a ride for his family and their four carts. And every time they turned him down, even when he asked for his family alone.

The same pure bloods that Reichsführer Heinrich Himmler had lauded for leaving Ukraine to repopulate Greater Germany were now unwanted, discarded, forgotten, and left to their own wits. Emil was at once discouraged, isolated, and yet unbowed; he had relied on himself in difficult situations before, hadn't he?

Never bet against me. I've gotten out of tougher situations than this.

———

The snow finally stopped on the morning of March 4, 1945, but howling east winds had caused drifting and stranded them another five days. Luckily for the Martels, the Soviets had been hampered by the same foul weather and were still encamped along the Oder River the evening of March 9, when Emil saw other ethnic Germans like themselves loading their wagons. The Martels had a final meal of mashed potatoes and sauerkraut and went to bed with plans to leave first thing in the morning.

When Emil got up at dawn on March 10, he could see other refugees already pushing their carts to Berlin. An hour later and knowing this might be the last time he would ever see his parents and sister, Emil fought off tears, hugging them and telling them each good-bye.

"We'll see each other again," Rese promised from her wheelchair. "I know it, just like Corporal Gheorghe said he knew he was going to live through Stalingrad."

He rolled his eyes but couldn't help smiling. "I'm counting on it."

With that, Emil began moving the last of their things into the three wagons on the sidewalk out in front of the tenement. The sun was strong, melting the snow, springlike, almost balmy after the cold blasts they'd survived in the prior months. He planned to follow the other refugees, heading south first, then picking up a main road heading west. With luck, they could make fifteen kilometers a day, which would put them at the German border in roughly eight days. *From there, we'll figure out how to get to the western Allies and—*

Emil felt a sharp poke at his back that almost knocked him into the little wagon. He got his balance, turned around to see what had hit him, and found two Polish militiamen standing there. One of them was aiming a rifle at him.

"German?" the rifleman said in German.

Emil nodded. *"Volksdeutscher."*

"Hands behind your head," he said. "You are coming with us. You have cleanup work to do. Here and then in the Soviet Union."

Stunned, Emil said, "No, no, my family, we were just leaving."

Adeline had come out of the building with the boys, her mother, sister, and Marie, who held the twins.

"You're not going anywhere but with us," the soldier said as the other one came around behind Emil. "March."

"Emil!" Adeline shouted in a panic.

"Let me at least say good-bye to my family," he said.

"No," the soldier said. "March!"

Emil felt another jab between his shoulder blades and started walking, feeling like he was outside of himself the way he'd been that fateful night in Dubossary, apart from his body, walking on the road to doom.

"Papa! Papa!" Walt and Will yelled.

Emil looked over his shoulder, saw them bursting into tears. Adeline ran up alongside the militiamen, her palms up in surrender.

"Please, he's done nothing wrong," she said in Russian. "He's not a soldier. We're farmers from Ukraine. Can't you hear our accent?"

"We don't care about your accent, and we don't care where you're from or what you do," the first militiaman said. "We have orders to find all Germans, including all *Volksdeutsche* men, and detain them until we can turn them over to the Soviets."

"No," Adeline said, terrified. "No, no, no, where are you taking him?"

"He'll help clean up Poland for a while," the soldier behind Emil said. "And then, far east. Probably Siberia."

"No!" Adeline shrieked, and grabbed the front soldier by the sleeve. "You can't do this! Please, my father never came back from Siberia!"

He threw her down in the snow and snarled, "We don't care, bitch."

Jolted by the fall, lying there in the snow, Adeline fought her way to her knees and screamed hysterically after him, "Emil! Emil! What do I do now?"

Emil looked over his shoulder at the love of his life and his dear sons coming to help her and bellowed, "Go west, Adeline! Go as far west as you can, and I promise I'll find you!"

Chapter Twenty-Four

Adeline felt her sons' hands on her, hugging her and trying to console her. She heard their voices asking questions but did not understand them and could not look at them. She just knelt there in the street, paralyzed and staring after the dwindling form of Emil, her husband, her life, being stolen from her when they were only minutes from making their final escape west to freedom. The sheer unfairness of the loss was magnified by the last sight she had of her husband—trudging forward into his fate with head unbowed and will unbroken.

I will remember that, Adeline thought, dazed. *I will hold that image in my heart until . . .*

In her mind, Emil's last words—*I promise I'll find you*—echoed against her father's last words—*I promise you all I will come back!*

But my father never came back, she thought bitterly, and felt more broken than she'd been in her entire life. *He never came back. He . . .*

"Adeline," Marie said. "Please, you've got to get up. You're upsetting the boys."

Though still in a daze, Adeline heard that clearly and looked up to find her cousin kneeling at her side. Marie was gazing at her with a concern and understanding born of the harshness of her own lost love. Then she felt a little hand patting on her other shoulder and looked around to see Walt there, crying.

"Is Papa coming back, Mama?" he choked.

Adeline hesitated, suddenly understanding that her faith in God, in life, in herself, lay in total jeopardy. She could feel the fear of never seeing Emil again like a night bird clawing at her heart, tearing at the root of the one thing that had always kept her going: her fervent belief that someday, somehow, their life would get better if she kept faith in God and her dream of that mythical green valley in the West.

"Mama?" Walt blubbered. "Please say he's coming back."

She licked her lips and swallowed before Will said, "He's coming back, Mama. Right? He's just going away for a while. Right?"

The shaky squeak in her youngest son's voice triggered something more powerful than her own fear or loss. A mother's instinct to protect her young surged through Adeline, obliterating for the moment her desperate need to cope and grieve.

"Yes," she said, opening her arms to her boys. "Papa's coming back. He will find us."

They rushed into her embrace, and she held them, not knowing whether to pray to God for strength or to damn God for robbing her of a husband and her sons of a father.

"Adeline?" Marie said again. "There's a truck coming. You need to get up."

She pulled back from Walt and Will, forcing a smile to her lips and a glint of optimism to her eyes as she said, "Well then, we'll just have to have our own adventure until your father comes to find us. Okay?"

The boys wiped at their eyes and their cheeks with their sleeves and nodded. She smiled again, stood, and brushed the dirt off her skirt before taking each boy by the hand, and with a nod of gratitude to her cousin, she tried to walk resolutely back to the little wagon and her mother and older sister.

———

Malia and their mother stood by their wagon, watching Adeline and the boys approach with piteous expressions on their faces. Her sister moved first, came to Adeline, and hugged her. "We're going to survive. He's going to come back."

"Of course he will," Adeline said.

Lydia showed rare emotion when she took her daughter's hand, kissed it, and said, "I never wanted this to be your burden, too, Adella. Never."

Adeline remembered her father being dragged into the night, vowing to return. She heard Emil's last words echo in her mind: *Go west, Adeline. Go as far west as you can, and I promise I'll find you.*

"I know," Adeline said, shaken inside again as she kissed her mother's cheek. "But I've seen how strong you were for us, and now I'll just have to be strong, too."

"Mama?" Will said, tugging at her skirt.

She looked down at her younger child. His face was streaked with dust and drying tears, but the terror of losing his father had been replaced by a surprising earnestness and interest.

"Are we going west without Papa?" he asked. "That's what he said to do, didn't he? Go as far west as we can, and he'll find us?"

Adeline gaped at him a moment, then looked over at the little wagons, already packed and ready to act on Emil's mad idea to make it to the western Allied lines and to surrender as refugees. She knew he was serious, but she kept thinking of the last time they'd been caught between two armies, the snowstorm, the warring tanks, and the brutal way Emil had lashed at the horses until they'd bled to save them.

Could she do that? Did she have that kind of courage and resolve? Had Emil been right? Was the only way to freedom through a hail of bullets and bombs?

"Mama?" Walt said. "Are we going? Or not?"

Her sweet, innocent boys were looking to her for guidance, and she knew the decision she was about to make might change everything about their young lives, for good or for bad. She felt anxious and alone, and then heard an explosion in the distance to the northwest that shook Walt, who held tight to her leg.

"I want to go back inside," he whined. "I don't want to be near tanks again."

Seeing how traumatized her son was, Adeline made her decision and looked at her mother and sister. "We won't go west if there's combat anywhere near us. I can't put the boys through it again. We'll stay put until things calm down and . . . things are safer."

"Oh," Will said, scrunching his brows. "But Papa said, 'Go as far west as—'"

"I know what he said, Will," she replied sharply. "But do you want to see what it's like to run on foot between the tank cannons and men from both sides shooting at us?"

He took a step back at the sudden, harsh change in his mother. "No, Mama."

"Good. Then I expect you and Walt to help me as Papa would want you to help me. We start by unloading the little wagon and bringing it all back upstairs."

When they clomped up the stairs past Emil's parents' apartment, the door flew open, and Karoline was looking at them, puzzled. "I thought you'd all gone for good."

"Soldiers took Papa," Will announced. "He's going to Siberia."

Emil's mother stared at her grandson, then saw it confirmed in Adeline's puffy eyes and almost fainted before she grabbed the door frame and screamed the news to Johann and Rese. When they'd come, Emil's father pushing his daughter in the wheelchair, Adeline told them what had happened just down the stairs when they'd been seconds from leaving.

Karoline took the news like one more club to her battered body and soul, dumbfounded at first at the unfairness of it, then angry, then bitter. All within a few moments, what had happened to her son had gone from shocking to confirmation of the unending suffering that was her lot in life.

"Why'd we come all this way?" Karoline asked Johann. "We could have stayed in Friedenstal, and Emil would have ended up the same way." She looked at Adeline. "You would have ended up the same way, Adeline, even if we hadn't come. This is what they do to our men and to us."

There was such compelling anger and defeat in Karoline's eyes, Adeline almost succumbed to the rancor that thrived in her mother-in-law's core.

Then Karoline spat, "Face it, Adeline. This is what they will do to your boys, too."

That rocked Adeline, and fury boiled out of her. "That will never happen, you evil-thinking shrew! I will protect them and get them west when the time is right. And your son? He's coming back to find us, because I know the kind of man he is."

Karoline's face twisted with mock pity, but before she could reply, Lydia, who was on the stairs at the edge of the landing, said, "You know, Adeline, that's what I said at the beginning and for too many years."

Adeline spun around and glared at her mother, shouting, "What? Should I think Emil's dead and never going to return when he's only been gone thirty minutes? I can't think that way, Mother! I won't give up hope! Not now. Not ever!"

Lydia bowed her head, and when Adeline swiveled back to Karoline, the older woman had lost some of her spite. "You can't give up hope. I did after

Johann had been gone six years. I gave up hope. In my mind, Johann was dead. Fifteen months later, he knocked at my door."

"And look at me," Johann said. "A wreck of a man."

"You're not a wreck," Adeline said. "And I promise you, Emil will not be wrecked, either."

———

Emil focused on putting one step in front of the other, trying not to let a predicament he'd spent a lifetime trying to avoid crush him before he could figure a way out and back to Adeline and the boys. As he and the two Polish militiamen walked farther and farther from his family through the streets of Legnica, he realized his mistake had been admitting his German heritage. He wasn't a soldier, but it did not matter. To them, he was the last vestige of a conquering army in retreat. He should have spoken to them in Russian, but he didn't, and now they could do anything they wanted to him and probably would. He was powerless in that respect, but not so powerless in another.

As he walked, he remembered what his father had told him not long after his return from the frozen East and one of the few times he'd spoken about his years in a Siberian prison camp, slaving below ground. Emil had asked him how he'd managed to survive. Johann had said some of it was luck and some of it was learned. Despite all his hard work growing up on a farm, for example, Johann was lucky in that he'd been a little chubby from all the good food he'd been eating before the Stalinists came to take him away for hoarding. The extra flab around his belly had allowed him to survive the trip east when so many died.

Emil thought about all the food they'd had and how much weight and strength he'd regained since Adeline found Esther. In that way, he was somewhat ready to survive a long journey. He put that in his favor.

His father had also said he tried never to speak German in the presence of any of the Soviet guards. It seemed to enrage them and often resulted in a beating. Emil decided to speak only Russian from that point forward. Maybe he could convince someone that these two had him all wrong.

Johann said he had trusted very few people in the camps. Everyone at first should be considered a potential informer. Trust should be something hard won. So was the ability to avoid illness. Emil's father had been fanatical about cleaning himself after leaving the mines and the latrines. He'd also forced himself to eat whatever he was given, no matter how grisly, and to drink the cleanest water he could find and lots of it.

"The important thing was to stay standing as long as you could," his father had said. "Every day you stayed alive, you had the opportunity to be set free or to escape. I escaped twice, but they brought me back and beat me senseless. Then I got sick."

That confession had surprised Emil when he'd first heard it. He'd never seen his father as the kind of man who would try to escape. But now that he was a prisoner himself, he thought he understood Johann at a deeper, gut level, better than he ever had before, and he vowed to follow those four survival tactics and others he had heard that day long ago.

I can only rely on myself, he thought. *But in a sense, my father has prepared me.*

Emil was certainly better prepared than the fifteen men in the back of the truck they threw him into an hour later. Nervous, thin, suspicious, they would not meet his eyes, as if they instinctually knew to trust no one now. He sat on a bench near the rear gate and saw other men being led to other trucks under armed guard.

The truck coughed to life after an hour of waiting. As they pulled away, putting more and more distance between him and his family, Emil swore he saw Nikolas and two other men he recognized from the trek and Camp Wielun climb into another waiting truck.

They began to drive east. With every kilometer that passed, Emil felt more and more betrayed by life. He'd spent almost a year since they'd left Friedenstal doing everything in his power to get his family west, and now he was heading in the exact opposite direction. To the north and east, he heard sporadic cannon fire and knew the Red Army was not far. Two hours later, approaching Breslau with the noon sun glinting off the Oder River, he could see the Soviets had the city surrounded. Mortar shells were exploding inside the fortress the Nazis had built.

They turned due north for several kilometers and then looped back toward the river. Not long afterward, Emil saw the first Soviet tank and then another and then seven, all of them rolling west, unimpeded. He watched them and the Soviet troop carriers that followed the tanks, knowing that he'd failed miserably. He'd wanted to get to the western Allies, and he'd come up short, got captured, and was soon to be delivered to Stalin's men. And Adeline, Walt, and Will were back there, right in the path of the tanks passing him, thrown to the wind and the wolves.

He remembered how the militiamen had pushed Adeline to the ground and tried to use his anger at that to weld in himself the belief that he would survive whatever he was going to have to face. But try as he might, Emil could not do it. He kept thinking about Adeline and the boys and felt in his heart the first acid trickle of despair.

———

That despair grew over the numbing six weeks that followed as Emil and hundreds and then thousands of ethnic Germans were put to work by the Polish militias, who treated them as slave labor. They were not trucked anymore but made to walk in long double lines under the supervision of armed guards, moving from one war-torn little town to the next, spending twelve to fourteen hours a day removing the debris of collapsed buildings and clearing roads so more Soviet troops could be brought to the battle lines.

Emil tried not to speak unless spoken to by one of the Polish guards and then only in Russian. But he listened in both languages and heard the news that the Allies were forcing Hitler back on every front. The Soviets were preparing to attack Berlin from the east while the Americans and British were fighting their way there from the west, though they appeared to be stalled by pockets of fierce resistance from the remaining Wehrmacht forces.

As March turned to April 1945, the brutal cold that had gripped all of Europe gave way to climbing temperatures that made the heavier clothes Emil wore intolerable. He took to carrying most of his clothes with him wherever he went and placed them where he could see them as he toiled. He thought of his father constantly, following Johann's lead, keeping his head down, laboring without comment or complaint, drinking only the water given to him by the guards, eating all the food given to him as well, and sleeping whenever and wherever he could.

The prisoners spent their nights in abandoned barns or in the woods, often side by side in the dirt, with the guards under orders to shoot any man trying to escape. Emil had been looking for a way and a chance to flee, but they'd been under tight control, no more than one hundred men in a group with eight armed militiamen watching.

Rumors spread that they were headed much farther east once the war ended, but they seemed to move between war-ruined town and war-ruined town in a lazy S pattern, sometimes north, sometimes south, and even a few times west. Emil began to hope he would be imprisoned somewhere close to Germany so if he did escape, he would not have to go far to find his family. But where would they be?

He'd told Adeline to go west, as far west as she could go, but now he feared he'd sent them into harm's way. He imagined them following his orders faithfully, walking west despite being shot at and dodging bombs, and tried to tell himself that they would somehow make it to the Allied lines. Or had he been a complete fool and sent them all to their deaths?

That last question gnawed at Emil whenever he lay down under the watchful eyes of the militiamen and escaped into sleep. He had nightmares in which Adeline, Walt, and Will were out in the middle of a muddy battlefield, hurt and screaming to him for help. But in those dark dreams, he always seemed to be behind a fence, gripping the barbed wire so hard, blood seeped down his hands as he screamed to them that he'd found them; he'd come west, and he'd found them.

———

Four weeks after Emil was taken, Soviet guards took over from the Polish militiamen, but his assignment was the same in every town they entered: clear debris, stack bricks, stay alive.

The first day under Soviet control, he heard a squat, flat-faced guard named Lebedev boast, "Stalin will have Berlin. It is certain. The Red flag will fly above the Reichstag by Workers' Day!"

"Maybe before Workers' Day," said his usual partner, Aleksey—a skinny kid, no more than twenty—who seemed to always follow the older Lebedev's lead.

The Soviets finally attacked Berlin on April 16, 1945. Two full army groups fought toward Hitler's capital from the south and the east. A third Russian army overran the Germans from the north.

Within four days, the city was encircled. The pitched and hand-to-hand battle with the last of Hitler's fervent loyalists unfolded in the same brutal heat Emil was experiencing. More than eighty thousand Red Army soldiers would die in the next ten days, wresting Berlin from Nazi control. Hitler committed suicide on April 30. His generals formally surrendered two days later, and the rough boundaries of East and West Germany were effectively set where the various Allied armies stopped moving forward.

The day the war ended, Emil was in a small town south of Kielce, Poland, stripped to the waist, moving busted concrete and brick in infernal heat, when he heard the same two guards talking.

"I told you the Red flag would fly on the Reichstag by Workers' Day," Lebedev said, grinning and lighting a cigarette. "I wish I was there to see it."

"I wish I was there for the party," his comrade, Aleksey, said. "I heard they're trucking in vodka, and any German woman is yours for the taking. No one will stop you."

"Instead, we watch these German swine pick up bricks and march east with them tomorrow, nowhere near Berlin. I saw the orders myself."

"How far?"

"Almost two hundred and fifty kilometers," Lebedev said bitterly. "Probably two weeks on foot to the train."

———

Two weeks? Emil thought morosely when he took his first hated step straight east early the morning of May 3, 1945. *And the Soviets are free to rape every woman they see. Including my Adeline.* The thought made him so sick and angry, he wanted to kill one of the men guarding him with his bare hands, but he knew he'd surely be dead the next minute. And where would that leave his family?

They were in marching formation, two abreast, and every few kilometers that day, they were joined by more groups of prisoners, many in German army uniforms, until Emil lost count at twenty-three hundred. One of them, unmistakably, was Nikolas. Emil could see him fifteen men ahead of him and to the left, limping only slightly.

The heat that day soared along with the humidity. The four times they were given water, Emil guzzled two-thirds of his ration and soaked his brim cap with the remainder so he could keep his head cooled. By three o'clock in the afternoon, it was brutally hot, in the upper thirties Celsius, not a cloud in the sky, and the weakest men among them began to stagger and drop. The man next to Nikolas was one of the first. Nikolas ignored his fallen partner and kept walking. The next man in line stepped over him as did the next eight.

Emil stopped, grabbed the man under the armpits, and tried to help him to his feet.

"Leave him be!" Lebedev shouted. "Keep marching. Close your ranks!"

Emil reluctantly let the man sag into the dirt, stepped around him, and hustled forward to close the gap in the line. He heard Lebedev shout at the fallen prisoner that he had one more chance to get to his feet. Then he heard the Russian shout for Aleksey to finish him off and throw him in the ditch. Glancing back, Emil saw the young soldier walk up and without hesitation put a bullet in the fallen man's head.

The gunshot caused prisoners ahead of Emil to panic and break formation. Several began to run. Other guards yelled in Russian and shot into the air to stop them, but that only created more of a riot up and down the ranks. One of the uniformed German prisoners decided to use the commotion as a diversion to try to escape, sprinting directly away from the march into a fallow field, heading for woods about a hundred and fifty meters out.

He'd made it more than halfway when Lebedev saw him, ran forward, dropped to one knee, aimed, and shot the runner in the back ten meters before he reached the trees. The sight of him pitching forward into a mist of his own blood was enough for the remaining prisoners to settle and scurry back into line. During the confusion, places were changed, including Emil's. When they started again, he looked to his left and found Nikolas limping beside him, a miserable expression on his face.

"You could have found somewhere else to stink, Martel," Nikolas said.

"How's the knee?"

Nikolas glared at him with utter loathing. "Getting better every day. Soon I'll be good enough to stick a knife in your back when you're not looking."

"Except I will be looking," Emil said. "And when you try, I will take that knife away from you, and I will stick it up your ass and give the blade a twist or two. You'll die shitting blood if you try, Nikolas."

That infuriated the bigger man, but he did not reply, just glared straight ahead now, gritting his teeth and limping on, stride for stride with Emil for hour after numbing hour until a halt was called in farming country. In eleven hours of walking, they'd covered nearly thirty kilometers and seen ten men die.

Lebedev pointed Emil, Nikolas, and the other prisoners toward a small loose grove of trees in a field that had been recently hayed. Aleksey went with them and allowed them to dunk their heads as they waded across a stream. Though dunking in the cool water was a relief, Emil collapsed almost immediately against one of the trees, grateful for the shade and the green grass; he knew he had to rest if they were going to march like this for two straight weeks.

Nikolas found another spot to lie down. Other men returned to the stream and drank from it, but Emil had seen cows farther out and decided it was too risky. Despite being massively thirsty, he waited two hours until a food-and-water truck came. Dinner was weak cabbage soup, a hunk of bread, and enough water to fill the can they'd been supplied with.

Emil wolfed down the food and water. He got back in line for more water, drank it all, and lay down for good before the sun was gone. Using his clothes for a pillow and hugging his water can and shoes lest they be stolen, he allowed himself to think about Adeline, Walt, and Will for the first time since they'd started marching. He fell asleep with their faces before him, saw himself hugging them, singing the boys a silent lullaby, and wishing them all a good night's rest.

Chapter Twenty-Five

May 12, 1945
Near Pulawy, Poland

The last part of the march was the worst for Emil. They'd done nothing but hike in the heat for the past three days, more often than not across fields and broken ground in order to keep the roads clear for Soviet military traffic. Prisoners were collapsing and dying by the hour.

Emil had woken up foggy, barely rested, and nauseated. He could already tell the heat was going to be relentless, and he wondered if he could keep going if they were in for a long march. His stomach was so upset, he couldn't eat his ration of bread, and he spilled half the water in his can before he took a step. By noon, they'd hiked ten kilometers, and the temperature had soared, with air so thick, there seemed to be a mist on the hazy low horizon.

One foot and then the next, Emil told himself. *One foot and then the next.*

But by early afternoon, sheer thirst was cracking his resolve. He looked everywhere for water. Passing a pond, he wanted to go to it and dive in as his sister had at the lake the day she lost her legs. But he could see that Lebedev and Aleksey were in no mood to see their prisoners do what they could not.

Emil's tongue and throat felt as parched as the soil in the fields they crossed. His eyelids were sticky with sweat and his lips crusted with salt. Several times he felt so dizzy, he feared collapse. *What if I fall and can't get up again?*

In the throes of heat exhaustion, his tortured body began to infect his mind. He heard Lebedev and Aleksey shouting, which became Captain Haussmann shouting at him for the first time in months. Try as he might, he could not prevent the terrible memories of that night from returning in full force. Emil staggered eastward in a feverish trance, seeing parts of that night as if they were happening all over again.

———

September 15, 1941
Outside Dubossary, Transnistria

"Okay," Emil said. "I'll do it."

"A wise choice," Captain Haussmann said, waving the barrel of his weapon at the terrified young man still huddled with the two young girls at the edge of the ravine. "Do it, then. Prove you're fit for the new Germany, farm boy."

Aware that Haussmann still had his weapon trained on him from just a few meters away, Emil felt himself harden and go to a mental place he'd been many times before. Growing up on a farm, he'd slaughtered animals, and that was how he tried to see the Jews as he turned to them that night. He tried to make them animals in his mind, not humans, and he was not human, either. Besides, if he didn't do it, the three children would die anyway, and Emil and his family's chances for survival along with them.

The young Jewish man was pleading with him again, begging Emil not to shoot as he walked forward, clear-eyed as he raised the gun and tried to take aim. As his sights settled on the Jewish boy's chest, Emil felt cold, ruthless, committed to murder.

"Do it, or I'll blow your head off!" Haussmann shouted behind him.

In his mind, as he started to squeeze the trigger, Emil had already killed the Jewish boy and the young girls so he could see his wife and sons again.

A shout rang out behind him.

"Captain Haussmann, stand down and lower your weapon!"

Feeling like he was still in a nightmare, Emil gaped over his shoulder. Silhouetted in the truck headlights' glare, an SS officer with a hawklike nose was striding toward them. Haussmann took one look, lowered his weapon, and snapped into a salute.

"Obersturmbannführer Nosske!" he cried.

Nosske pointed at Emil. "Lower your weapon."

Haussmann said, "I thought you'd gone to Kiev, sir?"

"Not yet," snapped Nosske, who seemed to be Haussmann's superior. "Were you threatening to kill this man unless he shot those Jews, Captain?"

Haussmann nodded with vigor. "I thought he needed to demonstrate his allegiance to the Fatherland, to—"

"He'll do it in a different way," Nosske said. "Reichsführer Himmler himself vomited when he saw fifteen men shot to death three months ago. His explicit order afterward was that no one shall be forced to participate unless they wish to."

"With all due respect, Lieutenant Colonel Nosske, this man is a coward; this man is—"

"Not going to shoot Jews unless he wants to," the SS assault leader said firmly. "Give him another job, Captain. Give him a shovel to bury them all and find someone else willing to shoot them, and do it quickly. We have two thousand more to dispose of before dawn."

Two thousand? Emil thought, now trembling uncontrollably and gaping dumbly at Nosske and Haussmann, who saw argument was futile and snatched the Luger from Emil's hand. He walked over to Helmut, the young guy with the missing tooth, and gave him the pistol. "Go ahead. Show the farm boy what a true new German looks like."

Helmut nodded, passed Emil with a look of disdain before walking right up to the three Jews. He shot the girl on the left first, then the one on the right, and then the suffering older boy. He used his boot to push their corpses into the darkness.

"Just like shooting hogs in a pen," he said to Emil before grinning at Haussmann and Nosske. "Sign me up. I could do this all day long."

Emil stared at the place where the young Jews had been huddled, begging for mercy, just a few moments before. He felt dazed and sickened. *I was going to shoot them. I was going to murder those children. How could I have . . . ? How . . . ?*

And then Emil processed the first thing Helmut had said and understood that he and the toothless guy had told themselves the same story: The Jews weren't human. They were animals.

"Martel!" Captain Haussmann shouted, snapping Emil out of his thoughts.

He turned to the SS officer and his commander, seeing Nosske gesture to a shovel on the ground. "Use it, or he *will* shoot you."

Emil nodded, lowered his head, and hurried to get the shovel. More rifle and pistol shots were beginning to ring out farther north up the ravine, and with them the cries of the doomed rose once more. It all made Emil feel like he'd gone to hell for reasons he did not understand, and he had to struggle to focus on Haussmann, who pointed south along the ravine.

"Go there and start shoveling that pile of lime onto last night's work," the SS captain said, his tone sewn through with disgust.

Emil wanted to ask how long he'd have to shovel before he could go home but thought better of it. He nodded and turned away, only to receive a kick square in the right butt cheek that made him stagger forward and almost fall.

Emil's instinct was to spin around and break Haussmann's skull with the shovel blade, but he knew if he did, he'd be a dead man. Instead, he straightened up, kept his head low, and limped toward the pile of lime in the shadows just beyond the headlights' glare. The night breeze shifted, came out of the southeast and the ravine itself. With the breeze came the reek of bodies that had rotted all day in the sun.

He retched and retched again. More rifle shots went off. More people were screaming. When Emil was able to stand, he could see north through the headlights the long line of Jews waiting to die. Most of them seemed resigned to their fate now, going to slaughter like animals. Only they were not animals.

Emil stopped breathing through his nose, went to the lime pile, and started shoveling, crying, unable to stop thinking about his decision to shoot the three Jews, and how quickly he'd gone from seeing them as people, children, to seeing them as animals, and how fast he'd thought of himself as a tool, an implement, not a person at all. Even if he'd done it for his family. He retched and sobbed as he threw the first shovelfuls of lime over the edge of the ravine and into the darkness and decay below. He felt in his heart as if he'd killed those three children himself. He'd been willing to do it, hadn't he? He'd absolutely decided to put a bullet in each of them, hadn't he?

Emil knew in his heart and his mind that he had decided and that he was a murderer. *I crossed the line. They were already dead. I was already living with it.*

But he'd been forced into it, hadn't he? He'd begged God not to make him part of it, but there he'd been placed, and there he'd decided to kill three children, finding a way to justify it beyond the gun at his head. *They were doomed to be killed no matter who pulled the trigger. They were animals. I was only a tool.*

No, they weren't. They were as human as your own flesh and blood. And no, you weren't some unthinking, unfeeling tool of destruction. You, Emil, were a cold-blooded murderer no different from Helmut.

He went on this way, torturing himself as he shoveled for hours and the shooting went on and on and on. Every shot made him flinch, made him relive the three children being executed. He thought of Adeline and wondered what she would have done in his place. He bowed his head, feeling like a lesser man when he understood exactly what her reaction would have been. Her thoughts would have been with the dying and the dead. Not herself.

Adeline would be praying for their souls, he thought, and felt confused, enraged, and small, a speck in time. *She'd be praying for their souls, and I can't see the sense of that anymore. Dead or alive, no one's listening.*

And with that, in the dark of the night as two thousand Jews lost their lives, Emil Martel's faith in a benevolent God, his belief in himself and in the common good of man, left him. The following day, on his way back to Friedenstal and his family, he would shake his fist at the sky and curse a cruel God for his sorry lot in life.

Emil tripped and sprawled facedown in the weeds of an overgrown field the prisoners were crossing, ripping him from his trance.

"Get up!" someone barked as he stepped over Emil. "Lebedev's coming!"

Forcing himself to his knees and then to his feet, Emil felt like he might go down again. But he gritted his teeth, got angry, and started marching once more.

He remembered that moment outside Dubossary almost four years ago when he'd lost his faith and realized his beliefs had not changed a bit since. There was no God. Despite what Adeline said, there was no help from on high. No one else could help him put one foot in front of the other. He had no one to rely on but himself.

And this march? With every step, he saw it more and more as punishment for being a murderer in everything but the pull of a trigger.

By sheer force of will, Emil kept putting one foot in front of the other for nearly three days after he collapsed in the heat. And for nearly three days, he obsessed about and suffered for what he'd become in Dubossary—a monster no different than Helmut or Haussmann.

I became a monster, and this is the torture I must go through if I am ever to see Adeline, Walt, and Will again, he told himself over and over again. *I just have to take the pain, accept the torture, and plod on.*

Every day, men dropped from exhaustion. Every day, men were shot for their weakness. The deaths alone kept Emil going when all he wanted was to lie down in the shade and sleep.

Near the end of the third day, lightning bolts had begun to crack nearby and thunder to shake the ground beneath Emil's weary feet. He did not care. Lebedev had just said they were a mile from the station where their train east awaited.

The last mile, Emil thought, and smiled wearily. *There were times when I wanted to quit and let them put a bullet through my head, but I'm here. I made it.*

Then the winds came with rain, blustery and drenching. Emil and scores of other prisoners took off their shirts and let the rain pelt the filth off them while they leaned back and opened their mouths wide to drink from the sky. Somewhere deep inside, Emil wanted to roar out in victory for having made it this far when so many men had fallen along the way—almost two hundred by his count.

But he knew that celebration would only attract attention, and his father's number one rule of survival in a Soviet prison camp had been to attract as little attention as possible. Emil stayed silent as they entered Lublin, which was like so many of the other small cities and towns they'd trudged through—in ruins or pocked with bullets or bomb-cratered. And just as they had in the other towns, people came out to jeer and curse at the prisoners in Polish and Russian, calling them "German swine" and asking them how it felt to be beaten and herded east.

"Enjoy Siberia, stinking Kraut!" one little boy yelled, and threw a rock at Emil, hitting him in the shoulder.

The kid let out a cry of joy that turned into a sneering laugh. Emil trudged on, less enthusiastic about the rain. *That boy could not have been much older than Walt, and he hated me. I never did a thing to that child, yet he hated me so much, he was happy to hit me with a rock.*

He was beginning to think that hate ruled the world. Hate was certainly in almost every terrible experience he'd endured in his life. He'd succumbed to it in Dubossary, hadn't he?

The cycle of mental suffering began all over again for Emil as they rounded a corner and were led into a rail yard where a long freight train awaited them, boxcar doors gaping wide. The rainstorm had passed and with it the short-lived pride of having survived the march. The shadows and darkness inside those boxcars spoke to Emil in a language he did not understand but felt like a slow sawing in his brain and belly.

Where would he be coming out of those shadows and that darkness? Worse, who would he be? Was he destined to die in the East? Or return like his father, a gentle man, but a broken one deep inside?

Lebedev and Aleksey called a halt. Emil stood there, closed his eyes for several moments, blocking out the train that would take him farther away, and summoned up the clearest image of Adeline and the boys he could muster. The one that came up was of them all the evening after she'd returned from Lodz with enough food to feed the entire family. Adeline had beamed that night. As weak as Emil had been after the fever broke for good, he'd felt stronger every time she smiled at him that night over dinner.

Well, isn't that what love does? he thought. *Makes you stronger?*

Lebedev began shouting out orders.

"Get your rations and get on the train."

"Where do you think it's taking us?" Nikolas asked Aleksey and Lebedev.

Emil hadn't seen them enter the train yard.

Aleksey smiled. "I understand you'll be given winter clothes when you arrive."

Lebedev snickered and added, "Don't let anyone steal your gloves, or your fingers will fall off in fifteen minutes' time."

Emil felt sick, closed his eyes again. *Siberia.*

"Get your rations and get on the train!" Lebedev shouted again. "I never want to see any of you filthy, worthless bastards ever again."

Having been through the train rides to Budapest and then to Lodz, Emil knew that getting a good place to stand was crucial to surviving what had to be a one- or two-week trip to Siberia, depending on the train's power and the track conditions. As the sun began to set, he got his rations and climbed into an almost empty car near the rear of the train. He took a position on the short side of the doorway and steeled himself for the long journey ahead.

———

May 18, 1945
Poltava, Ukraine

For three days, Emil fought for and held his position by the door. When it was shut, the air in the boxcar was stifling and rank, but he had a crack that allowed him fresh breathing air and a sliver of a view as the train rolled east between a crawl and a trot.

At those speeds in the pulverizing heat and humidity, the boxcars had become coffins. In Emil's car, five men weakened by the march had died. Men were expiring at higher rates in the other cars. He'd watched at least thirty corpses carried out.

That morning, as a body was being lowered from an adjacent boxcar, other prisoners were on the ground, relieving themselves and stretching their legs, when two men made a break for it. The Soviet Red Army soldiers guarding the train cut them down within fifty meters.

Hours later, Emil kept his lips and eye to the crack in the door and did everything he could not to think about the bleakness of his situation. It was one of the other things his father had told him about surviving the gulag. *The worse it was, the less you thought. You had to figure out a way to go down inside yourself, find a place no one could get to, and just be. Like a bear hibernating.* By that point in his captivity, Emil believed he'd found that place deep inside and was telling himself he could last a week, even two, in the train just by keeping one eyeball to the crack in the door, catching glimpses of the passing countryside, breathing fresh air, and not thinking at all.

The brakes squealed. The train ground slowly to a halt. When the door slid back, Emil threw his hand to his brow against the brilliant, hot sun, seeing that they'd stopped beside a long, wide, fallow field and beyond it another and another. He smelled horses and cattle and looked around, thinking that the land looked familiar. Too familiar.

The soldiers told them all to climb out and assemble in the field. When they did, a big muscular Soviet officer stood in the back of a lorry and spoke through an amplifier.

"Welcome to Poltava prisoner of war camp. You are here to make amends for Adolf Hitler's destructive acts of aggression against the Soviet people. Hitler took Poltava in 1941 and made it his base for bombers that attacked Stalingrad and Moscow and killed tens of thousands of innocent Russian people. The Allies had no choice but to bomb Poltava and its airfield, and there was a long battle here with your army. You are to rebuild what was destroyed. When that is done, you will go home. Not a day sooner."

Poltava. Emil knew where he was now and felt a little better. He was back in Ukraine, far-eastern Ukraine, almost to the Russian border, a good four hundred and seventy-five kilometers east-northeast from where he, Adeline, and the boys had set out on the trek fourteen months before.

I am a long, long way from where I left Adeline, but at least I'm not in Siberia, he thought. *Ukraine I can escape from. I've done it before. I can do it again.*

Though he was smiling inside at these thoughts, Emil kept his face grim as the soldiers got the prisoners in lines to receive clothes: a set of prison grays, including a cap, a jacket, and work boots. They were warned to protect their clothes. There would be no replacements.

After being deloused in tents by the railroad tracks and leaving their old clothes behind, they were marched into the city. Though the heat was stifling, the route unfolded along a babbling stream in a shaded forest that smelled of pine and wildflowers until the wind shifted and all Emil could smell was doused fire and chemical burn.

The trees ended. They walked out onto a rise in hot aluminum sunlight, which afforded them their first view of Poltava. The city was once home to three hundred thousand people, but more than 80 percent of it now lay in scorched ruin, a wasteland of war where fewer than six thousand people were eking out a living.

Emil looked down on the soot- and bomb-blackened maze of low broken walls, twisted steel skeletons, and ragged black spires jutting from the rubble as far as he could see and felt his bravado fade. Though he did not believe in God or heaven, his own eyes told him he was about to enter hell.

Chapter Twenty-Six

More than three and a half months after Emil was taken, the sun was rising over the building that had given the greater Martel clan refuge for nearly five months. Adeline and the boys were in the street out front with their little wagon and Marie's. Lydia and Malia, Emil's parents, and Rese were there as well with their loaded carts.

Karoline said, "You all should come with us. We'll be back in Friedenstal in a week. A place we know. A life we know."

"The Soviets are lying to you," Adeline said curtly. "You'll go back to a life worse than what we knew. And besides, Emil told me to go west and he'd find me."

Her mother-in-law looked like she'd tasted something foul before she said, "Face it, Adeline. Your mother's right. Emil is gone and not coming back. Just like your father."

"I don't believe that," Adeline said, her hands gathered to fists. "I'll never believe that."

"This is good-bye, then," Karoline said.

Adeline nodded and told Will and Walt to say good-bye to their grandparents and aunt. Rese had tears in her eyes, but Karoline hardly looked at them before tousling the boys' hair. After Adeline hugged Rese and Johann, Karoline said, "Come with me a moment, Adella."

"I'm not changing my mind."

"I know that," she said before leading her far enough down the street to not be overheard.

As sour as ever, Karoline looked her in the eye, and said, "Will you forgive me before we walk away from each other forever?"

Adeline knew exactly what she was referring to, that incident long ago when the first Waldemar was starving, and Karoline nevertheless drank much of the cream a friend had left for him two days before the infant died. For years, she'd held that against her mother-in-law, told herself that she could never forgive the spiteful bitch for that greedy, uncaring act.

But standing there, she listened not to her mind but to her heart. "I forgive you, Karoline. You didn't cause his death. My malaria did. He would have died with or without the cream. I held it against you for so long. It was unfair of me."

Her mother-in-law's features melted, and she grabbed hard onto Adeline's forearm before choking, "Thank you. I don't know what got into me that day. I . . . Take care of those boys. They've got Emil all through them, you know."

Karoline's hard expression returned before she nodded and went to her cart. She got behind the push bar while Johann took the front handle. Rese, sitting on the wagon, waved at them, her face red with pressure before she broke down sobbing.

"If Emil finds you, tell him to come find me," she said before her parents-in-law pushed and pulled their cart toward the train station and a ride back to Ukraine and little Friedenstal.

———

"Will we ever see them again, Mama?" Walt asked, tears in his eyes, as they vanished.

"I don't know," she said.

He seemed more upset, so she added, "If it's part of God's plan, we will."

She went to the handle of the little wagon, Emil's normal position, before looking back to Walt and Will at the push bar and then over at her sister and her mother and her cousin with her twins in her cart.

"Ready?" she said.

Lydia and Malia nodded. So did Marie.

Will said, "I'm ready to go west."

Walt, fretting, said, "But how will Papa know where to find us after we leave here?"

"I left a letter for him with the owner in case he comes here first," she said. "It says we're going to Berlin to get to the British or the American zones where we'll be waiting for him."

"He'll never get to read it," Lydia said.

Malia, who stood beside her at the push bar to their wagon, said, "Mother, you need to learn to keep your yap shut sometimes."

Lydia stared at her older daughter and then raised her chin and looked away, saying, "I don't know why they won't let us stay here."

Malia said, "No one in Poland wants us here. If we don't go back to Friedenstal, we have no other choice."

Adeline's sister was right. Like every other country Hitler invaded, Poland had decided to expulse all people of German heritage from its borders no matter their role in the war. They'd been given forty-eight hours to pack and decide to either return to the East on a train or go west on foot.

Marie had asked for extra time given Rutger's fever but was denied. The sick child was fussing atop Marie's little wagon, and Adeline's cousin was looking overwhelmed as they got ready to depart.

"Here we go," Adeline said. "Let's walk as far as we can today."

She picked up the wagon handle, gave one last glance east down the road to that corner where Emil had disappeared more than three months before, and then turned her head west and started walking. They'd gone less than a kilometer to the outskirts of the town, joining a steady stream of other refugees headed west, when Will said, "Mama, how far is Germany?"

"One hundred kilometers," Adeline said, already feeling her feet start to ache.

"And Berlin?" Walt asked.

"Nearly three hundred."

"Ahhh," Will groaned. "We're never going to get there."

———

They covered twelve kilometers by sundown that first day. Adeline did not have time to wonder if Emil was seeing the sunset somewhere in the vast Soviet east.

During the course of the day, she'd somehow become the de facto leader of the family and had to decide where they'd camp for the night and what they'd eat and where each of them would sleep.

Adeline had the boys dig out an oven for her in a stream bank, then made soup and heated the bread she'd made the day before and rationed the dried meat she'd bought back in March on the black market when the Reichsmark still had value. While Will and Walt fed the fire, she and Malia washed the dishes.

"Can you believe they're gone for good?" Malia asked. "Rese, Johann, Mrs. Sunshine?"

"I'll miss Rese and Johann," Adeline said.

"Something in my stomach says they're going to regret it."

"I told them that, but she wouldn't listen."

"What else is new about her?"

Adeline told Malia why Karoline had taken her aside.

"Are you trying to tell me she has a soul after all?"

"Maybe."

"Maybe people can change. Maybe people can surprise you if they live long enough."

Adeline was suddenly overcome with emotion and hugged her older sister.

"What was that about?" Malia asked when they separated.

"That was thanks," Adeline said. "For being you and being here and sticking up for your little sister. And because of what happened, what we heard earlier today."

Her older sister sobered. "I imagine there will be a lot of that."

"Not with me," Adeline said. "I'll claw and bite until they bleed if they come."

Later that evening, she lay between her sons on the ground, facing the last of the glowing embers in the fire and hearing Marie trying to soothe her twins. Rutger had developed a hacking cough during the day, and Hans had come down with the fever as well. But Adeline could not take her mind off the young refugee girl, no older than sixteen, whom they'd seen two Soviets drag off the road into a barn.

They had all heard her screaming, even the boys, who had been frightened and asked what was happening to the girl and why. Adeline had told them she didn't know and didn't want to know, and she'd told herself that she would not let it happen to her. No matter what, she would not let herself be raped by animals. But lying there on the ground, with a mad chorus of bugs and night birds calling to her from the creek bottom, she knew she had never felt so frightened and alone in her entire life despite her mother and sister being less than ten meters away.

Emil was gone and with him her unwavering faith in God and her ability to survive and keep her sons alive. During the entire trek out of Ukraine, her faith had stayed strong, and she'd believed that God walked at her side. Now, she realized it was Emil who had really walked at her side, and with him gone, she felt abandoned, thrown to the wind, forgotten by grace.

For the hundredth night since she'd last seen Emil yelling at her to go west, Adeline shut her eyes and prayed to God to save him and to take her and the boys safely west where he could find them. And for the hundredth night since she'd last seen him, she fell asleep, plagued by a dark silence that made her heart ache all the more.

———

The next day, Adeline and the boys pushed and pulled the little wagon for fourteen kilometers. The third day, they managed ten. The boys never complained, because they saw the thousands of other refugees just like them jamming the roads, all heading toward German soil. It rained for a while that third afternoon, which helped everyone but Marie's sons, who were burning up with fever and were weakened by the rattling, choking cough that ravaged their lungs.

They camped in an abandoned silo that night, and the sounds of the twins' whimpers and cries and Marie's soothing words echoed all around them. Marie's sons finally settled down. Adeline fell into a deep, dreamless sleep that was broken by machine gun fire. Bullets pierced the silo above them, letting thin shafts of sunlight in, and turning every one of them hysterical with fear.

The shooting stopped as quickly as it had begun. They heard men laughing. They all screamed that there were people inside. If they heard, they didn't care and raked the upper silo with a few more bursts before it stopped.

Will was crying and held Malia. Walt had gone quiet but held tight to Adeline. Lydia was sobbing. So was Marie, who crouched over her twins, protecting them.

Shaking from adrenaline, Adeline told Walt to stay with Will, went to the hatch door to the silo and pushed it open. She ducked her head out, seeing three Russian soldiers walking away, vodka bottles in their hands, machine guns over their shoulders. Beyond them on the road, hundreds of other refugees were already on the move, streaming toward the broken Fatherland.

When she turned back, Will was wiping the tears from his eyes. Walt sat on the floor of the silo, staring down, silent. Malia and Lydia were staring off into the distance. And Marie was still crouched over her little boys and crying in low, terrible moans.

"It's okay," Adeline said. "They're gone. Couple of drunken soldiers is all."

Adeline went over to her cousin, who continued to moan, crouched, and rubbed her back. "I said it's okay, Marie. They're gone now."

Marie's chest heaved, and she groaned. "Make it stop, Adella. Please make it stop."

"Hey," Malia said, kneeling next to her. "What's the matter, sweetie?"

Marie lifted her head at last, her expression tortured, her eyes like bloodred saucers. "My little boy's gone," she whispered, "and I don't know what to do."

Adeline was confused and then horrified when she looked under Marie at the twins, seeing Hans in his cloth diaper, squirming on his blanket, his chubby cheeks flush with fever, and his brother stiff, cold, and blue.

———

While Malia and the boys dug a grave outside, Marie stayed in the silo, all but ignoring the squawking little boy in her lap as she gazed dumbly at the shawl covering his twin.

Adeline remained at her side the entire time. "Hans wants to eat," she said softly.

"He wants to, but he doesn't when his fever's spiking like this," Marie replied in a daze. "Rutger did the same thing two days ago."

Walt stuck his head in. "It's ready, Mama."

Marie's face twisted in pain. She held out Hans to Adeline. "I'll carry Rutger."

"No."

"I'll carry my boy," she insisted.

Remembering the day that she buried her own firstborn, Adeline took Hans and watched her cousin wrap her dead boy in the shawl and carry him outside. When she went to lower Rutger into the grave, she almost fell in after him, but Malia grabbed her and held her tight.

Lydia began to recite the Lord's Prayer. Malia joined her. Adeline was unable to give much voice to the words while Marie sobbed out her heart and soul.

After they'd filled the grave, Marie said, "I'm not ready to leave him. I can't."

"You have to," Adeline said, handing Hans to Malia and going to her cousin. "You have another boy to think of and cherish."

"But I'll never be here again."

Adeline went to the grave, grabbed a handful of the earth, and wrapped it in her handkerchief. "You'll take this dirt with you, and when you find a home, you'll bury it and put up a cross so you can grieve properly. But for now, as hard as it is, you'll have to leave him behind and think about Hans."

Marie had a piteous look on her face as she took the kerchief that contained the grave dirt. She clutched it to her chest as she trudged toward her wagon. Adeline knew that hunched-over, tortured posture all too well and mourned for Marie, understanding that the only thing that would unwind her cousin's pain was time and the joy of other children.

———

July 2, 1945
Near Wykroty, Poland

Adeline and her family were less than twenty-six kilometers from the German border, trudging in relentless heat on a road jammed with refugees and Soviet army trucks, when Marie began to scream because Hans had stopped breathing. The panicked nurse tried mouth-to-mouth and beat on her son's chest. But her second boy was gone, and with him went Marie's mind.

After an initial torturous outpouring of grief, Adeline's cousin seemed not to hear anything said to her, even when Adeline told her the only place that she could bury Hans was under cinders by the railroad tracks. Her cousin watched blankly as Malia covered her second son and did not react when Adeline handed her a kerchief with the cinders of his grave in it.

Marie put it in her wagon beside the one with soil from Rutger's grave and then began pushing her cart vigorously toward Germany. Adeline and the boys struggled to keep up with her. Marie did not look back. Not once. Nor did she seem to cry.

An hour later, they reached a slowdown in traffic. A truck carrying young Soviet troops rolled by them and slowed to a stop. The soldiers were drinking vodka and singing. They noticed Marie pushing her cart, her blouse sweated through, her breasts swollen with milk. One of them called to her in Russian.

"Beautiful lady, why are you alone? Come in here with us, and we will party!"

Marie did not answer, just kept walking past them. The soldier got up and peered around the canvas at her.

"Did you see the size of her tits?" he asked his friends. "Bazookas!"

His friends roared with laughter and seemed not to notice Adeline and her boys as they walked past the truck. A few moments later, she saw other vehicles ahead begin to move and heard the brakes of the truck behind them sigh. It rolled past her, and she saw that same soldier hanging out the side of the truck.

"Beautiful lady!" he called as the truck passed Marie again. "You should not be alone like this. Come with us. We will have fun."

The truck stopped. If Marie heard him, she did not show it. She just kept walking in that same quickened pace she'd adopted since leaving Hans's grave. And Adeline and the boys again hurried by the truck and were ignored once more.

The soldier was, if anything, determined. When his truck went by Marie a third time, he held out a full bottle of vodka and said, "Beautiful lady, forget your miserable refugee life! Come with me. We will drink and party all the way to Berlin!"

The truck kept moving and got a good fifty meters ahead of Marie before it stopped. Adeline's cousin did not break stride as she abandoned her cart and started toward the truck. The soldiers saw what she'd done and started yelling encouragement and waving their vodka bottles at her.

"Come on, beautiful lady!" cried the soldier who'd been heckling her. "You'll never get a chance like this again!"

"Marie!" Adeline shouted. "Don't!"

But then the truck started up again, and her grief-shattered cousin broke into a run. The Russian soldiers went wild screaming and yelling to her. Marie sprinted and caught up to the truck. Hands reached out and hauled her up and inside.

A bottle of vodka was shoved into her hands while many other hands roamed over her. To the delight of the troops, Marie began writhing her body sinuously against their hands, tilted the bottle back, and started guzzling.

The truck sped up, and Adeline's cousin spiraled out of her life like a leaf caught in a gale.

Chapter Twenty-Seven

July 3, 1945
Poltava, Ukraine

In the five weeks since his arrival at the prison camp, Emil had learned to cherish the wind. Even the thought of it blowing against his skin was enough for him to survive the nights. The Soviets kept Emil, Nikolas, and six hundred of the remaining two thousand prisoners in the vast basement of the Poltava museum. The upper floors had been destroyed in the bombing.

They slept one hundred men to a room on long, low, crudely built wooden bunks with no mattresses. That many bodies in that confined a space created its own infernal heat and humidity, so, in the dense air, water dripped from the ceilings and upper bunks all night long. Emil couldn't decide which was worse, being outside in the raging sun, or in the dank hole of the bunkroom, crammed in with all those stinking men snoring, moaning, farting, weeping, and crying for deliverance in their sleep.

The sanitary conditions were beyond abysmal. Men went outside, sat on flat boards, and shit into a long trench that they dug and buried every three days. The city water was compromised. Prisoners began to fall ill almost immediately from giardiasis and dysentery. Emil could hear the afflicted men groaning and quick-footing it to the latrine all night long.

They slept in their clothes so they could be woken, brought up from the museum basement quickly, and then mobilized to march six blocks to a make-shift kitchen set up in front of the ruins of the Poltava city hall. Several of the remaining women in the city cooked for the prisoners, whose diet consisted of thin vegetable soup, a pound of bread to last the entire day, beets, potatoes, and the occasional chunk of boiled fatback.

Other men complained, but Emil closed his eyes and imagined every meal was cooked by Adeline. As he spooned the soup, he tasted her chicken soup with handmade egg noodles. When he bit into the bread, he imagined the strudel she used to make in the fall, filled with fresh berries picked from the vine. And when he put the fatback in his mouth, he swallowed it as if it were her finest schnitzel.

They were assigned to crews. The first few crews were put to work reconstructing the main waterworks, the city hall, and the museum.

Emil and Nikolas were assigned to a two-hundred-man unit charged with rebuilding the hospital. They had a hand in all of it at first: clearing the rubble from the ruins of the facility, digging out the remains of the foundation, and then building wooden forms to hold concrete.

When the forms were in place, Emil was put to work on a team mixing lime, clay, and fly ash for the cement, and then mixing that with sand, gravel, and furnace slag to form concrete, which was poured into the forms. The assignment kept him off to the side of the fury of activity on the hospital site, and he preferred it that way. The guards barely gave him a glance as he mixed concrete. He held his head down, worked hard, and kept his mouth shut.

I can survive this, he told himself over and over again those first few days. *I will survive this place, but only if I rely on myself alone. No allies means no betrayals.*

Emil also kept alert for opportunities to escape. So far there had been none. They were guarded at the hospital site. They were watched marching to meals and on their way back to the museum basement. Once down there and on the wooden bunks, Emil ignored the men shifting to either side of him and tried to fall straight asleep, hoping to be in a deeper, darker place when the night suffering began.

But in the middle of the night, when he'd been pushed or kicked or snored awake, he'd try to think of Adeline and Will and Walt to give him hope of making it through another day.

July 5, 1945
Cottbus, Germany

As they approached the first large town in Soviet-held eastern Germany, Adeline was still shaken by Marie's decision to jump into the truck with the Russians. But then, she'd look back at the boys, still pushing the cart. *What might I do if both of them were taken from me or killed?*

Those thoughts haunted her every step of the next four days, which unfolded in blazing heat and humidity. At a fork in a road that passed through woods near the town of Falkenberg, Adeline called for a rest. Her mother limped over and sat on a boulder in the shade.

"You can all go on without me," she said. "I'll live here."

Adeline sighed. "On that rock, Mother? In this forest?"

"No," Lydia snapped, and gestured to the road sign. "I am going into that town, finding out who is in charge, and asking for a place to stay."

"Mother," Adeline said, "we're less than two weeks' walk from Berlin. Two weeks from finding a way to the western Allies and—"

"Stop that nonsense!" her mother shouted, pounding her bony little fist against her thigh. "That was Emil's crazy idea, not mine and not yours. For better, for worse, we know how it works under Stalin. The sooner we settle down and adapt, the better. Admit it, Adeline, once and for all. Karoline was right. Emil is gone, just like his brother. He will never find a way back to you. Don't waste your life waiting for him. Your foolish dream of a green valley is over."

Adeline was surprised at the fierce bitterness that pumped through the old woman. "It is not over, Mother, until I say it is over. My husband, who I love and trust, told me to go as far west as I can, and he'll find me. I believed him then. I believe him now."

"I believed your father when he said he'd come back, too."

Adeline ignored her and looked at Malia. "We can find a place for her to stay, and you can come with us."

Her older sister smiled sadly and took Adeline's hand in hers. "My place is with Mother; you know that."

Adeline gazed at Malia, both of them blinking back tears. "I told you once I couldn't do this without you."

"I know, but now you have to," Malia said. "I don't want you to go, but you have to do what you think is right."

"We'll find each other again, won't we?"

"That's in the hands of a power far greater than us, dear," Malia said, taking Adeline in her arms. "But take my love with you wherever you go. And I'll take your love with me. And hopefully, someday, like your friend Mrs. Kantor, we'll be able to see the beauty in every cruelty we've had to endure. Even this moment."

Leaving her older sister's arms felt like roots were being ripped from her chest. That feeling amplified when Adeline went to her mother, who would not look at her as she said, "Don't promise me anything."

"I won't, Mother," Adeline said. "This is good-bye, then."

For a few gut-wrenching moments, she thought Lydia would be cold at their parting. But then her mother's shoulders trembled, and she got up to hug her daughter.

"You always were braver than me," Lydia whispered. "Like your father."

"I got the rest of me from you," Adeline said, her throat constricting as she felt how thin her mother had gotten on this most recent walk toward freedom.

When they broke apart, Adeline called to the boys to say good-bye to their *oma* and aunt Malia. Walt was stoic, but Will began to cry as he hugged Malia. And then they had to go.

"I can't sit here watching you leave," Malia said. "We'll each go our own way at the same time."

Adeline nodded, unable to stop the tears from flowing down her cheeks as she went to the front of the little wagon and picked up the handle. She wiped at the tears, then looked at the boys, forced a smile, and said, "Here we go. The Martels are off on another adventure."

With a weak last wave toward her mother and older sister, Adeline turned fully away, mentally chopping the ties, drenched with fear, but taking a step in her own direction and another and a third. She would later think that the first step she took that day, away from her past and toward an uncertain future, was like a leap between cliffs and the second-most courageous act of her life.

———

On July 16, 1945, Adeline, Walt, and Will walked down a road that passed through beautiful fields of ruby, purple, and white wildflowers glistening in a light mist and fog. The chill on the northerly breeze felt good after so many days walking in the heat. She smiled as the sun came and went, gleaming, giving her a show and making her realize just how much she loved flowers. Their hue, delicateness, and shape. Their tragically brief time on earth.

"It sure is pretty here, Mama," Walt said.

"It is," Adeline said.

"Is this our valley?" Will wondered. "I can't see any mountains."

"I can't see much of anything except flowers and fog, and that's enough for now," Adeline said, relaxing, feeling less anxious about their future.

Will ran off the road, picked her a bunch, and ran to catch up. "So you can look at them all day, Mama," he said, which got her choked up and more in love with her little boy than ever.

They reached the southeastern outskirts of Berlin about an hour later. What they saw in the next five hours made Adeline question her decision to leave her mother and sister behind. She had never been in a city as large as Berlin, so at first, she felt the excitement of newness. But as the fog swirled in and out and they walked deeper into Hitler's fallen capital, she soon realized that nearly ten weeks after the Nazi surrender, even with many streets cleared for traffic, Berlin remained a landscape of ruin, a deeply scarred and wounded place, a charred, haunted maze where the smells of bomb soot, burned chemicals, and death vied for dominance. Eighty-one thousand Soviets, one hundred thousand German soldiers, and one hundred and twenty-five thousand civilians had died in the Battle of Berlin, street by devastated road and building by rubble and wreckage. Depending on location and the wind, the stench of death rose and fell. Some bodies had evidently not yet been found, gathered, and buried or burned.

There were Red Army soldiers and prisoners everywhere, picking at the debris. They were stacking usable bricks and loading the rest into dump trucks. As she passed each knot of prisoners, Adeline scanned their faces, hoping against hope that she'd somehow spot Emil among them. But no one even resembled him among the men at hard physical labor.

Is this what Emil is doing? Is he like these prisoners?

In the ebb and flow of mist and fog, and the closer they got to the center of Berlin, the more the city was revealed as a ruptured, alien place with many of the structures being amputees, or skeletons, or debris. In that vast graveyard, she saw thousands of people living in apartments where some of the walls were missing, or under sheets and tarps amid the destruction. Adeline and the boys walked past hundreds of burned-out buildings, and women washing clothes in buckets of water from a hydrant, their children streaked with bomb soot and playing on mounds of shattered brick and bent steel.

She heard them speaking in German, all telling a similar tale of still being shell-shocked by the vicious street battle waged in Berlin during the last nine days of the war and worrying about their sorry lot in life now that Hitler was dead and the great Reich had been destroyed.

You have no idea of the suffering your Hitler caused, Adeline thought a little angrily. *Everything we have is in this cart, and I don't have enough food to feed my children tonight.*

One prisoner picked up a chunk of cement, turned, and walked at her with vacant eyes that made her shudder. He reminded her of Johann when he first came back from Siberia—a broken man—and she felt ill at the idea that Emil might return to her in a similar condition.

Adeline pulled and the boys pushed the little wagon a good three kilometers into the city before they were finally stopped at a Soviet checkpoint by a soldier who asked to see her papers. She spoke to him in Russian, which seemed to confuse him, as she lied and said she had no papers. She told him a convoluted story about being dragged out of Ukraine by the German army and getting separated from her husband.

"I was told he is here, working in western Berlin," she said in a pleading tone. "We are just trying to find him."

The soldier glanced at Walt and Will, filthy and exhausted by the last few weeks of walking. Adeline intentionally thought of Emil and summoned tears. The sentry got a disgusted look on his face and waved them through.

When she saw the first British soldier, she threw back her head and cheered. The boys looked at her like she was crazy.

"We made it, boys! We're where Papa wanted us! In the West, with the Allies!"

Adeline hurried up to a British soldier and tried to ask him where she could get food and shelter. But he did not speak German. When she heard her try in Russian, he pointed her back the way she'd come, shrugged, and turned away.

She pushed on, figuring she could find at least one American or British soldier who spoke Russian or German. Soon after, she and the boys were looking high up at the ruins of a church, seeing its spire split: one side was whole and barely scorched, and the other a blackened maw where some explosive from the sky had struck it a glancing blow, cleaving it in two. She couldn't believe how one side could remain untouched while the other was blasted and burned. She stared at the split spire for several more moments without understanding exactly why before pushing on.

Had it been a clear day, she might have used the sun as a guide to keep going west, deeper into the British Zone. But the skies darkened around noon and rain came. They ran, seeking shelter, abandoning all sense of direction and getting lost.

"Where are we going?" Walt asked as they huddled in an empty building.

"I don't know," Adeline said, so tired she felt confused now, unsure.

Will said, "I'm tired of walking, Mama."

"And I'm thirsty," Walt said. "And hungry."

Irritation and then anger bubbled inside Adeline. With the rain and the relentless uncertainty all around her, she almost took out her fear of not being enough on the boys: not being enough to make it to the West, not being enough to find Emil, not being enough to get food and water for her children. But she didn't. Instead, she took a deep breath and got them the last of the water from the wagon and the last of the bread she'd bought from a bakery outside the city.

———

The rain finally relented. They walked and soon found themselves in Tiergarten, a giant forested park that had been turned into a base for the British. Men were sawing down trees and clearing the land.

She tried two more British soldiers. Neither spoke German. But the second one understood some Russian.

"I need food for my children," she said.

"That way," he said, gesturing out of the park.

Not knowing that she was changing the course of her life, Adeline turned her sons and the little wagon in that direction. An hour later, they walked toward the bombed Reichstag, and she knew she'd gone the wrong way; a giant Soviet flag—bloodred with gold hammer and sickle—flew off the top of the damaged dome. The sun came out and hit the flag as it fluttered, causing it to glow brooding yellow and scarlet, like jaundice and fever. That's what tyranny was, Adeline decided, a sickness, a fever, a poison in the liver of mankind. The workers' flag, those foul colors, and the Nazi flag had waved above almost every injustice and harm she had ever lived through. Right then, she thought about turning around, going back into the British Zone and begging for food.

Walt said, "Mama, I'm tired of walking."

She heard him but did not answer.

"Mama," Will said. "I'm hungry and—"

Adeline couldn't take it anymore. She spun around and glared at her sons. "I know you're tired and hungry and thirsty, but I am not a magician. I cannot make things appear with the snap of my fingers or by closing my eyes and wishing it were so."

Unsettled by the unusually harsh tone in her voice, the boys retreated a step.

She saw them do it and felt terrible. She went to them, got down on her knees, and hugged them. "I will get us food as soon as I can. Please, I'm just as hungry and as tired as you are. Okay?"

Will squeezed her tight. "Okay, Mama. I'm not that hungry."

"Neither am I," Walt said.

Adeline rested her head on theirs a moment, realizing that once again her children might go to bed without a proper meal and a proper bed in which to sleep. In the shadow cast by the flapping Soviet flag, she felt cut off from everything she'd ever known and everyone she'd ever loved but for her boys.

She looked to the sky and said, "You've got to help us. We have no one else to turn to."

PART FOUR:
A TALE OF TWO
PRISONERS

Chapter Twenty-Eight

September 27, 1945
Poltava Prison Camp

Four months into his imprisonment, Emil awoke to the shouts of the Russian guards and realized he'd survived another night. He sat up, relieved to see that the men on either side of him on the bunk were moving as well. After lacing his boots, he shuffled to the staircase and climbed out into the dawn.

Emil lined up in the now-familiar formation, shivering in the cool fall air after the inferno of the basement. Nikolas stood three rows in front of him and to his left. They worked on the hospital but never together and had not spoken since June, which was how Emil preferred it. Two prisoners led a pony pulling a large wooden, four-wheel, flatbed cart into view.

The pony cart came empty and left the museum laden every morning and every evening. Emil saw the pony cart as he marched off to eat and as he marched back to sleep. Not once since he'd arrived back in May had he seen the cart depart the museum empty.

Every dawn revealed dead men in the bunks. Every dawn their corpses were dragged out of the basement, loaded on the pony cart, and taken to be buried in a field near the woods at the edge of the ruined city. The men who'd died at work during the day were loaded on the death cart and taken out in the evening by a second team of two prisoners.

The burial details were voluntary. Prisoners who agreed to handle the dead were rewarded with double rations of bread, soup, and fatback.

Despite his father's rule of eating everything offered to him, Emil had not volunteered for the detail even though it would have meant extra food. The idea of burying the dead brought back excruciating memories of that night in Dubossary.

He could also see that, despite the extra rations, the prisoners on the burial details did not last long. Disease was rampant in the camp. Handling the bodies struck Emil as a straight road to eternity. Like a many-headed hydra, the sicknesses came and went, only to return. Dysentery fluctuated between a scourge and an epidemic. Mosquitos thrived in the wet basement. Malaria reared and attacked. To prevent the spread of typhus, their hair was kept scalp-tight, and their clothes were boiled every other week to kill the lice that transmitted the disease. The Soviets tried to boil enough drinking water for the prisoners as well, but there were outbreaks of cholera.

Indeed, nothing seemed to stop the men around Emil from dying. Some two thousand men had entered Poltava with him. By his count, two hundred and fifty men had died since, leaving seventeen hundred and fifty of them to rebuild the city.

As Emil worked, as he marched, and as he slept, that fact kept worming around in his head: seventeen hundred and fifty men were left to rebuild a city of three hundred thousand people. *It's impossible. It would take us twenty years.*

He had been telling himself every morning that he was enough, that even if he could not escape, he could survive Poltava.

But for two decades? And what would I have to go back to?

Emil would be in his early fifties by then, close to his father's age when the Soviets let him go. His sons would be grown strangers. Adeline would have given up on him long ago and found another man and another life. And how would he ever find them in the first place?

Emil's confidence started to slip. He noticed how much weight he'd lost and with it some of his strength and stamina. Mixing concrete was hard labor, and he was unable to work at the same pace he had just the month before. His slowdown attracted the attention of the guards and the foremen, who berated him twice that afternoon to speed up the production of concrete blocks while the foundation cured.

Marching back to the museum that evening, chewing the last of his bread ration, Emil knew he'd broken two of his father's rules, work hard and stay unnoticed. But how was he going to work hard and stay unnoticed if they didn't give him enough to eat?

Twenty years with men dropping at this pace? he thought as he watched the burial detail set off with three more who died at work. *The numbers are wrong. They're lying. We won't last a year. I won't last a year. If I don't escape, I am going to die.*

Emil felt caged and had trouble breathing as he climbed down the stairs into the dreaded basement where he found a spot on the bottom bunk against the wall in the far corner where he would not have men to either side of him. Already feeling the heat building in the low-ceilinged room, he took off his boots, put them along the wall in a defensible position, and used the coat he'd been given for a pillow.

Closing his eyes, he remembered Adeline the day he married her, when his lips had touched hers at the ceremony's end and she was all he needed in life and their future had seemed impossibly bright. They had a small celebration afterward. Mrs. Kantor had hired an accordionist so everyone could dance. Emil had been nervous about slow-dancing with Adeline, but when she came into his arms, it was as natural as breathing. When their first dance ended, the accordionist played a toe-tapping tune that set their feet afire and made him deliriously happy, maybe the happiest he'd ever been.

"I love you, Emil Martel," Adeline cried at one point.

"I love you, too, Adeline Martel," Emil said. "You make me feel like I fell asleep in Russia and woke up in paradise."

Lying in his bunk in the prison camp, he drifted off to sleep, thinking, *You still make me feel like that, Adella. Be strong and wait for me.*

September 28, 1945
Gutengermendorf, Soviet-Occupied east Germany

The following morning, Adeline felt her heart swell with happiness as she watched almost eight-year-old Walt and almost six-year-old Will trot away from her down a grassy knoll and through a field of ripening sunflowers on their way to the rural village. It was a Friday, and this was their first day at school. They would be tested today and assigned to classes. Actual studies would begin on Monday, but she remembered her own first days of school and felt excited for them.

They'll love it, she told herself. *They're boys. They'll love it here, and I will learn to.*

They'd already adapted to so much, hadn't they? After sleeping outside hungry near the Reichstag, she'd found a shelter for refugees for two nights before the Soviet occupying authority sent them on a train to Gutengermendorf.

An elderly man named Peter Schmidt had begrudgingly picked them up at the station and taken them to his farm a kilometer and a half from the village. His wife, Greta, wasn't happy to have a family of three foisted on her on top of the Russian soldiers already billeted in their home, but she'd given Adeline and the boys their own room in an outbuilding that was clean and dry and safe.

Given her history, they put Adeline to work as a field hand. Within a few weeks, she had proved her worth, and the couple turned friendlier, especially when they discovered she was as skilled in the kitchen as she was weeding, scything, or threshing.

"They grow up fast," Mrs. Schmidt said. She'd come up behind Adeline as she held her hand to her brow and watched her boys exit the sunflowers, heading toward a line of elm and chestnut trees that marked the village boundary.

"Too fast, Frau Schmidt," Adeline said. "I wish my husband could be here to see this."

The elderly woman put her hand on Adeline's shoulder. "Almost everyone has lost someone they loved because of Hitler's war."

Adeline smiled sadly and nodded, knowing that the Schmidts' son had died on the western front the winter before, fighting with the Wehrmacht against the invading Allies.

"But maybe your Emil will be one of the lucky ones," Frau Schmidt said. "Maybe you will see him walking through the village someday. But you should not dwell too much on that kind of dream. That kind of dream, Adeline, can break your heart."

Adeline thought of her mother. "I know it can. The sunflowers?"

"We need every one of them down before nightfall. Peter says it's going to rain tonight, first real cool-off of the season." She paused. "You'll be needing us to watch the boys tomorrow night?"

"Please," Adeline said. "I can't tell you what a help that is."

"I'm glad to do it," she said. "When soldiers are drunk, they're savages."

Adeline went with two other field hands down into the sunflowers where she spent the day cutting their stalks and piling them into bundles and then hauling them up to the barn where they were hung upside down to dry before the seeds were harvested. She liked the work because it was familiar, and that gave her comfort and peace during the long hours of toil.

She sang and hummed old songs for hours until she remembered how Emil used to sing lullabies to the boys before they slept. It was the only time all day she stopped to cry.

The boys returned later in the afternoon, running from the village as she cut down the last of the sunflowers. They sprinted when they saw her, hugged her, and babbled on about the school, their teachers, their new friends, and could they go tomorrow to play with them in the village. It would be Saturday after all, no school until Monday, and Will's new friend had a real leather soccer ball. They were so excited and full of the newness of their lives, it was contagious, and she couldn't help but laugh and clap and want to ask them about every moment of their day since they'd been gone.

That feeling remained with Adeline through dinner and even afterward as she led the boys in the moonlight from the farmhouse back to the outbuilding where they slept. She felt satisfied with the day, almost content with her lot. She had worked hard doing what she liked for people she liked. They had fed her family well in return, and now she was going to sleep with a roof overhead and with her schoolboys at her side.

"Is this our pretty green valley, Mama?" Will asked before they went inside.

"It's pretty," Adeline said, yawning.

"No mountains and no big river running through it," Walt said in mild protest.

"Is it, Mama?" Will said. "I like it here."

She smiled at him. "Remember what I told you when you asked me that same question last year in Romania?"

"No."

"I do," Walt said. "You said, 'This is the green valley we are in today, and we should enjoy it.'"

"That's right," she said, and kissed him on the head, grateful that her older son seemed to be coming out of the shell that had formed during his repeated encounters with tanks and bullets.

———

Adeline slept fitfully that night but rose before dawn as she had nearly every morning since she'd gotten to the farm. She dressed quietly so as not to wake the boys and went out into the crisp air, smelling the fall and looking east for the first rays of the sun. She'd taken to imagining that they belonged to Emil, reaching out to her.

She helped pitch hay until three o'clock that Saturday afternoon when Will and Walt returned from playing in the village. After taking a shower, Adeline and the boys went into the farmhouse where Frau Schmidt had already cooked their evening meal: thin pork chops with onions sautéed with fresh black pepper, squash from the garden, and applesauce made from fruit gathered from the trees out back. It was so incredibly good, Adeline begged her for the recipe, which pleased the older woman all the more.

Kindness and good people still exist, Adeline thought as the farmer and his wife chatted with the boys about their new friends at school. Once again, in the company of her sons and this couple, she was content, almost at home, and it made her feel a little guilty and anxious. This farm, this village, weren't as far west as she could have gone, and she was not going to find the freedom that Emil longed for here. No matter how comfortable her life felt at the moment, the Soviets had only been in control of eastern Germany for less than five months.

Give them a little time, Adeline thought. *They'll ruin this place and the hearts of these good people, take their lands, cast them out, sow hate, and turn them against each other. It's guaranteed. It's what Stalin does. It's what tyrants do. And I don't want to be here to see it happen. I don't want the boys to be so beaten down by life, they—*

"Adella?" Frau Schmidt said. "Did you hear me say it's nearly five o'clock? Saturday night?"

Adeline's eyes shot to the clock. "Sorry. I was off somewhere," she said, getting up and hurrying to the sink to do the dishes.

When she was done and the boys were drying and stacking, she gave them each a hug and a peck on the cheek. "Mama will be home in the morning, and we'll think of something fun we can do together."

"Like what?" Will asked.

"Pick the rest of the apples," Frau Schmidt said. "Every tree. You'll get to climb the tallest ladders and eat the ripest fruit."

Both boys broke into grins, hugged their mother one more time, and went back to their chores. Frau Schmidt followed her out of the farmhouse and onto the modest front porch.

"Thank you," Adeline said again.

The older woman took her hands and said, "You've been through enough. We don't need to add insult to injury, do we?"

"No," Adeline said, and squeezed her hands. "I'll see you early. Make sure the boys keep their door locked."

"Early's good, and I will make sure they're sleeping it off."

Adeline went back to her room and put a blanket, a pillow, a bottle of water, and a small Lutheran Bible Frau Schmidt had given her in a large cloth sack. She put the sack over her shoulder and left the outbuilding and then the farmyard, headed down the knoll toward the cut-sunflower field and the village. She'd reached the stubble, scattering three roe deer that had come in for the seeds that had fallen during the harvest.

Then she heard men laughing and singing to her left. She looked across the northern hayfields to the dirt road that led from the village to the farm and saw the three Soviet soldiers who also lived with the Schmidts. The men were too far for her to see clearly, but she knew each of them carried a bottle of vodka issued to them by the Red Army. It was Saturday night, vodka night, payback for staying mostly sober the other six days of the week. It was also rape night, when the Soviet soldiers were free as a matter of unwritten policy to take any woman over the age of sixteen and under the age of fifty, consenting or not, as a spoil of war.

Adeline did not consent, and she would not be a spoil of war. She took her attention off the Russians and hurried on through the cut field and across the south hayfield toward that line of hardwood trees turning color. The air was already cooling. The light was soft and golden in the late-day sun. Horses neighed in their pastures, and cocks crowed in the distance. Far behind her, she heard her sons laughing as they played before dark.

———

Reaching the trees, Adeline stopped in the shadows beneath one old elm. She shut her eyes and listened and breathed, her nostrils open to the smell of leaves and cut hay. She could still taste the applesauce, and for a moment she could almost believe in a world without hardship and strife.

Then she heard the soldiers singing raucously in the distance, drunk already, soon to be fed and soon to be drunker and in search of a woman. Adeline stayed in the shade of the trees and walked the length of them behind houses that reminded her of the nicer homes in Birsula, and one in particular that always put her in mind of Mrs. Kantor's house. She did not stop to admire it but hurried on into thicker foliage until she was abreast of the rear of the old Lutheran church and out of sight of the main road that ran through the village.

Adeline continued past the church a good twenty-five meters, looked around to make sure she was alone, then squatted to pee before returning to the church. The small rear door was slightly ajar. She paused to listen and to peer at the narrow slices of the main village road she could see. No one was walking. No one was talking.

She dashed across the forty meters of grass that separated her from the door, pushed it open, slid inside, and then almost closed it shut. She turned, breathing deep and slow as she let her eyes adjust to the dim interior, seeing two women in their forties already camped in the pews forward and left, and a much younger woman midway down the center aisle on the right.

Adeline knew them by sight, if not by name. They all had Soviet soldiers billeted in their homes. One by one, more women entered the church by the rear door and began to stake out places to sleep. Adeline preferred a pew in the back right. Most of the women who sought refuge in the church were locals, either from the village or the surroundings. They knew who Adeline was, where she lived, and her circumstances. They treated her with civility but little warmth or friendship.

That was fine by Adeline. She was there for one reason: to sleep in safety so she could rise and go home early to be with Will and Walt while the Russians slept and suffered their hangovers and wondered where all the village women went on Saturday night. Let them. She was going to pick apples tomorrow and enjoy the bounty and beauty of harvest time before it was gone and snow blanketed the land.

There were sixteen women in the old church when one of the fathers of the two youngest girls wished them all good night. An older woman barred the door behind him. Adeline heard him bar the door from the other side and lock it in place with three different locks.

Adeline sat on the blanket, looking forward past the small knots of women whispering to each other. For a few minutes, she stared into the fading light at the altar and the shadow where the cross had hung high on the wall behind it.

When she could no longer see the shadow of the cross, she drank some of her water and told herself it had been a good day. Better than she could have hoped for.

But then she thought about Emil and felt a deep pain in her heart. When she was with Frau Schmidt or out working in the fields or with the boys in their room, she could keep thoughts of him at bay. But here in the gathering darkness of the old church, there was nothing to distract her, and her loneliness was almost overwhelming.

How long could she last, living on hope and a vow? She'd always told herself she wouldn't be like her mother, wouldn't live a life of hoping that every knock at the door was love returning, only to open it and endure heartbreak all over again.

When the darkness was complete and she could hear the other village women settling down to sleep, Adeline did the same, realizing that she had not opened the Bible while it was still light enough to read. But then again, she rationalized as she pulled the blanket over her and plumped the pillow, why should she pray when she wasn't getting answers anymore?

Drained by six days of labor, Adeline fell asleep quickly and into deeper, dreamless, merciful darkness.

She awoke eight hours later at the sound of keys turning in the locks and the bar being lifted from the door. The rear door opened and was left slightly ajar. She gathered her things immediately and went outside to watch the dawn and the first fingers of light reaching toward her from the east.

———

November 1, 1945
Poltava, Ukraine

The Soviet guards rang triangles in the darkness, the peals and pings penetrating the sleeping heads of the surviving prisoners. Emil roused groggily. The afternoon before, he'd suffered cramping and diarrhea and been terrified that he'd contracted dysentery, which was still taking lives throughout the camp. But he'd chewed a bit of charcoal to quiet his gut and slept through the night. He still felt lousy, but he had not stayed awake all night with his ass over a cold plank outdoors in the latrine.

"Get up!" the guards bellowed, ringing the triangle again. "Move!"

Emil forced himself into his pants and boots, still damp from the day before. Putting on the jacket and cap, he wondered how long the Russians thought they'd survive if they had to work in this kind of clothing in the middle of January.

They don't care if we live or die, he thought as he climbed the stairs out of the basement and stepped through the doors into brilliant light. Frost covered all the machines and equipment around the museum, sparkling in the floodlights' glare. With his clothes, socks, and boots still damp, Emil almost immediately started shivering and had to stamp his feet and swing his arms to stay warm while the basement emptied out behind him.

The burial detail was right on schedule. Two new prisoners led the pony pulling the death cart to the museum's freight entrance. They disappeared into the basement and quickly returned with two bodies, the lowest count in days. The guards ordered Emil and the other prisoners to march to a new mess facility in the basement of the city hall. As they started, he glanced at the men on burial detail. In the past two months alone, he'd counted almost one hundred and seventy more dead. They were now down to fifteen hundred and eighty men to rebuild the city.

How long can we last? he asked himself yet again. *How long can I last?*

As they climbed downstairs into the basement, Emil decided that he could last for today. Beyond that, he had no idea. But he intended to live through the day and see another tomorrow. Or die trying.

Standing in line, he heard the cooks complaining about not having enough wood for fuel. He took a bowl of hot cabbage soup, his daily ration of bread, a hunk of stale cheese, and the piece of cold sausage that was the best thing he'd had to eat since he arrived in Poltava. As he lingered over the sausage and soup, he remembered the scraps of lumber all around the hospital site.

As he was leaving, he asked a cook how much she'd pay for an armful of wood for her stove. She told him one ruble. It was one ruble more than he had, so he told her he'd bring her wood in the evening. Then he girded himself for what lay ahead and went back outside, where it felt even colder than before.

The darkness began to lift. He watched the eastern horizon as it brightened and felt better as his crew set off toward the hospital site. Emil had always thought Adeline glowed like the dawn, and nearly six months into his imprisonment, he seemed to sense her most at sunrise; or at least he thought of her most then, of her smile, and her scent, and the glint in her eye when she was teasing him. These memories would make Emil smile and get him through the fourteen-hour workday, just as they had on all the other fourteen-hour workdays.

And the memories did help him that entire morning. The month before, Emil had figured out an easier way to make cement and then concrete in larger batches by mixing it in a large metal horse trough with a one-meter length of wood he'd cut and fashioned as a mixing paddle.

The easier horse-trough-and-paddle method had boosted his production. And he'd been able to maintain his strength and weight. Better, the foremen and the guards weren't down his throat all the time. He was giving them what they wanted, and he was staying unnoticed.

So Emil was more than concerned when he saw someone much worse than a guard or a foreman coming toward his cement-block operation with a blueprint rolled up in his hand. It was the site superintendent, a big Russian named Ivanov, who had perpetual dark bags under his eyes and an endless series of cigarettes dangling, smoldering, yet somehow never falling from the left corner of his lips.

Emil had never actually spoken to Ivanov, but now the man in charge of rebuilding the hospital came in under the tin roof and right up to him. "You build my concrete blocks, yes?"

Emil was rattled by the big Russian's presence but nodded.

"I need more," he said. "Twice as many as you make for me now. No, three times. We are behind schedule. We have to close up a large part of the building before the snow flies. What do you need to triple your daily production?"

Emil did not expect to be asked and thought before he answered.

"Three men to help me," he said. "Warmer clothes and boots for them and me. Three times the block forms. Three times the materials."

Then he pointed to piles of lime stacked against the back wall of his work area. "I'll need a much larger storage shelter for the materials with walls and a roof and a covered, walled workspace big enough for three horse troughs like this one. And three boat paddles. And as it gets colder, we'll need a way to keep the concrete warm enough to set properly."

Ivanov gave him a look of reappraisal. "Nothing else?"

Emil hesitated, but then said, "Twice the rations. We'll need the extra food if you expect us to stay alive and working."

The Russian lit another cigarette, put it in the left corner of his lips, took a drag, and blew it out the right side. "Two men. You will have the rest of what you need. And if you are not making three times the blocks at this time next week, you will be taken out and shot."

Chapter Twenty-Nine

The superintendent was a man of his word. Within two days, Ivanov had expanded Emil's workspace and put up rudimentary walls and a longer, wider tin roof that extended over the storage area, which had a large, wide rear door through which the various materials could be brought in.

Early the third morning, his two men arrived a few minutes apart. The first prisoner in was a burly central Asian with a pumpkin-shaped head, an Uzbek named Krull, who said he'd been drafted into the Soviet army and sent to fight in Poland. When the Red Army launched its attack on Berlin, he'd had enough of war, went AWOL, and got caught heading east.

"I got east," Krull said. "Just not far enough."

The second man through the door was the last person Emil wanted to see. Nikolas had to stoop and duck his head to get through the smallest of the three doors. He'd lost a lot of weight and still limped.

He grimaced at Emil. "What are you doing here?" he said.

"I work here," Emil replied. "Just do what I tell you and we'll have no problems."

"I don't take orders from you, Martel."

"Yes, you do," Ivanov said.

The site superintendent had just come through the door with guards behind him carrying winter clothing and boots. "You will do exactly what Martel says when he says it. Is that clear? Or would you prefer to work outside all winter?"

Nikolas wasn't happy, but he said, "I'll stay."

———

The heavy boots and clothes were a big improvement in warmth, and the walls and roof kept them less exposed to wind and weather, which worsened through November 1945. But tripling the output had Emil working harder than ever, moving enough raw materials, and water, and mixing and pouring to feed Ivanov's demand for concrete while winter growled louder and louder from the north. On his way back to the city hall basement and his evening meal, he'd linger and pick up an armful of scrap lumber and tote it to the cook for another ruble in his pocket.

Day after day, Emil told himself it would get easier, that he'd find a way to make more concrete blocks and work less. But he didn't or couldn't. Even with the bigger troughs to mix in and the paddles, he, Nikolas, and Krull were working so hard to make the quota, most days after gathering wood for the cooks, he was left too tired and too hungry to think clearly, even with the double rations.

The rest of the prisoners in camp got more winter gear soon after Emil's crew did, and they were all given an extra quarter ration of food to offset the demands of toiling in the cold. But the warmer clothes and the extra food could not extinguish the diseases that continued to smolder, catch fire, and sweep through the basement of the museum and through the other nearby basements where the rest of the surviving prisoners bunked.

Three dead one morning. Two that evening. Three the next morning. Five in the evening. Then typhus reared its head again. Six men were found dead the following morning. Five in the evening. Nine the next morning. Emil heard the pony pant with effort and the burial cart's axle groan when it left with two new prisoners who'd volunteered for the detail.

The Soviets responded to the typhus outbreak by forcing the men to strip off their heavy clothes, which were soaked in a boiled lye solution. After they were put through yet another delousing shower, they were forced to put the wet wool clothes back on and wear them through the day in the cold so they would not shrink. Men began to contract pneumonia.

"Every one of us is going to die," Nikolas said bitterly later in the month, as they mixed their ninth big batch of concrete for the day. "It's just a matter of time."

"It always is," Krull said.

Nikolas sneered at the Uzbek. "Who asked you?"

He shifted from Russian into German, lost his grit, said, "I don't feel right here, Martel."

"Who does in this hole?"

"It's more than that: inside and up here," Nikolas said, touching his left chest and forehead. "Everything feels heavy and dark. I keep having nightmares and thoughts that won't stop. They're all telling me it's just a matter of time."

"Like Krull said, it always is," Emil said.

Nikolas shook his head violently and shouted at him. "You don't understand! I'm doomed, and so are you, Martel! We were doomed for our sins, doomed the moment we took the gun and decided to pull the trigger on those Jews. This is just one step down into the deep hell that awaits us after we shit or cough ourselves to death!"

The triangle began to ring outside, signaling the end of the workday. Emil's heart ached as he finished pouring the last of his concrete. He tried to think of Adeline, but her image would not come to him because Nikolas's words kept ringing in his head.

Doomed the moment we took the gun and decided to pull the trigger . . . This is just one step down into the deep hell that awaits us . . .

He recalled that night in Dubossary, saw Haussmann aiming his Luger at him, and felt himself change his mind and decide to pull the trigger on those poor Jewish kids all over again. Emil heard echoes of his own voice, then the SS officer's, and then Nikolas's.

Okay, I'll do it.

Wise choice.

Doomed the moment we took the gun and decided to pull the trigger.

As he was walking behind Nikolas to the mess hall, eating, and then marching back to the museum, those three voices would not stop playing in Emil's head. They continued in the basement, in the dark, and as he fell into a restless sleep where he was plagued by nightmares, sweats, and cramping in his chest so painful, he thought he was having a heart attack.

Eight men died that night. Six succumbed at work the next day, and twelve passed from typhus before the following dawn. There were too many corpses. The burial cart could not hold them all, and the pony was having so much trouble, they put a third man on the detail to push. Even so, two bodies were left behind. The last Emil saw of them, crows were pecking at their eyes.

Doomed . . .

———

December came in cruel and stayed that way, another step down into the hell Nikolas foretold. The temperatures nose-dived. It began to snow. Ivanov drove them to keep up the pace of production as the walls he was erecting were nearing completion. But they were having trouble keeping the workspace warm enough to cure the concrete, until Ivanov had a woodstove brought in.

A week passed and then two, and the pace of the dying only slightly fluctuated. Emil figured that they were losing more than one hundred men every week now. As Christmas approached, he believed that of the two thousand men who had walked into Poltava the prior May, fewer than a thousand remained alive.

We were doomed for our sins.

To combat those thoughts, Emil told himself there was no God, no heaven, and therefore no hell. There was just what happened in front of your face, and you were the only one who could do a thing about any of it. But the pains in his chest would not go away, and the black thoughts that enveloped him would not subside. He tried to believe that he was enough, that he was Emil Martel, damn it, a man who'd stood up to terrible times and events before. He told himself he could still survive Poltava, even if his own eyes said he was lying.

On December 19, 1945, Nikolas began to cough and feel feverish. His work slowed. Ivanov was furious. He wanted to have the hospital enclosed and the roof on by New Year's.

"Pick up the pace, or I'll find someone to replace you in here, and you can go back outside with the others," Ivanov said, and left.

They worked sixteen hours that day and the four days after. Emil did not remember gathering wood or eating or returning to the museum at night. His life became the triangle ringing, climbing from the bunk into the dark and bitter cold, and then mixing and pouring for hours on end, his tired, polluted mind telling him over and over that he was doomed by forces he did not understand for deciding to kill the three Jews, a belief reinforced every time Nikolas coughed up blood.

In the end, the feverish pace was too much for Krull. With no warning, the Uzbek Red Army deserter made another run for it while they were marching back to the museum in a snowstorm the evening of December 23, 1945. The guards laughed, ran after him, and knocked him down with the butts of their rifles. Krull got back up and started running again. They shot him in the back.

Nikolas was marching and coughing in front of and to Emil's right. He looked over his shoulder at Emil and croaked, "I told you. Just a matter of time now."

———

The triangle began ringing and pealing early on Christmas Eve morning. Emil felt dizzy as he dressed and climbed from the basement. Every muscle in his body was knotted and aching.

I don't know how much longer I can take this, he thought, then went off into the series of thoughts that had become his obsession. *Nikolas is right. It's only a matter of time now. I am doomed for what I've done. Doomed.*

Outside the museum, the snow had intensified, and the wind was picking up. Emil had to hold up his forearm and squint to see Nikolas limping into position, bent over, and coughing. The pony, the death cart, and the three men on the death detail were like ghosts passing in the blizzard, leaving the museum with only seven dead that morning.

The construction superintendent was waiting for them in the work area.

"I'll need nine more batches from you," Ivanov said. "Nine more and we'll be ready to hoist in the trusses and put on the roof."

"We're down a man," Emil said.

"And I can't spare you another until tomorrow," Ivanov said, and left.

Nine with just two men? Emil went to work without further comment or hesitation, shoveling materials into the wheelbarrow and dumping it into the horse troughs. Nikolas, however, seemed in a trance, limping at half his normal pace while stopping every few meters, racked by coughing fits. Hours later, Emil was finishing the seventh batch and was ready to pour the concrete into the molds, when Nikolas went into a violent hacking jag behind him.

He heard something fall and twisted around to find Nikolas gasping on the ground, blood trickling from the corner of his mouth.

"Martel," he rasped.

Emil didn't want to but went over and squatted next to the man as he fought for air.

"Tell me," Nikolas said.

"Tell you what?" Emil asked.

Nikolas choked and coughed so hard, his eyes went buggy, and his face flushed purple before he managed to say, "Tell me I can be forgiven for what I've done. Tell me I'm not going straight to hell for killing all those Jews."

Emil looked into his frightened eyes and shook his head. "I can't forgive you, Nikolas. I can't even forgive myself for what I've done."

Nikolas became even more terrified. "No," he gasped, then made a gurgling noise before he coughed and choked out a gout of frothy red blood that ran from his lips down his chin.

Nikolas's tortured eyes fixed on Emil a moment, then rolled to one side and went dull.

———

December 24, 1945
Gutengermendorf, Soviet-Occupied east Germany

Later that same afternoon, Adeline was pulling an apple cake from Frau Schmidt's oven and trying to stay cheerful even though it was Christmas Eve and Malia's birthday and she hadn't heard from her husband in nine months.

Putting the cake on the stove top to cool, Adeline heard Will and Walt giggling in the other room.

Herr Schmidt had taken them into the woods earlier and cut down a small tree. The boys were helping him decorate it with tinsel and ribbon and antique ornaments that had been in the Schmidts' family for ages. Outside it was beginning to snow.

"I wonder how long the Soviets will let you celebrate Christmas," Adeline said to Frau Schmidt, who was slicing bread on a cutting board. "It was banned for us."

The older woman stared at her. "Banned? Not even Hitler did that."

"Hitler's not Stalin," Adeline said. "Stalin's worse."

"I wouldn't let my boarders hear you say that."

"Never," Adeline said. "Soon there will be secret police."

"No," she said. "No more Gestapo."

"It will be a Communist Gestapo whatever they name it, and within a matter of months, they will have your neighbors, old friends even, ready to inform on you so they're not shipped east."

Frau Schmidt sat on a chair near the fire. She gazed into it and then looked at Adeline. "Will you inform?"

"Never," Adeline said immediately. "Whispers like that took my father away forever. I won't do it to someone else."

"Good," the older woman said. "Then we can trust each other."

Will came into the kitchen. "It smells so good in here! Can I have some cake?"

"After dinner," Adeline said. "Out of the kitchen now."

"Awww," he said.

Walt said, "Told you."

"Told you," Will said in a mocking tone as he walked past his older brother.

"The chickens and the potatoes should be done, Adeline," Frau Schmidt said, using her cane to get back to her feet.

Before she could answer, they heard the sound of boots on the front stoop, and the three Soviet soldiers billeting with the Schmidts entered. Kharkov, a captain in his midtwenties, came in first. Adeline saw the glaze to Captain Kharkov's eyes almost immediately and the broad, uncharacteristic smile he gave her and the bottle of vodka in his hands. She looked away and took a long, shaky breath. Frau Schmidt glanced at her in warning. He was a danger to Adeline. She felt it, too.

"Smells good!" Captain Kharkov said as the other men joined him, both junior officers, both younger. "When do we eat?"

Each of the other soldiers had been drinking as well. Each carried bottles two-thirds full.

"We're pulling the birds out of the oven right now," Adeline said, turning to the larger of the two ovens and opening it, revealing two golden-brown birds stuffed with onions and surrounded by red potatoes.

She set the pan on the counter and went about moving fresh bread and dishes of steaming boiled cabbage and brussels sprouts from the Schmidts' garden on the long oaken table before returning to the birds. Using a sharp knife, Adeline quickly dismantled the birds into pieces and slices that she piled on a platter.

Frau Schmidt called out, "Dinner, Peter!"

———

Herr Schmidt soon arrived with two large bottles of homemade beer and took a seat at one end of the table with his wife at the opposite end. Captain Kharkov sat on one of the benches with his junior officers. Adeline sat by Frau Schmidt with Will to her right and Walt to Will's right, opposite the Russians.

Adeline looked at all the food a moment and remembered the Christmas Eve before, when they'd had so very little to eat. She knew she should be happy, grateful, but as the roast chicken and the side dishes were being passed around, she could not help but think of Emil and what horrors he might be facing alone. A ball of emotion welled in her throat.

The Russians spoke among themselves as they ate and drank. Adeline was thankful to see they were nursing their vodka, not guzzling it like some Red Army soldiers she'd seen and even Marie, her own cousin, all tortured souls, bent on oblivion. But tonight, the three at the table felt harmless enough that she began to relax.

Still, her plan was to act as if the holiday were a Saturday night. It would be cold in the church, but she would bring her heavy clothes and blankets, and Christmas Day would be dawning before she knew it. She wanted to be back before the boys woke up. Though Adeline did not have the money to buy her sons presents, the Schmidts did, and she wanted to see the expression on Will's and Walt's faces when they opened—

"You are lucky, Adeline," Captain Kharkov said, startling her from her thoughts.

She looked over at him with a puzzled expression.

"Your sons," he said. "You have them with you while my good wife and baby boy are alone in Leningrad."

"I am lucky," she said. "I'd be luckier if my husband wasn't in a prison camp."

"That's true," Kharkov said, and poured himself another finger of vodka.

"I'm full," Will said, rubbing his stomach after he'd cleared his plate.

"No room for your mother's kuchen?" Frau Schmidt said.

Will frowned. "I didn't say that."

"You're sure?" Adeline teased.

"Mama!" Will said. "That's not nice."

Adeline smiled, got up, and returned with the cake. The boys each grabbed a slice. Will destroyed his in three bites. Walt took his time, nibbling on his as the plate went around the table. As Frau Schmidt passed the plate with the last piece on it to Adeline, Captain Kharkov finished his vodka and poured another finger.

"That was an excellent meal," he said, speaking in Russian and raising his glass to the Schmidts and to Adeline. "We thank you because it reminds us of the perversity of a system that allows two old, relatively useless people like the Schmidts here to own so much land and to reap so much bounty from it."

Adeline realized he'd been saying this directly to her because the Schmidts didn't speak Russian. She flushed and looked away from him.

Kharkov went on. "Under our system, in the old days, the Schmidts would be judged 'kulaks': people who have grossly overbenefited from the labor of others. In the old days, they would have been thrown off this land. Isn't that true, Adeline?"

Adeline looked up to find him studying her. "Yes."

She knew she should have left it at that, but she added, "And the land would have been given to idiots who knew nothing about farming. No surprise that they produced nothing, and people starved."

Captain Kharkov's eyebrows flickered, but he said nothing, just gazed at her a few more moments before downing his glass and pouring himself another. Adeline got up and cleaned the kitchen until it sparkled. She dried the carving knife last, turned from the sink, and said, "Okay, boys, time for bed."

"It's only just dark," Captain Kharkov said. "Sit, have another drink with us."

"The beer has already made me a little tipsy," Adeline said. "Will? Walt?"

Will yawned as he got up. "I am tired."

"Me, too," Walt said. "Mama, will we get Christmas presents tomorrow?"

"We'll see," she said, smiled at them all, nodded to Captain Kharkov. "Sleep well. We'll see you all tomorrow."

"Tomorrow," Kharkov said. He poured another drink and saluted her as they went out the door into the snow.

———

A half inch had fallen on the bare ground, enough to make the landscape look pretty and safe as Adeline and the boys went to the outbuilding. She got them changed, and as they had almost every night since Emil disappeared, they held hands and prayed for him before she had them climb into the bed.

"Tomorrow is Jesus's birthday," Will said. "He was born with donkeys."

His mother smiled and said, "Sort of."

"And we believe what Jesus taught," Walt said. "That's why we celebrate Christmas, right, Mama?"

Adeline hesitated, but then nodded. She was going to tell them good night and leave but changed her mind and picked up the Bible Frau Schmidt had given her. She flipped to the book of Luke and read them the story of the Nativity.

"See, there were donkeys," Will said when she finished.

"Yes, there were," Adeline said, laughed, and kissed her younger and then her older son on the head. "And sheep and other animals."

She kept the light on long enough to put on her coat and to gather up the quilt, two blankets, and the pillow and the wool knit hat Frau Schmidt had given her. She turned to tell them good night, only to see them already sleeping. She thought of Emil again, how he would never know moments like this, and despite the wonderful food filling her belly, she felt robbed of love and time.

Adeline went out the door into the short hallway, shut it, and locked it, thinking, *They robbed me; they robbed my sons; and they robbed Emil. They're still robbing us!*

Outside, the snow was still gently falling. Adeline looped around the barn to get her bearings, then set off by dead reckoning through the darkness and the snow toward the tree line that marked the village. She wandered off course twice before finding the leafless trees and following them past the backs of the village homes before coming parallel to the old church.

As was her custom, Adeline went beyond the church to pee and then went to the rear door, finding it ajar. But when she pushed open the door to listen for the sounds of other women, she heard nothing. The glass windows of the church had been boarded over for the winter, so once inside, she felt comfortable digging around in her bag for a candle and some matches with the door shut but not barred in case another woman wanted refuge for the night.

She lit the little candle, which threw enough light that she could see her breath in billowing clouds and confirm that the church was indeed empty. She shivered and understood why. Boarded up like this, the building got little or no heat during the day. In fact, it felt colder in there than it had outside in the falling snow.

Adeline went to the pew where she normally spent her Saturday nights and started preparing her bed. As she did, she thought about Walt saying, *And we believe what Jesus taught, right, Mama?*

She sat a moment with her hands clasped and felt torn between wanting to go down on her knees and pray and fearing to pray because she would not be heard or heard in the wrong way as she'd been that day near the Reichstag when they had no food and no shelter. In the end, she bowed her head and asked God to forgive her for not praying much of late.

"It's been hard without Emil, Lord," she whispered, that ball of emotion swelling in her throat again. "Taking care of the boys and working for the Schmidts . . . I'm grateful for the roof over my head and the good food we eat. I am. But please watch over Emil, wherever he is. Protect him, Lord. He's a good man. The only man I've got or want. So please, bring him back to us, and keep me and the boys safe in the meantime."

She bowed her head and sighed before unfolding the quilt and blankets. She was arranging the pillow and about to blow out the candle when the rear door pushed open and someone shone a flashlight inside. Several of the women who took refuge in the church had flashlights, so she stood there, waiting to see which one had decided to brave the cold.

Captain Kharkov stepped inside, looked around, saw her standing in the candlelight. He smiled drunkenly and held up the nearly empty bottle and waved it around at the interior of the church.

"How romantic, Adeline," he said. "What a perfect place."

Chapter Thirty

Six hours earlier, that same Christmas Eve
Poltava, Ukraine

Watching Nikolas die in front of him shook Emil in ways he did not expect. He had hated the man in life, and yet he felt some pity for the way Nikolas left it, terror filled and unforgiven, sure that he was about to face judgment.

I'm not facing judgment, Emil thought after covering Nikolas's body and dragging it outside to freeze. *There is nothing beyond this life. The only thing you can rely on is yourself.*

Emil worked until he almost dropped that day but relied on himself to reach the concrete quota Ivanov had set. He sat by the little woodstove after pouring the last of the concrete into the block molds. He closed his eyes.

I am enough. I alone can survive . . .

The triangle began to ring, signaling the end of the workday. Emil opened his eyes in a daze, feeling in his chest and in his head the same darkness that Nikolas had described, so heavy and cold, he did not know if he could get to his feet. He did, finally, but he was dizzy and had to hold on to the wall before he could gather up his hat and gloves and go out into a full-on blizzard. Nikolas's corpse was already almost buried in the falling snow.

"Line up!" the Soviet guards shouted. "Marching formation!"

Emil went to one of the guards he was familiar with, pointed out Nikolas's body, and was told the burial detail was coming. He paused to watch the snow build on Nikolas's frozen body, then took the dead man's place in line. He'd gather wood scraps tomorrow.

Trudging through the storm to the city hall basement to eat, Emil felt like he might collapse at any moment. His mind and inner voice turned reptilian, bent on survival, and goading.

One foot in front of the other. One foot . . .

I am enough. I am Emil Martel, damn it. I am . . .

And then Nicholas's words, *We were doomed the moment we took the gun and decided to pull the trigger.*

At the same time Emil was hearing the echoes of Nikolas in his mind, a prisoner several rows in front of him staggered and collapsed in the snow. A guard went to the downed man and kicked him. When he didn't respond, the guard dragged him to one side and left him.

Barely able to stand himself, Emil gazed dully at the new corpse, hearing Nikolas again in his head, *It's just a matter of time.*

The prisoners began moving. Emil tried to follow them, one foot, one step, one foot, one step. He got dizzy again, wobbled, and almost went down. Black spots appeared and swam in his vision. He thought he was going to lose consciousness and die in the snow, another frozen body on the death cart, and panicked, tried to will himself alert. Emil staggered finally and went down on his knees. He had nothing left. He surrendered.

I can't do it. I am not enough. I'm just a man. I'm sorry, Adeline. I can't do this alone . . . I need help. I need . . .

A hand grabbed him roughly under the armpit and jerked him to his feet. It shocked Emil back to semi-alertness, and he looked in confusion at the guard.

"You're not dying on me today," the guard said. "Ivanov wants you kept alive."

Emil felt his balance return, said, "I'll be better once I've eaten."

The guard nodded, said, "The mess is just ahead there."

The line slowed at the entrance to the city hall's basement. The area was lit by floodlights. Emil had his head down, defeated, cut off from hope. He felt like he had nothing left to fight with beyond his ability to stand up and move with the line toward food and sleep. He knew he was so weakened, he would die if disease hit him.

Maybe it would be better. Less torture in the long run for Adeline and the boys. And if I'm going to face judgment, I'd rather do it sooner than later.

Emil got wobbly again, his despair deepening and widening before yawning bottomless with sheer desperation and fear. Feeling like he was falling away into the darkness, he did the only thing he could think of: he threw back his head, exposed his face to the driving snow, and raised both arms to the night and the storm.

"You hear me?" he croaked. "If you do, take me sooner than later."

———

The line moved again toward the stairs. Emil dropped his arms and slouched forward a step. Why was he even bothering to eat? It was over. He'd lasted seven months. He could not do it alone anymore. And God? God was just a story in a—

"The bee is a miracle," he heard a man say in German, but in an odd, thick accent. "No bee, no flowers, no fruit, no beauty, no life."

The line moved a foot. Emil went with it, lifting his head and turning to search for the source of the voice.

Out of the blizzard, a pale apparition appeared: a prisoner caked in snow led the pony and the death cart coated in hoar, with four bodies already aboard and two other prisoners helping from the back, driving the wheels and the weight through fifteen centimeters of snow.

The lead prisoner had his hood up as he tied the pony to a post about twenty meters from Emil and turned to the two others, saying, "Eat honey and you'll live a long life. It's a gift from God. Makes you strong. Makes you live long. We'll eat first? Then the graveyard, yes?"

Emil squinted, shook his head in disbelief, but then, as if drawn by some magnetic force, he left his place in line and walked toward the men of the death detail as they made for the back of the meal queue.

Emil followed them, calling out, "Corporal?"

It was windy, howling. The three prisoners kept walking.

"Beekeeper," Emil shouted. "Survivor of Stalingrad!"

Two of the men continued on. But the one who'd been leading the pony stopped, pulled back his hood, and turned to look at Emil with a puzzled and then amused expression, as if someone had whispered a joke in his ear that he was only now getting.

311

"Martel," Corporal Gheorghe said, grinning at him. "I said I'd see you again, and there you stand!"

———

Gutengermendorf, Soviet-Occupied east Germany

Captain Kharkov shut off the flashlight, put it in his pocket, and strolled in Adeline's direction, holding his vodka bottle in one hand while unbuttoning his long coat with the other.

"A perfect, perfect place," the Russian said. "I'm surprised none of us thought of it when we tried to figure out what became of all the good women of Gutengermendorf on Saturday nights. But your tracks in the snow did not lie, and here we are."

"No," Adeline said. "Not with me."

Kharkov smiled and kept coming. "Oh yes, with you. This I am allowed. You, fair Adeline, are a spoil of war, an older, more experienced spoil of war. And one I will enjoy greatly, because even if it is as cold as a witch's tit in here, I know it will be so deliciously warm beneath your skirt. A treat for both of us on Christmas Eve."

She said nothing but felt the fear and the shame already bubbling in her. He'd come to the end of the pew where she slept and saw the bedding laid out.

"You thought ahead," he said, drinking the last of his vodka. "How lovely."

The Soviet officer tossed the bottle into the next pew and started toward her, unbuckling his belt, long coat open.

"Don't, or—"

"Or what?" he said, only to come up short, a meter from her, staring at the carving knife she held in her hand.

"Or I'll cut you into pieces," she said. "I'm good with a knife."

Kharkov smiled. His eyes went half-lidded as he took a step back. "I'm sure you are. I saw you take care of that chicken. But I'm not a chicken, Adeline, and your knife doesn't scare me."

He reached inside his coat and came up with a pistol that he pointed at her. "So drop it, and let's get down to pleasure, shall we?"

"I have a husband," she said, not lowering the knife.

"I don't care."

"You have a wife, a baby."

"Not tonight," he said, smiling.

Adeline swallowed and said, "If you come any closer, I will kill you. So shoot me. Get it over with. I'd rather be dead than let you on top of me."

That enraged Kharkov, who thumbed off the pistol's safety. "You think I won't?"

"Go ahead and shoot me," she said again. "The town will hear the shot. They will investigate you for murder. You'll be sent to the gallows, and your young wife will know you not only as a rapist, but a cold-blooded killer on Christmas Eve. And when you're in your cell, waiting to die, you'll be like Raskolnikov in *Crime and Punishment*. You read it. Of course you did. And you remember how the murder ate up his mind. Like a cancer before the gallows. Is that what you really want, Captain Kharkov?"

The Soviet officer glared at her, the pistol trembling in his hand, before aiming past her and shooting. She jerked, startled at the gunshot, and slashed the knife in front of her, sure that he was coming for her now.

But Kharkov had already left the pew and was storming away. Wrenching open the rear door, he snarled, "German bitch," before slamming it behind him.

Adeline stared after him for a second before running to the door with the knife still in her hand and throwing the bar. Then she began to shake so hard, she had to stumble back to her pew and sit for fear she'd collapse. Tears came and the loneliness, followed by the certainty that a man like Kharkov would not let this stand. He would find a way to attack her or punish her.

It took a long time, until the candle was nearly spent, before she truly believed he would not return, and she was able to calm herself down enough to take the carving knife and slip it under her pillow. Then she took off her boots and put on her extra wool socks and her knit hat before blowing out the candle and snuggling into the blankets.

To get her mind off Kharkov, she tried to summon Emil's image. Instead, she asked herself who she would be if another year passed and she was lying in this pew next Christmas Eve with no word from him. The lonely world that question suggested frightened her so much, she curled into a ball, and fell asleep praying that a year from now she would be in his arms.

Poltava, Ukraine

In the basement of city hall, Emil gulped down his soup and tore into the extra bread and boiled brisket, onions, beets, and cabbage they were given in a nod to the holiday. Every few moments, he'd lift his head to reassure himself that Corporal Gheorghe really was there, across the table, and eating just as voraciously.

Emil felt better than he had in weeks, and he realized it was just because the mad Romanian soldier was with him, not a friend really, not even an acquaintance, just a familiar face and odd voice in a cold, distant place on Christmas Eve.

When he'd slurped the hot soup and eaten half of his double rations, Emil said, "How did you get here?"

"The sun, the stars, the moon—"

"Right," Emil said, cutting him off. "Just give me what happened here on earth."

"But it always begins up there."

"I'm sure it does, but start when we left you a hard day's ride from the Romanian border."

Corporal Gheorghe thought about that and then smiled. "You have a sister-in-law, I remember. Still sweet as honey?"

"Malia, that's right. Tell me from there."

"She married?"

"Not the last time I saw her."

The corporal smiled, tapped his lips, and then explained that shortly after the Martels rode on to Romania, the Red armies that had pursued them suddenly halted to resupply just shy of the border. Romania's leaders saw the writing on the wall and decided they were better off flipping their allegiance from Hitler to Stalin.

"I got orders to surrender to the Soviets and tell them we fight for Moscow now, not Berlin," he said. "But when I walked up with a white flag on my gun, they arrested me, sent me to prison camp in Ukraine, but not this far east."

"What happened?"

The Romanian grinned. "I escaped after four months, started home to become a beekeeper, walked ninety kilometers, and got caught. They sent me to a second camp. I escaped again."

He tapped a finger on his left temple, just below his scar from Stalingrad. "That time I got smart and walked mostly at night. I almost made it to the Romanian border."

"But caught again," Emil said, shaking his head. "And they didn't shoot you?"

He laughed. "Can you believe it? They said no more Ukraine for me, that I was going far east to work in the mines. But instead, they brought me here five days ago. It's good, I think."

"There's nothing good about this place," Emil said, then described the disease and mortality rate among the prisoners. "It's a death trap. You'd be better off in the mines."

"I heard that the first day when I raised my hand for burial detail."

"For the double rations?"

"That, too," he said, then leaned forward and whispered. "A secret? The burial detail is how I escaped the first two camps. Join the detail. We'll escape together."

Emil shook his head. "You'll kill yourself touching those bodies."

The Romanian tapped his temple again. "Not if they're frozen, Martel."

Emil thought about that. "Maybe. But why the burial detail? How do you escape?"

The corporal leaned forward even more. "Russian guards? They fear ghosts because there are too many dead in one place. They won't go to where the bodies are actually dumped. In a snowstorm, we can run."

Emil crossed his arms. "They'll catch you on foot. They did it twice."

"Not on foot this time," Corporal Gheorghe insisted. "That pony is stout, almost as big as a horse. We'll ride him. We'll find train tracks, find a train, jump on, go west."

For a moment, Emil embraced the idea of escaping with the Romanian. He was only half-crazy, and he'd predicted they'd meet again, hadn't he?

What if he's right? What if we could . . . ?

He thought of the pile of dead bodies he might see in the morning and have to bury. It made his skin crawl.

"I can't do it."

Corporal Gheorghe tilted his head, the smile back. "If you can't, you must. It is always so. Come, we will escape together. We will go find your wife and her sister, sweet as honey."

Emil swallowed hard. "There are reasons I can't join that detail."

"What reasons?"

Feeling his heart and breath start to race, Emil realized he'd never told any-one about Dubossary. But gazing back across the table at the corporal, he felt compelled to describe that night, to confess to another the depth and nature of what he'd done.

Over the next twenty minutes, he told Corporal Gheorghe the story of Dubossary up to the moment Captain Haussmann handed him the Luger and ordered him to prove his German allegiance by shooting the three young Jews. But then the triangle rang, telling them to leave the mess hall and prepare to march to the museum basement.

"What did you do?" Corporal Gheorghe asked.

"I—"

"Move!" a guard shouted, and then pointed at the Romanian. "There are still two bodies out there. One on the road. One near the hospital. Go get them."

He got up, staring at Emil. "Join the burial detail. You must tell me what you have done."

With that, he walked away. Emil watched the Romanian leave, noting for the first time how light on his feet the man was, so fluid in his movements, he seemed to glide. By the time Emil went out into the blizzard, which continued without relief, the death cart was gone, and with it, Corporal Gheorghe, who suddenly felt like his last hope.

But the burial detail?

As he marched back to the museum, the thought of loading bodies on that cart, frozen or not, made Emil feel like he'd been locked in a space so tight, he could barely breathe while invisible hands laced his stomach in knots.

Christmas Day 1945
Gutengermendorf, Soviet-Occupied east Germany

Adeline awoke shivering in the dark church, sat up, and saw light streaming under the rear door. She almost got up to gather her things and return to Walt and Will. Instead, she wrapped her blankets around her shoulders, got on her knees, and prayed for safety for her, the boys, and Emil.

When she stood to fold and pack, however, Adeline did not feel safe. Not with Captain Kharkov and his men still living in the Schmidts' home. That sense built as she left the church and trudged back through town and up the knoll to the farm.

It had snowed seven centimeters overnight before the temperature climbed above freezing. Now a dank drizzle fell, and she walked through slush.

"Merry Christmas, Mama!" Will and Walt cried when she unlocked the door to their room in the outbuilding.

They jumped off the bed and ran into Adeline's arms. She held them tight and kissed them each on the cheek before saying, "Merry Christmas to both of you dears."

Will stepped back. "Do we get presents?"

She smiled. "I understand Frau and Herr Schmidt found presents for you under their tree last night."

Due to the circumstances, they were forced to break custom and celebrate on the morning of Christmas day instead of Christmas Eve.

"Really?" Walt said. "What?"

"Get dressed, and we'll go and see."

Will was dressed sloppily in seconds and bounced up and down as Walt went through the process with more time and care.

"C'mon, Walt," Will moaned.

"You want me to go barefoot?"

"If you have to."

"I don't have to, and I won't," his older brother said, pulling on his shoes.

"Mama!"

"Calm down, Will," she said. "The presents will still be there waiting."

"But I'm waiting!"

"And I'm done," Walt said, getting up to grab his warm coat.

Will ran to the Schmidts' house and disappeared inside while Walt held Adeline's hand and walked with her.

"Mama?" Walt said. "Is Will always going to be in a hurry?"

She thought about that and smiled. "I think so. It's his nature."

"He's always going so fast, he makes me dizzy sometimes."

Adeline laughed. "Yes, he makes me dizzy sometimes, too."

They kicked the slushy snow off their boots before they went into the farmhouse. Frau Schmidt had been up cooking sausages from the pig they'd butchered the month before. The smells in the house were delicious as she glanced around, happy not to see any of the Soviet soldiers up and about, especially Kharkov.

"Merry Christmas!" Frau Schmidt cried from the kitchen, where Will was already munching on one of the cookies.

"Merry Christmas!" Adeline replied.

"Mama, can I have a cookie, too?" Walt asked.

"Of course," she said. "It's Christmas Day."

He took off his coat, hung it, and kicked off his boots before trotting through the main room into the kitchen to get his cookie. Adeline followed him, happy to see the fire dancing in the stove, and how warm and inviting it all was.

Herr Schmidt was drinking hot tea. When the boys were finished with their cookies, he said, "I think I saw presents for the Martel boys under the tree."

Will and Walt looked to their mother, who nodded. "Go ahead."

They ran to the other room and found two small presents wrapped in butcher paper. Will and Walt opened them and drew out two wooden spinning tops that Herr Schmidt had carved for them.

He showed them how to get them going and how they could battle each other. Their shrieks of laughter and triumph when one knocked the other top over made Adeline feel better than she had since Emil was taken.

Outside, she could see that the drizzle had turned to snow again. Herr Schmidt, going to look out the window at a thermometer, saw the temperature was dropping, which he told the boys was a good thing for their other present.

"Another one!" Will cried. "Where?"

"In the barn," he said. "Get your coats and hats on, and I'll show you."

Walt said, "You want to come, Mama?"

Adeline had heard from Herr Schmidt what else he planned to give the boys the week before and nodded. "I do."

"I'll have hot tea and cider waiting for you," Frau Schmidt said.

They dressed and went out into the lightly falling snow and the deepening cold. They'd only been in the house an hour, but the slush mixed with the new snow was freezing already, turning crunchy and slick, perfect for the boys' big present.

Herr Schmidt had the sled up on a bench in his barn. It had belonged to his son when he was a boy. The farmer had fixed it up the week before. It had a seat, two runners, and a rudder to steer and slow it. He showed them the runners—wood with screwed-in metal edges and another strip of metal down the middle—and how to turn them with the rudder.

"Who's first?" Herr Schmidt said. "Walt?"

Adeline's older son appeared uncertain. "Will can go first."

Will grinned and nodded. "Yes, please."

The old farmer led them out of the barn, back into the snow, and set the sled at the top of the knoll above the snow-covered field and the village beyond. Will got on it and held the rudder with both hands.

"How do I get it going?" he asked.

"I'll push you," Herr Schmidt said, put his boot on the back of the sled, and gave a big shove.

With a whoop, Will went flying down the knoll and out onto the flat before crashing. Adeline had a moment of panic until her younger son rolled over onto his knees and threw his arms in the air, laughing.

The sled had a rope that allowed Will to pull it uphill. Walt looked scared before he went, but with Herr Schmidt's coaching, he, too, went sailing down the knoll and onto the flat. He didn't crash, jumped up, threw his head back and yelled, "I love this!"

When he got back to the top, he said, "Your turn, Mama."

"Yes!" Will said.

"I don't think . . ."

"It really is safe," Herr Schmidt said.

Reluctantly, Adeline sat on the sled, watched the farmer show her how to use the rudder, and then screamed with delight as he gave her a shove, and laughed as she started accelerating down the hill. She kept the rudder steady and flew even farther than the boys out onto the flat.

Gasping, delighted, Adeline lay back for a moment, staring at the snowflakes falling, and felt as alive as she ever had, until she thought of Emil and felt guilty for enjoying anything while he languished in a prison or worse. But she refused to ruin the boys' holiday, so she got up and dragged the sled to the top of the knoll.

The boys kept sledding, but it had gotten too cold for Adeline. She went back to the farmhouse to help Frau Schmidt in the kitchen. But as she passed the barn and happened to glance at the upper windows of the house, she saw Captain Kharkov at one of them, glaring out at her.

She dropped her eyes, feeling the joyous state she'd been in vanish because she knew in her heart that the Soviet officer was the kind of man who kept score. She'd one-upped him, and he would want to make things even.

As she entered the house, Adeline made a decision and went straight to Frau Schmidt to tell her what happened in the church the night before.

"I can't believe I'm saying this, because you have been so very good to us, Frau Schmidt," Adeline said, "but as soon as I can find another place to live, the boys and I will be leaving you."

Frau Schmidt saddened, but then came over and hugged her.

"I understand," she said. "But please don't become a stranger."

———

Poltava, Ukraine

The blizzard broke at dawn on fierce northwest winds that brought piercing blue skies and breathtaking cold. The sun threw rose patterns across the swirling winter landscape. Twenty-eight centimeters had fallen overnight. Where the snow had come to rest leeward, it was powdery and relatively easy with the pony to get the death cart to roll.

But where the wind had drifted the snow, Emil and Corporal Gheorghe had to break trail and shovel so the wheels, axles, and the bottom of the cart would not bog under the weight of the eight prisoners who'd died overnight. The corpses were stacked two by two and four high, frozen together in a gruesome stack.

Before going to sleep on Christmas Eve, Emil had decided not to join the burial detail and Corporal Gheorghe's escape scheme. But the Romanian, using a flashlight, found his bunk and shook him awake at five o'clock.

"I'm the only one on detail," he'd said. "Corporal Gheorghe needs Martel. And Martel needs Corporal Gheorghe."

Seeing there was no quit in the man, Emil had gotten up and dressed before following him up the stairs and out into minus-twenty-degree air. Every joint and bone in his body ached from the impossible workday before, but he helped the Romanian load the frozen bodies, including Nikolas who had turned pale blue. Two Soviet guards watched and followed them as they led the pony and cart south, a different direction from the east-west marches he'd taken twice a day since arriving.

Emil had never been to the graveyard or even to this part of the ruined city before, so he looked around with interest, seeing large pieces of Poltava that were still snow-covered wastelands, no signs of human activity at all. But here and there, he'd catch sight of civilians scratching out a life in the frozen demolition zone. Several of the children were boys as young as his own, filthy, cold, and hollow-cheeked.

As they left the city with two Soviet soldiers trailing them, Gheorghe said, "The guards don't speak German. Finish the story. The Nazi gives you the pistol, says shoot the three Jews. What did you do?"

Emil stopped the pony as they came to the edge of a large snow-covered field with dense forest on the far east and south sides. The sun was fully up now, reflecting off the snow, glary, almost blinding. He squinted, saw more drifts ahead, and bare ground and dead grass in places where the wind had scoured a high point.

"Stay in the grass. We'll dig out drifts if we have to," Corporal Gheorghe said as if reading his mind. "Tell me the story. He has a gun to your head?"

Emil took several deep breaths, trying to keep his head turned away from the Romanian and facing the bitter wind. But the raw gale, driving loose snow, forced him to turn toward the corporal and face the truth.

"I decided to kill them, Corporal. I told Haussmann I would do it. In my heart, it was already done. I walked right up and tried to aim at the teenage boy. I was squeezing the trigger."

As they reached the middle of the field, Emil explained how a senior officer had intervened because of Himmler's policy and how he was sent instead to shovel lime on the hundreds of Jews who had died the night before.

"I prayed to God not to be a part of killing Jews," Emil said bitterly, "but I wasn't heard. Instead, that gun was put in my hand, and I made a decision to kill those kids. I shoveled lime the entire night. There were so many men shooting and so many innocent people dying that I stopped believing in the common goodness of men. And I stopped believing in my own basic goodness because I had decided to kill those innocent people, children. As I shoveled, I knew I should have been praying over the bodies in the ravine, but I couldn't because I no longer believed in God."

———

The guards called a halt at midfield, said they would wait for them here.

"Where do we bury them?" Emil said.

"We don't," Corporal Gheorghe said. "The ground's frozen. We'll dump them at the back of the opening along the edge of the woods there. Crows and wolves will do the rest."

"Really?" Emil said, disturbed.

"This is why Russian guards are so afraid of the place. They won't go down there. In a good storm? We'll go down there, take the pony off the cart, and we'll escape and get a strong head start with the snow covering our tracks."

Emil did not reply at first, still feeling like he needed to unburden himself.

"I hadn't prayed again until yesterday, Corporal Gheorghe," he said as he led the pony and the cart down the descending ridge where the snow was shallow. "And today I wish I hadn't. I'm right back to believing that God does not answer, does not exist, and most men are not good by nature, including me."

"Then what are most men by nature?"

"Beasts. They may act like they're good. But it only takes a threat to their own life to lose that, to become a different creature like I did, not a human, a savage, an animal."

The Romanian kept walking. The pony blew through its nose and kept plodding.

Emil could not stand the silence. He said, "Maybe I deserve this. Maybe I am here to be punished. Maybe I am not meant to be forgiven. Maybe I am meant to live out my days dragging dead, diseased bodies to the wolves and the crows. And maybe Nikolas was right. I was doomed the moment I took the gun and decided to kill those three kids."

They reached the bottom of the hill and a part of the field where they were sheltered from much of the wind. The snow was deep and powdery. The pony was able to easily pull the cart and seemed to know the way toward a cove-shaped clearing along the wood line.

"I'm doomed," Emil said, and shook his head. "Just like these men we're dumping."

As they entered the small clearing, Corporal Gheorghe said, "Doomed for what? You did not pull the trigger. You did not kill anyone."

Emil looked at him angrily. "But I *decided* to kill them. In my mind, I'd *already done it.*"

"But you did not shoot."

"Because of that SS colonel. If he had not been there, I would have shot them. I would have. I chose to kill those innocent people after praying and not being heard. I got so angry at God for not hearing that—"

"Didn't God?"

Emil frowned. "Didn't God what?"

The death cart's wheels began to bog in deeper snow, and the pony struggled. The Romanian didn't reply as he went around the back of the cart to push.

Emil joined him, saying again, "Didn't God what?"

"Hear you."

"No, I wasn't heard!" Emil said sharply. "If I was heard, do you think I'd be here?"

"I can't answer that, but I can tell you that you *were* heard."

"Ignored, then."

"No, no," the Romanian said as he strained to keep the death wagon moving. "You begged God not to make you a murderer. Then you showed courage telling that Nazi, no. You believed God's word, Commandment Six. You said you would not kill."

"But then I changed my—"

"Stop! When you said no, did you know Heinrich Himmler had a rule that no one would be killed if they refused to kill a Jew?"

Emil thought about that. "No."

"And so, when you refused, you risked your life to do the right thing and accepted the consequences of saying no. From where I'm standing, I think you showed your true self to the Almighty One that night and you were rewarded for it."

Emil couldn't think that way. "I changed my mind. I was going to shoot them."

"But you were stopped, yes?" the Romanian said as they neared the back of the clearing. "You did not have to kill because you did the right thing. Can't you see the hand of God in that, Martel? Bringing that officer to stop you from murdering the three Jews? I am not a smart man, but I see the Universal Intelligence's hand in that as plainly as I see this Christmas morning and you."

Emil stared at the snow ahead of them, trying to filter what the corporal had just told him.

For more than four years he had blamed, then denied God for making him decide to kill those Jews. But now, he *could* see the work of a greater power in all of it. He didn't have to kill that night because he had refused to do the wrong thing in the first place. Emil's heart pounded. *I was heard. I was.* Emil felt breathless as he looked over at Corporal Gheorghe, thinking of him no longer as some head-injured madman, but as a strange and divine messenger of salvation.

"You believe that?" Emil said finally.

Nodding, the Romanian said, "I think the Almighty One spared you after refusing to kill the three Jews. See? You were a hero to God. And to your wife and sons and to your sister-in-law, sweet as honey."

Emil blinked. A hero? He shook his head.

"A hero doesn't give up, and I gave up yesterday," Emil said. "I was weak. Lost. I reached my limit. I said I could not go it alone anymore."

He smiled. "See? You have a hero's heart, but you are a man. You have limits. Even you can't go alone, can't do everything by yourself. What did you do when you gave up yesterday?"

Emil thought back. "I had this terrible weight in my chest, and I prayed for it to go."

"Yes. You showed faith, prayed. Asked for help with your burden. It's good. Now, ask the Divine to walk by your side. You will never be weak or lost again. With the Almighty as an ally, even a crazy beekeeper with a dent in his head can survive the Battle of Stalingrad!"

The pony stopped with a snort, and the cart came to rest in the axle-deep snow.

"Far enough," the Romanian said, and went around his side of the cart. Emil did the same. It was only then that Emil saw all the wolf tracks and crow feathers and the odd bone or two sticking up out of the snow about three meters in front of the pony, whose flanks twitched and shivered.

"We just dump them here?" Emil said.

"They'll never know. We turn the cart around, we push, they fall, we leave."

They led the pony in a tight circle and then released the lever that held the bed of the cart down and pushed up on the end closest to the pony. The stack of eight bodies slid off into the deep snow. Nikolas's corpse landed faceup.

"We should go now," Gheorghe said. "That way, the guards won't be suspicious."

Emil barely heard the Romanian. Seeing his past in a completely different light now and no longer imprisoned by that night in Dubossary, he walked over by Nikolas's corpse and the bodies of prisoners he did not know. On Christmas morning 1945, after more than fifty months of denying God, Emil began to pray, asking the Almighty to walk by his side and to accept the departed souls of the corpses he was about to turn over to the birds, the wolves, and the wind.

Chapter Thirty-One

January 25, 1946
Berlin, Soviet-Occupied east Germany

Adeline climbed down off the crowded train with two large, empty canvas bags and the purse Frau Schmidt had given her as a parting gift. She walked outside the station where teams of men under Soviet guard were working to patch bomb holes and erect new ironwork. Outside, she was shocked. The last time she was in Berlin, the summer before, she and the boys had to weave in and around the destruction, which seemed everywhere. Now, but for the skiff of snow, the streets were mostly clear, and traffic was flowing.

She got out a notebook in her purse and checked an address. She asked a police officer how to get there and was relieved to find it was only twelve blocks away.

Walking into a raw north wind through Berlin on that dank, cold day, Adeline thought to herself once again that it really was remarkable what a month could do to your life. The day after Christmas, Frau Schmidt had helped her go to the local committee in the village to seek a lodging reassignment.

When the clerk asked why, Frau Schmidt said, "To keep from being raped."

The clerk, a woman, had immediately softened. "I'll see what I can do for her."

"She's a wonderful cook, too. It's a crime having her as a field hand."

The clerk knitted her brows, then tapped her lips. "How good a cook?"

Frau Schmidt said, "She can make a stringy old hen taste like a spring chicken. She makes wonderful noodles and apple cake."

The woman said, "Let the poor thing speak for herself. Do you speak Russian? Know any Russian dishes?"

Adeline smiled and nodded. "I speak fluent Russian and know many Russian dishes from a kitchen I used to work in back in Ukraine."

The clerk sent her immediately to a large home at the edge of town, the billet of the ranking Soviet officers in the area, including a Colonel Vasiliev, who was in his sixties, corpulent, and curt. But he loved the pork chop and spicy applesauce dish Adeline prepared for him for lunch, and hired her on the spot.

When Adeline happily hurried back to the clerk's office for a housing reassignment, the colonel had already called ahead. It was done. She could move the very next morning to new quarters in a room in a house on the village's main street, not far from the school.

———

Reaching the address in Berlin that Colonel Vasiliev had given her, Adeline remembered how relieved she'd been when she reached the Schmidts' house that day and found Captain Kharkov and the other officers had not returned. Frau Schmidt had been upset that Adeline was packing already but pleased at the change in her fortune.

Adeline told the boys only that she'd gotten a job cooking and they had to move into the village, closer to their friends from school, which they liked. They had so little to their name, it did not take more than an hour for her to get their things into the little wagon, which Herr Schmidt helped load into his larger wagon.

"Can we come back to sled?" Will asked.

The old farmer smiled and patted him on the head. "Anytime you want."

"You're always welcome, Will, and you, too, Walt," said Frau Schmidt, who insisted on riding into the village with them so she could see how they'd be living.

They set off in the last twenty minutes of good light as fat snowflakes filled the frigid air. Halfway to town, Adeline saw Captain Kharkov and the other two Soviet officers walking up the road toward them.

When Kharkov spotted Adeline, Will, and Walt and their little wagon, he stood in the road blocking the way. Herr Schmidt reined his horse to a stop.

"What is this?" Kharkov barked. "What is happening here?"

"They have been given new quarters in the village," Herr Schmidt said.

"I was never apprised of this!"

"Orders of Colonel Vasiliev," Frau Schmidt said. "She cooks for him now."

———

In Berlin weeks later, Adeline grinned, recalling the fury in Kharkov's face as he stood aside and glared at her.

I beat him twice in three days, she thought proudly, before walking up to a Soviet soldier standing before the door that matched the address she sought. Adeline showed him her papers and the official letter from Colonel Vasiliev granting her entry.

The Russian guard, who could not have been older than nineteen, nodded and handed them back to her, saying, "Buy me a little chocolate in there, yes? The food we get is dung."

"No promises," Adeline said.

He sighed and opened the door into a commissary for ranking Soviet officers. She entered, and the door closed behind her. Adeline took a look around and felt as if her breath had been stolen.

The room was long and wide, with a low ceiling, and shelf after shelf after shelf bulging with food. And not just the staples. There were freshly butchered meats, beef and pork, and fowl; and herring and other fish chilling on ice; and cheese and honey; and twenty different kinds of vodka and four cigarette brands. They even had the specific beluga caviar the colonel had placed at the top of her shopping list.

After a lifetime of want and lack even in the best of moments, Adeline found that being there in the officers' commissary, amid the dizzying array of delicacies and endless choices, was almost overwhelming. She'd known that people high up in the Communist system lived differently than the ordinary people they claimed to support. She just had not understood how well they lived while others like her had suffered for decades.

Adeline did the numbers in her head as she shopped. Near the end of her list, she realized the colonel had given her more than enough cash to cover the purchases. And she had a little money of her own. She paid for Colonel Vasiliev's list of groceries and acted as if she were going to leave, then made a show of staring at the list and groaning.

"I forgot a few things," she said. "Can I leave the bags here?"

The cashier, a bored female Red Army soldier, shrugged. Adeline quickly returned with a jar of blueberry jam, three large chocolate bars, one small chocolate bar, and a wedge of cheese. She paid for them with her own money because she knew the colonel or one of his staff would check the receipt against the cash she returned. After paying a second time, Adeline rewrapped her scarf against the cold and went outside. The same young Russian soldier was standing there, stamping his feet and looking gaunt and unhappy.

"Here," she said, giving him the smaller chocolate bar.

The soldier broke into a grin, thanked her, and snatched it from her.

Tearing at the wrapper, he said, "It's true, you know?"

"What's true?" she asked.

After popping the candy between his lips, chewing, and swallowing with great contentment, he said, "In the Soviet Union, if you have chocolate, vodka, or cigarettes, you can change a yes to a no and a no to a yes."

She thought about that and smiled. "What's your name, Private?"

He hesitated. "Dimitri."

"Have a nice day, Private Dimitri," she said. "I don't want a yes or a no changed today."

The Soviet private cocked his head at her, a little puzzled, before Adeline turned and walked away carrying her shopping bags, one in each hand to maintain balance on the slippery roads and sidewalks. She thought of Emil for only the second time that day. In their new home—a single, large room in the house of a widow younger than Frau Schmidt—she'd continued her habit of rising at sunrise and facing the East to think about Emil and his promise to find her.

But during the day, when she was cooking especially, she'd found it best to push thoughts of him aside. The fact that she had the ability to not think about Emil for hours at a time made her feel horrible deep down and . . . Adeline stopped, realizing she'd taken a wrong turn or two somewhere and was disoriented and then lost.

A girl walking by gave her different directions back to the train station. Two blocks along that route, she saw a queue of people waiting outside a building that had a white flag with a red cross on it fluttering above the door. Having endured such lines as a refugee in Wielun, Adeline figured they were waiting for medical attention.

But when she asked an older woman at the end of the line, she was told that most were waiting because they had been separated from loved ones during the war. The building housed the International Red Cross, which was taking names and addresses of people to be printed on big lists that would be posted in public places in the Soviet, British, French, and American zones.

Adeline stood there, debating whether to stand in the line. Emil had been taken east. He'd said he would look for her in the West. But who knew when or if he'd ever get a chance to look for her and the boys? And who knew if these lists would still be up somewhere five or ten years on? She shook off these doubts and others that wormed through her and took her place in line.

It couldn't hurt. Could it?

Chapter Thirty-Two

February 3, 1946
Poltava, Ukraine

The weather had shifted in late December, turning as cruel as it had the year before. There was near-constant snow, too much of it to make a run for it even with the pony, and days on end when the thermometer outside the cement works failed to rise above negative twenty Celsius. With windchills exceeding forty below zero at night, Emil and Corporal Gheorghe had decided it would be suicide to try to escape. They would wait for a thaw to reduce the snowpack and then a trailing storm to cover their tracks.

At Emil's request, after another of his workers died, the Romanian corporal came to toil in the cement-block shop. They gathered scraps of lumber from around the site for the cooks. And they continued to work the burial detail together, pushing bodies off the pony cart with the rise and fall of the sun. In early January, the bodies would have vanished almost overnight. Now they lingered for days in various stages of desecration. So many men were dying, the wolves and crows could not keep up.

Of the more than two thousand prisoners who had walked into Poltava in May 1945, three hundred and eighty remained alive and working to rebuild the city so they could go home. And there seemed little slowing to the spread of disease or the variety of death. When one outbreak ended, another began.

"We'll all be dead in six weeks," one of the other concrete workers said before exiting the shop to go out into the cold.

Corporal Gheorghe was pushing a wheelbarrow of lime to his mixing trough and smiled after the man. He tapped the dent in his head and nodded to Emil.

"He will be dead in six weeks because he says he will be dead in six weeks," the Romanian said, shaking his head and then laughing. "Why doesn't he ever say, 'In six weeks, I will run in fields of honey clover chasing a sweetie girl'?"

Emil snorted with laughter, seeing that image in his mind as he used the wooden paddle to stir his final batch of cement for the day. "Because one is likely and the other is fantasy?"

"Both are fantasies; both are dreams of what could be," the corporal said seriously as he dumped the lime in the trough. "Either can become real. Eventually. But people never learn this. They never realize that the Divine, the Almighty One, God, is listening to their hopes and dreams and trying to help. For good or for bad. Death or fields of clover. It is our choice."

"Is it?"

"Everything is our choice. Did you not choose to think about Dubossary differently?"

"Yes."

"And did it not make a difference?"

It was true. Ever since Corporal Gheorghe had shown Emil a different meaning to his story of Dubossary, he'd felt better mentally and emotionally than he had in the more than four years that had passed since that terrible night.

"A big difference."

"There you go, then."

"But that was the past," Emil said, pouring more fly ash into the concrete mix. "How can thinking change the future?"

"Not change, influence," Corporal Gheorghe laughed as he picked up his paddle and stirred. "The way you think about Dubossary now will influence your life in the future, won't it?"

Emil felt that was true also, but he couldn't put his finger on why exactly. That irritated him, but he nodded.

The Romanian said, "And if you ask yourself today what your opportunities are, will you see them? Will you find them in the future?"

"What opportunities?"

"Any opportunity. A chance to escape, for example. If you think about it now, will you be looking for the chance in the future?"

He thought about that. "Yes. I will be."

"It's the same with everything else," he said. "What you seek is what you will find, but only if you hunt it with all your heart and mind."

"Not always," Emil said.

"Always," Corporal Gheorghe insisted. "The problem is, most people get frustrated when they do not find what they are looking for or don't do what they are trying to do easily and in a short period of time. They give up after a couple of failures or a couple of years of struggle. The dream that once lit up their heart now begins to darken it, and their thinking changes. They lose faith far too early. They believe far too early that their dream can never exist. The problem is they haven't stayed true to their heart long enough for the Almighty One to move the moon and stars so the dream they seek can come into being. Once disbelief takes hold in their heart and thoughts, the Almighty hears it and gives up trying to help them. That's why dreams don't come true. It's why you have not become more in your life, Martel. It's why you haven't lived up to your name. And it is why I *will* become a beekeeper."

The corporal was smiling, which made Emil angry. He stopped pouring concrete into the molds. "What do you mean I haven't lived up to my name?"

"You keep trying to be a farmer, but the surname you use—Martel—is telling the Universal Intelligence a different story."

Emil stared at him in total confusion. "What story?"

"Martel means 'hammer' in old French. Even if you were good at it, you were not meant to be a farmer. You are meant to be a builder. You are meant to be the hammer, not the plow."

For a moment or two, Emil struggled with the Romanian's thinking, but then felt like that was also true. He'd always loved building things, even as a child. When it came right down to it, he even liked the process of mixing cement and making blocks.

He studied Gheorghe again. "Where did you say you learned all this stuff?"

The corporal stopped stirring and leaned over the handle of his paddle. "You remember me telling you and your family about Private Kumar? The Indian who was with me in the trenches at Stalingrad?"

It had been nearly two years since that night when the Romanian soldier had appeared out of the creek bottom, bearing stolen honey wine, but Emil recalled much of the story.

"Didn't he die? Blown up in the first attack?"

The corporal nodded sadly. "Because he believed he was going to die. He told me before it happened, and so it was. Private Kumar knew all this wisdom from his grandfather in India, and yet he died because he could not believe in a dream of a life beyond the battle. He died because in his heart he believed in the dream of his death. I know it is strange and disturbing to think this way. But I know it is true. I dreamed of a life as a beekeeper and believed that in my heart even before the mortar bomb hit me. It was why I was able to walk through the battle. It is why I will survive Poltava, return home, and become a beekeeper."

"Because you still hold that dream in your heart where it can't be taken from you?"

He smiled and started stirring again, saying, "Now Martel begins to understand."

The other man building concrete blocks returned, and they fell into a silence. Corporal Gheorghe seemed perfectly content as he worked. But Emil struggled with the Romanian's way of thinking the rest of the day. A small part of him wanted to believe it. The bigger part of him was deeply skeptical.

Later, as they were gathering scrap lumber for the cooks at the mess hall, he said, "So explain to me how this works. Did Private Kumar believe God was behind all this?"

"Not God in the way we were taught," he said, waving a piece of wood around at the falling snow. "This is the Divine. Everything is the Divine, the Almighty One, the Universal Intelligence. You, me, everything."

"I have no idea what you are talking about."

Corporal Gheorghe frowned but then put his hand on his chest, shut his eyes, and rocked his head back so the snowflakes hit his face. A moment later, he opened his eyes, lowered his chin, and gazed in a warm and calming way that made Emil feel strangely connected to him.

Gheorghe said, "Private Kumar believed that everything in life was, when it came right down to it, one thing, a supremely intelligent, universal force he called the Divine or the Universal Intelligence, or the Almighty One. I am part of the Divine. You are part of it, too. Everything is part of this life force you can call God, if it is easier to think that way. You are part of God, and God is a part of you. It's why the Divine understands your thoughts, dreams, and emotions, Martel. The Almighty is in you, and you are in it."

Emil chewed on that as they carried armloads of scrap lumber to the mess hall. After they'd given the wood to the cooks, gotten their pay, and sat down with their meal, Emil said, "You didn't say 'prayers.'"

The Romanian paused his soup spoon in midair, looked at Emil, puzzled. "Prayers?"

"You said God hears our thoughts, dreams, and emotions, but you didn't say prayers."

"Oh," he said, and put a spoonful of soup to his mouth. "According to Private Kumar, the Divine hears and understands prayers and thoughts, but they are not God's primary languages."

"Okay," Emil said. "What are the primary languages of God?"

Corporal Gheorghe smiled, put his hand on his chest, and said, "Whatever emotions you carry in your heart, Martel, especially love. God listens loud and clear if you feel love. The Almighty also knows if you are feeling good. The Universal Intelligence responds when you are happy or courageous or even if you are just calm. It understands when you are grateful for the miracle of your existence and rushes to help you when you have a dream that helps other people. The Divine hears all the languages of the heart and beauty."

The corporal sobered and pointed at Emil's chest. "All languages of the heart, Martel. Private Kumar said if you are dark in your heart, with too many bad thoughts circling in your mind, God also listens. When you suffer and curse your life, the Almighty listens closely. When you have no goodness in your heart or your prayers. No love. No calm. No desire to help others. No thankfulness for the miracle of your life. When you hold things like hatred or anger in your heart or envy or comparison, when life is all about how everything is unfair to me, me, me, the Divine understands those ancient languages of self-destruction, too. The thing is, the Universal Intelligence will help you even if your dreams come from a dark place, but the dreams will end up destroying you in the process. If you don't believe me, think of Hitler or any other tyrant."

Gheorghe returned his hand to his heart. "So live here, Martel. Love life like it is a miracle every day, every moment, and dream in a way that helps others, and the Divine will hear you and you will walk through battles untouched and have anything your heart desires."

Emil didn't know if he believed half of what the Romanian was telling him, but he said, "Even beehives?"

Corporal Gheorghe laughed and shook his spoon at Emil. "Yes, lots of beehives to make lots of honey because it is good for people. Makes them strong and live long."

———

After they had eaten and taken the pony cart and the dead to the sheltered cove by the big field, Emil went to his bunk with the Romanian's words still whirling and echoing in his head. It was a lot to take in, but when he began complaining to himself about the hardness of his bunk, the dankness of the room, the men still dying around him, and how much he missed Adeline and the boys, he stopped. What if God, or the Divine, or the Almighty One, or whatever you wanted to call it, was listening to the dark emotions he was feeling in his heart?

Instead, he tried to be grateful for the bunk and the dank room because he was not lying out in the snow; and to be thankful for the dying men around him because they reminded him that he was still alive, that he still had opportunities, that he was going to find a way to escape.

Emil imagined the coming thaw, the trailing storm that Corporal Gheorghe believed would come after the thaw, and the two of them bolting from the haunted burial grounds on pony-back, in the falling snow at dusk, avoiding dogs, getting to a train, and fleeing west. His heart warmed, and he felt excited at these dreams all the way down into sleep.

When he awoke the next morning to the sound of the triangle ringing, he tried to picture Adeline's green valley: the mountains and their snowcapped crags surrounding a lush, emerald-colored basin where wheat grew like a weed and a crystal river flowed through, feeding it all. He saw himself with a fishing pole standing by that river and started the day with a smile.

Emil emerged from the basement in the darkness before dawn, February 4, 1946, and saw ten bodies frozen in the snow by the pony and the death cart. No other prisoners would volunteer for burial duty, so Emil and Corporal Gheorghe got behind the cart and pushed while the pony pulled it across the icy ruts and deep snow in the big field above that cove in the trees. There were so many dead to pray for now, Emil feared using up his prayers. And how was he supposed to feel good about this?

"I'm beginning to believe you are right about a lot of things, or Private Kumar was," Emil said as they prepared to tip the bodies over. "I see clearly now that my prayers were answered that night in Dubossary because I felt calm about doing the right thing. God answered, and I did not have to kill those three kids."

"That's right."

"But what about the Jews praying that night?"

"What do you mean?"

"The Jews were begging God for their lives, too. I heard them, and the Almighty did not answer. He didn't answer the people who died in the death camps, either. What would your Private Kumar have said to that?"

The Romanian stared ahead for a long moment and then shook his head before releasing the latch and heaving his shoulders against the underside of the death cart. Emil threw himself into it as well, and with a thud, the ten frozen bodies fell into the snow.

Emil stood there, looking at the corporal when they lowered the bed of the cart and latched it. "Why didn't God answer them? Why didn't the Almighty answer the millions of Ukrainians who starved to death under Stalin?"

The Romanian looked pained as he said, "You are asking if I know the intent of the Universal Intelligence, and I do not. But maybe the millions in Ukraine died so people like you would run like a nomad when you got the chance to make a new life in the West. Maybe so many Jews died so the ones who survived would become the toughest, strongest people on the face of the earth, people who would help make sure there were no more death camps or starvation. Ever."

As they headed back to the hospital site, Emil thought about those nomads and survivors, felt a pang in his heart, and understood that even if Corporal Gheorghe was right, even if the starved went west and prospered and the Jews who survived became the toughest people on the planet, they would all still be human, and they would all still have broken hearts over what was done to them and to their families.

———

For nearly two weeks that February, the weather dried out, but the cold lingered, deep and bone-numbing. The death detail beat down a hard track through the field and into the clearing where they continued to dump a steady five bodies a day.

Emil could see the snow settling in the forest, but the skies were so clear, he and Corporal Gheorghe would have been easily tracked and caught if they had made a run for it. With each day that passed, he felt a little more doubt creep into his thoughts and felt a deeper shade of darkness in his heart.

But Corporal Gheorghe remained steadfast. "A thaw and a trailing storm will come."

In the middle of the month, the trailing storm came for Emil in his dreams. He saw himself and the Romanian leading the pony cart into the clearing as flakes quickened to steady snow. The wind turned blustery, threw a curtain of white between them and the Russian guards as they released the pony from the cart, climbed aboard, and galloped off. The snow was knee-deep, but they seemed to flow through it like spirits as they vanished into the forest and the night.

And then it was dawn, and snow was still falling, and the pony was sweating hard. They broke free of the trees, only to see a train stopped on the tracks. Men were ahead of the locomotive, moving a fallen tree off the rails.

The men boarded the train. Emil and Corporal Gheorghe took off in a low crouch toward the nearest hopper car. Emil reached the ladder first, remembered his maimed sister, and grasped each rung for dear life. The train heaved and began to move as he climbed.

"Martel!"

Emil looked down, saw the Romanian had only one hand on the ladder and was struggling to keep pace with the train. Emil stretched out his hand. But the corporal let go and fell. Emil dove after him into darkness.

———

At the sound of the triangle ringing, Emil bolted upright. Why hadn't someone woken him earlier? He jumped up, put his heavy clothes on, checked for the hundred rubles he'd saved from an entire winter selling scrap wood to the cooks, and ran up the stairs and out into the bitter cold for formation. The pony cart was there, but it was empty.

Emil was surprised. It had been a good five weeks since they'd had a night where no prisoners died. One of the guards who usually accompanied the burial detail in the morning was standing there near the cart.

"None?" Emil said in Russian.

The guard shook his head, said, "Good for you, but find someone who wants to eat double rations to help you tonight and to make cement. The Romanian was transferred."

Emil felt his stomach plunge. "Transferred? Where? Why?"

"He was sent south to a high-security camp on the Sea of Azov before he could try to escape from the burial detail. That's how he escaped prison camps twice before. Did he tell you that?"

The guard was studying Emil closely now.

"No," Emil said. "All he talked about was honey and becoming a beekeeper."

The Russian arched one eyebrow. "Well, that's one nice dream that's not coming true. At least not where he's going. Line up. You have food to eat and blocks to build."

As he'd done every day since his arrival at Poltava, Emil tried to follow his father's rules for survival. And with a nod to Corporal Gheorghe, he tried to feel grateful at the mess where he ate his double rations alone and tried to believe in his heart that he would escape.

But marching to the cement shop, Emil felt alone again. By midday, he was admitting that he missed the Romanian and the interesting angle he had on nearly everything in life.

Yes, he'd taken a hit to the head. But the injury seemed to have awakened the Romanian to a way of thinking Emil had never been exposed to before, a way of seeing the world as more than it was, a place where everything was connected and where dreams did come true, a place where imagination, faith, and effort collided with the spark of God's grace to become whole and real and good.

For reasons he couldn't explain, Emil felt flooded with warm emotions thinking this way. He teared up and almost cried. But not with grief or longing or pain. He was sitting there in the squalor of the concrete works amid the disease-ridden and hopeless destruction of Poltava, wanting to sob with joy because he realized Corporal Gheorghe had left him a different person, changed in ways he never expected, feeling blessed and humbled at how miraculous everything around him now seemed.

The drab wooden walls. The dwindling piles of gravel mix, slag, and lime. The mixing troughs. The building block molds. The hospital under construction outside. The terrible food. The museum basement. The ruins of Poltava. The dead men. The corporal. His own life. His love. His children. His wife. His destiny. His escape.

Emil told himself he had only to pick one path and follow it, trusting in his heart that it would lead him where he wanted to go. Every step west to freedom. Every step west to Adeline and the boys.

———

The sixteen days that followed Emil's awakening to endless possibilities were as dry as the sixteen that had come before. And his fellow prisoners were back to dying at a rate of five to six a day. But Emil ignored it all. He went to work in the cement shop and toiled on the burial detail afterward, knowing that the trailing storm was coming because a trailing storm always comes.

He said it to himself over and over again while looking to the skies and at everything around him in a continual state of wonder. Even the dreaded museum basement, the coffin of so many men, had come from someone's dreams, he realized. Emil continued to gather wood for money and to pray over the dead when he dropped them. He went to sleep, grateful for every moment of his day, and he woke up the same way.

It took until the end of February for the thaw to come and the middle of the first week of March 1946 before Emil heard whispers of a coming storm. Within two days, it was all the guards and the foremen were talking about. A blizzard was forecast with heavy snowfall, bitter cold, and high winds. All work would have to be suspended until it passed.

Before dawn on March 9, 1946, Emil woke up, sure that deliverance was upon him, that this morning or this evening he would get his chance to fulfill Corporal Gheorghe's dream of escape. When he exited the basement, snow was already falling steadily, enough to blur tracks. The wind was picking up as well, and there were two bodies waiting on the pony cart.

I'm leaving this place this morning, Emil vowed over and over again as he walked toward the cart. *I will not sleep in that basement tonight or ever again.*

He reached the cart and saw an unfamiliar guard there, a big Russian woman instead of the usual male soldiers who accompanied him.

"I'm with the burial detail," Emil said in Russian.

"Not today," she said. "Today you are coming with me. Get in that truck there."

"But the bodies," he said. "It's not right they should be here like this all day."

"Why?" the guard said. "Do you think they care whether they're eaten by wolves this morning or this evening? No. Get in the truck."

"Where am I going? I work at the hospital site, making concrete blocks."

"Not today, because you are almost out of lime and a shipment is coming in."

Emil knew that they were indeed running low on lime. He glanced at the pony and cart and told himself he'd be back before dark. He'd go alone to the boneyard, he decided before climbing up into the back of the transport. He'd escape that very evening.

Three other prisoners soon joined Emil in the back of the truck. They were driven to the mess hall to eat early and were done by the time the other two hundred and forty-nine men still alive in the prison camp were lining up outside.

They got back in the truck and started to drive. Emil closed his eyes, saw himself in that dream he'd had before Corporal Gheorghe was transferred. He was racing in the low light toward the side of the slowly moving train, ready to grab a rung.

Emil was emboldened by that vision. *Tonight's the night,* he thought, and felt grateful for it in his heart. *Tonight, the Almighty sends me a miracle.*

But when they reached the rail yard and he saw the freight cars full of lime on a spur line that ran beside and beneath a covered loading dock, and the dump trucks on the other side of the dock waiting for the lime to be transferred, Emil began to doubt the job could be done quickly at all.

———

Indeed, ten backbreaking hours later, Emil and the other three men were only just starting to attack the second railcar of lime. The storm had already dumped twelve centimeters, and it was still snowing hard. He had an hour left until darkness. He kept looking to the big Russian guard, hoping she'd call work for the day. But she didn't budge.

Finally, he went over to her. "I have to be back for the burial detail."

"I was ordered to keep you here until it's done," she snapped. "Someone else will take care of the bodies today."

The guard said it all with such finality that Emil turned around, knowing he was defeated, at least for that day. In the past, he would have been enraged at his misfortune, one more example of his brutal, sorry, unlucky life. But he didn't allow anger to consume him. He just went back to work, knowing that if he did not escape today, he would escape tomorrow. He felt it in his heart and with every fiber of his being.

Darkness fell. The wind swirled snow. Another train rolled into the rail yard on tracks beyond the covered spur line and the loading dock where Emil was shoveling lime into wheelbarrows and then truck beds. Determined to finish so he would not have to return in the morning, he had not taken a break since talking to the female guard more than an hour before.

Emil walked up to her now and said, "Permission to piss."

Before she could reply, there was a startling *clang!*

One of the dump trucks leaving the docks had slid on ice and hit another one trying to enter. The guard trotted that way.

Emil called after her. "Permission to piss!"

"Granted!" she yelled, and began to run toward the two drivers, who were out of their cabs, and looking ready to fight.

Emil climbed down off the loading dock onto the coupling between two of the freight cars and jumped off the other side of the spur line, landing in snow about twenty meters from the other train, which had stopped. He started to unbutton his fly, when a strange sensation came over him, sent prickles up his back.

And then Emil knew why. The other train. If he was right, if he'd kept his bearings, the train right in front of him was headed west.

He had a split second of indecision before he remembered how Corporal Gheorghe said that dreams almost always come true in ways you don't expect, that the Universal Intelligence almost always has a better plan in store for your visions. He'd imagined the pony and a crazy ride and having to stop the train by downing a tree. This way was simpler. This way was easier.

Emil remembered telling Adeline that he'd know the way to freedom when he saw it, and now, freedom was right there in front of him for the taking.

The westbound train started moving, the wheels screeching and drowning out the shouts coming from the Russian guard and the two drivers back by the loading dock. Feeling himself explode with happiness, Emil sprinted to the train, grabbing onto and clambering up the nearest ladder.

The train car had no roof. It was a hopper car and nearly filled with snow-covered coal. As the train gathered speed toward a lighted section of the rail yard, Emil threw himself into the hopper and lay flat on the coal, facedown, telling himself over and over to have faith, to believe it was done, that he was already gone.

He felt the train pick up speed, heard voices, but no shouting. And then everything went dark and stormy around him, and all he could hear was the clacking of rails and the whistling and moaning of wind. Emil got up on his knees finally and saw the lights of Poltava fading through the curtain of falling snow behind him.

After two hundred and ninety-five days in purgatory, after watching nearly one thousand eight hundred of his fellow prisoners die around him, and after transporting and praying over many of their bodies, Emil rocked back his head and threw his arms and hands wide to the snowing skies, knowing for certain that through a man's unrelenting heart and God's mysterious grace, dreams really can come true.

Chapter Thirty-Three

March 9, 1946
Gutengermendorf, Soviet-Occupied Germany

Some seventeen hundred kilometers away, Adeline tucked the boys into bed, kissed both on their foreheads, and quietly left their bedroom, knowing they'd both be asleep in moments. She went to the kitchen where Katrina Holtz was drinking tea.

"Are they still here?" Adeline asked the middle-aged owner of the house.

"Been and gone, disappointed as usual," Frau Holtz said, and laughed.

"Should I go tell Erica to come up?"

"No, she says she rather enjoys it down there. Gives her time to read."

While the two young Soviet soldiers billeted across the hall from Adeline had shown no interest in her, Frau Holtz's seventeen-year-old orphaned niece, Erica, had definitely attracted their attention. Six nights a week, Erica was around and pleasant with the Russians, but in no way led them on. On Saturday evenings, however, her aunt put her in the basement in a space hidden by a tall, wide set of shelves jammed with jars and books and tools.

Adeline no longer felt threatened enough to spend her Saturday nights in the old church. Working for Colonel Vasiliev had seen to that, giving her an invisible but strong and clearly understood shield of protection. As long as she applied her cooking skills and kept the colonel fat and happy, she believed she'd be safe. And Vasiliev had given her free rein to go into Berlin to shop at the Soviet officers' commissary, where she often purchased items for herself, the boys, and for Frau Holtz and Frau Schmidt.

She rarely went up to the Schmidts' farm anymore, however; Captain Kharkov was still living there, and she preferred to avoid him. But Adeline ran into Frau Schmidt in the village every so often and had learned she needed baking chocolate for her husband's upcoming birthday.

"I'm going to make a surprise delivery to Frau Schmidt," Adeline said to her landlord. "I promise I won't be long."

"You're sure?" Frau Holtz said. "It's Saturday night."

"I'll go the back way across the fields. No one will see me, and I'm sure the Soviet officers who live with her have already gone into Berlin for a night of carousing."

She could see her landlord disapproved but left the kitchen, put on her boots and her coat with a block of baking chocolate in the pocket before wrapping her warm scarf about her neck and head. Stepping outside the front door of Frau Holtz's low, mustard-colored house, Adeline took a deep breath of chill air, pulled on her mittens, and waited for her eyes to adjust. She turned left, went through the big swinging gates, and padded in five centimeters of new snow past the big brick barn where she'd stowed their little wagon.

Raising the latch on the smaller, rear gate, she went out under the bare limbs of the elm trees and out into the field. The quarter moon overhead reflected off the snow, giving her just enough light to start toward the knoll and the Schmidts' farm. She was less than halfway across the field when she had her first thought of Emil that day.

———

Adeline halted in her tracks because she realized she had not woken up early and gone outside to look east for the dawn. When had she stopped doing that? Yesterday? The day before?

Feeling hollow, Adeline understood it had been more than a week since she'd gotten up to pray and to look at the few pictures she had of Emil. The weather had been horrible last week. That was true. But it had been clear since. She had no excuse. And she'd forgotten to pray with the boys before bed!

She bowed her head, closed her eyes, and tried to see Emil's smiling face. She could remember him the day they'd met quite clearly, such a young, tough, and shy man who'd already survived so much. She could remember how he loved to laugh and sing and dance when he had a little beer or homemade wine in him. But the only other clear memory she could summon was his anguished face as the Polish militiamen dragged him away.

Go west, Adeline! Go as far west as you can, and I promise I'll find you!

Out there in the cut and snowed-over sunflower field, Emil's words echoed in Adeline's head as she opened her eyes and started walking again, trying to calculate how long it had been since he'd been taken from her. When she figured out it was almost a year to the day, she stopped again, her mitten traveling to her mouth, trying to stop the sobs of loneliness and unknowing that erupted from her. *Is he alive? Where is he? In Siberia? In one of those mines?*

The thought of her beloved Emil enslaved, working in a cramped, hot tunnel below a frozen wasteland, almost took Adeline to her knees. But then a gust of wind blew a mist of snow in her face, shocking her and making her realize she was cold. Shivering cold.

Adeline tried to run to heat up her body, but the snow was too deep in places, and a ring of questions began to form and repeat in her head: Was Emil alive? Would she ever see him again? If he lived and somehow found her, would she even know him when she saw him? Would the boys? A year or two, of course. But ten years? A decade of not knowing?

When she finally crested the knoll and was walking past the Schmidts' barn, she was trying to tell herself that she could last ten years if Emil could. *But what if Emil can't last? At what point do I give up?*

Her mother had never given up, and her father had never come home. Emil's mother had given up on ever seeing her husband again, and he'd shown up on her doorstep, alive but broken.

Walking to the front porch of the farmhouse, she wondered what her life would be like if that was Emil's fate as well and sensed an almost crushing burden on her shoulders. She shook it off immediately. It did her no good to think like that. She had to keep faith that he'd come back whole. In the meantime, she had to live for her boys, keeping their father's memory alive in their hearts. *But if I have trouble remembering his face, how can they?*

Adeline was about to knock, when she heard piano music playing. She ducked down and looked beneath the shade to see the farmer and his wife sitting side by side at the piano. Frau Schmidt was playing, and her husband was watching her with such deep, undying love that Adeline was moved to smiling through tears. They'd been married for nearly forty years. They'd been through terrible tragedy, and yet their love hadn't just survived; it had deepened and flourished. *Isn't that a cause for hope?*

She considered not knocking and leaving the couple alone. But then the music stopped, and she could hear Herr Schmidt clapping inside.

Frau Schmidt was thrilled when Adeline did knock on her door, greeting her like a long-lost daughter and kissing her on the cheek when she gave her the chocolate. Herr Schmidt said he was calling it a night and went upstairs. Captain Kharkov and his men were thankfully on leave in Berlin.

Adeline said that she couldn't stay long, that she had to get back in case one of the boys woke up, but she ended up spending an hour with her friend. She listened to the older woman's fears about her husband's health and shared some of her own.

"I sometimes wonder who I will be without Emil," Adeline said.

"You will be you," Frau Schmidt said softly.

"What?"

"You are already without him, Adeline. So you will be you without him in the future, and from what I've seen, being Adeline Martel is more than enough for anything life wants to throw at her."

She hugged the older woman and thanked her for her kindness and support.

"I thank you," Frau Schmidt said, hugging her back. "You are a good friend."

Adeline felt better as she left the house. Knowing the Soviets were in Berlin, she decided to take the lane back to the village. Dogs barked in the distance. The snow creaked beneath her boots, but there was a nice smell in the air. Spring was coming.

She heard Frau Schmidt say, *Being Adeline Martel is more than enough for anything life wants to throw at her.*

Is that true? Adeline wondered. *So far, yes, but—*

A car engine turned over. Headlights came on ahead of her on the lane, blinding her. She threw up her sleeve to block it, hearing a car door open.

"Frau Martel?" a woman's pleasant voice said.

"Yes?" Adeline said uncertainly, and stopped. "Who are you?"

"Lieutenant Eloise Gerhardt with *Kommissariat 5* of the *Deutsche Volkspolizei*, the People's Police," she said. "I'd like a few words with you, please. Come, I can drive you home while we talk."

Adeline hesitated.

Lieutenant Gerhardt's voice grew sterner. "Frau Martel, do as you are told. You do not have a choice in this matter."

Adeline resigned herself and walked through the headlights' glare to see the party officer was a big stocky woman in a gray-green woolen long coat. She had short dark hair, a square chin, a prominent nose, and hard eyes.

"Please," Lieutenant Gerhardt said, gesturing to the open rear door. "You first."

Adeline reluctantly climbed into the sedan, seeing a man was driving the car. The policewoman got in beside her, saying, "Keep the interior light on, and drive Frau Martel home the slow, long way, please. We have much to discuss."

The driver grunted and put the car in gear. The overhead light went on.

Lieutenant Gerhardt smiled. "You will answer my questions truthfully, yes? It will be bad for you otherwise."

It was only then that Adeline realized that *Kommissariat 5* of the People's Police meant she was talking with a secret police officer of some sort, like the one who'd taken away her father so long ago.

"Yes?" Lieutenant Gerhardt said, her tone now colder.

"Yes," Adeline stammered. "If I can."

"Good. You cook for Colonel Vasiliev?"

"Yes. And for several of his ranking officers."

"You often go to Berlin to the special commissary there at the colonel's request?"

Frowning, wondering why she was being asked that, Adeline said, "Yes. He gives me a list and the money. I go and come back. There is always a receipt."

"You admit you are a frequent visitor of the commissary on Colonel Vasiliev's behalf. More frequent than almost any other customer. Did you know that?"

Adeline shook her head. "No."

"It is true. The party keeps track. You see, your colonel is a glutton. He sees himself as better than the others who shop there, and he takes advantage of his position to fatten himself."

Adeline said nothing.

Lieutenant Gerhardt smiled. "And you take advantage of your position as well, don't you, Frau Martel?"

She didn't know what to say.

"You always seem to forget something after you have paid for the colonel's needs," the secret police officer went on. "Then you buy what you want and give the sentry a bribe on your way out. Or you buy something for someone like Frau Schmidt or Frau Holtz and then bribe the sentry on your way out. Yes?"

Adeline swallowed hard and then nodded. "Yes. I . . ."

"You are a black marketeer, Frau Martel. That is a crime against the party and the state. You could be sent to prison like your husband and have your children made wards."

"No, please," Adeline said, panic-stricken. "They were small things. Treats for my young sons. Some things Frau Schmidt needed. She's old and—"

"The party does not care about Frau Schmidt's age or her needs," Lieutenant Gerhardt said sharply. Then her face softened. "But it does care about you, Adeline. So you are going to stop your black-market activities, and you are going to tell me what Colonel Vasiliev buys on a weekly basis, or does out of the ordinary, or says when he is drunk and full of your food. Do you understand?"

Adeline did understand. She'd grown up under Stalin. She knew how Communists turned neighbor against neighbor, worker against boss, husband against wife, sowing fear into the culture in a way that stifled all thought. And when they had enough on you, for crimes you did not even commit, you were sent away, never to return.

"Do you understand?"

"Yes," Adeline said, bowing her head. "I understand."

"Good," Lieutenant Gerhardt said. "Isn't this where you live coming up ahead?"

Adeline felt so disoriented, she had to look twice before nodding. "Yes, there, with the big gates and the barn."

The driver pulled over. Adeline reached for the door handle, only to feel the secret police officer's hand like a claw on her shoulder.

"Another question before you go," Lieutenant Gerhardt said, and smiled in that knowing way Adeline had already learned to fear. "In Berlin, you put your name and Frau Schmidt's address on a list with the International Red Cross."

How does she know that?

"Yes," Adeline said, nervous again. "The list is for refugees, families trying to find one another. I put Frau Schmidt's address because I didn't know how long I'd be at my present place."

The secret police officer said, "Why would you do such a thing?"

"I put it there, hoping Emil might see it someday."

"In Berlin? When he is in the East?"

"I . . ."

For several long moments, Lieutenant Gerhardt said nothing.

Feeling her throat close, Adeline quivered with emotion, forcing herself to look the woman right in the eye. "I want my husband back. Is that so wrong, Lieutenant?"

"No, but if I were you, I'd stop thinking about him ever coming back. From what I understand, the prison camp where he was sent is riddled with disease. Men dying every day."

"Emil?" she said, hearing her voice shake.

"I don't know. All the party has been told is that there's hardly anyone left alive there. I'm sorry, Frau Martel. But the sooner you deal with the fact that he's dead or soon will be, the quicker you can get on with a new life. You can get out of the car now, Frau Martel, but we will meet next Friday after you leave work, yes?"

Adeline felt dazed by the news of Emil's fate—*a prison camp riddled with disease . . . men dying every day . . . hardly any prisoners left.* She nodded dully and opened the door. When she went inside, she did not answer Frau Holtz, who called from the kitchen, asking why she'd been gone so long. She just hung up her coat and scarf, took off her boots, and went into the bedroom.

Closing the door behind her, she stood in the darkness, listening to the sounds of her sons sleeping. Emil's sons sleeping. Adeline started to cry but steeled herself enough to undress and climb into bed. Walt stirred and rolled over beside her. She stared into the blackness, hearing Lieutenant Gerhardt's soft, brutal voice.

I'm sorry, Frau Martel. But the sooner you deal with the fact that he's dead or soon will be, the quicker you can get on with a new life.

Adeline wrapped the pillow over her head with both arms, bit into the fabric, and finally let herself scream.

Chapter Thirty-Four

Emil was shivering so hard atop the coal car, he could not control it. His heavy wool clothes were now caked with wet snow, and he was exposed to the howling wind. What was he thinking when he climbed on this train? He might have escaped the prison camp, but he was going to die soon if he didn't get to some kind of shelter.

Emil had tried digging in the coal, figuring he could bury himself under it and leave an airhole to breathe through. But down a few centimeters, he hit a layer of ice frozen into the coal below. He tried kicking at it with his boot, only to succeed in knocking himself off balance and almost falling off the side of the train, which stopped often at crossings but overall moved much faster than the one he'd come east on. He believed he was close to seventy-five kilometers away from Poltava now, maybe more.

The shivering got worse. His thoughts were becoming foggy. He knew he was minutes from freezing to death. Hearing brakes squeal and the train slow yet again, Emil began crawling until he reached the rear of the hopper car. He spent the moments before the train came to a full stop bending and unbending his fingers, trying to get blood into them, making them functional before he climbed down the ladder.

Emil jumped off the low rung into deep snow. Slogging rearward, he grabbed a rung on the front ladder of the next hopper car and climbed up, only to find it as full of coal as the first one. The train was still stopped. But for how long?

Longer than you can last in this cold, Emil.

His fingers screamed, but he forced himself down the ladder and again slogged toward the rear of the train. It began to move.

Barely able to see, he held out his hands, tried to anticipate the ladder. The one at the rear of the second hopper car slipped through his gloves, and the train began to pick up speed. He snagged the front ladder on the third hopper but couldn't hold on.

Knowing he was about to be left behind in the storm and the darkness to die, Emil put his hand on the side of the third car, waiting to feel it end before he reached higher and grabbed at the oncoming ladder of the fourth car with both aching hands. He caught an upper rung with his left and the side of the ladder with his right and was immediately dragged along as Corporal Gheorghe had been dragged in his dream. The Romanian had let go in the dream, and Emil had jumped after him into darkness.

But not this time. With everything Emil had left in him, he held tight with his left hand and stabbed up his right, finding a higher rung. With two more brute strength moves upward, his boots found the ladder's lowest rung.

Coated with snow, battered by wind, gasping, sweating, he hung off the ladder like some giant white cocoon for almost a minute. When his teeth began to chatter, he climbed again. At the top of the ladder, Emil reached over the side of the car, feeling for coal. He felt nothing but wind, so he straddled the side of the coal car and reached down as far as he could with his right foot.

Nothing. Was it empty? At least partially.

Figuring he could at least get down out of the wind, Emil brought his left leg over, and dangled by his fingers a second before letting go. He fell three meters and hit heels first in snow on steel. The shock went up both his legs, buckling them. His upper body crashed so hard, the wind was knocked out of him, and for a few moments he thought he'd cracked ribs.

When Emil finally managed to sit up, however, he realized he'd been right. Here, in the pitch darkness deep in the front right corner of an empty hopper car, he was well sheltered from the northwest wind. And the snow seemed to be lessening.

Heartened by that, he struggled upright and cringed before spreading his legs wide and leaning his back into the corner, brushing at his clothes and trying to get as much of the wet, caked snow off him as possible. The first few chunks he put in his mouth and sucked out the moisture to quench his thirst. Then he unbuttoned the coat and lifted his shirts and sweater to expose his belly to the cold, hoping that some of the sweat on him would escape.

Stay as dry as possible. Move to stay warm. Survive, he thought.

When Emil believed he'd gotten most of the snow off his outer clothes, he began kicking the snow on the floor of the railcar away from his corner and soon created a knee-high arched wall of snow in front of him. Ducking down in the darkness, he felt as if the wall had cut even more wind. He lost track of time, building the wall to chest height.

Brushing the snow off his clothes yet again, Emil winced at the sore ribs as he finally lowered himself to the floor of his little fortress and leaned back into the corner. The wind was almost completely gone now, and it was no longer snowing. He closed his eyes, telling himself he'd have to eat at some point. He had money from selling scrap wood to the cooks, more than one hundred rubles in a buttoned shirt pocket. Now he just needed a place to spend it.

Vents began to form in the cloud cover. Through one, he saw the quarter moon, and for reasons he did not understand, he felt warmed seeing it and warmed further when the clouds fully parted and he was able to locate the North Star. *I can navigate and walk at night if I have to.*

After taking off his coat to shake the remaining snow off it, Emil sat on the steel floor in the corner of the hopper car and dozed despite the constant aching cold beneath him. Then he felt and heard the brakes slowing the train yet again.

———

This time lights appeared. They were pulling into some kind of station. Able to see now, he spotted another ladder, this one on the opposite interior wall of the hopper. He knew he should stay where he was, cover himself with snow, and hide behind the crude wall he'd built.

But if he did not know where he was, how could he figure out where he was going? For all Emil knew, he might be on his way to Moscow or Leningrad. He buried that thought straightaway. Although the tracks they'd ridden had curved and meandered, the North Star did not lie. They'd been heading steadily west.

But how far west?

Unable to tamp down his curiosity, Emil climbed out of his snow fortress and sneaked across the car. He climbed to the top of the inner ladder, nervous because the lights were so bright. Part of him wanted to take a quick peek. But he figured that might create a flash of movement and attract attention. As slowly as he could, Emil raised his eyes just above the side of the hopper car and scanned left and right before slowly lowering his head.

He was in a large rail yard with many freight cars on other tracks. There were men working on a loading dock well ahead of him. The men were so far away, Emil decided to take another look and saw a sign in Russian that he understood. He knew where he was now: Lubny. They'd gone through the same station heading east to the prison camp. A good nine hours had passed between that train leaving Lubny and arriving in Poltava. He had no watch but knew that nine hours had not passed since he'd escaped.

Maybe four. Maybe five. In any case, Emil was heading west much, much faster than he ever could have hoped. And for the first time since he'd escaped, he allowed himself to think of Adeline, Walt, and Will.

Where would he start to look for them? In Legnica? Back in Poland where he'd been taken? But he'd told Adeline to go as far west as she could, and he'd find her.

He heard voices: men speaking in Russian. He eased his head up one more time and spotted two Soviet soldiers walking alongside his train by the coal car he'd escaped in, four ahead. One of them climbed the ladder of that car and looked around before descending.

They came a car closer. The other soldier climbed up to look inside.

"*Nyet,*" he said in a whiny voice. "Only coal."

"You heard what they said; he jumped on this train," his partner said in a much deeper voice. "Unless he fell, he's here."

Emil slowly lowered his head and climbed down the ladder. He stared at his boot prints in the snow on the bottom of the empty hopper and understood he'd blown his chance. If he'd stayed behind the wall of snow and buried himself, he might have made it.

"Your turn," he heard the whiny soldier say, followed by the sounds of boots squeaking in the snow and gloves scraping up the side of the hopper car just in front of Emil's.

He stood there on the floor of his own car, shaking his head at his sheer stupidity. He was going to be caught and sent back to Poltava. Or worse, like Corporal Gheorghe, he was going to be sent somewhere worse.

"This one's empty other than snow," the one with the deep voice said.

"I got this one," the whiny soldier said.

Emil closed his eyes. He'd escaped not only to find Adeline and the boys. With the number of men succumbing to disease around him, he'd escaped to live. *But now I'll be sent back to die.*

The train lurched forward a meter and stopped. The soldier on the ladder cursed. Emil was thrown off balance but stayed upright.

"That hurt my shoulder," the whiny soldier cried angrily before the train lurched and stopped again. "You go up it."

Their voices were close now, right on the other side of the hopper car wall. The soldier would climb up, look in, and see Emil directly below him. It would all be over. He'd fulfilled Corporal Gheorghe's dream of escaping by train, but his own dream of going west and reuniting with his family was about to be snuffed out.

"The hell with it," the soldier with the deep voice said. "I'm not breaking an arm or a leg over some escaped POW. If he's in any of these last cars, he'll be dead by morning. Temperature's supposed to dive, hit thirty below."

———

Emil's heart felt like it was trying to smash its way out of his chest. He could hear their footsteps. They were walking away!

The train lurched and began rolling again, picking up speed, and he was beyond Lubny, heading toward Kiev, the biggest city in Ukraine. Emil held on to the ladder and began doing slow squats, up and down. If the temperature really was going to plunge to negative thirty, he would have to move all night. The best way would be like this, stable, slow, and steady.

As he fell into the rhythm of it, Emil began to think forward to Kiev. Darnitsa, the central station, would be heavily guarded by Soviet soldiers. They would search the cars, wouldn't they? He decided he had to act as if they would search every car. At first, he considered getting off the train just east of Kiev.

Then he thought, *What would Corporal Gheorghe do?* And came up with a bolder plan.

He laughed at the idea and then loved it and how giddy it made him. Closing his eyes, he could remember only one other time in his life when he'd felt like this: the night he and Adeline were married, a night his heart had bubbled with joy.

Emil could suddenly see that night as if it were happening all over again. He saw himself kiss Adeline at the end of the ceremony. He saw himself dancing with her to accordion music, gazing into her loving eyes, his hands about her waist.

Still holding that ladder in the hopper car, Emil realized he wasn't that cold as long as he stayed in that memory. He kept his eyes shut, hearing the jaunty, upbeat accordion music in his mind as he let go of the ladder and began to dance.

———

For hours on end, Emil danced and laughed with his imaginary Adeline, sometimes thrown off his feet and falling into the snow on the floor of the hopper car as the train rounded a tight bend. But he didn't care. In his mind and in his heart, Adella was with him and they were celebrating and that was all that mattered.

Even so, at dawn, he verged on delirious. He'd been awake more than a day by then, ten of those hours at hard labor shoveling lime and six of those hours dancing with the memory of his bride. And the Soviet soldiers had been right about the cold. He didn't know if the temperature was thirty below, but his mitts kept sticking to the steel ladder, and the snow had turned crusted and crunchy. His feet ached. So did his lower back.

At the first sign of light in the sky and with the train still moving, Emil shook off the daze and climbed the interior ladder of the hopper car. At the top, he looked around, seeing the all-too-familiar landscape of rural western Ukraine, with vast fields bordered by thin hedgerows and coated with snow as far as the eye could see. He was surprised that the land triggered a wave of nostalgia in him. A memory surfaced from childhood, shortly after his father pulled him out of school to work on the farm. He remembered being sad at leaving school, which he'd enjoyed, but also being thrilled to follow his father out into the fields with a long day of work before them.

He thought of his father, mother, and sister and wondered if he'd ever see any of them again. Were they with Adeline? Or had they gone back to Friedenstal as his mother had wanted? Were they somewhere to the southwest of him a hundred kilometers? Even if they were, he decided, he was still going west. He was still fulfilling his dream.

———

An hour later, with Emil crouching below the lip of the hopper car, the train pulled into a freight yard at the central rail station in Kiev. It was windy, brilliantly sunny, and bone-numbingly cold. Seeing men scattered about working in the yard and no soldiers, he heaved himself up and over the side of the hopper car and almost slid down the exterior ladder. He moved quickly away from the train, thankful for the brisk wind, which was swirling the snow, erasing his tracks. After getting behind other boxcars, he spotted a pickax almost buried in the drifting snow and grabbed it.

Emil threw it over his shoulder and walked down the tracks toward the main station building. Another rail man exited a door at the top of a low flight of concrete stairs. He smiled, ran up them past the man, and caught the door. He stepped inside a long narrow hallway, let his eyes adjust to the dimness, and felt an unfamiliar yet welcome sensation brush across his face, hearing noises he hadn't heard in more than a year. Once he could see, he started walking toward the source of the sensation and the noises: the considerable gap between the threshold and the bottoms of the swinging double doors at the far end of the hallway through which a steady stream of heat flowed and the bustle of a crowd echoed.

Near the end of the hall, a door stood ajar on his left. He pushed it open and found an empty room with wire-mesh lockers, probably for the rail workers. He went in, seeing a lavatory with a deep sink and a mirror off the locker room. Emil pulled off his wool hat and moved to the mirror.

For the first time in more than a year, he saw his own face and condition. It was a shocking reflection. Adeline would not have known him if he'd asked her to dance. He barely recognized himself.

Emil had lost more than twenty-five kilos. His shabby, worn prison clothes hung off him like a scarecrow's outfit. His hair and beard were bristly and cut unevenly. His cheeks were hollow. His teeth were yellowed. His facial bones stood out against his skin, which was scabby, drawn down, and filthy with grime. His eyes, sunken, dark, and hardened, troubled him most.

Knowing he was taking a terrible chance, but also knowing he could not go into the central station in Kiev looking like someone who'd just dug himself out of a grave, Emil struggled from his coat, sweater, and shirts. With every breath, his ribs seemed to move like so many player-piano keys against the skin of his bruised, chaffed, and lesioned torso.

He turned on the faucet and stuck his head and face under the ice-cold water. He scrubbed for a good ten minutes, dunking and dunking until his true features were revealed. *There,* he thought, looking in the mirror again. *Adella and the boys would almost know me now.*

With that, he caught something come alive in his eyes, a glint where there had been none. It reminded Emil of the plan he had come up with the night before. He smiled, headed into the locker room, and went through the lockers, finding a faded blue workman's coverall, a pair of work boots newer than his own, and a shirt and a wool peacoat far less filthy than his prison-issue jacket.

As Emil dressed in the stolen clothes, he felt no remorse. He'd been unjustly thrown in a prison camp for a year, needed the clothes, and figured life could be unfair to someone else for a change. He threw his old clothes into an empty locker after he'd retrieved his rubles and put the wad of notes in the pocket of his pants beneath the coverall. Only then did he leave the room, surprised that no one had bothered him. Then again, according to the clock and the schedule he'd seen on the wall, the day shift had started less than an hour before.

Emil left the pickax in the hallway and went through the doors out into the organized chaos of Kiev's central train station. The crowd of voices babbling. The colors so brilliant after so many months of gray. The wondrous smells of fresh food cooking. The harried faces of people returning to their lives or boarding trains to start new ones. For a moment, it was all so overwhelming, Emil had to put his hand on a wall to keep from falling.

Hunger pangs brought him back to his senses. He followed the irresistible smells into the ticketing-and-waiting area where he knew vendors would be selling food. He found at least ten of them, mostly women, and forced himself to look at everything they had before ordering black tea, two small rolls of bread, and a chunk of dried sausage. There were many other, richer, and sweeter items he would have much rather had as his first meal out of captivity, but Emil was nervous his gut would revolt if he did. He found a bench and ate his food sparingly. A soldier walked by, never giving him a second glance.

Emil ended up spending three hours wandering around the train station, watching, listening until he knew when the next freight and passenger trains west were leaving. He had more than enough money left to buy his way to Poland but feared having to reveal his lack of documents to do so. In the end, he retrieved the pickax and went back out into the freight yard.

It was still bitterly cold and windy. He found the freight train he was looking for and tried the sliding doors on several boxcars before finding one unlocked. He acted as if he were digging a hole with the pickax outside the car until the train started to move.

Emil was climbing inside with the pickax, when he heard shouts. He got in, looked out, and saw workmen running at him. One was yelling, "Hey, that's my coat!"

"I left you mine!" Emil cried, shut the door, and threw his weight against it as the train picked up speed.

Emil left that train at the very next stop. He could not chance that the workmen were calling ahead about a thief and stowaway. After dark, he caught the next freight train going west and got off at the next stop. It became a pattern and a way of survival for Emil over the next ten days.

Not only could he find food, water, and warmth in the train stations and depots, they offered him the chance to listen to the rumors and the propaganda swirling through Ukrainian society in the aftermath of the Soviet reoccupation. Everything he heard convinced him that the new life under Stalin and the Communists was the same as the old one: based on fear, tyranny, and the destruction of anyone who had an original thought or dream.

On the eleventh morning of his escape, March 20, 1946, the weather finally broke warm. On the eleventh evening of his escape, shortly after he'd crossed the Polish border and slipped out of a freight car in the town of Chelm, Emil was captured by local police.

He'd prepared for this possibility as part of his plan and began acting a little odd like Corporal Gheorghe, speaking Russian, telling them he was a survivor of Stalingrad who'd been blown up in the first wave of attacks and then walked through the battle unscathed. He was just trying to go home to find his wife and sons where he left them in Legnica. The soldiers didn't believe him and put Emil in a jail with others awaiting deportation back to the East.

The rest of the men in the jail were miserable and angry. But Emil stayed remarkably calm, believing that this was just a detour on the road to his dream. He was going west. He was finding Adeline, Walt, and Will.

The very next day, he was saved from deportation when guards asked him if he had ever worked on a farm. Still acting like a man who'd taken shrapnel to the head, Emil nodded and was put on a truck with twenty other men who'd escaped various prison camps. They were all taken to a new camp and put to work with other men planting row crops.

Eight weeks later, in late May 1946, Emil heard that the baker in the camp kitchen needed help. Although he had chopped firewood for a bakery when he met Adeline, he had no experience at actually baking. Emil learned fast. For the next four weeks, he arose at three o'clock in the morning and went to the bakery to mix dough and heat the ovens. He ate fresh bread the entire time, gained weight, and made friends with the baker, who had worked for a time in Germany before the war.

In late June, a rumor and then a fact swept through the camp. The planting season was over and so was their usefulness. The work camp was about to close. The prisoners were to be put on trucks at dawn and then on trains headed east.

If Emil was ever to go west, ever to find his family, it had to be now. He thought like the mad Romanian and came up with a relatively simple plan that he reluctantly shared with the baker, along with a request: that the baker exchange his Russian rubles for Polish zlotys so he could buy a train ticket home to his family.

In the end, the baker agreed to his proposal with a shrug, a wink, and a nod. Emil broke his normal routine that night and did not return to his bunk after mixing and kneading the dough and then leaving it to rise. Instead, around five thirty the morning of June 29, 1946, he lay down on the warm floor of the bakery's back room, behind the ovens, and "fell asleep." He waited three full hours after the trucks and the other prisoners were gone before leaving the bakery with the baker yelling after him. A Polish guard came. The baker told him he'd found Emil sleeping in the back room when he was supposed to be on the truck with the others.

Emil was taken before the camp's commanding officer, where he again acted shell-shocked and said only that he'd fallen asleep and didn't mean to miss the train. The camp commander had wanted to leave the rural area as quickly as possible and was furious at this snag in plans.

When he was asked what to do with Emil, now that the camp was officially closed, the commander thought about it, and then said, "Take the brain-damaged idiot outside the gates; give him a swift kick in the ass; and let him go become someone else's problem."

Emil Martel goes west and finds his wife and sons, he thought, hearing Corporal Gheorghe's voice in his head as he hurried away from the prison gates, massaging his sore rump, and giving thanks to Jesus, God, the Divine, the Universal Intelligence, the Almighty One, the stars, the moon, and the planets over and over again until he was long out of sight.

———

With the warmer weather and wanting to avoid all human contact, Emil slept in forests by day and walked mostly at night for almost three weeks, navigating by the stars to put as much distance as he could between himself and that last prison camp outside Chelm. He waited until the morning of July 19 to walk into the farming community of Pulawy, northwest of Lublin, Poland, and ask to buy a ticket to the last stop before the German border.

The clerk gave him a strange look, but said, "That would be Rzepin."

"Rzepin, that's the place," Emil said. "My great-aunt lives there."

The clerk was skeptical but sold him the ticket. After buying food for the ride, Emil took a window seat, put his hat over his eyes, and slept as the train took him across the country. He had to change trains twice, once in Warsaw. His plan was to leave the third train at Rzepin, then cross the German border in the dark on foot.

Twelve hours after he'd started, however, when the third train of his trip made an extended stop in the city of Poznan, Emil recognized possibility when he saw it. It was early evening, still a few hours from darkness, and he had grown hungry again. Emil left the train, entered the main station, and saw a large group of men, close to fifty of them, gaunt, shabbily dressed, and sitting cross-legged on the floor under the watch of three Soviet armed guards.

He bought the usual staples of his bland diet and asked a clerk at the ticket counter who the men were and was told they were German prisoners of war going home. There had been some sort of agreement just reached that allowed for a prisoner swap. These men, all originally from western Germany, were going to be swapped for eastern German prisoners of war.

Feeling breathless, and remembering again how the Romanian was always talking about the opportunities laid before you when you have a clear vision of where you want to go, Emil said, "You mean they are all going to west Germany?"

"To Braunschweig in the British Zone. I assume that's west."

Emil thanked her and moved to one side where he could eat and watch the German prisoners and the Soviet soldiers. The men sitting cross-legged on the floor all seemed relaxed, happy to be going home, even if it was as prisoners.

And why not? Emil thought. *They might be in prison in the West for a while longer, but when they're out, they'll be free men. You can't say that about the men coming the other way.*

Then he remembered something else Corporal Gheorghe had told him about most people seeing the door of good fortune open, but then not acting, not walking through the door, not taking a chance, only to see the door slam in their face.

You decide; then you act. You choose faith; then you walk through the door.

Another, larger group of German prisoners came into the station with their fingers laced behind their heads at the same time the conductor entered from trackside to call for all passengers westbound. Emil made his decision and acted in faith, stuffing the rest of his food in the pockets of the jacket he carried.

The original three Soviet soldiers ordered their prisoners to stand and lace their fingers behind their heads at the same time the bigger group tried to move past them to get better seats on the train. There was some bumping. Grumbling.

Cursing. In the mild upheaval, Emil slipped in among the prisoners and laced his fingers behind his head.

———

No one checked Emil's documents before he boarded the train. If they had, he would have shown them his ticket to Rzepin and gotten off at the next stop. Instead, the train was waved through at the German border, picked up speed, and took Emil swiftly west.

He modified his cover story on the ride, telling the men who asked that he was Corporal Emil Martel, an ethnic German who fought for the Wehrmacht. He'd survived Stalingrad and fought at the Dnieper River where he lost his documents before being captured and put in a prison in a place called Poltava.

"But you are not German," sniffed one of the men. "Why are you here with us?"

Emil fixed him with a steady gaze, then smiled, and offered him some dried sausage. "No, I'm not German. But Reichsführer Himmler himself thought I had purer Aryan blood than most. Because of it, my family was protected by the SS and brought to Germany. They are waiting for me."

The man seemed slightly taken aback and accepted the meat. "Where?"

"Braunschweig," he said. "They're in a camp near there for refugees."

"British Zone," the man said, his suspicions dulling as he chewed some of the sausage. "That's not far from where they're taking us."

"I'll just be happy knowing my family is near and safe until I am freed."

An hour and a half later, the train passed south of Berlin and Adeline and the boys. Emil would later figure out that he'd gone within eighty kilometers of them.

The train finally stopped east of Wolfsburg. Emil and the other prisoners were ordered out onto the narrow platform while the three passenger cars they were riding in were transferred to another engine. It was sweltering hot by then, and the prisoners were irritable and restless when they were told to show their documents before getting back on the train.

Emil went boldly near the front of the line, ready to bluff his way on. But he'd no sooner told the soldiers that his documents were lost at Stalingrad than he found himself ordered to stand over against the wall of the train depot. The car behind the locomotive was filled with prisoners before the soldiers checking documents moved on to the next car in line.

Emil watched them carry the table forward and set it in front of the open door to the car before ordering the man next in line to present his papers. No one seemed to be watching him, so he strolled down the platform, jumped off the far end, and crossed the tracks in front of the locomotive, waving at the engineer.

He hurried along the opposite side of the train to the third passenger car, which was empty. Crouching, he climbed inside, hurried down the aisle, and took the third seat before ducking down and waiting.

He heard the table being moved into place outside the train car. When the first prisoner entered the car, Emil made a show of tying his shoe before sitting up. When he glanced at the man taking the seat beside him, he saw the prisoner he'd given sausage to earlier in the day. The man nodded at him and looked away.

Sweating from the heat and the risk he'd just taken, Emil pulled his cap down and pretended he was sleeping until the train finally left, heading south. Less than thirty minutes later, the train veered west and slowed to a stop amid rolling farmland. Emil could see a stream running through a lush field and could not help thinking of Adeline's green valley. Was he close at last? Was she already there?

But then a Soviet soldier came through the car from behind Emil.

"Get out your papers again!" he shouted. "Show me your papers! If you wish to cross into the British Zone, you must have your papers out and ready. Now!"

Chapter Thirty-Five

December 24, 1946
Gutengermendorf, Soviet-Occupied east Germany

Adeline awoke at five o'clock that Christmas Eve morning and eased out of bed, feeling as if her legs and arms were made of lead. Her head was pounding and groggy as she dressed in the dark, left the room, and got her coat and canvas shopping bag.

She trudged out into the cold, heading to the station and the five-thirty train to Berlin. She wanted to be first in line when the officer's commissary opened at seven. Then she could be back in time to prepare lunch and the evening meal for Colonel Vasiliev and his officers, and still make it home before dark to celebrate the holiday with the boys.

Waiting alone on the platform, stamping her feet to stay warm, Adeline felt alternately irritable and deeply, deeply sad. At first, she tried to blame it on the terrible sleep she'd been getting lately. But after she got on the train and closed her eyes, the real reason for her depression wormed its way forward.

The Christmas Eve before, after she'd held off Captain Kharkov with the butcher knife in the old church, she'd asked herself who she would be if another year passed and she found herself lying on a cold, hard pew with no word from Emil.

A poor, lonely woman, she thought. *That's who I am a year later. A poor, lonely woman, who can't face the fact that she's probably a poor, lonely widow clinging to false hope. It's what Lieutenant Gerhardt hints at every time I see her, isn't it? Emil has died of some disease, and I am forced to spy on everyone. My housemates. My neighbors. The colonel and his men.*

What kind of life is this? And who are Walt and Will becoming? Are they being told at school to spy on their friends? On me?

It all made her angry, bitter. She wondered what the last two years and nine months were really about. They had survived the Long Trek and the last year of the war, only to be cruelly split apart. She had tried to go as far west as she could, only to not go far enough. She had tried to live her life quietly, keeping her faith in Emil's return, only to face rapists and secret police who said her faith was foolish and misplaced.

What have I done to deserve this? Adeline asked herself. *Why in God's name am I being punished like this?*

———

By the time she reached the central station, Adeline knew she wasn't being punished in God's name. She was being punished in Communism's name, in Joseph Stalin's name, just as she had been punished in his name when they took her father away nearly two decades before.

Sent to the East. Thrown to the wind and the wolves. Never to be seen again. Like Emil.

Adeline felt something shift inside and realized sadly that she didn't have the emotional strength to put a question mark on that last thought. After drinking tea and eating strudel from one of the few vendors already open in the Berlin central station, she set off through the streets toward the officer's commissary, suddenly missing her mother, Malia, and her brother, Wilhelm.

What's become of them? Where are they? In that little town where I left them? Will I ever see or hear from them again? Or are they gone from my life? Never to be seen again. Like . . .

Adeline stopped herself from using her husband's name, but she saw Emil clearly in her mind, then, as he was the last time she'd seen him, being led away by the soldiers, and bellowing at her to go as far west as she could and he'd find her. Try as she might, she could not stop herself from bursting into tears. That was probably the last time she'd ever see him. That was the image that would stay with her until she was old, wrinkled, and dying with the question of Emil's fate still in her heart. Would she ever know what became of him?

That question drove her deeper into the darkest state of mind she could ever remember, a despair so complete that she barely noticed the familiar soldier at the commissary door.

He said, "I need chocolate for my lady friend tonight. And any kind of cigarettes."

"Chocolate and cigarettes of any kind will get me a visit from the secret police."

"I had to talk," he said. "I told you that. They threatened my sister."

"They always threaten someone, don't they?" she said, and went inside.

Adeline moved through the shop quickly, knowing exactly what she wanted, and why. When she was finished, the voice in her head she called her safer-self told her to go to the checkout, to pay, and leave. But she got angry at that voice. She'd been listening to it for years. It was the same voice that said she didn't deserve to eat when she was starving, the same one that blamed her for the first Walt's death; the one that never failed to remind her that she was a refugee, someone no one wanted; the voice that whispered she was not as good as the people around her; the one that said don't take chances, go along, protect yourself, protect the boys; the voice that always spoke out of fear.

Adeline stood there a long time, staring off into the middle distance before she finally asked where that voice had gotten her. Was she any safer than she'd been when she walked away from her mother? Other than the roof over her family's head, a warm place for them to sleep, and a job that fed them well, she knew the answer was no. As long as she was here, living under the Soviets, dealing with people like Lieutenant Gerhardt, the answer would always be no.

Deep in her gut, Adeline felt the anger change, become defiance, and defiance felt good, so good she pulled out a pen. She scrawled a few more items on the list, then got them and put them on the counter along with everything Colonel Vasiliev had ordered. She added her money to the total and paid.

Outside, she handed the guard a chocolate bar. "If you tell the lieutenant about this, I will never buy anything for you again. Merry Christmas."

"You can't say that now."

"And yet I did," she said, and walked off toward the train station.

Eight hours later, Adeline pulled a roasted capon from the oven in the kitchen off the Soviet officers' formal mess that she called the "white room" because Colonel Vasiliev had insisted on having white tablecloths to match the walls and floor. She moved the bird to a smaller oven to stay warm along with covered bowls of freshly made egg noodles with onions and two loaves of Russian brown bread freshly baked with little slices of garlic the way the Soviet colonel liked it. She opened the large caviar jar and poured the contents on a plate along with Vasiliev's favorite crackers and four different kinds of cheese. Two bottles of vodka and three bottles of Riesling wine were already in a washtub out in the white room, packed in ice.

After setting the long table with fresh linen, silverware, and crystal, Adeline cleaned the kitchen to a shine. When she was finally done, she decided not to think about the things that were wrong with her life. Just for today, she'd go home and make every effort to celebrate the season with Walt and Will. And maybe she would take up Frau Schmidt on her offer to come and spend the holiday evening with her and Herr Schmidt again.

Thinking how excited the boys would be for their presents and feeling much better than she had all day, Adeline put on her coat, gloves, and scarf and went out into the frigid air. The late-afternoon winter sky had turned a thin blue that spoke of colder temperatures to come. She'd no sooner rounded the corner than the dreaded black sedan pulled up beside her. The rear window was already rolled down.

"Frau Martel," Lieutenant Gerhardt said as if they were dear friends. "How lucky for me to catch you. Please get in. I'm sure you have much to tell me after your holiday shopping spree."

Adeline had anticipated a visit from the secret police. It was why her canvas bag was empty. It was why she'd left her gifts behind, hidden in a cupboard in the pantry of the Soviet officers' mess. She climbed in and closed the door. They stayed parked, the engine idling, the same dour driver smoking at the wheel.

"What's in your bag?" Lieutenant Gerhardt said.

Adeline showed her it was empty and then handed her the receipt for all the items she'd purchased earlier in the day.

Lieutenant Gerhardt studied the list, her jaw stiffening. "The colonel buys all this?"

"No, there were other requests from at least six of his staff officers in there," Adeline replied. "They all paid with their own funds. Good vodka mostly."

"Name them. Break their purchases down for me."

Adeline did, adding one or two of her items to each of the officers' lists, and waited while Gerhardt scribbled in a brown notebook, then said, "What else?"

"I cooked, cleaned, and left," Adeline said. "The officers won't sit down to eat for at least another hour."

Lieutenant Gerhardt continued to write, not looking up at her as she said, "You disappoint me, Adeline. I have asked you repeatedly to stay and listen to the conversations at the table."

"And I have," she said. "Is it my fault they only talk of women, food, drink, and how soon they can all go home to Mother Russia?"

The secret policewoman raised her head. "Why did you not stay this evening?"

"It is Christmas—"

"These feeble customs will no longer be recognized by the party, Adeline."

"I got up at three o'clock this morning. I have worked hard for twelve hours, Lieutenant. I am going home to my sons now, and here's a secret you won't have to dig out of someone else: I will follow feeble customs not recognized by the party tonight and tomorrow, which Colonel Vasiliev has given me off for equally feeble reasons."

Gerhardt set down her pen and gazed hard at Adeline for several long moments before leaning toward her, murmuring, "Do not mistake my gentle tone for weakness, Adeline. I am the party here, and the party never forgets. That's how it works."

Adeline knew she should shut up at that point, but she stared evenly at the secret policewoman and said, "I think I know that better than you, Lieutenant. I've lived under the Soviet system for most of my life. You're just getting started, which means the file they have on you somewhere is still slim, but growing fatter every day, week upon week, month upon month, year upon year. Until they no longer have use for you."

The secret policewoman sat back, studied her in reappraisal.

"You do not like living here, do you, Adeline?"

"I like my job. I like cooking. The school is good for my boys."

"But things could be better for you, couldn't they?"

Adeline felt uncomfortable, as if she sensed a trap of some kind.

"I have no complaints, Lieutenant," she said.

Gerhardt's smile was thin. "I think not. I think you have many complaints. But you are smart, Adeline. No one ever hears you say them out loud."

Adeline said nothing.

The secret policewoman watched her, smiling as if she could read her thoughts.

"A warning, Adeline. Every day the border with the West hardens."

Adeline frowned. "I don't understand."

"Towers and fences are being built along the border. They have dogs patrolling in places now, with more being trained. And every day, more and more people trying to run west without permission are being shot. Especially refugees."

"I don't know what—"

Gerhardt's smile evaporated. "Think twice before you are tempted, Adeline. I tell you this for your own good, as well as the good of your sons."

"I still don't—"

"You rarely speak of Frau Schmidt anymore."

Adeline felt like she was being jerked in multiple directions. "What's there to tell? She's old. Her husband is sick. I go sit with her from time to time."

"And the Russian officers who live there?"

She could see Lieutenant Gerhardt wasn't going to leave without something to chew on, so she said, "One of them, Captain Kharkov, is a rapist."

The secret policewoman's chin retreated. "A rapist?"

"He tried to rape me last Christmas Eve in the church where I used to hide on Saturday nights and holidays. I held him off with a butcher knife."

Lieutenant Gerhardt's thin smile returned as she opened her book, saying, "Good for you, Adeline. I'll make note of that."

When the secret police car drove away, leaving her at the curb, Adeline made a show of heading toward home before looping back to the kitchen to retrieve her gifts, which she put in the canvas bag along with whatever other delicacy struck her fancy in the pantry. She left the Soviet officers' billet for a second time, feeling more than a little rebellious and brazen at the way she'd handled Lieutenant Gerhardt and taken food from the Russians.

But why the warning about the border hardening? Did the secret police-woman know that Adeline had crossed into the British Zone in Berlin the year before? Or did she just take Adeline's defiant tone as evidence she was unhappy enough to make a run for it?

In any case, it didn't matter. By the time she reached home, the idea that people were being shot every day trying to cross the border was enough to snuff the idea from her mind.

Her landlord, Frau Holtz, was just leaving with an overnight bag, headed for Berlin to visit relatives with her niece. The Russian soldiers had already gone to the city.

"Looks like it's just us for Christmas, Mama," Walt said.

"Can we go cut a tree?" Will asked.

"Our room's too small for a tree. But no glum faces now. We have been invited to the Schmidts', just like last year."

The boys cheered. Walt said, "Are we getting presents like last year?"

"Maybe," she said, and smiled.

"Can we go sledding?" Walt asked.

"I'm sure."

"At night?"

"No, there's no moon tonight. It will be black as ink. But get your things together, and maybe you can sled before it turns dark."

Ten minutes later, they were dressed in their warm clothes and out the door, with Adeline's canvas sack filled with food and gifts. They took the long way around and reached the Schmidts' farmyard as the sun was dropping toward the hazy horizon, sending slanted light through the leafless trees. Frau Schmidt was thrilled they had come and told the boys they could use the sled until dark. Thankfully, Captain Kharkov and his friends had long since departed. Adeline stayed out with the boys through their first run. Seeing them hike back up the knoll through the snow felt good deep inside her chest. How they'd grown in just a year: Walt was nine now, and Will seven.

"Mama!" Will cried. "Did you see how fast we went?"

"A speed record!" she called back. "I am going in with the Schmidts now. Don't kill yourselves!"

"We won't!" Walt yelled back.

Adeline smiled and walked a few light and unburdened steps. Then the reality that they were spending another Christmas without Emil brought her mood crashing down, just as it had crashed down a thousand times since he was taken. She trudged toward Frau Schmidt's front door, almost overcome by sadness and gloom, worse than what she'd endured early that morning when depression had seemed like a shroud around her. Her longing for Emil now felt sewn through her, like strings on a marionette she'd once seen. She wanted to stop and pray for her husband's safe return but did not know if she had the strength.

Finally, and barely holding back the grief welling up inside her, Adeline stopped walking. She closed her eyes and prayed to God to watch over Emil's soul and to tell her if he was dead so she could make her peace with the end of him and the perpetual love she'd always feel for him no matter what life had in store for her next.

Tears dribbled down Adeline's cheeks as she went up the stairs and inside the Schmidts' warm and welcoming home. The tree was waiting for the boys to help with its decorating. Herr Schmidt looked better than he had in weeks and was building a fire.

In the kitchen, Frau Schmidt was working at the oven. When she heard the door shut, she turned, saying, "Adeline, did . . . Are you all right?"

"I'm trying, Greta!" Adeline said, and then burst into tears.

As her husband rose in concern, the older woman rushed across the room to Adeline. "My dear, whatever's the matter?"

"It's always hard this time of year, not knowing," she wept. "And that evil woman Lieutenant Gerhardt told me Emil was put in a camp where disease has killed nearly everyone. He's been gone since March last year, and I have no word whether he's dead or alive."

Frau Schmidt hugged her, saying, "I can't imagine. But you have your sons. No matter what, you'll have Emil's spirit in them."

Remembering that her friends had lost their son in the war, she stopped crying and pulled back to look at the elderly woman, who had a wistfulness about her.

"Thank you for reminding me how lucky I am, Greta," Adeline said.

Will burst into the house. "Mama, come quick. You've got to see the sky. It's so . . . I mean, you won't believe it!"

She hesitated, wiping at her tears with the sleeve of her coat.

"Go on," Frau Schmidt said. "Your sons are giving you a present you won't believe. Could there be anything better than that?"

Adeline gazed at her, smiled softly, and shook her head. "Thank you," she said again.

Buttoning her coat and putting her scarf over her head, she went outside where Walt and Will were peering up in awe. She followed their gaze and gasped.

The sun had almost sunk below the horizon, but its dying light was throwing fire at five clouds stretched out in long, thin spirals, painting them in rich reds, golds, and purples, like so many ribbons festooned in the sky above them, slowly rotating as if blown by a spiraling breeze. Smiling up at the ribbon clouds, Adeline felt her sons come in beside her and wrap their arms around her waist.

"Merry Christmas from heaven, Mama," Walt said.

Adeline felt the tears flow again and hugged both her boys tight, still watching the sky when she heard the door open and footsteps on the porch.

Frau Schmidt said, "Will you look at that!"

"Isn't it incredible?" Adeline said, looking over at her friend and smiling.

"Peter!" Frau Schmidt called. "Come look before it's gone!"

Her husband came out, struggling into his jacket but stopping when he looked up and saw the ribbons. His jaw hung loose a moment. "My God, I've never seen anything like that in my life."

The colors in the clouds changed with every minute that passed, turning redder and more purple than gold, and then only purple before darkness took the gift of the ribbons in the sky and made them a cherished memory.

"Did you like your present?" Will said as they walked back toward the farmhouse.

"One of the best presents ever, thank you," Adeline said, hugging both boys tight.

Frau Schmidt was already back puttering in her kitchen when they entered. And Herr Schmidt was still in his heavy coat and winter hat, squatting to light the fire, which began to dance in the stove while Adeline and the boys took off their winter clothes.

"That will feel good in about fifteen minutes," Walt said.

"I just like watching fire," Will said.

"Everyone does," Herr Schmidt said, closing the stove door and tousling Will's hair before removing his hat and coat. "Would you like to sing some carols?"

Both boys clapped and looked to Adeline, who was not entirely in the mood for singing. But she nodded. "That would be nice."

Frau Schmidt called out, "Peter!"

"Greta?" he said.

"You said there was something in the post for Adeline."

"Ahh," he said, wagging his finger as if just remembering. "I put it here, I think." He reached into his coat's inner breast pocket and came out with a slim envelope. "I don't know why they sent it here. You've been gone almost a year."

Equally puzzled, Adeline took it, seeing the typed address with her name, care of the Schmidts, and a return address, "IRC-DPC-Alfeld."

The boys went into the kitchen where Frau Schmidt was pulling cookies from the oven.

"Where's Alfeld?" Adeline asked as she turned the envelope over, seeing the flap was partially unsealed or had been resealed poorly.

"No idea," Herr Schmidt said. "Then again, my memory is not what it used to be."

Putting a finger under the raised flap, Adeline tore it open and retrieved a single sheet of paper before unfolding it. She began to read the typed letter. As she did, her free hand started to tremble and then to travel shakily to her lips. Her eyes blurred before she rocked back her head and threw up her hands, screaming in a mixture of disbelief and pure joy.

"My God, boys, it's from the International Red Cross! Papa's alive and free! He's waiting for us in the West!"

The boys began to jump up and down and scream with her.

"Where is he?" Will cried.

"A displaced persons camp in a place called Alfeld! The British Zone!"

Walt calmed down and looked confused. "How did he get there?"

She looked at the letter through tears that she had to brush aside to reread it. "It doesn't say. It just says he's waiting for us to write to him."

The Schmidts shared in their happiness, which was contagious that night. They ate and drank and toasted before Herr Schmidt went to the piano and played a jaunty tune Adeline did not recognize. But it had a toe-tapping quality that reminded her of the song an accordion player had performed at her wedding and how she and Emil had danced to it like they'd gone to sleep in Russia and woken up in paradise.

She held her hands out to Will and to Walt.

"What are we doing?" Walt asked when she began to tug their arms this way and that.

"We're dancing," she said. "We're dancing the night away because your father is alive!"

PART FIVE:
THE LAST GREEN
VALLEY

Chapter Thirty-Six

March 13, 1947
Gutengermendorf, Soviet-Occupied east Germany

Adeline closed the door between the kitchen and the dining area in the Soviet officers' billet, checked the sugar beets she had stewing to make fresh molasses, and then dug out Emil's fourth letter to her. When she opened it, her hands trembled, but not with the shock and ecstatic wonder that had erupted through her when she first learned he was alive and living at a displaced persons camp fifty kilometers south of Hanover, Germany, near the town of Alfeld.

Adeline was thrilled to get this latest letter, of course, but she was also anxious to see that—once again—someone had opened the envelope and read the contents before she had the chance. Lieutenant Gerhardt, no doubt. The secret policewoman had known the Red Cross had written to her back on Christmas Eve. That was why Gerhardt had warned her about trying to go west.

Since that letter, the woman had gone out of her way to let Adeline know that she was reading every word that passed between her and Emil. The secret policewoman knew that he had escaped Poltava, come all the way across Ukraine, Poland, and eastern Germany, then smuggled himself into the British Zone with a group of returning army soldiers and the invaluable help of one who liked sausage and gave Emil documents to wave at a border guard before his final crossing.

"Your husband is a criminal, an enemy of the state," Lieutenant Gerhardt said several times. "And you will be a criminal and an enemy of the state, Adeline, if you decide to run to him with your sons."

Gerhardt seemed to enjoy saying these kinds of things to Adeline, who knew the secret policewoman was trying to goad her into a revealing reaction. But she had grown up understanding that, in this sort of situation, the best reaction was either no reaction or a well-placed deflection.

"I am filing the documents for the three of us to join him legally," Adeline said every time Lieutenant Gerhardt brought up Emil, their letters, and her suspicion that she was preparing to try to leave Soviet-occupied east Germany.

"They'll shoot your sons as you run," Gerhardt said when they last spoke.

But so far, the secret policewoman's suspicions were just that. Lieutenant Gerhardt may have read every word that passed between Adeline and Emil, but she had not figured out that not only were they declaring their love and describing their lives and longings for reunion in their letters, they were speaking in a "mirror code" they'd used earlier in life when dealing with Communist authorities. All the speaker or writer had to do was mention a mirror or a reflection or something silvery like the surface of a lake or river, and the listener or reader would know that the sentences that followed were the exact opposite of what was intended. The use of the words "I do" in a sentence indicated that the lying had stopped, and they were now telling the truth.

Adeline, in her first letter to Emil, wrote:

> My dearest love,
> You don't know how overjoyed I was to receive your letter on Christmas Eve. The boys were so happy, they were jumping up and down and screaming at the tops of their lungs! I looked in the mirror that night and thought how I wished you would come here to be with us. Our lives are so much better than they were in Friedenstal. We are happy here. No one listens to our conversations like the old days. I do think of you every hour while I work in a kitchen cooking. Walt is studying geometry, and Will is learning to read. Until we are in each other's arms, I do love you with all my heart. Your Adeline

Now Adeline read Emil's latest response, which made her stomach hollow and shaky with adrenaline.

> My dearest Adeline,
> I pray you are well and happy, and the boys grow strong. There is a silvery pond near the camp, and I often stare at it, wondering if I should not wait here, if I should try to come to you and the boys. The border is almost completely closed now. I heard that the only way across for refugees in either direction is the official way. At the pond yesterday, I thought if life is the way you describe it, I want you to stay there and I will make the journey east to you. Slow down your plans and wait for me to knock on your door soon, or to call you before I come in at the train station there. Know that I do love you and I am in great spirits, hoping to see you very soon. Hug and kiss the boys for me. Your adoring husband, Emil

———

Adeline put the letter down on the table and put her face in her hands. If she'd read the letter correctly, Emil was not telling her to wait for him to come to her. He was telling her that she, as a refugee, had to sneak across the border as soon as possible because there were still places where it could be done. But she had no idea where to cross where there were not already fences or patrols or dogs or towers or all four that she and her two young boys would have to avoid and evade.

Emil's words from long ago echoed in Adeline's memory: *At some point, you'll have to decide where you want to spend your life—in slavery or in freedom—and if you choose freedom, you'll have to run through a no-man's-land with bullets zinging around your head to get there. I don't think there's any way around it. If we want that life, we'll have to risk death for it.*

Adeline glanced at the clock in the kitchen at the Soviet officers' billet and saw it was almost noon. Colonel Vasiliev and his staff were in Berlin overnight. Once the molasses was done and poured into two glass jars, the afternoon was hers.

After the jars were sealed, she left them on the table and decided to go for a walk to try to get her thoughts straight. Putting on her coat, she wandered through the village and found herself turning onto the road that led up to the Schmidts' farm. She hadn't gone more than a hundred meters when she saw Lieutenant Gerhardt's car rolling her way.

For a second, she considered walking into the woods to avoid the secret policewoman but decided that would be about the worst move she could make. Adeline stood there, waiting for the black sedan to pull up beside her. The window rolled down.

Lieutenant Gerhardt smiled thinly. "I would think you'd be in the kitchen, Adeline."

"I was given the afternoon off."

"Yes, I know. How was your trip to the commissary yesterday?"

"Later than I'd planned because they've changed the hours," Adeline said, and handed her the list as well as the receipt.

Gerhardt scanned the list. "Cigarettes?"

Adeline had prepared for that question. "The colonel started smoking again."

"Hmm," Lieutenant Gerhardt said, nodding. "And where are you going?"

"I'm out for a walk. It's the nicest day we've had lately."

"I wouldn't know." Gerhardt sniffed. "I've just come from your friend, Frau Schmidt's. Her husband has taken a turn for the worse. A stroke, the doctor thinks."

Adeline tried not to react, but did, wringing her hands. "Then I could be of help to her. May I go, please?"

"I hear your husband is thinking of joining you?"

She nodded. "That is his thinking."

"He is not worried about being sent east if he comes here?"

Adeline didn't know what to say, then blurted out, "I think he's more worried about not seeing me and my sons."

"As he should be," Lieutenant Gerhardt said, and rolled up the window.

———

The car drove off. Adeline stared after it, feeling more and more anxious. Ever since Emil had contacted her, she had been trying to meet the midday train so she could talk to people in the stream of homeless refugees who came to the town to beg and barter and see what they knew about leaving the Soviet Zone safely. But every time she asked, she had gotten little solid information. And every time she opened her mouth to query another person, she risked one of them reporting her to someone like Lieutenant Gerhardt.

Emil wants me to run, but he can't tell me how, she fretted before turning and hurrying up the road to the lane that led to the farm. She knocked on the door a few minutes later. Frau Schmidt opened the door, saw her, and smiled sadly.

"You heard?" she said.

"About Peter? Yes. Where is he?"

"Upstairs with the doctor," the elderly woman said, a tear dribbling down her cheek. "He doesn't know who I am, Adella."

Adeline hugged Frau Schmidt, who hugged her back twice as hard. When they parted, the farmer's wife sat at the table and folded her shaking hands, saying, "It gets worse. The party believes we are too old and now too infirm to farm. As you predicted, we are to be moved."

Adeline's heart ached for her friend. "I'm so sorry, Greta."

The doctor clomped down the stairs. He glanced at Adeline, greeted her, and then spoke with Frau Schmidt about her husband's condition. He'd given Herr Schmidt a shot, and he was sleeping. He cautioned her not to try to feed her husband anything other than water until he returned the following day and left.

The elderly woman went upstairs to check on her ailing husband and then came back down to the table, saying wistfully, "I wish we'd done it last week before he . . ."

"Done what?" Adeline asked, looking at the clock and seeing she had another hour or so before the boys got out of school.

Frau Schmidt hesitated before saying, "Tried to go west. We have relatives near Dusseldorf. But now . . ."

Adeline debated, and then said, "What does Lieutenant Gerhardt ask about me?"

"She wants to know if you are going to try to leave and go west."

"And what did you say?"

"You're going through the proper application process."

Feeling relief as well as a thrill of anticipation, Adeline reached over to cover Frau Schmidt's bony hands with her own and looked into her friend's eyes. "Can you tell me where you were going to try to escape? And how?"

Greta swallowed hard and nodded. "But I have no idea if it will work, Adeline."

———

Five days later, on March 18, 1947, Adeline arose at two thirty in the morning and roused her boys. Walt came awake groggily while Will groaned, "Why are we up so early, Mama?"

She whispered, "Quiet. We're going to see Papa."

Will took the pillow off his head. Walt snapped alert. "Really?"

"It's now or never," she whispered, and touched them both on the cheek. "Get dressed in your warm clothes. Lace your boots tight. We're going to be taking a long walk. And please, quiet as a mouse when you come outside. We don't want to wake our neighbors or their dogs."

Will said, "Mama—"

"Not another word until I say so!" she hissed. "Do you understand?"

Both boys shrank but nodded. It was rare to see their mother so intense.

"Good. Wait for me outside. Close the front door slowly behind you."

Adeline left the room as quietly as she could, put on her coat and boots, and eased out the front door, leaving it ajar. It was above freezing and nearly pitch dark, with only a sliver of a waning crescent moon above, when she went to the front gate and opened it on hinges she'd oiled two days before. Then she padded over to the big sliding doors across an arch of the brick barn. She'd oiled the wheels on those doors, too, and pushed them smoothly aside before retrieving their little wagon packed with their essential belongings covered by two blankets.

Adeline found the boys by the stoop and motioned to them to follow her. They went down the street to the other side of town and the small train station there. The three-fifteen to Berlin was late and largely empty that morning. The conductor recognized her when she paid for the tickets.

"The early train and with the little ones today?"

"We're going to spend the day and evening with my sister and mother in Falkenberg," Adeline said, and stared at the boys in a way that told them not to correct her.

"You'll be there before ten o'clock," he said. "You'll have to buy Falkenberg tickets in Berlin."

As the train began to roll, Adeline could see he wanted to linger and talk, but she got out one of the blankets and put it over their laps.

"Let's get some sleep," she said to the boys, and promptly closed her eyes.

She waited to pull the boys close to her until the conductor had walked off. She kissed each of them on the head, closed her eyes again, and imagined rushing into Emil's arms, envisioned them all rushing into Emil's arms, a family again. Once she saw that clearly in her mind, she began to pray to God over and over to make it real. She smelled Emil's scent and felt his big arms around her. She heard his gruff voice telling her how much he loved her and how they would never, ever be apart. She surged with joyous emotions and saw herself in his arms again and again and again. The entire hour-long ride, while the boys drifted off and slept, she kept seeing herself in Emil's embrace and thanking God for making it real, for bringing them back together after more than two years of separation and longing.

———

It was still pitch dark when they arrived in Berlin at four twenty-five that morning. She shook the boys awake and then folded the blanket and put it back in the little wagon.

"Are we there yet, Mama?" Will asked grumpily.

"Another train, a walk, and a train," she replied, pulling the little wagon down the platform into the central station. She checked the schedule, seeing the train she wanted was leaving at four forty-five on the far track.

"C'mon boys, push," she said. "We have to hurry now."

The station was surprisingly crowded for that early an hour. They wove through the crowd, seeing two soldiers smoking cigarettes and chortling about something over near the main entrance. Adeline kept glancing at them until they reached the correct track, turned their backs on the soldiers, and hurried toward a ten-car train.

The first car was packed. So was the second. A conductor was smoking outside the third car.

He was in his midtwenties with a sparse beard and acne. He turned surly the moment he saw Adeline and the boys coming down the platform, pushing and pulling the little wagon.

Grimacing, he pointed his cigarette at the wagon. "Where do you think you're going with that? And you'd better have papers if you're going through to Wolfsburg."

"Oebisfelde," Adeline said.

His chin retreated as he puffed and shook his head. "Last stop before the British Zone. You're not getting on my train, lady. I know what you're up to. If I let you on and don't report it, I'll end up on a shit list. And aren't you putting your kids in danger, trying something like this?"

Adeline looked over her shoulder and saw no one coming.

"Not if we're not caught," she said. "And you won't end up on that list. I promise."

"Why would I ever take the chance?"

Adeline reached beneath the bottom blanket laid across their belongings in the cart and came up with two jars of molasses. "I made this from sugar beets I gathered myself."

The conductor looked at the jars and laughed. "That wouldn't get one of your kids on."

She grimaced but reached beneath the blanket again and came up with a bottle of whiskey and a carton of Turkish cigarettes that had cost half her last paycheck at the Soviet officers' commissary. She held both out.

"They're yours if you let us on, help put our wagon in the baggage car, and help take it off in Oebisfelde. The whiskey now. Cigarettes when we leave you."

The conductor chewed his lip a second, then dropped his cigarette and ground it with his heel before taking the bottle. "You and your brats wheel the wagon down there."

———

Five minutes later, Adeline and the boys were inside the crowded sixth car, seated on the side opposite the platform. Will and Walt were so tired, they fell asleep

390

against her as soon as she spread the blanket over them. She wanted to do the same, to seek refuge from her growing anxiety, to make her mind stop racing. But she could not.

Adeline stayed hypervigilant, listening to the people talking around her and wondering whether they, too, were making a run for freedom.

The train began to move. The boys shifted in their sleep against her, and it took everything Adeline had to fight the fear that built in her in tandem with the speed of the train. When the conductor came by to punch their tickets, he already smelled of whiskey.

"How long?" she asked.

"We've got clear tracks," he said. "You'll be there around five minutes to six, just before sunrise, in time for them to see you and shoot you when you make your run."

He walked away, seeming almost amused. Adeline felt a caustic taste in the back of her mouth as she did the math against the sunrise, which a book in the Soviet officers' billet said would be at 6:23 a.m. Subtract half an hour, and the conductor was right; they would be arriving in Oebisfelde at the crack of dawn. With every step she and the boys took after leaving the train, the light of day would grow along with the chance of discovery, the chance of gunfire, and worse.

I should have come earlier! I should have taken the midnight train to Berlin!

But the midnight train would have been more crowded, and the central station most certainly so. They would have ended up in Oebisfelde at roughly three a.m. with only a sliver of a waning moon above. *How would we have seen? How would we have known we were going the right way?*

She did not own a flashlight and had feared stealing one from the officers' billet, only to have its light betray them as they ran for freedom. In the end, she decided a night run was not worth the risk. Now, however, as the train hurtled toward dawn, she was feeling regret.

No, she thought, clamping down on the emotion. *I have to believe this is the right time and the right way to go.*

Adeline closed her eyes and was actually starting to doze when she heard the conductor's question echo in her mind. *Aren't you putting your kids in danger?*

She came to again, alert, tense, her chest heaving when she glanced at Will and then Walt, feeling her heart pang with alarm for them and for her. They *were* in danger, terrible danger, all of them. They'd been in peril from the moment they'd left the house with the wagon. If they were caught, the Soviets could separate her from the boys. They could send her east to a work camp and Walt and Will to an orphanage. With every kilometer that passed along the route heading west-southwest from Berlin toward Oebisfelde, the border, and the British Zone beyond, her anxiety rippled through fear toward terror.

What if I'm shot? What if the boys are shot? And I'm not?

Adeline's mind reeled and threw her back more than a decade, seeing herself as if from the ceiling of their flat in Pervomaisk, where she'd held the first Waldemar in the moments after he'd died and she'd known what it was to have something ripped from her heart, an agony so complete and devastating, she'd wanted to lie down and die right there.

———

In the train, Adeline gasped at the wrenching emotion of that horrible memory.

"Mama?" Will said, jerking her back to reality. "Are you okay?"

"Yes, I . . . ," she said, her heart thumping and her stomach churning when she gazed down at her dear little boy in the dimly lit railcar. "Why?"

"You cried out. You said, 'Waldemar.'"

"What?" Walt said, rousing.

"Nothing," Adeline whispered. "Go back to sleep, both of you."

As the boys readjusted and snuggled against her, she tried not to think about the cold sweat on her brow and the nausea in her stomach and the weakness in her chest and legs at the thought of one of them dying before she did. *I can't take that. I can't do that again, Lord. I can't.*

Adeline realized she'd been holding her breath and forced herself to take in one inhalation after another after another. And as she did, for reasons she'd never be able to fully explain, she thought of four lines in Emil's third letter: "Remember that Corporal Gheorghe? The Romanian with the dented head and the honey wine? I saw him again. He said to say hello to Malia if you have the chance."

Corporal Gheorghe. Of course, she remembered him. How could she not? His hypnotic eyes and the way he talked about the Battle of Stalingrad, how he'd woken up after being shelled in the initial Soviet attack, how he'd seen the world differently, and how he'd known without a doubt that he would survive to tell the tale. That unwavering belief had seemed to protect the Romanian as he'd walked on through the bloodiest battle ever fought on earth.

I have to believe like that, Adeline thought. *I have to believe with every fiber of my being, with no doubt that we'll make it. No doubt.*

Adeline suddenly understood that if she really had no doubts, none whatsoever, she'd be calmer and make better decisions in the waning darkness and waxing light that lay before her and her beloved boys.

No doubts, Adella. You're already there.

She closed her eyes and repeated the words again and again as she drifted off, dwelling on that vision of reunion she'd held on to on the train to Berlin, feeling Emil's powerful arms surround her, protect her, hold her to his chest while she—

"Lady," the conductor said, and shook her shoulder. "Wake up. Oebisfelde, next stop. We need to get you and your wagon off fast. Understand?"

Chapter Thirty-Seven

March 18, 1947, 5:47 a.m.
Oebisfelde, Soviet-Occupied east Germany

"Understand?" the conductor repeated, irritated. "And I want my cigarettes."

Adeline's throat started to constrict, and her heart was racing again. Thoughts about losing another child returned. They tried to paralyze her.

Stop it. No doubts, Adeline. You're already there.

"You'll get the carton once we're off," she said. "Boys, wake up. We're going for our walk."

"A walk?" the conductor snorted. "Lady, when it counts, I'd be in an all-out sprint. The Russians shoot first and—"

"Stop," she said as the boys slowly came to. "Please, sir. For their sake."

"Yeah, yeah," he said, and walked toward the back of the car.

Will said, "I'm thirsty, and I have to pee, Mama."

"I do, too," Walt said.

Adeline was folding the blanket and realizing that she'd forgotten to pack water.

"We'll pee when we get off and find some water before the next train," she promised.

Will groaned. "When's that?"

She started to snap at him but stopped herself. "Sooner than you think."

The train slowed. She looked out, trying to see back east, trying to find the dawn and finally spotting its pale purple hint far across a grain field covered in an inch of new snow.

"Here we go," she said, getting them out into the aisle and following them toward the rear exit. "The traveling Martels are off on another adventure."

"You always say that," Will said.

"Because we're always traveling," Walt said with an air of condescension.

Adeline looked outside again, catching the silhouettes of rooftops before the train came to a stop with a squeal and a hiss at a two-story brick station with a single platform lit by gas lamps and the cracking dawn.

"C'mon, now," the conductor said. "Fast."

She climbed down, telling the boys to stay on the platform, and then ran after the conductor, saying, "Are we the only ones getting off here?"

They reached the baggage car, and he stopped, saying, "The only ones crazy enough on this trip. Most people take the earlier train to Oebisfelde and try in the dark."

"But I was told there were trees that would hide us."

"There used to be trees you could sneak through to get across the border unseen," he said as they got the wagon down. "They cut them down last week, and they've started to dig up the stumps. It's becoming a real no-man's-land near the border."

No doubts, Adeline. You're already there. Already in Emil's arms.

"Thanks for the information," she said, handing him the cigarettes. "And your kindness."

Adeline expected him to say something snide. Instead, he took the cigarettes, sighed, and said, "Good luck to you, lady. And your kids. Someone told me if you see the medieval tower in the town, you've gone too far, and they'll probably see and stop you before you can even try to start walking toward the border."

"Good to know," she said, and set off toward the boys with the little wagon.

The conductor climbed aboard the first passenger car. By the time Adeline reached Will and Walt, the train was pulling out, leaving them alone on the platform, with the eastern horizon now pale purple slashed with moody reds.

Will danced around and said, "I'm thirsty, and I have to go pee."

"So do I," Walt said.

"You can't go here," she said. "Outside."

They pushed and pulled the cart through the empty station. Adeline noticed the wagon felt odd, as if one of the wheels were out of line and dragging as they went out onto snowy steps that overlooked the intersection of a road running west parallel to the railroad tracks and another that wound south into the town, which was where Frau Schmidt had said to go.

"They'll stop you at the border if you try the paved road next to the rail tracks or the paved road on the south side of town," Frau Schmidt said. "But Peter and I were told that midway between the two roads, there's a diagonal alley to your right. It will lead you to a lane that cuts west through farmland to the town of Danndorf, about four or five kilometers away.

"Just before the border itself, on your left about one hundred and fifty meters, you will see a two-story house where Soviet soldiers watch the lane and the paved road to the south. But the lane goes into trees that shield the border near there. If you can get to those trees without being seen and stay hidden, they won't see you cross until it's too late."

But the trees have been cut down!

———

"Mama!" Will whispered, dancing about. "I have to pee as bad as that time you made me pee in the jar."

Walt said, "I have to pee but not that bad."

"Go," she said, pointing to her right. "Over there, while I get the wagon down the steps."

The boys hurried down the stairs, over to some bushes, and unbuttoned their flies. She tried to ease the wagon down the steps, but the weight got away from her, and it went bouncing down into the slushy street with four big thumps and a crack.

"What was that, Mama?" Will whispered.

She pushed on the wagon, felt it roll, and said, "I don't know."

Will finished and hurried to her. Adeline glanced east at the red-and-purple horizon growing brighter and felt panic again. She looked back toward Walt, who was just standing there by the bushes, peering around as if they had all the time in the world.

"Let's go, Walt!" she hissed.

"He's always like that," Will said as Walt startled and ran toward them.

Adeline could almost make out her older son's features in the dawn light when he puffed up to them. She knew their chance for easy freedom was slipping away, second by second.

"Both of you behind the wagon," she said. "Quick now. And if you see an old tower ahead of us, tell me to stop."

They made it two steps before the arm that held the front right wheel to the wagon snapped and the wheel fell off. The wagon tilted and sagged on top of it. Adeline stared at the broken wheel lying in the slush.

"What do we do?" Will asked.

Adeline wanted to cry. But sunrise was coming. She had to act, and fast.

Going around to the wagon's opposite side, she saw that the front and back wheel arms were bolted into rectangular support structures, each made of four wooden bars. The longer sides of the rectangle were bolted across the bottom of the wagon about fifteen centimeters apart. The shorter wooden bars were bolted over and into the crossbars.

Adeline noticed a gap of perhaps five centimeters between the short bars and the bottom of the wagon and was inspired. Finding a large rock, she used it to pound at the left, top, side rail and soon had it separated from the wagon.

She beat down the nails so they would not cut her, then fed the rail through the gap in the front-wheel support from the left side to the right. The rail now stuck out from the bottom of both sides of the wagon a good thirty centimeters.

Adeline got a piece of rope she'd used to bind some of their things in a bundle, cut it in two, and used the pieces to tie the rail in place on both sides of the wagon. It took far too long. The sun was rising as she finished. For a moment, she thought about turning back, but the idea of being in Emil's arms would not let her.

"Walt, come around front and take the handle. Will, you still push."

With that, Adeline went around to the right side, squatted to grab the rail, and lifted it and the wagon's front end, becoming the fourth wheel. She had to adopt an awkward position to do it, bent over, taking most of the weight in the mid and low back, which almost immediately began to protest as they started down Bahnhofstrasse, the street that wound away south from the Oebisfelde train station and the frontage road that ran west toward the border.

They passed between rows of smaller homes interspersed between large brick-and-stucco buildings. Adeline barely gave them a glance. Sweat was pouring off her brow into her eyes, making it difficult to see as she tried to crane her neck to gaze ahead and down every side street they passed, looking and listening for anything that might indicate the approach of a patrol.

"That smells good," Will said as the aroma of baking bread wafted on the wind.

Somewhere in the distance, Adeline heard a sound like wood striking wood, followed by a long rushing sound that took her breath away. *That was a gunshot!*

Part of her wanted to turn around, but she didn't.

No doubts, Adeline. You're already with Emil.

One block. Two blocks. Three blocks. Her back and hands were on fire. She peered ahead and up, trying to spot that medieval tower before they went too far and missed that diagonal alley that led to the farm lane heading west.

But what about the trees?

They walked on, the remaining three wood-and-tin wheels of the little wagon sliding in the slush as they went through a roundabout at the intersection of two roads. They continued south on Lessingstrasse as more sun poured into the town. Why hadn't they encountered anyone else?

"Mama," Will said.

"I told you—"

"The tower, Mama," Walt said.

Adeline saw Oebisfelde's medieval tower in the distance, tall, peak-roofed, with big windows thrown wide at the top.

She set down the rail and the front end of the wagon, spinning around and picking it up again before crying, "Back the other way, boys!"

She hurried them out of sight of the tower toward that roundabout. Before they reached it, she spotted an alley on their left cutting diagonally northwest. At the end of it, she could see where the buildings stopped and met empty ground beyond. *Is the lane there?*

As far as Adeline was concerned, it was. She puffed with effort as they moved the little wagon into the alley and up its length, passing the backs of homes where lights glowed and children laughed and cried.

Nearing the end of the alley, Will said, "Mama? I'm thirsty, and that lady's getting water."

He was pointing at the dim figure of an old woman cranking a bucket from a well in the yard of the last house on the right. Adeline stopped as the woman poured water from the well bucket into another.

"Excuse me, ma'am," Adeline said. "Can I bother you for some water for my sons? We've come a long way, and they're very thirsty."

The old woman looked at them and then at the little wagon.

"No," she said. "I'm sick and tired of helping the traffic."

Before Adeline could beg, she'd turned, walked down the side of her home, and disappeared into the shadows.

———

"Here we go again, boys," Adeline said, and lifted the wagon as the rising sun lit up the snow-clad meadows and overgrown fields beyond.

"Mama, I'm thirsty," Will complained.

"We're all thirsty, Will," she snapped. "Please, help Mama and be quiet. I promise to get you water as soon as I can."

Frau Schmidt had said there was a dirt road running north-south that they would cross to get to the farm lane. Adeline could see that road now, just beyond an open-faced shed in the old woman's yard that had firewood stacked inside. They passed the shed. Across the north-south road and slightly to her left, she spotted the two-track lane heading west.

She'd taken the first step out of the alley toward the lane when she heard the clop and jingle of an approaching horse.

She glanced to her right, seeing a swarthy man driving a horse and cart loaded with large milk cans. He was almost upon them and waving wildly at her.

"Can't you see?" he cried, pointing out into the farmland. "There's a Soviet patrol coming in from the guardhouse! Get back and hide!"

Adeline did not wait to look and spun around to pick up the wagon's front right corner from the reverse direction. "Go back again!"

Will and Walt could see the fear in her face and pulled until they were back into the alley. The man on the horse and cart went by, waving at her to get into the old woman's firewood shed. Adeline grunted with effort as they hauled the wagon behind the shed and urged the boys to follow her into it.

"Don't move!" she gasped. "And not a peep now from either of you!"

Adeline could see in their faces that the boys understood they were in danger, but they said nothing when she motioned them to crouch behind the woodpile while she peered over it.

The shed was flimsily built, with gaps between most of the planks on the rear wall, which faced the dirt road, the lane, and the farmland. At first, she saw nothing. But then, coming out of a low spot about five hundred meters west of town, she saw four Soviet soldiers with guns and fixed bayonets urging a group of prisoners with their hands behind their heads back toward Oebisfelde. Beyond them another kilometer or so, she made out the roof of the two-story guardhouse. The patrol had to be coming from there.

In minutes, they were near enough for Adeline to see that there were twenty prisoners, fifteen men and five women, and to hear the soldiers berating them in Russian, calling them traitors to the new order.

"Don't move," she whispered to the boys, and stayed frozen herself as she watched the prisoners come so close, she could see the terror plain and gutting on their faces.

To a person, they were filthy. Several bled from facial and head wounds. Adeline tried to breathe shallow and low when the patrol reached the end of the lane, less than twenty meters away. The prisoners were ordered to turn right and march south toward the tower. The breeze carried their sour odor as they walked around a bend in the road and vanished from her sight.

For two seconds, she lay there, panting with relief. Then she heard a voice, not in her head speaking words, but in her heart spurring emotion that she understood completely.

This is your chance, Adella! Take it!

In the most courageous act of her life, Adeline pushed herself upright off the firewood stack, got the boys to their feet, and said, "Let's go see your papa."

———

Adeline bent over and picked up the rail and the front end of the wagon once more. They dragged the wagon back into the alley before she stood straight and set her gaze west, beyond the fields, beyond the Soviet guardhouse to a distant line of trees, three, maybe four kilometers away. That had to be the other side of the border.

Her lower back began to burn again as they pushed the wagon across the dirt road onto the lane, which was flanked in places by low rock walls. When they were one hundred meters out from town, Adeline straightened enough to glance south toward the medieval tower and saw someone moving in its open window.

She swallowed hard and had to will herself not to scream at the boys to abandon the wagon and the last of their belongings and make an all-out sprint for the border. Having grown up in big open spaces like this, however, she knew a running horse got noticed whereas a drifting cow rarely drew attention. With that in mind, she kept them moving at a slow, steady, maddening, and backbreaking pace. Time dragged, but soon they were two hundred meters from town and then three and four. The farther they went down the lane, the more Adeline felt as if her arms were being yanked from their sockets. Her lower back was still barking at her, and she had to rest every hundred meters to tolerate the pain.

Five hundred meters west of town, as they came up out of that low spot the patrol had passed through, she stumbled and felt as if something sharp had been stuck between her shoulder blades. Adeline gasped, dropped the rail, and was almost overcome with an agony she recognized from her many long days bent over in crop fields. She hunched there, trembling.

"Mama!" Walt said. "Are you okay?"

Adeline couldn't talk as she forced herself to straighten up and then rotate her shoulders back and her shoulder blades down. A few seconds later, she felt her spine shift with a crack. The pain lessened, and she stood there panting, wiping at the sweat pouring down her forehead and swallowing at the nausea in her throat.

"Mama?" Will said.

Before she could answer, Adeline heard a volley of gunshots from back where she'd last seen the patrol. Panic began to well in her. *Are they shooting the people who tried to cross the border last night? What will they do to us? They wouldn't shoot the boys, would they?*

For a moment, she was frozen in place. *Should we go on? Or turn back?*

She thought she heard a woman scream before a second round of gunshots went off.

Walt said, "They're not going to shoot us, are they, Mama?"

She saw how scared he was, and it shook her.

"No," she said, aware of the squeak in her voice. "Here we go now."

Adeline took two deep breaths and then squatted gingerly to pick up the rail. She raised the front end higher than she had before, pinning the rail across her lower thighs, not caring that the wagon's balance was off as they walked out to eight hundred meters and then a full kilometer from town. The sun had risen higher now. The snow had begun to melt in earnest.

With every step, more of the two-story farmhouse that served as the Soviet guardhouse came into view off to the south-southwest. By the time they were less than five hundred meters from the guardhouse, she could see the stumps of what had been the forest that was supposed to shield them as they crossed the border. Some of the stumps had been turned up out of the ground. She could see their root systems blocking the lane beyond the driveway to the guardhouse.

Turn around, Adeline! a voice in her head cried. *They'll shoot you! They'll shoot the boys!*

But she knew that if they stopped now, they had no chance of being with Emil before sundown, maybe ever. Another voice, stronger and more powerful, began to speak to her.

No doubts now. Have faith, Adella. Walk right by that guardhouse the way Corporal Gheorghe walked through the Battle of Stalingrad and survived the Elbow of the Don.

An odd little smile began to form on her lips. To her surprise, the pain between her shoulder blades, in her lower back, shoulders, and hips eased as they walked nearer.

Then the frightened voice flared up when she realized the guardhouse was not one hundred and fifty meters south of the lane. It was much closer, no more than fifty meters to their left. On its ground floor, there were two large glass windows facing the driveway.

They're going to spot you, Adeline. They're going to shoot you before you find . . .

Adeline stopped to rest and to shake off the feeling of despair. She looked right at the windows from less than seventy-five meters, and, imagining the beekeeper, she smiled.

Have faith, Adeline thought over and over as they came abreast of the driveway and the upturned stumps blocking the lane. Still smiling, she glanced at the windows and saw two Soviet soldiers in the left one. They were in some kind of argument with a heavyset man wearing a homburg and a dark long coat. One of the soldiers looked their way. She smiled as she took her eyes off the window.

"We'll go around, boys," she said, trying to sound confident as she veered the wagon around the root balls to see that the lane beyond the stumps was split in two.

The left way turned south toward the improved road. The right track was muddy, rutted and gouged in places, and blocked by more uprooted stumps in others. The right lane seemed to peter out altogether near the far end of the stump field.

Have faith, Adeline thought, peering forward and believing she could see a clear path through the stump field, across the border, and into thick trees on the other side. She glanced back over her shoulder at the guardhouse windows, seeing all three men facing her and the boys now, but still in the midst of argument, with the man in the homburg waving his hands all around.

"How far are we going, Mama?" Will asked.

Adeline smiled, shifted her grip on the rail, and said, "To those trees out there."

"That's not far," Walt said.

"Half a kilometer. No more. Like walking to school from Frau Schmidt's."

She looked back a third time when they were a hundred meters out from the guardhouse and could no longer see the lower windows, which meant the men could no longer see her and the boys. Adeline's heart began to soar as they kept moving the little wagon across the ruts and around the stumps, heading steadily west.

It's done, she told herself as they walked another fifty meters toward freedom. *We're already in those trees out there. We're already on that train to Alfeld. We're already with Emil.*

A gunshot split the cold morning air, a crack and whoosh that seemed to go right by them. Adeline startled, cowered, and then twisted around as another shot went off from back by the guardhouse. She couldn't tell who was shooting at them or where they were firing from.

But there was no doubt about the man in the homburg and the black long coat, who was running up the drive now, waving his arm and shouting at her. "Halt! Stop!"

Her eyes widened. *He's secret police!* she thought.

Positive now that they were going to be caught or shot, Adeline felt her faith turn to abject terror, as if she were about to be burned alive or drowned before her sons. She lunged forward against the rail, screaming at the boys. "Push! Run! Fast!"

Within twenty seconds, her lungs felt ready to burst, and her leg muscles turned rubbery. For a moment, she could not find the way through the stumps.

"My God!" she gasped. "Help me! Please!"

She took a few more steps and saw a path through the maze. She hauled the little wagon and her boys down it, looking back with three hundred meters left before the trees, and seeing that the man with the homburg was well out the driveway into the stump field and gaining on them.

Realizing he was going to catch her at this pace, Adeline surged with an emotional energy that she'd never felt before and never would again, a mother determined to save her children, a wife desperate to hold her husband again, a woman fueled by fear, by love, and by prayer.

Her vision tunneled. Her hands ached, her shoulders howled, and her back felt ready to break in two places. But her legs had returned and kept driving as she yelled again and again at Walt and Will to keep going, to not give up.

Suddenly, they were almost there. Less than two hundred meters. Even through the stinging sweat in her eyes, Adeline could see where the stump field stopped at a brush line with a few scattered trees beyond that before the real forest began.

A gun barked. She swore the bullet passed right by them.

Fighting hysteria, she screamed, "Stay low and don't stop, boys! Just keep going!"

Another flat gunshot sounded before three more followed in slow, deliberate, aimed succession as Adeline, Walt, and Will propelled the little wagon toward that brush line, those sparse trees, the woods, and freedom.

"Where's that man?" she yelled.

"He's getting closer, Mama!" Walt cried.

Adeline put her head down and used those words like the whip Emil used on the horses during the tank battle, goading her through the next hundred meters. It felt like an eternity before she could see the end of chaos and want, right there in front of her.

In moments, they were out of the stump field, stumbling across a small path and then plunging down another that wound west through matted dun grass, willows, and thorn brush before entering the thick woods. At the edge, she looked back to see the man in the homburg still out there in the stump field, still coming after them, maybe one hundred meters behind them.

"Just a little farther, boys!" she said, plunging into the woods.

The forest was shadowed and stark, with snow dusted across the floor and tree limbs. The path widened ahead, becoming more of a used lane again. It wound into pines and past a small millpond on their right. At the other end of the pond, there was a bench. Surely that would be far enough.

Reaching the bench, Adeline looked back once more, and saw no one running after them through the trees. Her leg and back muscles knotted and spasming, she allowed herself at last to slow, stop, and let go the rail. Only then did she collapse on the bench and take her crying, terrified sons into her arms. Only then did she break down, sobbing for joy.

"We've done it!" she blubbered, squeezing them close to her, and then laughing hysterically. "We believed and we're free, boys! Free! And we will see your father before the sun goes down!"

Back down the trail, a branch snapped.

Chapter Thirty-Eight

Adeline whipped her head around and saw the man who'd chased them. He was limping toward them, his coat muddy and open, his homburg muddy and in his muddy hand, his face mud streaked, florid, and sweaty as he shook his head.

She pulled the boys even tighter as he gasped angrily, "*Fräulein*, why didn't you stop when I yelled at you to stop? Look at me. I've got mud everywhere."

"They were shooting at us," she said coldly. "And you can't make us go back."

"Shooting at you?" he said, cocking his head at her. "Can't make you go back?"

"That's right," she said forcefully. "You'll have to kill us before we do that."

To her surprise, he threw back his head and roared with laughter. "So you *didn't* have permission to cross?"

Adeline said nothing.

"Of course, you didn't," he said, putting his muddy hat on and clapping his muddy hands in delight. "Do you know how lucky you and your boys are? Those people who were caught last night? Four of them were repeat offenders, who were shot in Oebisfelde shortly after the guards spotted you coming out of the town. You came out so close to the patrol that passed you that the guards assumed you'd already been stopped and cleared to cross."

She stared at him in disbelief. "But they shot at us from the guardhouse. You chased us."

He laughed again. "Those shots were the guards taking target practice. They weren't aiming at you. They felt sorry for you having to carry the wagon.

They sent me to help you." He smiled. "I'll still help you. Where are you trying to go?"

She broke down crying at that, then gathered herself. She swallowed hard, wiped the tears from her eyes, let the boys go, and got up on quivering legs. "A town called Alfeld?"

"I can't help you get all the way there, but Danndorf and the train stop aren't far."

Adeline was suddenly trembling head to toe, more exhausted than she thought she'd ever been. When he said he'd be the fourth wheel, she nodded in gratitude and followed him and the boys on toward Danndorf.

When they arrived, they drank from a fountain and went into a café-bakery where Adeline bought bread. When the owner heard they'd just escaped the Soviet Zone, he gave the boys small sweet cakes and let her use his telephone to call the Alfeld displaced persons camp.

She was told Emil was at work in the fields and left a message to tell him that they had made it across the border, and they would be arriving at the train station there soon. The good Samaritan cleaned the mud off his clothes and helped her get the broken wagon to the local train stop.

When they finally were on the platform and she was thanking the man, Adeline realized she'd been so worked up about actually escaping, she'd never asked his name. When she did, he smiled.

"My name doesn't matter. You and your boys are safe and where you're supposed to be."

She got the chills at that, and said, "May God watch over you, sir."

"Hearing your story, I'd say he watches closely over you, ma'am, and your sons and your husband," he replied before strolling away, chuckling to himself.

Adeline watched him go, feeling a tingling sensation as if the tips of feathers were softly brushing her entire body.

"What are you thinking about, Mama?" Walt asked.

She smiled and teared up as the Samaritan disappeared from view. "I was thinking about grace, God's love, and how truly blessed we are to have it."

Alfeld, British-Occupied west Germany

Emil paced up and down the train platform in the afternoon spring light, feeling as nervous as he'd been working up the courage to ask Adeline out on their first date. He kept inspecting his reflection in the station window. He'd had plenty to eat in the refugee camp, but he hadn't gained back half the weight he'd lost during his imprisonment and escape.

Would Adeline recognize him? Would the boys?

It did not matter. He would recognize them. He would have recognized them even if they'd been separated a decade. He was certain of it.

Emil walked back to the end of the platform, looking south, trying to make another train appear. For the longest time, he saw nothing but the rails disappearing around a far bend. In years past, he would have grown more anxious, more fearful of imagined disaster with each passing minute.

But since escaping to the West, Emil had never been calmer or more self-assured. He'd survived the worst that life could throw at him, and those trials and his time with Corporal Gheorghe had changed him, made him stronger and humbler and more aware of the power of dreams and the magic of life all around him. He appreciated every sunrise and every sunset and was grateful to the Almighty for every gift he was given in between.

He'd also practiced seeing Adeline and the boys and himself together in his mind while feeling how intensely good that would be in his heart. In the displaced persons camp, he had declared to any and all who would listen that he would find his family. And when he'd found Adeline and the boys through the International Red Cross and they began communicating in code, he'd openly declared over and over again that his family was not staying in the East. They were not living under Stalin anymore.

Shifting his weight back and forth from one leg to the other, Emil summoned every bit of strength and certainty he had and uttered a vow he'd repeated ten thousand times in the past year.

"They're coming west," he said firmly. "They're coming to freedom. They will not be stopped. We will never be apart. Ever again."

A faint whistle blew, and with it his heart raced, his eyes watered, and his stomach fluttered like birds flushing. He heard the train's rumble build before the locomotive appeared and sped toward him. He suddenly knew in his heart they were on the train, and it took everything in his power not to run right at it.

The engine slowed and rolled past Emil, followed by the first passenger car, and the second, and the third. He scanned every face looking out at him and didn't see any of them as the train came to a stop with the baggage car in front of him. His emotions started to sink, but he was already telling himself that they would be on the next train, when the baggage car's door slid back. The little wagon was right there, missing a wheel, but without a doubt it was the one he'd built for the boys so long ago.

"Emil!"

"Papa!"

He spun around, and the dreams and spirits of hope that had lived in him for more than two years became real and human again. Adeline was jumping down from the first car with Walt and Will right behind her. They ran at each other and fell into each other's arms.

Emil held Adeline tight when both their legs wobbled and they sank to their knees, hugging and kissing each other. The boys came in to hold them, all of them shaking, sobbing, and bursting with a happiness so beautiful and pure, none of them would ever forget it.

"We'll never be apart again," Emil said. "I promise you that."

"Never," Adeline said.

"Never," Walt said.

"Never ever," Will said.

They held on to each other as if they'd all arisen from the dead, barely hearing the conductor put their little wagon beside them. Finally, when the train began to pull out of the station, Adeline drew back her head from the crook of Emil's shoulder, blinking away her tears and smiling in awe as she gazed up into his eyes and saw they were burning with brilliant love for her, just the way she'd dreamed it.

Overwhelmed, she choked, "Our life is a miracle, Emil!"

"One miracle after another," Emil said, and kissed Adeline like it was the very first time.

Chapter Thirty-Nine

September 23, 1951
Aboard the USS **General R. M. Blatchford**

Fog had formed after sunset and turned the cloudy night as black as any Emil Martel could remember. Nearing midnight, it grew dank cold, the kind that gets in your bones, but he refused to leave the foredeck of the troop transport where he stood near the bow, peering west, eager for any sign of light.

Earlier in the evening, there had been many other pilgrims on deck with Emil, all looking for that first glimmer of new life. But one by one they'd slipped off to their cabins, and now there remained only a handful still keeping watch.

Adeline came up behind him and put her arms around his waist. "You don't want to come to bed? They say we can't get off until morning anyway, and my stomach is at it again."

"I want to see this," he said. "I want you and the boys to see it, too."

"Okay," she said, snuggling up against him. "Then I'll wait with you and pray my dinner stays down for the first time since we got on this ship."

"That would be a gift."

"Wouldn't it?"

———

As far as the Martels were concerned, every day that had followed their escapes from Communism and their reunion in the West had been one more miracle, a gift from God for which they were deeply and constantly grateful. Emil and

Adeline had not cared that they all lived for a short time in cramped quarters at the displaced persons camp. And they did not mind toiling out in the fields as hard as they had under Stalin while the boys attended school. The food was infinitely better, and they were together again, free to make something out of their second chance at life.

Adeline told Emil everything that had happened to her and the boys after he was dragged away by the Polish militiamen. Emil gave her an edited version of events after he was taken. He described the long march to the train that took him to Poltava. He told her about living in the basement of the museum with two thousand other men and the diseases that had ravaged his fellow prisoners. He even told Adeline a bit about Corporal Gheorghe and how he'd come to Poltava and how they'd been on the death detail and planned to escape together, only to have the Romanian transferred to another prison camp with higher security. And he described in detail how he'd escaped and rode trains west.

But Emil still felt he could not tell Adeline about the massacre in Dubossary and how he was able to confess to the Romanian corporal but not to her. He didn't want to hurt Adeline or make her feel less about him in any way. He felt she'd been through too much already.

During the summer of 1947, the Martels were moved to more-permanent housing in Lütgenholzen, south of Hanover and about two hundred and fifty-five kilometers west of Berlin, where Emil and Adeline continued to work in the fields while the world tried to find permanent homes for them and for the millions of other people displaced by World War II and its aftermath. Many refugees were going to South America, including Argentina. Others had their sights on Canada and the United States.

The Martels wanted to go to North America, but they needed a sponsor, a relative or someone residing there and willing to give Emil a job and his family a place to live for a year while they got on their feet. They also needed to show that they were in good health. Adeline had never felt better as they settled into their new life. Walt and Will grew, put on weight, and made big strides academically in that first year. But Emil's health was not good. He suffered abdominal pain and was often violently ill with vomiting and diarrhea. He turned jaundiced and weak.

In the summer of 1948, Emil collapsed in the fields and was rushed to a hospital where doctors discovered eggs and larvae in his stool. Whether it was from the pig manure Emil had spread in the fields or from the garbage and rancid food he'd had to eat at times during his escape from the prison camp, the doctors determined he was infected with a tapeworm that had attacked his liver, leaving him near death. They rushed Emil into surgery and went in through his back, removing two ribs to get at his liver. When they reached it, the doctors were horrified to find a baseball-sized tapeworm surrounding one lobe.

After they removed the parasite and left the wound open to drain, Emil hovered near death for days. Adeline and the boys kept vigil over him, but never once lost faith that he would survive.

———

When Emil finally awoke, he was weak but happy to be alive. Within a day, however, he'd turned agitated and gloomy, not like his post-escape self at all.

After a week, as he lay in bed, his torso wrapped in gauze, Adeline asked him what was bothering him. Somehow, Emil understood that he would never know peace unless he stopped hiding part of his past from her.

"I will only speak about this once," he said, "but you deserve to know. Do you remember when we first returned to Friedenstal, and I took the wagon and horses and went to Dubossary to get roofing supplies?"

Adeline did remember and felt her stomach grow queasy. "What happened?"

Over the course of a long afternoon while the boys were in school, Emil told her everything: how he'd been stopped leaving town by then captain Haussmann; how Haussmann had forced Emil and other ethnic Germans to go to a remote ravine where members of the SS were shooting Jews; and how he'd begged God not to make him participate; how Haussmann had handed him a Luger and told him to prove his loyalty to the Reich by shooting a Jewish teenager and two younger girls; how he'd refused at first; and how Haussmann had put a gun to his head; how he'd changed his mind so he could see his own family again; and how he was preparing to shoot, when he was stopped by Haussmann's superior who invoked Himmler's order that no one be forced to kill Jews; and how instead he'd spent the night burying the hundreds shot there.

"But make no mistake, Adella," Emil said. "I made the decision to kill them before I was stopped. I didn't see God's hand in Haussmann's superior showing up until I was at my worst moment in Poltava and Corporal Gheorghe showed me that I had done the right thing, and even though I'd decided to shoot, I was prevented from doing it."

Adeline had listened in growing dread of what Emil might have done until he'd described the entire sequence of events. Hearing how the Romanian who'd survived Stalingrad had saved Emil's mind and soul in the prison camp completely erased her fears.

"Corporal Gheorghe was right," she said, squeezing his hand. "You refused, Emil. You didn't know about Himmler's order, and yet you refused. That took staggering courage, my love. The kind of courage that most men lack. I'm . . . I'm proud of you, Emil, proud to be your wife."

Emil felt his eyes mist. "I'm proud to be your husband. I have never known anyone as courageous and loving and good as you."

"Stop."

"It's true. We are all together because of *your* courage and *your* refusal to quit."

Adeline smiled and brushed away a tear. "Thank you."

They held hands for several minutes, just loving each other before Adeline said, "Do we know what happened to Haussmann?"

Emil nodded. "I saw it in the newspaper. After we left the refugee camp outside Lodz, he was transferred to a combat unit. He survived the war, was arrested, and was going to be tried at Nuremberg as part of the *Einsatzgruppen* case. But he committed suicide in his jail cell before the trial began."

"Coward."

"Yes. But I don't want to talk about Haussmann or that night in Dubossary ever again. Okay?"

She nodded. "And thank you for telling me."

———

On the foredeck of the *General R. M. Blatchford*, Emil and Adeline heard a horn blare in the darkness and the fog. Within minutes, they heard a bell clanging.

"We're close," Emil said. "We have to be."

"I'll get the boys while my stomach's still calm," she said, kissed him, and walked away.

Emil continued to peer off the bow, sure that he'd be seeing lights by now. But like everything the past three years, events were happening much more slowly than he wished.

They'd finally found a sponsor the year before, one of Adeline's long-lost uncles who owned a farm and needed help because his son was about to be drafted. In return for two years of Emil's labor, the family would receive lodging, food, and a small stipend to use to get on its feet after the work obligation was fulfilled. With the sponsor in place, the Martels were moved north to yet another displaced persons camp where they studied English and their immigration application wound through the maddeningly slow process of verifying their identities and pasts.

Finally, nine days before Emil would come to be searching for lights beyond the bow of the ship, and after living as refugees for more than seven years, the Martels went to Bremerhaven, boarded a transport that had brought US occupation troops to Europe, and finally set sail west. During the week-long voyage to America, Adeline was seasick almost every day. Still, she, Walt, and Will made deep, lasting friendships among the other ethnic Germans aboard. His family aside, Emil had kept largely to himself, spending every afternoon on the foredeck near the bow, watching the sunset and dreaming about their life to come.

Emil did not see himself being a full-time farmer again. Not for long, anyway. As Corporal Gheorghe had noted, deep down he was a hammer, not a plow. Despite being imprisoned in Poltava, he'd actually enjoyed seeing buildings materialize right in front of his face, the magic of one man's dream set down on paper and made real by a crew of men's hard work and skill. He'd decided long ago that he believed at least part of what Corporal Gheorghe had taught him. Was the world, the universe, all one entity? Was God inside him? Was he inside God? Emil still struggled with those questions. But the Romanian was right about one thing: all it took to have a good life was a cheerful, grateful mood, a clearly envisioned, heartfelt dream, and the willingness to chase it with an unwavering belief in its eventual realization.

Emil's dream for years had not been to just survive in the West. He wanted to live and to thrive there, making fair money for a fair day's work, giving his wife a safe, comfortable life in a home of their own, and providing his boys with the formal education he'd never had and the opportunity to go their own way when they were ready. More than that, secretly Emil desired a car. He'd fallen in love with automobiles while living in Germany and liked to imagine himself driving around wherever he wanted to go, as free as a man could be.

———

On the deck of the troop transport, Adeline returned with the boys, about to be fourteen-year-old Walt and about to be twelve-year-old Will, both of whom were wrapped in blankets and grumpy at being awakened in the middle of the night.

"I can't see anything," Will said.

"I'm tired," Walt said, yawning. "I want to—"

"There!" Emil said, pointing out over the bow where a light had appeared, faint at first, but growing, and then another followed by dozens more as the fog swirled and lifted a little. People began to clap and cheer. Others went to find their families. As tugboats came to pilot the ship through the Verrazano Narrows, the foredeck became crowded with refugees cheering each glimpse of New York City through the ever-changing fog.

The ship slowed on entering Upper New York Bay, came to a complete stop, and lowered anchors shortly after one a.m. The fog had lifted to thirty feet, and they could see lights on all the shores around them.

Emil was about to say that this was as good as it was going to get for the night, when the breeze picked up and the fog swirled before a vent formed high in the sky to the northwest, revealing the lit torch and the hand of the statue.

People began to gasp all around the Martels because the vent was growing with each passing moment, revealing the arm, the face, and then the crown of Liberty. Emil lost it then, grabbed Adeline and his boys, held them tight, and broke down sobbing.

As everyone on the deck around them roared their delight or dissolved into tears at their own deliverance, Emil choked, "We did it! We made it!"

"Your dream come true, Emil," Adeline said, kissing him. "Right there in front of you."

By then, the fog had blown away to the east, revealing the lady in all her glory. Emil stared up at the statue in awe, shook his fist, and whispered, "Freedom. All a man could ever want."

"We still have to find Mama's green valley," Will said.

"This is enough," Adeline said, also unable to take her eyes off the statue. "I don't need the valley."

"But we're going there the day after tomorrow, aren't we?" Walt asked.

"We get on the train the day after tomorrow," Emil said, and kissed Adeline. "Then we'll have a three-day ride."

"To the beautiful green valley?" Will asked.

"It has to be," Walt said.

———

Four nights later, when the train pulled into the depot in the tiny town of Baker, in far-eastern Montana, a freak, early-autumn storm was bombarding the area with snow. Adeline's long-lost uncle was waiting with his Jeep. The little wagon had been left behind in Germany in favor of a single wooden crate of belongings that they lashed to the roof and drove off through the storm to the farm where they were to live and work for the next two years.

The storm was howling when they reached the farm and were shown to a bunkhouse where they collapsed in exhaustion. When Emil awoke at dawn the next morning, the storm was over, the temperature was falling, and the sun was shining brilliantly on the bleakest, most barren, snow-blasted landscape he'd ever seen.

"We're in Siberia," he muttered in disbelief. "What the hell have I done?"

For the next month, as the boys started school in town and Emil learned the workings of the farm, he became convinced that he had made a gigantic mistake bringing his family to America, to Montana, and especially to Baker. That conviction grew as winter set in and the true cost of feeding and housing an extra four mouths became clearer to Adeline's uncle and his wife, who complained often about the amount of food Will and Walt were consuming. Emil tried to work as hard as they would let him and told himself that they'd be off the farm within a year.

By February 1952, however, his frustration deepened. Their sponsors had stopped paying Emil's full wages, saying they had to keep some of the money back to make sure everyone was fed. Then their sponsors' son was given a 4-F at boot camp and returned home. In early March, Adeline's uncle told her they did not have enough work and food. She and her family had to leave the farm and make their own way. Adeline and Emil needed to find jobs, and fast.

Rather than fight the situation, rather than be angry and bitter about the short hand he'd been dealt yet again, Emil drove straight into Baker and discovered that the town's first hospital was being built. He found the foreman and spoke to him in broken English, asking for work. The foreman told him the only job he had to offer was as a laborer and concrete mixer.

"Concrete mixing? That I know how to do from building a hospital in the Russian prison camp I escaped from," Emil said, smiling.

"You escaped from a Russian prison camp?"

"Yes. I know cement from this time."

"Then you're hired."

Chapter Forty

The Martels rented a small house in Baker within walking distance of Emil's work site. Adeline found a job cleaning rooms at the only motel in town for fifty cents an hour. Walt officially changed his formal name from Waldemar to Walter and found work after school at the butcher shop and at the movie theater as a projectionist. Will changed his name from Wilhelm to William and called himself "Bill." He bagged groceries at the local store and swept the theater floors.

They pooled their money, saving until they could afford to buy a small lot across from the high school and pay to have a basement foundation dug and poured. Emil worked at the hospital site and other projects during the day and, with Bill, put down a subfloor on top of the foundation in the evenings. They also installed plumbing, electrical lines, and a woodstove in the basement.

The Martels lived in the basement the entire winter of 1952–53, enduring minus-thirty-degree-Fahrenheit nights and big snowstorms. But it was their basement, and Emil and Adeline could not have been happier. And little miracles continued to unfold all around them.

Walter happened to mention that the butcher often threw away the pigs' heads and hocks because no one wanted them. Adeline couldn't believe it and asked him to bring them home. She made headcheese, soup stock, and braised hocks in the basement that winter. Emil liked to joke that they ate so much free pork, he felt like they'd left Ukraine and ended up in hog heaven.

The only thing missing for Adeline was her mother and sister, with whom she kept up a correspondence made intermittent and difficult by the closing of the Iron Curtain. Everything they wrote was being read. Lydia was sickly, and Malia's life was consumed caring for her.

They had no word from Emil's parents or his sister, none since Adeline had watched them leave for the train back to Friedenstal. He began to think of Karoline and Johann the way he'd come to think of his older brother, Reinhold: spirits lost to him in the wind.

But by Christmas 1953, the house was done, and they were celebrating the fact that it would soon be paid for. There was also a 1947 Chevy sedan in the driveway. Emil's bosses marveled at the sheer effort the man put out day after day in bitter temperatures, often gloveless as he mixed cement or helped frame up a new wall.

Adeline continued to clean at the motel and to work her wonders in the kitchen. She also became an active member of the local Lutheran church. Bill enjoyed working with his father more than he did attending school, but Walter blossomed in the classroom.

Indeed, in the spring of 1956, a little more than four years after he arrived in America with only a smattering of English, Walter was named the valedictorian at Baker High School two months before graduation. During those years of studying and watching his father work construction, he had grown interested in architecture. Walter applied to two schools and was accepted to both.

After their escape from Soviet control, the Martels had vowed never to live apart. Around Easter that spring, Emil, Adeline, and Walter boarded a train bound for the University of Chicago. They wanted to see if they thought they could live in the Windy City while Walter studied at one of the greatest architectural schools in the world. But after less than a day and a half on Chicago's South Side, they all felt claustrophobic and voted unanimously to leave on the very next train headed back to Montana.

———

About a month later, in mid-May, Emil and Adeline were driving west to Bozeman, a place they'd never been, to try to find a house there to live in. Walter would be attending the School of Architecture at Montana State University, and they wanted to keep the family together. They'd left Walter and Bill in Baker the day before because the boys had final exams and work they could not miss.

They battled typical spring weather in Montana the entire drive: rain, then sleet, then intense periods of wet snowflakes that plastered the windshield and forced them to slow because cars were sliding off the road.

"Do you remember all the wagons we had to pull out of the mud on the Long Trek?" Emil asked. "When we were fleeing the bear and running with the wolves?"

Adeline smiled. "If I close my eyes, I can remember it all. The mud. The cold. The bombs. The tanks. The good and the bad."

"Luckily, there are much better things to think about in America."

"Thank the good Lord for that."

Near Big Timber, the weather began to show signs of breaking, with thinner clouds racing across the sky like moody red fingers. Adeline found them hypnotic. As they approached Livingston, she began to drowse and then dozed off.

Maybe it was those clouds in the sky; maybe it was Emil's talk of the Long Trek, but Adeline dreamed vividly of that day they left Friedenstal with her mother and sister in the wagon behind them and years of uncertainty and suffering before them. Will was curled up in her lap, and she was feeling every bump in the road through the wagon's flat wooden seat, when Walt asked, "Where are we going, Mama?"

———

A horn blared loud enough to jolt Adeline wide-awake.

A big truck honked its horn a second time and swerved around them in driving sleet and rain on a steep and winding road that was barely visible through the windshield.

"Emil?"

"I'm okay."

A sudden flash of lightning revealed they were in a densely wooded mountain pass. The flash was followed almost immediately by a thunderous explosion as loud as the tank cannons they had dodged outrunning Stalin's armies. The blast shook the car.

"Maybe we should get off the road!" Adeline yelled.

"I can't!" Emil said. "There are cars behind me and there's nowhere to get off!"

The rain stopped slashing the car for a moment, and she could see a pale cliff jutting out of the forest high above them and looking for all the world like the silhouette of a frog. Two turns past the frog rock, the road flattened, and the rain began to pour again.

"Bozeman two miles," Adeline said, reading the sign.

"There's an exit ahead," Emil said before sheets of rain came and the wipers failed.

He rolled down the window and stuck out his head, squinting into the rain as he braked and took the exit, which put them on a gravel road that turned left beneath the highway. He pulled over under the bridge, started fiddling with the wipers, and got them working again.

Back in the car, Emil drove forward to a T in the road, intending to make a U-turn. He saw a signpost with the names of ranches and arrows pointing in either direction. The bottom sign pointed right and read "Montana State Ag Fields."

"There," Emil said. "Looks like we can drive right to the school from here."

Another rain squall swept over them as they drove down a long gravel road that broke away at right angles but kept trending west. At one point, they could see the highway to their right before they dropped into a ravine. The road got bumpy on the way down and looked almost washed out on the way up the other side.

"Maybe we should turn around," Adeline said.

"The sign says it's right in front of us," Emil insisted, and floored the accelerator.

They shot up the other side, fishtailing in mud and bouncing through potholes and puddles that spattered the windshield brown and killed the wipers again. The rain was still coming when they reached the top, and Adeline could see through the muddy windows that they were on a plateau of sorts with a ranch yard on their left and a barbed-wire fence across the road just beyond with a sign that read "Dead End."

Emil said nothing, just started to jam the transmission into reverse, when Adeline threw out her hand and said, "Wait!"

She was staring through the cleaner parts of the windshield at beams of sunlight shining through breaks in the storm beyond the plateau. Feeling compelled and trembling head to toe, Adeline opened the car door, climbed out, and looked west, gasping at the breathtaking valley that unfolded before and around her in a hundred shades of green.

Several of those pillarlike sunbeams shone down on farm fields already emerald with the shoots of spring wheat. Other beams illuminated the twisting, lime-colored lines of leafing cottonwoods and quaking aspens along creeks that braided across the valley floor toward the cow town of Bozeman and a river called the Gallatin she could see sparkling in the distance.

Emil's door opened behind her, but she did not look back at him. She was too enthralled by the clouds lifting with every second, revealing the six mighty mountain ranges that surround the Gallatin Valley, their foothills emerald and sea green with new grass and blooming wildflowers rising to jade-and-olive pine and spruce forests that climbed the rugged flanks toward impossible crags freshly blanketed in snow and piercing the bluest sky she'd ever seen.

Emil came up beside Adeline as overwhelming love and joy burst from her heart and tears began to stream down her cheeks.

"It's so beautiful," she whispered, feeling humbled and awestruck. "Like God painted it for me, Emil. So much more than I ever could have imagined."

"Look behind us."

She turned to look back across rolling, grassy hills, toward the mountain pass they'd come through. The storm was in full retreat now, with lingering broken clouds and scattered showers that caught the noonday sun and threw a massive arching rainbow across the east end of the valley that was quickly joined by a second rainbow at a different angle, and then a third. From beginnings miles apart, their multicolored arches seemed to erupt out of the verdant hills, to soar, collide, and shimmer red, blue, purple, and gold with sheer, stunning intensity.

"I've never seen anything like that in my entire life," Emil said as he put his arm around Adeline's shoulder.

She put her arms around his waist and laid her head on his chest, watching the rainbows pulse and radiate for almost a minute before they faded to pale, colored glimmers and then to cherished memories.

"We are never leaving here, Emil," Adeline vowed, looking west again at the last green valley of their long and improbable journey.

"Not until the day we die," Emil said, and held her tight.

Chapter Forty-One

But for occasional short trips and after returning to Baker to pack their things and sell their home, Emil and Adeline Martel never did leave Southwest Montana's Gallatin Valley. And from that point forward, after all the hardships and tragedies they'd endured, nearly everything the Martels touched seemed to turn to gold.

Before Walter and Bill started school in the fall, Emil had bought a lot in Bozeman and started building a new home within walking distance of the university.

After he finished with his house, he recognized an opportunity when three small lots went up for sale near the Dutch Reform church on the less-tony north side of town. Reasoning that the aging Dutch farmers who lived west of Bozeman might like a small home to retire to near their place of worship, Emil took a risk, bought all three lots, and started building the first house with Bill helping after school.

They were putting up roof trusses when a Dutch farmer came along and asked if the house was for sale. Emil said it was. The farmer asked the price, didn't flinch at it, and handed Emil a twenty-dollar bill to hold the house until his wife could see it. The next day, the farmer and his wife returned, asked several questions, and went to the bank for a check for the full price.

Emil Martel & Son Construction was born and capitalized in one day.

———

When he wasn't working on the houses his father was building, Bill, at sixteen, tried to get a job building the field house at Montana State University. When the contractors turned him down, he walked away, vowing to build projects bigger than any of them could imagine.

The following year, Bill quit before graduating high school, went to work full-time for his father, married his teenage sweetheart, Lynell Lewis, and never looked back. The Martels were soon so busy and so successful, Adeline and Emil were able to sponsor her brother, Wilhelm, to come to the United States after finding his name on a Red Cross list of refugees. But she could not convince Malia to come, even after Lydia died in 1964.

Walter finished college, married Deeann Kessler, and worked for several years as an architect in Billings until Emil and Bill asked him to join their expanding company in 1967. Martel Construction grew at an even faster pace until near disaster struck.

Driving home after a late night putting together construction bids, Walter was T-boned by a drunk driver running a stop sign. He had to be cut out of the car and lay in a coma for two days with a head injury. It would be a year before he could work full-time again.

In February 1971, Emil was stunned to learn that his older brother, Reinhold, who'd been conscripted into the German army and vanished during the war, was alive and free after spending twenty-six years in a gulag in Siberia, cutting timber for lumber. Emil and Adeline immediately bought airline tickets and flew back to Germany as US citizens. They visited Reinhold, now sixty-five, in West Germany where he had been reunited with his family, who had also managed to end up on the right side of the border.

Seven years later, Emil and Adeline returned to West Germany because Reinhold had tracked down Rese and gotten her a three-month travel visa. They were there when she arrived. Both brothers were so rocked to see her that Adeline joked that they almost had to be hospitalized for too much happiness. Then Rese told her two brothers that their father had been savagely beaten by Polish militiamen on the way back to Ukraine in June 1945. Johann did not survive the journey. Back in their home in the tiny farming village of Friedenstal, which had been renamed Tryhrady by the Soviets, Karoline dwindled and passed away in the early 1960s.

Rese told them she was happy under Communism, but soon enough, Emil and Adeline figured out that she had succumbed to bitterness and alcoholism. She was drunk nearly her entire time with them and refused their offer to sponsor her to come to America, preferring to return to the hell she knew rather than move to the paradise she did not. It was the last time Emil ever saw her. Rese died in the early 1980s.

On their return flight to the States, Emil asked himself why some people were willing to uproot and chase freedom at all costs while others were content to stew in their misery. That led to thoughts of Corporal Gheorghe, and he wondered yet again what became of the Romanian who'd helped save his life in Poltava and made him truly aware of the miracles and opportunities unfolding everywhere around him.

In 1979, twenty-eight years after their arrival in New York Harbor, the Martel brothers were able to offer their father a buyout and a pension so he could retire in style.

"Retire? What would I do all day?" Emil asked.

"Go fishing, Papa," Bill said. "You've always liked fishing, and some of the best fishing in the world is right here."

Emil did like fishing, and he was tired of banging nails at twenty below zero with no gloves on. After some thought and several talks with Adeline, he took his sons' offer.

With part of the lump sum the boys paid him on day one of his retirement, Emil bought a gold Cadillac that he proudly drove around Bozeman and the Gallatin Valley, fishing poles in the trunk.

Emil, meanwhile, lived to see Martel Construction prosper, to witness his sons have children, and to see his entire family, including Reinhold and his new wife, gathered at his home, laughing, telling stories, drinking the wine he made in the basement, and savoring Adeline's cooking.

Walter worked with Bill for fifteen years, until a dispute with a union in 1982 resulted in one of their construction trailers being firebombed with Molotov cocktails. For Walter, who'd been shaken by tank cannons as a child and was sick of the fighting between union and nonunion labor, it was the final straw. He went to Bill and said he was done and asked to be bought out. Bill was not happy. He felt abandoned by his brother but raised the money. For three years afterward, there was no contact between them, which greatly troubled Emil and Adeline, who prayed that they would come to peace with each other.

In 1985, Emil had to have gallbladder surgery, ordinarily a two-hour ordeal. But the surgeons faced complications from his earlier tapeworm surgery, and he almost died on the operating table. Nonetheless, when Bill and Walter walked into his hospital room together shortly after he awoke, he told Adeline it was one of his happiest days ever.

In 1987, Emil was diagnosed with terminal lung cancer, which caused him to reflect on his remarkable life. He, of course, had come to believe that it is only rare individuals who can rely completely on themselves. At some point, most people will face obstacles or situations that seem impossible to overcome unless they have the stubborn will to dream and learn to humble themselves and rely on a greater power as they work to make their vision real.

He noted often that everything difficult he'd had to do seemed to have prepared him for the next difficult thing. Being imprisoned now seemed to have been one of the best things that ever happened to him because, after his escape, he had never looked at life the same way again. Every moment, every opportunity he'd been given after Poltava was a gift—from God, the Almighty One, the Divine, the Universal Intelligence, or whatever Corporal Gheorghe wanted to call it—and he gave thanks for those gifts by being happy and cheerful about nearly everything.

Soon afterward, at seventy-five, Emil passed on, a content, fulfilled man who'd seen his adult life begin under brutal oppression and unfold in poverty and starvation, only to have it end in freedom, blessed with abundance beyond his wildest dreams.

———

Every morning before and after Emil's death, Adeline got out of bed in Bozeman and went down on her knees, thanking God for their miraculous good fortune. She ended her day the same way. People who knew her for decades said she was relentlessly cheerful and grateful for every blessing she'd been given in life.

She was also determined never to go hungry again.

Adeline had a big garden in her backyard where she grew bumper crops of vegetables that she canned for winter and huge cabbages she used to make sauerkraut. Emil had dug her a root cellar where she buried potatoes and onions in the winter. She adored the kitchen the boys built for her, and it became a hub of family and friends where everyone was welcome and well fed, especially her grandchildren, whom she doted on.

She attended Lutheran services every Sunday. She loved going to have her hair and nails done at a beauty parlor. And because she'd never had a doll as a child, Adeline amassed a large collection that was her pride and joy.

Walter and his wife traveled to Europe in 1993 and were able to visit Adeline's older sister in the former East Germany. Malia had lived a hard life but still retained her amused optimism and odd perspective. She died two years later at age eighty-seven and is buried alongside her mother in Falkenberg.

Around that time, Adeline was interviewed by the *Bozeman Daily Chronicle* as part of its Fourth of July package. In the article, she recounted her suffering and starvation in Ukraine, the ordeals of the Long Trek, the family's separation when Emil was sent to Poltava, his escape from Communism, her escape from Communism, and her endless gratitude for the country that had finally taken them in.

"God bless the United States of America," Adeline said. "Only in America is a story like ours possible."

Indeed, Adeline would live to see Bill driven to success by a small, empty, wooden packing crate he kept outside his office door. The crate once held the last of the Martels' belongings when they sailed for the United States. Like the little wagon in his memory, the crate was a constant reminder to Bill of how desperately poor his family had been when they sailed into New York Harbor, and how far they'd all come since then.

She watched Bill and his sons build Martel Construction into a vibrant enterprise with residential and commercial projects in the United States and abroad. She also saw Bill and her grandsons give back for their good fortune, partially paying for and building, among other things, an addition to Montana State's Bobcat Stadium. In gratitude, the school named the stadium's football gridiron "Martel Field" after Bill.

In her later years, Adeline became more and more homebound, though she would continue to entertain her friends and family in her kitchen, where she would feed them her famous apple cake. If they were lucky, they'd hear snippets of her harrowing adventures on the way to the last green valley or one of her frequent observations about life.

"You know, I used to think life was something that happened to me," she told one old friend as she was beginning to fail. "But now, I know life happened for me."

They were out in her garden, and she was smiling at how it teemed with life.

Looking back, Adeline said she could see the entire incredible arc of her journey, how everything that happened to her and Emil had indeed seemed to prepare them for the next, more difficult challenge, both of them learning and adapting the entire way.

More than fifty years had passed since she and the boys escaped the Soviet Occupation Zone and reunited with Emil, but she still marveled at the events of that day.

"If that old woman had given us water from her well, we never would have been warned by the man driving the milk wagon to hide in that shed, and we probably would have walked right into that Soviet patrol," she said. "And if we hadn't gone for the border when we did, so close to the patrol passing with the prisoners, the Soviet soldiers in the guardhouse would not have thought we had the correct documents to cross the border and would not have sent that muddy angel of a man to help us get the wagon to the train station. The border guards would have stopped us, and who knows what would have happened?"

After marveling over that story, her friend asked Adeline to describe the most important things she'd learned over the course of her long and remarkable life.

Adeline thought about that for a little while before saying, "Don't chew on the bad things that happen to you, dear. Try to see the beauty in every cruelty. It sets you free. Forgive hurt if you want to heal a broken heart. Try to be grateful for every setback or tragedy, because by living through them, you become stronger. I see the hand of God in that.

"I also see his hand in every right step and every wrong one we took in our lives, all somehow moving us forward, but sometimes around and around and around like a leaf I've always remembered seeing blowing in the wind the first day of the Long Trek. We were blown along like that leaf, dancing, spinning, and rolling toward this life we were dreaming of. And here I am so many years later, still living that dream. It really is a miracle, isn't it? And now the only miracle left for me is to die and be taken in the arms of God."

Nine months later, on April 5, 2006, some two weeks shy of her ninety-first birthday, with Bill and Walter and their families gathered around her, Adeline Martel passed on as all great and wise heroines eventually do, her soul leaving her body on her final breath, thrown to the cosmic wind only to be guided by grace, a refugee spirit soaring toward salvation, her Lord, and her beloved Emil, waiting for her in a new and permanent Eden.

AFTERWORD

I hope you were as moved, inspired, and transformed by the Martels' story as I was hearing it for the first time. Working on their tale over the past two years has been one of the great honors of my career, and I will remain forever grateful to the entire Martel clan for trusting me to bring Emil and Adeline to life.

A question I hear a lot is how much of my historical fiction novels are based on fact.

Without dissecting every twist and plot turn, in the case of *The Last Green Valley*, I can tell you that Joseph Stalin did indeed starve more than four million Ukrainians to death during the Holodomor of 1932–33. Stalin also imprisoned and enslaved millions of people in the aftermath of World War II. Under the Soviet dictator's orders, many of the ethnic Germans who went on the Long Trek ended up being shipped to Siberian work camps. Untold numbers of those prisoners never returned.

Historians believe that between twenty and twenty-five thousand ethnic Germans perished on the Long Trek from Ukraine to Hungary, and on the trains that took the refugees north from Budapest to Lodz, Poland, which became known as the Ellis Island of the Third Reich.

The SS processed more than three hundred and fifty thousand ethnic Germans in Lodz under purity and immigration laws crafted by Heinrich Himmler and enforced by his "Reich Commission for the Strengthening of Germandom." The majority of these refugees were given clothes and homes that once belonged to Jews.

According to Yad Vashem, the Israeli Holocaust Memorial, some eighteen thousand Jews were massacred by the SS's *Einsatzkommando 12* of *Einsatzgruppen*

D in fields and ravines outside the town of Dubossary in early to mid-September 1941. Ethnic Germans who were members of the *Selbstschutz*, like the character Nikolas, were said to have participated in that atrocity and dozens of others across Ukraine after the German invasion.

Later in her life and after Emil's death, Adeline told one of her granddaughters that several weeks after they returned to Friedenstal in mid-August 1941, Emil took a trip with the horses and wagon to buy roofing supplies for the house he was building. She said Emil returned two days late and was as shaken as she had ever seen her husband, who told her he'd been forced by the SS to bury Jews and refused to talk about it ever again. Adeline never said where Emil went for his supplies, but Dubossary was and is the closest large town to their village.

Emil Haussmann was a captain in *Einsatzkommando 12* of *Einsatzgruppen D* at the time of the Dubossary massacre and served under Lieutenant Colonel Gustav Nosske, who was later tried at Nuremberg and imprisoned for his war crimes. Haussmann was promoted to major in the SS for his efforts in the early days of the "Final Solution" and the so-called "Holocaust by Bullets" that unfolded in Ukraine and Transnistria after the German invasion in June 1941. Three years later, Haussmann was part of an SS team that traveled with and protected the pure bloods of the Long Trek. He did kill himself before his trial at Nuremberg.

In the months prior to the German invasion of the Soviet Union, Heinrich Himmler did watch political prisoners being shot as a test for implementation of the Final Solution. Himmler was reportedly so shocked, he vomited, and later issued an order that no one be killed or sent to a concentration camp for refusing to murder Jews. He wanted true believers behind the guns.

During the Nuremberg trials, multiple Nazi war criminals tried to claim they were forced to participate in the Holocaust, that they had no choice at all. As part of that defense, their own attorneys searched repeatedly for evidence of anyone who had refused to kill Jews and was subsequently murdered or imprisoned under Hitler's reign. They were unsuccessful.

Historians believe that western Allied soldiers may have raped as many as eighty thousand German and ethnic German women during the last part of the war and its immediate aftermath. They believe Soviet soldiers may have raped more than one million German women in that same time period.

Beginning in 1952, as the Iron Curtain lowered and as part of an effort to stop people in East Germany from fleeing west, the border at Oebisfelde where Adeline ran for freedom was hardened to include watch towers, fences, walls, anti-tank ditches, and minefields. After the fall of the Soviet Union and Germany's reunification, the fortifications were torn down, and the fields she and her sons crossed were restored enough that I was able to walk much of Adeline and the boys' escape route, though the terrain and vegetation had no doubt changed.

———

In mid-May, Southwest Montana's Gallatin Valley is indeed a landscape painted in greens and one of the most beautiful places in the world. At the east end of the valley, where I live, double and triple rainbows often form after thunder-and-hail storms at that time of year.

Bill Martel is eighty now, retired, a widower, and still lives part-time in Bozeman, where I met him for the first time in November 2017. Walter Martel is eighty-two, retired, and still married. He and his wife moved farther west to be near their children and grandkids. They live in Hamilton, Montana.

In August 2018, after I retraced most of the Long Trek's route through Moldova, Romania, Hungary, and Poland, the aging brothers and I went to Ukraine, where we drove ten hours up a terrible road to Friedenstal/Tryhrady to visit the ruins of their childhood home. Seeing the exact place where their run to freedom had begun, both men were cast back in time and overwhelmed with emotion at the incredible distance they had traveled in their lives.

Two days later, in order to save them a thirteen-hour drive one way up an even more terrible road, I chartered a plane to fly us from Odessa to Poltava to see the site of the former prison camp. We found the city hall where Emil had eaten and the hospital he'd helped rebuild.

The Poltava Museum of Local Lore was there, too, restored but closed to the public when we tried to enter. We walked around and found the museum director, Oleksandr Suprunenko, who at first refused to let us in due to ongoing construction. Then he learned that Emil had been a prisoner there, worked on the burial detail, and had sold the cooks firewood before escaping. The director laughed, told us his mother was one of those cooks, and led us on a private tour of the museum.

Suprunenko showed us photographs of gaunt and haunted prisoners rebuilding the museum. He took us to the basement and told us that, due to rampant diseases and death, the Soviets closed the Poltava camp in mid-1947, just a few months after Emil's escape. The few survivors were sent to other camps to the east, some as far as Siberia, before other prisoners were brought in to live on another site and to finish rebuilding the city. Hearing that in the room where their father had slept before and after his daily trips with the death cart, Bill and Walter broke down crying.

They said that Emil rarely spoke of the prison camp, but there was no doubt that he left Poltava a far different man than the one who went in. Before his imprisonment, Emil had done little of note, doubted God, and believed that the best way for him and for his family to survive the Communists and the Nazis was to rely on himself, keep a low profile, and have little apparent ambition. After Poltava, however, their father turned deeply spiritual and daring. Emil seemed to see miracle and opportunity everywhere he looked and took massive risks that he was rewarded for throughout the rest of his life.

"Something or someone changed my dad in that camp," Bill said. "What? Who? How? I don't know. He wasn't a big talker. But he had to have had allies in the prison camp. One or two men he could talk to and trust. I guess you'll have to figure out a way to explain it."

I already had a sense of what, who, and how, because the month before, in Barlad, Romania, I interviewed ninety-eight-year-old Gheorghe Voiculescu, whose experiences and outlook on life would form the basis of Corporal Gheorghe's character. Mr. Voiculescu was sharp, funny, and truly seemed to glow and radiate goodwill as we spoke.

He distinctly remembered talking to and helping ethnic Germans on the Long Trek as they went west in the spring of 1944. Before then, Voiculescu had fought at Stalingrad in the brutal battle at the Elbow of the Don, where he was concussed and wounded by shrapnel from a mortar bomb. He told me he woke up from the blast and knew with absolute certainty that he was blessed, that he was going to live through the war, and that he was going to become a beekeeper. Voiculescu did walk through the rest of the battle unscathed, with Soviet soldiers and tanks running right by him, when so many around him died.

At the end of the war, Voiculescu escaped from two Soviet prison camps before being sent to a high-security camp on the Sea of Azov. He was released after four years of hard labor. Upon his return to Barlad, Voiculescu was hailed as a hero for being one of the few survivors of the Elbow of the Don. In recognition, he was promoted to and retired from the Romanian army with the rank of colonel.

Voiculescu worked for a time in a factory after his release but used much of the money he earned to finally fulfill his dream of becoming a beekeeper, which was a lifelong passion. Constantly extolling the wonders of honey, royal jelly, and beestings, he outlived three wives and celebrated his hundredth birthday in April 2020.

The real Corporal Gheorghe was, without a doubt, one of the more remarkable and enlightened individuals I have ever had the privilege of meeting.

———

Two mornings after we visited the prison camp and wondered about Emil's transformation, Walter and I were leaving Ukraine to fly to Germany and Poland to follow Adeline's escape route, and Bill was going home to Montana.

At breakfast at the airport before our flights, the Martel brothers told me that no matter what had really happened to their father in Poltava, they felt like they'd come full circle in their own lives, at peace with all they had endured, blessed for all they'd been given, in awe of their parents' love, courage, and determination, and profoundly and endlessly thankful for the long, perilous journey they took as boys, when their family risked everything and ran with the wolves in search of freedom.

Sitting there with Bill and Walter at the airport in Kiev, moved and inspired, and just a few days before I started writing down the story of Emil and Adeline Martel, I scribbled in my notebook the words that I'll use to finish their tale.

"This is an American story, an immigrant story, a spiritual and universal story. May we all dare to chase such dreams, experience such grace, and lead such miraculous lives."

—*Mark Sullivan, Bozeman, Montana, July 21, 2020*

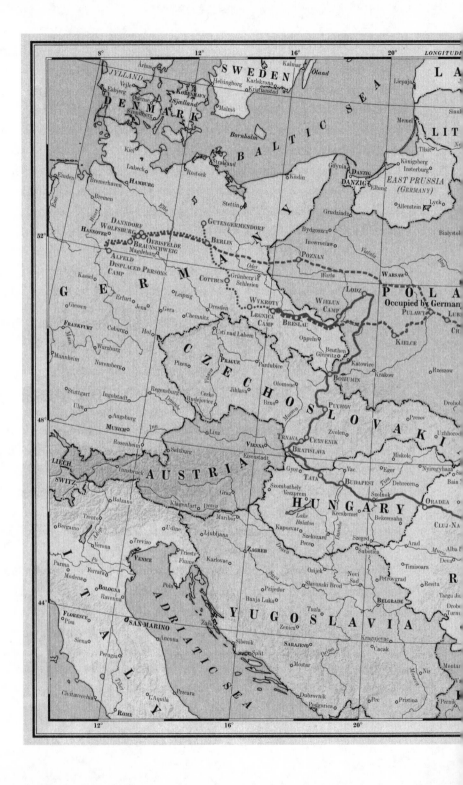

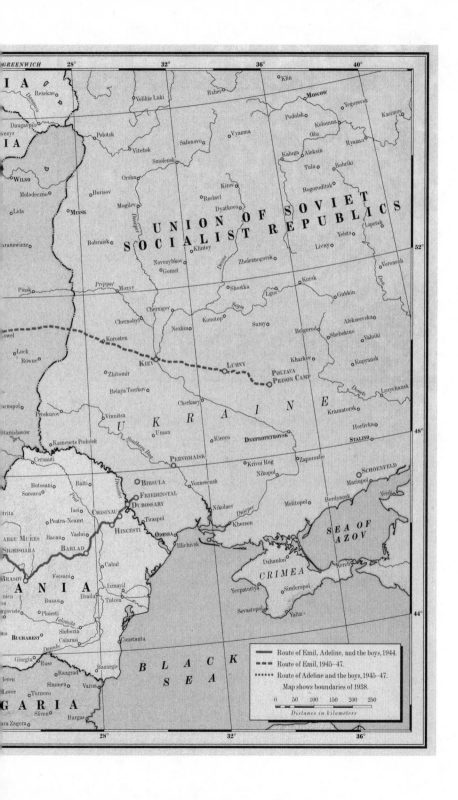

GREENWICH 28° 32° 36° 40°

52°

48°

44°

UNION OF SOVIET
SOCIALIST REPUBLICS

UKRAINE

ROMANIA

BULGARIA

BLACK
SEA

SEA OF
AZOV

CRIMEA

Rezekne
Daugavpils
Dunaburg
Okezys
WILNO
Molodeczno
Lida
aranowicze
Pinsk
Łowel
Łuck
Równo
arnopol
Proskurov
Stanisławów
Cernauti
Botosani
Suceava
trita
Iasi
Peatra-Neamt
ARGU MURES
SIGHISOARA
BARLAD
Bacau
Vaslui
Focsani
Buzau
BRASOV
Giurgiu
leven
Lovec
ara Zagora

Velikie Luki
Polotsk
Vitebsk
Smolensk
Orsha
Borisov
MINSK
Mogilev
Bobruisk
Novozybkov
Gomel
Mozyr
Pripyat
Chernigov
Chernobyl
Nezhino
Korosten
Zhitomir
Belaya Tserkov
Vinnitsa
Uman
Kamenets Podolsk
Balti
BIRSULA
FRIEDENSTAL
DUBOSSARY
CHISINAU
HINCESTI
Tiraspol
ODESSA
Illichivsk
Cahul
Izmavil
Braila
Tulcea

Klin
Rzhev
Moscow
Podolsk
Vyazma
Safonovo
Kaluga
Tula
Roslavl
Kirov
Dyatkovo
Klintsy
Zheleznogorsk
Shostka
Seym
Konotop
Sumy
Cherkasy
Kirovo
PERVOMAISK
Voznesensk
Nikolaev
Kherson
Dnieper
Melitopol
Nikopol
Krivoi Rog
DNEPROPETROVSK
Zaporozhe
Berdyansk
Mariupol
Dzhankoi
Yevpatoriya
Simferopol
Sevastopol
Yalta
Kerch
Yeisk
SCHOENFELD

Yegorevsk
Kazinov
Kolomna
Oka
Ryazan
Aleksin
Bobriki
Bogoroditsk
Yelets
Lipetsk
Livny
Voronezh
Kursk
Lgov
Gubkin
Belgorod
Shebekino
Valuiki
Alekseevska
Kharkov
LUBNY
POLTAVA
PRISON CAMP
Kupyansk
Lyzychansk
Kramatorsk
Horlivka
STALINO
Donets

KIEV
Desna
Southern Bug
Ialomita
Slobozia
Calarasi
Constanta
Bazargic
Razgrad
Ruse
Shumen
Varna
Burgas
Sliven

Danube
BUCHAREST
Ploiesti
goviste
nieu
ea

Pruth
Dniester

Dnieper

Desna

Livny

	Route of Emil, Adeline, and the boys, 1944.
	Route of Emil, 1945–47.
	Route of Adeline and the boys, 1945–47.

Map shows boundaries of 1938.

0 50 100 150 200 250
Distance in kilometers

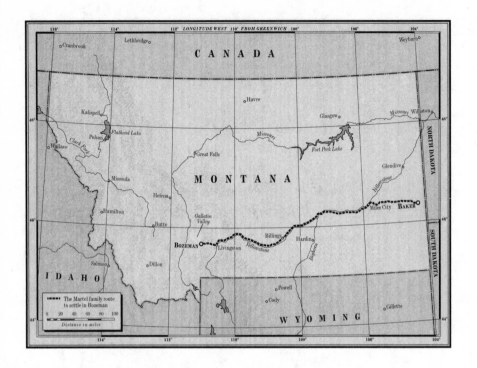

The Martel family, before the Nazi invasion, Pervomaisk, Ukraine, March 1941.

The Martels, shortly after being reunited, Alfeld, western Germany, March 1947.

DISCUSSION GUIDE

1. *The Last Green Valley* is a work of historical fiction, inspired by a true story. Do you feel that the story is authentic? How well do you think the author told a compelling story while also sticking to historical facts?

2. Have you or your family members lived through World War II? Have you or your family immigrated to the US? How do your memories or family stories reflect the emotions in this book?

3. Given the hardships the Martels had already endured, what emotional reserves do you feel they had to call upon to remain hopeful and stay on their trek to freedom?

4. Rese almost dies after suffering through a horrific accident. Emil almost starved to death and faced an unforgivable ultimatum at gunpoint. The family endures unimaginable peril on their journey and at the hands of the Nazis. What does it mean to be brave in the face of death?

5. There is a moment when Major Haussmann helps Rese after her accident. What do you think the author intended by choosing to portray such an evil man in this light? How did you feel about Haussmann's action in contrast with the ultimatum given to Emil?

6. Karoline is sometimes very cruel to Adeline, who is the mother of her grandchildren. Why do you think this is? What do you think of their reconciliation before they part ways?

7. What are your thoughts on Corporal Gheorghe's philosophy of life and how it influences Emil?
8. When Emil and Adeline are torn apart, what gives Adeline the faith and strength to carry on? What makes her so sure they will be together again?
9. What is your "green valley"?

ACKNOWLEDGMENTS

I am hugely indebted to a host of people who helped me in the research and writing of *The Last Green Valley*.

Foremost in that group were Bill and Walter Martel and their families. I thank the entire Martel clan for sharing their Emil and Adeline stories with me. I pray I did them justice.

In Romania and Moldova, my enormously resourceful guide, Florin Burgui, was able to track down a handful of people who either survived or witnessed the Long Trek of ethnic German refugees in the spring of 1944. They included Victoria Chmara, age ninety-one; Nicolae Hurezeanu, ninety-five; Ioan Muth, ninety-five; Gheorghe Voiculescu, then ninety-seven; Valea Uzului, ninety-four; and Victor Caldarar, ninety-six. Thank you for sharing your memories.

I was also aided by Flavius Roaita at the National Museum of Romanian History in Bucharest, Ottmar Trasca of the George Baritiu Institute of History in Cluj-Napoca, Romania, and Ramf Dan, a Romanian historian who interviewed more than two hundred and fifty survivors and witnesses of the German retreat from Ukraine. Historians Corneliu Stoica, Dorin Dobrincu, and Lutz Connert helped me understand the plight of people sent east by the Soviets after the end of World War II and those who never returned.

In Hungary, historian Eva Kuierung gave me insight into the transit of ethnic German refugees through Budapest on their way to Poland. In Ukraine, Dr. Sergey Yelizarov, an expert on ethnic German colonies, guided us to the remains of the Friedenstal colony, and to Poltava, where Oleksandr Suprunenko of the Poltava Museum of Local Lore helped us understand the conditions and challenges of the prison camp during the time Emil was held there.

Red Famine, Anne Applebaum's book about Stalin's starvation of Ukraine, gave me a good idea of what the Martels went through before the war. I was aided in my understanding of the Holocaust and Soviet and German rule in Ukraine by the works of historians and writers Wendy Lower, Gail Gligman, Alexander Dallin, Joshua Rubenstein, Ilya Altman, Eric C. Steinhart, Diana Dumitru, Ray Brandon, Daniel Joseph Goldhagen, Gerald Reitlinger, Sefer Zikaron, Walter Koenig, and Avigdor Shachen. Thank you all.

The writings of Dr. Alfred de Zayas gave me a deeper understanding of the expulsion of ethnic Germans across Central and Eastern Europe between 1944 and 1948. The research of Dr. Eric J. Schmaltz of Northwestern Oklahoma State University gave me insight into the SS transfer of ethnic Germans to the Warthegau region of Poland and their indoctrination into Hitler's Greater Germany. I appreciate the guidance.

Silvia Lass-Adelmann was my translator for research at the Political Archives of the German Foreign Office in Berlin concerning the Long Trek. I was also helped by archivists at the Romanian National Archives in Bucharest, at the US Holocaust Museum in Washington, DC, and at Yad Vashem, the World Holocaust Remembrance Center in Jerusalem.

I am blessed to have gone to O&O Academy in India to learn the principles of the spiritual philosophy of "Oneness" from my incredible teachers Krishnaji, Preethaji, and Kumarji. All three sages ended up influencing my depiction of the character Private Kumar. My experience at O&O also informed many other parts of this book and ultimately changed my life for the better. Bless you all.

Thank you to my early readers: Damian Slattery, Connor Sullivan, and Betsy Sullivan.

I am grateful for Danielle Marshall, my editor at Lake Union Publishing, who has had unshakable belief in this project since the beginning, and to Mikyla Bruder, publisher of Amazon Publishing, who has also been a big supporter of the Martels' story. Thanks go as well to developmental editor David Downing, copyeditor Jane Steele, and production editor Nicole Burns-Ascue for making the story stronger and the prose tighter.

Blessings also to my incredible publicity team—Ashley Vanicek at Amazon Publishing and Dana Kaye, Julia Borcherts, and Hailey Dezort at Kaye Publicity. I appreciate your getting the word out!

And a big double curtain-call bow to my literary agents, Meg Ruley and Rebecca Scherer, for reading and rereading and rereading the various drafts of *The Last Green Valley*. Your eyes and sensibilities make me a better novelist. Thanks also to Jane Rotrosen, Sabrina Prestia, and everyone else at the Jane Rotrosen Literary Agency who keep my writing dream alive.

ABOUT THE AUTHOR

 Photo © 2020 Elizabeth Sullivan

Mark Sullivan is the acclaimed author of more than twenty novels, including the #1 Amazon Charts, *Wall Street Journal,* and *USA Today* bestseller *Beneath a Scarlet Sky,* which has been translated into thirty-seven languages and will soon be a limited television series starring Tom Holland. Mark also writes the #1 *New York Times* bestselling Private series with James Patterson. He has received numerous awards and accolades for his writing, including a WHSmith Fresh Talent selection, a *New York Times* Notable Books mention, and a *Los Angeles Times* Best Book of the Year honor. He grew up in Medfield, Massachusetts, and graduated from Hamilton College with a BA in English before working as a Peace Corps volunteer in Niger, West Africa. Upon his return to the United States, he earned a graduate degree from the Medill School of Journalism at Northwestern University and began a career in investigative reporting. An avid skier and adventurer, he lives with his wife in Bozeman, Montana, where he remains grateful for the miracle of every moment. For more information visit www.marksullivanbooks.com.